The Best
AMERICAN
SHORT
STORIES
2021

GUEST EDITORS OF THE BEST AMERICAN SHORT STORIES

1978 TED SOLOTAROFF
1979 JOYCE CAROL OATES
1980 STANLEY ELKIN
1981 HORTENSE CALISHER
1982 JOHN GARDNER
1983 ANNE TYLER
1984 JOHN UPDIKE
1985 GAIL GODWIN
1986 RAYMOND CARVER
1987 ANN BEATTIE
1988 MARK HELPRIN
1989 MARGARET ATWOOD
1990 RICHARD FORD
1991 ALICE ADAMS
1992 ROBERT STONE
1993 LOUISE ERDRICH
1994 TOBIAS WOLFF
1995 JANE SMILEY
1996 JOHN EDGAR WIDEMAN
1997 E. ANNIE PROULX
1998 GARRISON KEILLOR
1999 AMY TAN
2000 E. L. DOCTOROW
2001 BARBARA KINGSOLVER
2002 SUE MILLER
2003 WALTER MOSLEY
2004 LORRIE MOORE
2005 MICHAEL CHABON
2006 ANN PATCHETT
2007 STEPHEN KING
2008 SALMAN RUSHDIE
2009 ALICE SEBOLD
2010 RICHARD RUSSO
2011 GERALDINE BROOKS
2012 TOM PERROTTA
2013 ELIZABETH STROUT
2014 JENNIFER EGAN

2015 T. C. BOYLE
2016 JUNOT DÍAZ
2017 MEG WOLITZER
2018 ROXANE GAY
2019 ANTHONY DOERR
2020 CURTIS SITTENFELD
2021 JESMYN WARD

The Best AMERICAN SHORT STORIES® 2021

Selected from
U.S. and Canadian Magazines
by JESMYN WARD
with HEIDI PITLOR

With an Introduction by Jesmyn Ward

MARINER BOOKS
An Imprint of HarperCollins*Publishers*
Boston   New York

marinerbooks.com

ISSN 0067-6233 (print)
ISSN 2573-4784 (e-book)
ISBN 978-1-328-48538-0 (hardcover)
ISBN 978-1-328-48539-7 (paperback)
ISBN 978-1-328-48341-6 (e-book)
ISBN 978-0-358-57841-3 (audio)

Printed in the United States of America
      1 2021
      4500834534

Contents

Foreword

I<small>T'S NO SECRET</small> that the stories in *The Best American Short Stories 2021* were first published in the year 2020. Some were likely written before then. 2020 was more beast than year. In early spring the rapid spread of coronavirus upended daily life, and the majority of the world found itself hunkered down at home. A new language sprang up: "flatten the curve," "social distancing," "self-isolation," "bubble," "herd immunity." People watched in horror as the number of cases and, tragically, deaths spiked higher. There were runs on toilet paper, hand sanitizer, Clorox wipes. People subscribed to Zoom, became bakers of sourdough bread, cut their own hair or grew it long, oversaw homeschooling, dabbled in armchair epidemiology. People ordered groceries online and disinfected each item before eventually learning that the air was the enemy (the *air*, of all things). Too late, people donned face masks when they had to come in contact with others outside their "bubble."

I am not someone who flourished in 2020. To be honest, reading large amounts of short fiction during a pandemic proved challenging for me. Doing large amounts of anything productive was difficult. However, I did master worrying, doomscrolling, snacking, wasting time, going for long walks, and the art of cocktail mixing.

For a story to resonate with me, it had to feel urgent during a time when even going to the post office held real danger. A story had to ring loudly with some kind of deeply necessary truth or humor or wisdom.

As the planet did battle with the enemy, we as humanity became more of a "we." Scientists working continents apart shared invalu-

x   *Foreword*

able data. Biotech firms joined together to create vaccines that are now rolling out at a stunning pace, at least in this country. (I write this in April 2021. May the situation change and the inequity of vaccine access plummet by the time you read this book.) Technology enabled us to communicate with sick loved ones isolated in hospital rooms or in care facilities, a cruel mercy. Newspapers waived subscription fees so that more people could stay updated about the constantly unfolding crisis. Friends and family gathered virtually. I myself had a novel out in August and did a virtual book tour, an odd and oddly intimate experience. There I sat in my attic office, my readers in their own homes but also inches from my face. Outside, the world was quiet and nervous. Our fragility and vulnerability became inescapable. Fear is a uniting force, and I have never felt the world so united.

And yet I have never felt this country so divided. The face mask became a badge of one's belief system: protect oneself and others nearby and wear a mask, or espouse a certain level of "personal freedom" and go without. In 2020 it became even clearer how unequal this "we" always was and continued to be. A disproportionate number of people of color grew sick and died. Workers lost their jobs and got evicted at a frightening rate. Women left their jobs in droves to stay home and tend children, who were mostly forced to attend school online. The vulnerable remained who they always were and were punished, and it was infuriating.

In her introduction, this year's guest editor, Jesmyn Ward, eloquently describes the pervasive seasickness of this past year. Ward chose a wondrous mix of stories. They carry certain marks of their time, if not of the pandemic specifically. We live in a moment rife with the global threats of nationalist extremism, climate change, racism, economic inequality. It is an anxious moment, and the anxiety is unlikely to substantially abate anytime soon. In these pages are pleading attempts to be heard and seen (Eloghosa Osunde's queer narrator states, "I will insist on my space") as well as desperate incantations against being erased, extraordinary moments of reimagination, inventive tales of escape. One look at the titles alone—with words like *miracle, escape, paradise,* and *last days* — reveals a steady gaze upward and outward.

In many of these stories, characters pass along crucial knowledge to younger generations. Brandon Hobson's narrator, an indigenous grandfather, writes to his grandchildren: "You must know the history of removal, and this is my own history." Nicole Krauss begins her piece: "We were European Jews, even in America, which is to say that catastrophic things had happened, and might happen again." The reluctant inheritance of another's pain is a common theme here. Rita Chang-Eppig's young character begins to bleed from her face on hearing about Saint Francis: "I was listening to the story . . . and I was overcome by compassion for him, so I started crying. I didn't even realize." Jamil Jan Kochai's narrator is the teenage son of an Afghan immigrant struggling with PTSD after being tortured in the Soviet war: "He is about to tell you a story that is either upsetting or horrifying or both, which isn't fair, because you are a son and not a therapist." An eighth-grade biology teacher issues kind warnings to a misfit student in Kevin Wilson's story: "If you give people something easy, they'll take it," he tells the boy, and years later the man's death is unspeakably devastating.

Some of these characters seek safe haven, even if only in their minds. Jenzo DuQue's young Colombian boys "had imagination. For every intersection we could not cross, another was invented . . . a portal to another world." Gabriel Bump's protagonist, who has "ambiguous brown skin," confesses, "There's my power glowing in the abyss, protected by Paleolithic megasharks." Security and freedom are always elsewhere for these characters.

Somehow, in some way, characters unearth hope in all its forms. I will not spoil Tracey Rose Peyton's moving story about the end of Rodney King's life, but I will tell you this: the ending will change you. In David Means's innovative "Clementine, Carmelita, Dog," the new seasons bring new sensations, and the world of animals comes to life in cycles that are heartbreakingly drawn.

Here are new but fully developed, confident writers such as Vanessa Cuti, Jane Pek, Christa Romanosky, Shanteka Sigers, Stephanie Soileau, and Madhuri Vijay. Here are newly minted and established masters like Brandon Hobson, Yxta Maya Murray, George Saunders, Bryan Washington, and C Pam Zhang. These stories gave me the chance to align my own anxious, isolated heart with others. More than once I could feel these stories in my body. My breath caught, my pulse sped. They bowled me over with their beauty, authenticity, imagination, and strength. I'm grateful to have been able to help gather these important voices in one place, especially during such a troubled time. And I'm thrilled to offer them to you.

The stories chosen for this anthology were originally published between January 2020 and January 2021. The qualifications for selection are (1) original publication in nationally distributed American or Canadian periodicals; (2) publication in English by writers who have made the United States or Canada their home; (3) original publication as short stories (excerpts of novels are not considered). A list of magazines consulted for this volume appears at the back of the book. Editors who wish their short fiction to be considered for next year's edition should send their publications or hard copies of online publications to Heidi Pitlor, c/o The Best American Short Stories, P.O. Box 60, Natick, MA 01760, or files as attachments to thebestamericanshortstories@gmail.com.

HEIDI PITLOR

Introduction

THE LAST YEAR bewildered many of us. The institutions we believed would protect us faltered, one after another. Casual cruelty, callousness, and gross ignorance became barely remarkable. Hundreds of thousands of Americans died in the COVID pandemic, so many of them brown and black and poor. We who were left were unmoored by this storm: our world shaken, seared by wind and rain, tossed by grief in a sea of loss. This year set the ships of our lives adrift, and the pandemic isolated us from one another, so that we spun and listed alone. The world we knew changed irrevocably, and in the midst of the storm that has upended us, it is nearly impossible to chart the new world that is. So many of us lost so much in the past year. We lost people we loved: we lost their slow smiles, their particular, musical laughter, their insightful questions, their silly jokes, their watchful eyes. The boats of our days capsized, and the sea of loss vomited up flotsam and debris, which we clung to so that we might believe, for a moment, that we were not alone, and that we might survive this.

That which sustained us, the rafts we depended on to keep us from sinking into the watery depths of our loss, was narrative. At the beginning of the pandemic, some of us watched *Tiger King,* half horrified, half gleeful, and wholly entertained by captive cats and terrible men. We read Brit Bennett's *The Vanishing Half* and marveled at women bent on the impossible task of escaping race and gender in America. Millions of us watched *Bridgerton,* relieved to find ourselves in a pastel-limned romance, sweet and shallow, swept into a story of people finding companionship and passion and healing in one another, through love. We read *One Story* and *Zoetrope* and *The Paris Review* and *The New Yorker* and *McSweeney's*, and we lingered on the short stories therein, read them once, and then, when we couldn't stop thinking about the characters and the worlds they existed in, we read them again. Throughout this terrible pandemic year, this year of low after low, we clung to story. Story sustained us, and we gripped the planks of narrative so that in the immersion into story, we might have togetherness and hope and drama and laughter and beauty, might revel in all that binds us together as human. This is what kept us afloat on the sea of grief.

When I was a child, my grandmother Dorothy was the first person who taught me something of the power of narrative. She was a natural-born storyteller. She taught me that stories could shore us up, lead us to unexpected revelations, enable survival and beauty all at once. At family gatherings, at birthday parties and Fourth of July cookouts and Christmas Eve celebrations, my grandmother told stories. She was good at it: she set the scene, detailed characteristics, embodied characters, switched voices for dialogue. Once she told me the story of my great-great-grandfather's death. He was out in the piney Mississippi woods before his moonshine still, which was set up in the shadows of the trees: the still was hot, singeing the moss and earth. Pine straw crunched beneath my great-great-grandfather's feet when he heard, carrying high through the tops of the branches, the whistles and shouts of the revenue agents, searching for stills. His lookout, my great-grandfather Harry, hadn't yelled an alarm, hadn't let my great-great-grandfather know that men were searching for him. The revenue agents, sweaty at the neck, faces glazed with the hunt, smiles set in rictuses of pleasure, shot my great-great-grandfather, who ran, who tried to hide in the shadows of the forest. Those revenue men would not have looked at my great-great-grandfather and seen the man who built a one-room schoolhouse to educate black children in 1940. They would not have seen the man who owned acres of land, granted them in perpetuity, a man who was determined to parcel out all he had to his children so that they might own some piece of this red-sanded, green-fringed, singing earth when he was gone. They would not have known he could read the weather in the clouds, tell the future in a flight of birds. The revenue agents would have looked at my great-great-grandfather and seen this: a short colored man with skin of river sand and black, almond eyes who was breaking their law.

"Daddy was looking for Mama," my grandmother Dorothy said, a crooked grin on her face, a strange smile punctuating this terrible story. "That's why he didn't call out in time." I was surprised at this turn, even as a child, ready as I was to settle into the sorrow of my great-great-grandfather bleeding, breathing cold while crows rustled and cawed in the leafy wisps of the branches. It was only when I was older and had spent years thinking about storytelling and stories, trying and failing and trying again to write good stories, that I understood this strange ending. I realized that with the telling of our family stories, my grandmother Dorothy had taught me so much about fiction, about what I valued in novels and short stories. How I wanted a story to be bracing, disorienting, and immersive. How I wanted it to grip me like the sea, pulling and pushing brine and bubbles up my nose, down my throat, leaving the taste of salt on my tongue. How I wanted it to scour me clean so that I forgot myself in the embrace of the wave, of the story.

My grandmother Dorothy taught me that narrative could be a different kind of sea—not the sea of loss, of grieving, but instead a life-giving, life-affirming ocean. Her stories made me value this: language that evokes and renders sharply and beautifully even as it confounds. Tales that surprise and subvert the reader's expectations. Fiction so well told that it subsumes a reader's awareness to the world of the story. When my grandmother Dorothy told me about her father's failed lookout, I understood that her shift in focus to my great-grandfather Harry wasn't rueful, and it wasn't darkly comic. Instead, my grandmother Dorothy was leading me to the image of the man, the emotion of the man, the heart of the story underneath; she led me to that ending so I could see my great-grandfather Harry, lean and light, wearing pants patched at the knees, feeling a rash of hornets in his chest rising up, panic and sorrow, as he found my great-great-grandfather, silent and still now, and thought about his future wife, my great-grandmother, Mary, short and broad-faced; how in that moment he could see her sure, blunt-fingered hands, and how he felt a smudge of the pain she would feel when he told her about her father, her silenced father.

I tried for years to apply my grandmother's lessons about what makes a good story to my own fiction. I failed. My first attempts at short stories were meandering long scenes. Maudlin characters never spoke; instead they stared pensively at swaying trees and wetland grass. There was never more than one character in them, so there was never cause for dialogue. The characters never even spoke to themselves. They sulked under willow trees or drove cars over bayous and thought deep thoughts. These early forays into fiction were objectively terrible. After much trying and failing, I wrote one good story about a trucker on a long-distance cattle haul, inspired by one of my neighbors in DeLisle, and then I wrote ten bad stories. Even after years of writing fiction, of finally finding my way to novel writing, a form that seems a little less restrictive and more forgiving, I still struggle with writing short stories. Writing a good piece of short fiction is difficult. This is one of the reasons that it has been such an honor to read for this collection, to see what mavericks of the form are creating, how even during pandemic and pandemonium, they are creating art that we will return to again and again, beyond this year and into the future.

I brought my need for narrative to sustain me, to keep me afloat in this year of insurrection and alternative truths, of rampant illness and death, to this endeavor of choosing this year's best American short stories. I read, and I held my grandmother's lessons about what makes for good story close to me. There were so many good short fiction pieces to choose from, stories peopled by compelling characters, rich with startling language, stories of intricate present worlds and riveting tensions. These were stories so good I almost felt the presence of the authors in the room with me, murmuring, and once I was done, the writers and their characters remained.

The first story I read from this strange year was "Clementine, Carmelita, Dog," by David Means. In this story Means allows us to inhabit the world of a dog who wanders through the lives of humans, humans who are struggling with loss, adrift in their own storm-tossed seas of grief. The dog binds them in her singular experience, and in doing so allows us to see something of ourselves in her and in her humans. The more I read, the more I encountered stories that shocked me out of my own experience and completely immersed me in another. In "The Last Days of Rodney," by Tracey Rose Peyton, I found myself living with Rodney King, an exhausted and tender man, bound by his own history and trauma, as he approaches death. In "In This Sort of World, the Asshole

Wins," by Christa Romanovsky, I hustled and hallucinated with a woman struggling with the weight of the world, with her own powerlessness, her own resolve, her own substance abuse. This immersion in other people through short stories fed something in me; it sated a very human need to sink into another's reality, to inhabit another's experience, and in doing so to understand my own little world, my own wandering, bewildered self a bit better. In these stories I experienced companionship and communion in words. When I read their last lines, when I ascended out of their worlds, I could breathe a little easier in my own skin, my own life, because I knew kinship.

I read more, and I encountered stories that twisted the realities of the worlds the characters inhabited, that turned surreal and beautiful all at once; these stories drew me into difference. In "To Buffalo Eastward," by Gabriel Bump, a man driven by heartbreak and loss careens through a nonsensical, charged landscape, drinking and doing drugs with strangers, sneaking into office buildings; the whole time he is searching for something to ease his loss. In "Playing Metal Gear Solid V: The Phantom Pain," by Jamil Jan Kochai, a boy plays a military video game set in the Middle East; the game expands, turns surreal, and he enters the world of the game to save his uncle, to save his father, and in some ways to save himself. In "Our Children," by Vanessa Cuti, a mother divorces and remarries, and on a camping trip that she takes with her family, she decides to abandon her children and her stepchildren to the woods: she leaves them, and the world that she inhabits when she drives away from them is dangerously alluring, terrible, and distorted. These stories, which take place on the labyrinthine roads and office parks of America, in the solitary rooms of the pandemic, rooms lit by the blue glow of virtual space, and then in the suburbs and wilderness of this country, all provided me with maps to different realities, different ways of being. In each of these stories a transformation of place occurs, and reality changes from familiar to menacing, from known to unknown. These changes mirrored the world I lived in during the past year, and while disorienting, these stories, these surreal transformations of world and circumstance and character, made me feel less lonely.

In my reading, I found compelling stories that not only transported me to surreal realities but also moved me through time. In "Portrait of Two Young Ladies in White and Green Robes (Unidentified Artist, circa Sixteenth Century)," by Jane Pek, one immortal being speaks to another who gave up her immortality, and in speaking to her beloved's ghost, this immortal sends a missive over the centuries, which becomes a testament to the undying nature of love. In "Love Letter," by George Saunders, a grandfather in a dystopian future (a future that seems to be a speculative outcome of our own terrible, post–January 6 insurrection present) writes to his grandson in an attempt to give him some advice, some words that might save him. Both of these artful, beautifully constructed stories tell a tale of time, of how it is mutable, alive, mysterious, and real. How all we have in this strange and bewildering present are those we love, and how even when the times turn terrible, that love remains. In this pandemic year, this was a particularly valuable lesson to read and remember, lost as we all were in the tumult of time, the uncertainty of living through a moment that felt novel and familiar at once in its unpredictability, in its ugliness, in its loss.

Young people figure prominently in many of the stories I chose for this collection. The young protagonists at the center of these stories are desperately grasping toward adulthood. Perhaps I chose these stories because this year, in many ways, made me feel unmoored in a way I hadn't since I was a teenager. As I came of age, half aware of the pressure of society and culture around me but fully cognizant of their weight, I found myself wandering, aghast. The young people in these stories are compelling and unruly and imperfect, and perfectly heartbreaking. The characters in "Biology," by Kevin Wilson, are a teacher and a student, both attempting to navigate the brutality of the world and still hold on to their innate tenderness, and it is very moving. The young people at the heart of "The Rest of Us," by Jenzo DuQue, are not so lucky: the world proves too much for them, and they break, turn nihilistic, with the seeds of caring and kindness buried deep within them. "Little Beast," by C Pam Zhang, follows a group of girls turned terrible, both to others and themselves, in an unjust world. In "The Miracle Girl," by Rita Chang-Eppig, two sisters grapple with miracles, identity, and the messy permutations of sibling rivalry and love. In "Switzerland," by Nicole Krauss, an older woman recalls her youth at a boarding school in Switzerland with a group of girls wizened beyond their years, full of bluster and bravado as they struggle to hide their naive hearts, to exercise some sense of agency in a world that abuses them and renders them powerless.

In "You Are My Dear Friend," by Madhuri Vijay, a young au pair adopts an older child, an intelligent, sharp-eyed girl, who acts out her sense of dispossession, her sense of powerlessness, on the au pair. All of these stories reveal painful truths about what it is to be a child in this world. The struggles that these young characters face dismantled me, and then the careful consideration of the ways they coped or didn't cope, of how they survived, pieced me back together again, and left me a bit more clear-eyed than before.

Some characters were more opaque, less open, raw, and vulnerable than the younger characters I encountered; some were even downright unlikable, but they were still irresistibly compelling. The daughter-in-law in Yxta Maya Murray's "Paradise" is plainspoken and immediately sympathetic, while her father-in-law is brusque and unyielding and racist, but the story peels away the layers of his personality so that by the end we feel empathy for both of them. The same is true of both characters in "Palaver," by Bryan Washington, which follows a mother and son who spend much of the story speaking past each other, around each other, through each other, until, after so much fumbling, they find their way to truth and truce. In Stephanie Soileau's "Haguillory," we meet an older man who is obstinate, close-minded, his heart damn near calcified, who changes, just a hairbreadth, after a chance encounter. Each time these characters surprise us by exposing a flicker of vulnerability, they demand we look beyond their thorny outsides to their soft insides. These characters, like all the people I encountered in my grandmother's stories, are deeply flawed and deeply conflicted but still empathetic at heart, still recognizable, and we as readers are able to see ourselves in their humanity and their inhumanity.

Finally, some stories enthralled me because they surprised me. Many of them surprised me in terms of language, language that was layered and textured and rich and took unexpected turns and played with rhythm and phrasing. Some of these same stories also surprised me in terms of endings, in how plot evolved in the world of the story. In "Escape from the Dysphesiac People," by Brandon Hobson, the main character, an indigenous boy, runs away from the dysphesiac people, white Americans, who stole him; his escape is both surreal and hypnotic, due to the rhythm and building of the prose. In "Good Boy," by Eloghosa Osunde, a queer Nigerian man tells the story of his liberation, a tale that is largely concerned with the title character reconciling, in an unexpected way, with his father, who shunned him. Everything about this character is unexpected, from the way he uses language to the way he exercises agency in his life. In "A Way with Bea," by Shanteka Sigers, a teacher, her elementary school student, and the student's brother all change in unpredictable ways as the story progresses to its devastating, tender end. In these tales, the surprise of the flowering of a human being, the evolution of character, reminds me that this too can be true of human beings in real life. At the same time that we are capable of devolution in private and public life, we are also capable of empathetic evolution and change.

In the end, I hope this collection offers you the opportunity for immersion, for surprise, for travel, for awe. I hope that as you sink into world after world, become character after character in these stellar stories, you can forget yourself, and then, upon surfacing, know yourself and others anew. I hope that return offers you some sense of ease and, as the best fiction does, a sense of repair. I hope that we get more from these writers, these blazing voices, as many of them are at the beginning of their careers. I am honored to have read their work, and I hope that you feel the same after you read this collection.

JESMYN WARD

The Best
AMERICAN
SHORT
STORIES
2021

To Buffalo Eastward

FROM *McSweeney's*

So, THE SUNRISE outside Ann Arbor—I figured I'd say something about that. I was in my parked car, reclined all the way, feet pressed against the radio, thinking about falling asleep there, outside that gas station. I was less than halfway to where I was headed when I saw the sun come over the pines, when I decided to keep going, when I decided to stop smoking, after just this last one.

The cigarette bounced out my rolled-down window, caught a breeze, floated into grass sparkled with dew. I had started, miles before the sunrise, to describe things in my head as *sparkled, dazzled, majestic,* and so on. Water and seagulls underneath the Mackinac Bridge during last night's sunset—that was glitter. I had crossed the bridge; I had decided to stop smoking, after just that last one. That cigarette hit a car's windshield and flew into the straits. In my rearview mirror: sparks and a swearing woman. She passed me on a slight curve, flipped me off, sped onto an exit ramp. I'd expected as much. Once, back home on our major road, a woman threw a hamburger against my window, made me swerve a bit.

There was a bookstore in Ann Arbor. Before another sunset, I stood looking at the novels and short stories and no one asked if I needed help. A person in college-themed sweatpants dropped their stack on my feet. I joked that my feet were made of titanium. The person in college-themed sweatpants laughed and invited me to a party, wrote an address in my phone, smiled after the books were rearranged in their arms. I told them my schedule was tight, which it wasn't, was never.

Outside the bookstore, in my car, I read about this new drug for depression and anxiety. It was a shot for which you had to pay thousands of dollars. I wondered if I needed a shot like that. One of my problems is not understanding my problems. I sat with my therapist and talked about childhood memories. I have problems telling stories. I get on one track and backflip to another, running in the opposite direction. One second I'm pulling a freight train from Kansas City to Las Vegas. The next second I'm in southern Indiana, headed to Atlanta. I know that's a problem. I wish I understood it. I watched a man in glasses leave the bookstore with a paper bag. I watched the paper bag rip. I laughed hard enough to cough. That was another thing wrong with me: laughing, at first, when someone needed help. I'd laugh before helping. I'd still help. I'd laugh first. Coughing in my car, I wondered if they had shots for whatever was wrong with me. The man didn't want help. He waved me away, grumbled into his fallen books, adjusted his tie, swore with a Nordic-sounding cadence, yelled at a bus for almost breaking his legs.

That was the bookstore in Ann Arbor.

At a liquor store in Ann Arbor, I weighed a plastic bottle of vodka in my hand. I picked up a bigger bottle and held it like an old cat.

In a grocery store parking lot in Ann Arbor, I slept and dreamed that all my pants were back home, folded and forgotten in my drawer. There was loud music in my dream and I was naked, not having a good time, getting yelled at by a disembodied voice.

Outside a house party in Ann Arbor, I counted people on a porch, counted people through the front window, counted people dancing, counted people talking, hugging, drinking, shaking hands.

Outside a house party in Ann Arbor, I pulled away.

I found a motel near the highway, off the southbound side.

Here's my point: that was day two.

I woke up in the darkness. Soon there it was: my life, it seemed, coming over the pines.

Day three would find me pulling into Buffalo around dinnertime.

There was a bookstore in Toledo, the Maumee River, places to sit along its banks, bars with small TVs showing baseball and game shows. Toledo seemed like enough for me. I carried my book and beer to the water, wanted a peaceful moment to watch smoke waft from the industrial parts of town into my lungs. I said something about America's decline to myself, out loud.

"Excuse me?" a jogging man said, slowed down in front of me, blocked my view.

"Nothing," I said. "Talking to myself."

"You can't drink here," the jogging man said, still jogging in place.

"I'm not drinking," I said.

"I'm not stupid," the jogging man said.

"I don't know you," I said.

The jogging man scoffed, continued on his way, glanced over his shoulder, made sure I wasn't following and foaming out of my lips.

Here's how I look: tallish; medium-brown freckles around my nose and eyes, on my ears; a broad nose with a little point, a little hook; strong-chinned; weak-bodied; soft, thin, broad-shouldered; my nails get too long before I chew them down; my foot arches are too high; without thinking, I walk on my toes; if I'm not mindful, my eyebrows can meld into a single thicket.

I have this ambiguous brown skin. People wonder if I'm Egyptian, Aboriginal, Brazilian, Mexican, Dominican, half of this, a quarter of that.

I have this long hair that grows up and out in curled waves. People don't know what to make of it. In middle school, this classmate would pull at my hair, try to yank strands out, hold my curls up to the light.

When I was little, people thought my mother was my nanny. My mother was a dean at Upper Peninsula State College. She taught classes on economics, gave lectures on employee happiness. She wrote a book about suicide rates in Silicon Valley. She told me to find pleasure in work, keep an eye on your heart and soul. She grew up in the projects in Chicago, would always tell me how she grew up in the projects and could whoop my ass. Once we tried to visit her childhood home in Chicago. We parked our car outside a chain-link fence with no buildings behind it. It was the largest empty lot I had ever seen. The city had blown up my mother's childhood home. They were going to build condos and offices, hair salons and organic grocery stores. Parked outside that chain-link fence, my mother cried about history. All her family was dead and buried in modest graves in Chicago, Harlem, Oklahoma City, and Georgia. When she felt like it, my mother could grow an Afro with gray streaks blaring from her temples.

Before I left, my mother gave me an industrial wrench for protection, in case my car broke down in Ohio and some local boys wanted to take advantage.

My father asked me to procure sports memorabilia, bring it back at Christmas, wrap it up, make it nice. In our kitchen, my father had a coffee mug from every NHL team, most MLB teams, half of the NBA, some NFL. He wrote a book about traveling to professional sports arenas around America. He wanted to write a screenplay about himself and sell it to Hollywood.

For years my father reported on high school sports for our local newspaper. Then, when the newspaper folded, he wrote a sports column for a local website. Then, after the town turned Republican, he started folding political jokes into his analysis, speaking truth to power, rambling on about the declining American mystique, eroding values. He resigned after someone mailed a dead rat to our house. We moved at night. That was a few years ago. We all cried in my mother's car.

I majored in European history, worked at UPSC's library, lived at home, hung around people and places I had always known.

I finished my beer on the Maumee. I found a route to Cleveland that took me along Lake Erie at a slow pace, through lowlands and forests.

There was a bookstore in Cleveland. There were stacks so tall you needed a ladder to reach the top. I asked a man with a ponytail if he could help with those Raymond Carver collections up there. He was a carpenter, not a librarian, he told me as much, hand on his hip, other hand holding Joyce and Morrison. He told me to climb the ladder myself, it wasn't that high, I wasn't that small.

When I came down, the man asked me to drink with him. He knew a spot next door, with TVs and boiled hot dogs—Cleveland against Minneapolis, which I knew before he told me. I looked at my wrist, forgot I'd left my watch back home with Pidge, as a way for her to remember me.

Pidge had kissed me before I left Michigan, on a gravel road, under a moon-draped evergreen, between two small lakes.

Whenever I texted Pidge on the road, I would think about turning around and driving back, which Pidge didn't want, because

Pidge has a fiancé. I would tell her about driving back. She'd call me "stupid" and "emotional."

One night back home, I stood outside my parked car, leaned against my hood, keeping track of an owl hooting its way across the lakes. Pidge was supposed to meet me at midnight. We were supposed to drive down to Kenosha, get an apartment, get two kittens, work from home, write books, cook global cuisines. Pidge was supposed to leave her fiancé. I waited until three in the morning. When she came in to work the next day, carrying her coffee and handmade satchel, I asked her to lunch. She declined with a thank-you. When I saw her after work, walking across the quad, I asked if I could call her later that night. She held my hands and apologized, said I couldn't, sorry.

"Huh?" the carpenter asked.

"Nothing," I said. "Talking to myself."

"Do you need a drink?" the carpenter asked. "I need a drink."

"I need to get to Buffalo," I said.

"That's close," the carpenter said.

He ordered two Miller Lites for himself, opened both, sipped both, opened his Joyce, laid it out between his arms, kept it open with his elbows. I wanted vodka. I wanted to know how this carpenter managed all these things at once. I imagined his works as solid—bookcases and skyscrapers, barns and avant-garde chairs. Minneapolis hit a home run into shallow left field. I ordered a Miller Lite. The carpenter flicked up one elbow, took a sip, and turned the page.

I waited for the carpenter to tell me something. Two women walked in falling over, held each other up, almost didn't make it to the bar, winked at us, blew us kisses, fell over laughing. I looked up at the screen, watched a batter get hit on the foot by a fastball. I figured I could leave at any moment and no one would notice. I worked through my next steps.

First, make it out of Cleveland alive.

Second, get some lunch on the way to Buffalo.

Third, call Flip when I got close.

Fourth, live in Buffalo.

First I had to finish my beer.

"What's he reading?" the two women asked at the same time now, standing behind me.

"Joyce," I said. "I think."

"*Dubliners!*" one woman said.

"*Finnegans Wake!*" the other woman said.

I tried to find a difference between their faces, their hair, their dark eyes made darker by the lightless bar. Both had black hair straightened flat, small eyes close to their noses.

The carpenter drained one can, then another. He turned his head away and belched into his armpit.

"*Ulysses,*" the carpenter said, closed the book, showed them the cover.

"Yes!" one woman yelled.

"I said yes!" the other woman yelled.

"I will yes!" one woman yelled.

Two outs into the third inning, the women introduced themselves. My eyes had adjusted to the darkness. Now I could see unique lines and blemishes on their cheeks and necks. Whenever they laughed, I noticed the different ways their teeth zagged. They wore matching blue lipstick. Their touches on my shoulder were different weights, whenever the carpenter made a joke about literature and the women couldn't hold firm on their feet, needed me to keep them up. We had arranged ourselves in a small circle. The carpenter and I had our backs to the game. We ordered more beer. We went around and said our names.

"Sancho," the carpenter said. "Sancho Panza."

"And I'm Daisy Buchanan," one woman said, laughing, heavy hand on my shoulder.

"I'm Jordan Fucking Baker," the other woman said, emptying a beer can into her face.

"What about our real names?" I asked.

"I'm Daisy Buchanan," Daisy Buchanan said. "I'm alone and boring."

"That's unfair," Jordan Baker said. "That's a shallow interpretation."

"I'm Daisy Buchanan," Daisy Buchanan said. "I'll steal your man. I'll steal your car."

"I'm Sancho Panza," Sancho Panza said. "I work for an idiot, a monster, a liar."

"Who are you?" Jordan Baker asked me, leaned forward on her stool, winked.

I tried to remember all the books I loved, all the characters I couldn't forget. I imagined myself back home, years ago, a child, kneeling in my mother's small library, thumbing through the hardcover and paperback rows. I heard my mother's feet come up the stairs, kick at the door, soft, nice. I heard my mother telling me to get out with my grease-stained fingers, my mud-stained shoes. I remember the book I had hidden in my shirt when she pushed me out, locked the door.

"I'm Invisible," I said. "I'm the Invisible Man."

"The lights!" Daisy Buchanan yelled.

We emptied our beers, ordered more, asked for a plate of hot dogs with mustard slathered on the buns.

During the seventh-inning stretch, Jordan Baker explained how love evaporates.

"It's like this friendship," Jordan Baker said. "After a while, if it's not going to work, you start to hate each other. You get annoyed every time they want to dance with you at a party. You hear them crying in the bathroom after another yelling match, and you get annoyed because they're crying and you have to make them feel better, tell them you're sorry. You hate them. Still, you're friends, best friends, because if you spend that much time with someone, those many years, you have to care about them, even if you hate them, even if you can't eat at the same time as them because they chew with their mouths open and smack their lips like they've always done. Still, one day you decide to leave. Still, it hurts. Even if you hate them, it hurts."

I expected Jordan Baker to slow down, stop talking. She didn't stop. Instead I excused myself, waddled to the bathroom, wiped my eyes, told myself not to cry in front of strangers.

I splashed hard, cold water on my face, slapped my cheeks, told myself I wasn't going to die alone.

Pidge isn't why I left home. Pidge didn't force me to Buffalo. Still, I would've liked Pidge to come with me. I thought we'd have fun driving with the windows down, trying out new lives.

Pidge's fiancé teaches in the engineering department. He studies ice fishing and climate change. Pidge has a picture of him on her office desk. He's shirtless on a mountain, smiling, trying to cover his belly fat with his slim arms. He's a nice-looking guy. His students nominate him for teaching awards. Once he answered when I called Pidge's cell phone. She was taking a nap. He asked to take a message. I told him Pidge had overdue books and the fines were starting to get serious. He apologized. I apologized. He hung up. I held the phone to my face.

Pidge would leave me notes on her library cards. They would say things like "You're my primary source" and "Check me out any day."

Once Pidge kissed me in the Medieval Medicine section.

When I got back, it was Daisy Buchanan's turn.

"It's like waking up from a nightmare," Daisy Buchanan said. "It's three in the morning, you're sweating. Your nightmares were about falling into a canyon, flying into the sun, whatever. You're up and looking around, gasping for air, all this sweat on your back and face. And then you hear this voice telling you it's okay. It was just a nightmare, it's okay. This voice is close to your face, tickling your ear. It's telling you to go back to sleep. It's okay. It's just a nightmare. And calm comes over you like a cold snap."

"I've heard that voice," Sancho Panza said.

"Then one morning," Daisy Buchanan continued, "you forget your lunch at home. You drive back from work. You open the door. And that calming voice is naked in your kitchen, making pancakes with your naked next-door neighbor."

At the top of the ninth inning, Minneapolis had the tying run on first base, with some power at the plate. Sancho Panza crushed a beer can flat between his palms. He flung the disk at a trash can fifteen feet away. He missed; we booed; he went out for a cigarette; we followed. Jordan Baker sat on a fire hydrant, rubbed her face, stamped a fallen branch to pieces.

"We need an adventure," Daisy Buchanan said.

"We could go to the harbor," Sancho Panza said.

"What's at the harbor?" I asked.

"Water," Sancho Panza said. "A lake. Waves."

"I've seen enough lakes," I said. "I'm sick of water."

"Sometimes," Jordan Baker said, "I feel like floating until I sink."

"No water," Daisy Buchanan said. "Let's climb something."

"I know roofs," Sancho Panza said. "I have keys and back doors."

"Once," Jordan Baker said, "in high school, I watched a woman ride a motorcycle into a pool. I bet that's happening somewhere tonight."

"You're right," Sancho Panza said. "We need transportation."

*

We emptied the junk from my backseat, mixed it with the mess in my trunk—books, clothes, chips bags, candy wrappers: my life laid bare for them to inspect and handle. We found a liquor store up the road, bought pints of flavored schnapps. We listened to country music. We tried to guess the words to songs we hadn't heard before, wouldn't hear again. We missed a turn. We didn't talk about our unpaid tab at the bar. We didn't talk about one another. There was nothing to know. In my front seat, Jordan Baker tapped on the glass, told us life was a series of fishbowls. Behind me, Daisy Buchanan and Sancho Panza rubbed at each other, made kissing noises.

"Here!" Sancho Panza yelled. "Turn! Park!"

We parked and looked up at an office building—a three-story structure made of windows and thick black metal strips.

"There are people," I said, pointing at workers in suits and dresses, carrying briefcases, trudging around, slumping into cars.

"Nine-to-five," Daisy Buchanan said. "I couldn't do it."

"They sell metal pipes," Sancho Panza said. "Some of them sell potato chips, I think."

"How do you know?" I asked.

"This is mine," Sancho Panza said.

"You own this building?" I asked.

"Other buildings too," Sancho Panza said. "A pizza place, that bar, that bookstore."

"You have an empire," Daisy Buchanan said.

"I am benevolent," Sancho Panza said. "I am cruel only when the hour demands it."

Sancho Panza had a key to a back door. He challenged us to race up a metal stairway. We passed a man smoking a cigar and crying into his cell phone. We passed a well-dressed couple laughing and pressing into each other. We exited onto a wide roof, where a woman in a skirt was juggling three empty beer bottles. Startled, she fumbled her trick, disappeared into another doorway, another staircase.

Here Sancho Panza reached into his pocket and materialized four pills, each a different brilliant color. Now someone commented on the view, how flat and boring it appeared, a repeated system of low buildings and mediocre trees. Now we took the pills.

That wasn't the first time I had taken pills from a stranger's pocket. In high school, around a campfire, on a small, abandoned island, a girl's older boyfriend asked if we wanted to feel the universe against our minds. "Sure," we said, bored, a little drunk, smiling at one another through the low flames. That island was abandoned in a bureaucratic sense. Somewhere, down an untraceable line, someone had stopped paying taxes on the land; somewhere, a bank sent a hollow person to put up foreclosure signs on the island's banks. We had never known the delinquent landowner.

There was a home yards away from the campfire. There was another up from the dock, a short hike uphill. Around the campfire, we took the pills and went into the closer house. Whenever we were bored and a little drunk, sick of staring at fire and embers, talking about fishing and car crashes on the hairpin turn near town, we'd stand up and walk into the home. Yes, the home was abandoned in the bureaucratic sense. Most nights and days, no one walked around in there, picking things up, putting things down, calling through doors and walls, walking carefully up the stairs. Still, a mattress sat, soiled and deflated, in the living room. Words spray-painted on the walls almost covered all the exposed wood beams. This was an abandoned house on a small island: everything you'd imagine. Our pills kicked in, we wrestled into a big pile in the second-floor bedroom. Later, we all linked arms and looked out a broken window onto our lakes. The late-night stillness heightened our experience, as if the water was one big mirror that could swallow our souls, the ghosts inside us. We waited for sunrise in the living room, standing in a line, arm in arm, looking at the dirt- and dust-covered floor, looking. The girl's older boyfriend saw a muskrat playing in the sink. No one else saw it; no one else looked. Instead, we saw snow falling, soft flurries taking long, curved routes to the water and dirt. We stayed like that until the flurries turned into a solid white sheet, cascading down on us. The pills wore off when it was too late. Sober, in the morning light, we had to shovel snow from our boats before they sank. We had to think of excuses for our parents. The girl's older boyfriend panicked, started pacing around and talking about cops coming on boats and helicopters and submarines. He started telling us about microphones in tree trunks, cameras in vermin. That muskrat! He yelled about that muskrat until we subdued him in well-formed football tackles from multiple angles. We put our hands over his mouth. We finished shoveling our boats after he went back to sleep. We left him there. Once I saw him pushing carts around the grocery store. I saw him on a tractor riding through town. I saw him, from a bridge, running across a frozen river.

Back on the roof in Cleveland, Sancho Panza wanted to know if the pills were working—could we feel ourselves turning inside out, exploding like a flower?

"I could wake up in Egypt," Jordan Baker said.

"What difference would it make?" Daisy Buchanan asked.

"I'd have all the sand I could want," Jordan Baker said.

"There's sand in Ohio!" Daisy Buchanan said.

"Not the same," Jordan Baker said, sat on the ground. "It's just not the same."

I found myself yards away, walking in a circle, counting my revolutions.

I found myself running into Sancho Panza, knocking him over.

Sancho Panza grabbed my ankles, begged me not to let him drown.

I had my hands on Sancho Panza's collar when I noticed the sky, swirling and wavering, preparing to rupture. Out there in the distance, toward downtown, the sky sucked up tall buildings.

"It's coming for us," I said.

Sancho Panza had stopped swinging at my throat and screaming. He went limp, took deep breaths, turned an ear to the roof, coughed, and spit up thick brown mucus.

"They're working," Sancho Panza said. "I think they're working."

Daisy Buchanan and Jordan Baker appeared, flanked me, trained their large pupils on my cheeks.

"Look," I told them, "this sky is bad business."

They jerked their heads upward, gaped at moving clouds.

"Don't you see it?" Daisy Buchanan asked.

"Of course," Jordan Baker said. "It's right there. Of course."

"My school bus," Daisy Buchanan said. "Right there. I'm right there waving for help."

"That's my submarine," Jordan Baker said. "Those are my specimens."

I couldn't explain how their eyes and minds were playing tricks. There wasn't a school bus; there wasn't a submarine. Above our heads, there weren't roads or seas or highways or rivers. It was all teeth and tongues.

Sancho Panza, reanimated, grabbed my leg, tried to climb up.

"My uncle," Sancho Panza said, drooled. "There was Easter breakfast at his farmhouse."

"I didn't finish my homework," Daisy Buchanan said. "Why can't I finish anything?"

"At these depths," Jordan Baker said, "we know more about the moon."

"You don't see it," I said. "You'll never see it."

"There's my daughter," Daisy Buchanan said, pointed behind us without looking. "Just like me: late and unprepared. And that face. Just like mine. Look how she hates it. Look how she can't stand it."

"Sunlight doesn't penetrate," Jordan Baker said. "Not this deep. Not under this pressure. It's all scientific, these things I don't understand. There's my power glowing in the abyss, protected by Paleolithic megasharks. It's all academic. It's all too scientific for me to understand."

"What?" I asked.

"Nothing," Jordan Baker said. "What did I say?"

"Uncle," Sancho Panza said, "why didn't you save me any coffee cake?"

We spent hours like that: talking and not understanding one another's eyes. At some point we left the roof, went to a lower floor, used Sancho Panza's master key to open offices and inspect other people's lives. We took framed family photos off desks, held them, and cried. We found liquor bottles in bottom drawers, took long sips. We found charts and graphs and memos; we felt connected to important happenings. In a large office, we found a list of underperforming employees. In a small office, we found a vision board with a spaceship and tiny glow-in-the-dark stars.

We finished in a conference room. Somewhere along the way, Jordan Baker had assembled a collection of stolen blankets. We all said goodnight. We kissed one another's hands. We pulled the blankets over our heads and blocked the rising sun. Curled against these whacked-out strangers, I felt a unique warmth, one I hadn't known before. I felt clear and directed, anchored. I had found peace. Here, I belonged.

I closed my eyes.

Instead of sleeping, I saw Pidge sliding across a frozen lake in her purple boots, twirling, extending her arms, teasing me, saying I couldn't keep up. Under her winter cap, her blond hair stiff against her neck. Her small frame puffed by her jacket and snow pants. Her nose crooked from a hockey fight, still black-and-blue. Her chipped teeth jagged in her smile. Brown eyes, almost black. She was sliding toward me now, getting smaller, getting faster.

That was Pidge during a break in a blizzard. Her fiancé wasn't her fiancé yet. Her fiancé was her boyfriend, out of town and stuck there because the blizzard was everywhere in the upper Midwest. We had brought bags of frozen burritos and beer to Pidge's apartment and holed up with movies and video games. Pidge, during her hockey game, had called an opposing player unkind names. They'd settled it with fists to the face and stomach. They'd both lost, busted up parts of their bodies and pride. I'd offered to help Pidge convalesce.

During a break in the blizzard, we bundled up and went for the lake.

Pidge sliding toward me, kicking up snow and ice, busting forth in a beautiful mist.

Pidge laughing at my unsteady feet, my wobbling.

Pidge confused—how could I not skate? Growing up around all this frozen water. How could I not skate?

Pidge slowing down, putting her heels down, kicking snow onto my legs.

Pidge spearing me to the ground.

Us cold on our backs.

Me asking if she was okay, putting my arms around her.

Pidge laughing, laughing, laughing, laughing.

Me slipping as I stood up.

Pidge staying down there, rolling around, laughing still.

I awoke to a man screaming, standing in the conference room doorway, spilling his coffee down his shirt.

Sancho Panza told me to run. He cupped my check with his hand. He'd handle it. Fly. Take your life. Jordan Baker and Daisy Buchanan were already gone. I could see their hair strands tangled in their blankets. I ran past the screaming man, ducked into a stairwell.

On my way down, I passed a man and a woman talking about running away, starting a new life, antiquing, scoring big at an auction, building a house in a tree.

On my driver's-side window, a note was written in blue lipstick. It read: "Invisible Man, make it where you're going."

The Miracle Girl

FROM *Virginia Quarterly Review*

ON THE FIRST DAY of her stigmata, Xiao Chun's palms bled so much that the school sent her home early. Xiao Xue sighed at this turn of events and gathered her things to follow her sister. Xiao Chun was already prettier, smarter, and more obedient—she just had to be holier too.

Wong Daifu, the village doctor, made a house call when he heard about the strange condition. He squinted at the puncture wounds, which were not round and smooth but thin ovals with fringes of red, protruding skin. "And you're sure she didn't hurt herself accidentally?" he asked.

"We were in class when this happened," Xiao Xue replied for her sister, who sat with her back straight and ankles crossed. "Me and the sixth graders were doing math with the teacher. She and the eighth graders were reading the Bible on their own. Suddenly she fell out of her chair and started flopping around."

"Then I don't know." He instructed Xiao Chun to keep the wounds bandaged and prescribed some herbs to prevent anemia.

That night, after getting shuffled off to bed, Xiao Xue heard her parents talking. "This is all because of the missionaries and their crazy school. I never heard of any bleeding palms before those foreigners got here," her father said.

"Keep your voice down," her mother said. "They've been kind to us. The food they give out isn't bad, and the girls are learning English. So what if we had to convert?"

He snorted loudly. "Either they want to give us food or they don't. Non-Catholics don't deserve to go hungry any more than Catholics do."

Xiao Xue wrapped her arms around herself and tried to sink deeper into the bed that she and Xiao Chun shared. Her sister was already asleep, kicking the blanket off the both of them little by little. The damp air chilled Xiao Xue's skin. A damselfly hurled itself against the window, its rapid wings making a sound like uncooked rice being spilled.

Xiao Xue didn't remember being particularly hungry before the foreigners came—not full, necessarily, but also not hollow the way her neighbors described. They'd fled to Taiwan from the revolution in China when Xiao Xue was a baby. She couldn't imagine lying awake from stomach pangs, feeling her blood thin into air. Yet the more the foreigners insisted that the villagers were poor and hungry, the poorer and hungrier the villagers seemed to become, as if they were living through some reverse loaves-and-fishes miracle. She once said as much to Xiao Chun, but her sister just rolled her eyes. "I guess you forgot the part about Mom scraping food from her plate onto yours."

When Xiao Chun kicked again, Xiao Xue snatched roughly at the blanket. Though Xiao Chun didn't react, Xiao Xue could tell she had awakened. "Does it hurt?" Xiao Xue asked.

"A little," Xiao Chun said, "but that doesn't matter. I feel so close to Jesus, you can't possibly understand. I feel his pain and his love for all of us."

Xiao Xue wormed closer to her sister, who had unwrapped one of the bandages and was admiring the wound. "What about if I do this?" she asked, pressing her finger into it. The flesh was warm and limp. The blood smelled like spring flowers newly broken through the earth.

"It doesn't matter."

Xiao Xue wiped her finger on the blanket and flipped onto her other side. Within minutes she was asleep. At some point in the night, she awoke and squinted at her sister. She was still admiring her hand. In the half-light from the hallway, the hole gleamed like a droplet squeezed from the heart of the sun. Would she feel warmer if she curled herself around the wound? she wondered. Would she shine with Jesus's love?

*

On the second day of the stigmata, the teachers called an assembly. They helped Xiao Chun onto the stage, which was just six milk crates turned upside down and pushed together. She was wearing a billowy white dress with little blue roses at the waist that one of the teachers had brought to school. It was the prettiest dress Xiao Xue had ever seen. The teachers explained that someone was coming from far away to investigate, to make sure that the stigmata were real. "Of course, we know that Xiao Chun isn't faking," Sister Eunice said to the students. "We were there when she fell to the ground. We witnessed the miracle with our own eyes."

One of the boys behind Xiao Xue muttered something about girls and bleeding. Sister Eunice cleared her throat. "This is no joking matter. Only those with unshakable faith and goodness experience the stigmata. All of you here should aspire to be like Xiao Chun."

Xiao Xue nudged Ye Jing's shoulder. He had been gawping at Xiao Chun since the assembly started. Not that he didn't gawp at her normally, a fact her mother sometimes teased him about ("Too bad you're younger than Xiao Chun," she liked to say to him. "Otherwise you two would make a cute pair"), but now he appeared transfixed. When he didn't respond, Xiao Xue elbowed him in the ribs.

"Stop," he said.

"Come to my house today," she said.

"I have to look after my grandfather."

"My sister will be there. Wong Daifu ordered her to go home directly after school."

He thought for a moment, longer than she would have liked. "I can't," he said finally, and she felt disappointed and relieved at the same time.

Onstage, Sister Eunice was retelling the story of Saint Francis. While fasting on a mountain, she said, growing more and more impassioned, Saint Francis was visited by a six-winged angel bearing the marks of the Crucifixion. His heart brimmed with both grief and joy, for he was both saddened by the angel's suffering and grateful that he had been chosen for this vision. Suddenly wounds appeared in his hands and feet. His side began to bleed as if pierced with a spear.

"Her eyes! Her eyes!" one of the students yelled.

Blood was dripping down Xiao Chun's pale, heart-shaped face. She seemed surprised by the development, cupping her bandaged palms in front of her chest, mouth slightly open. But she couldn't catch all the tears—they rolled over the sides of her hands, seeped through the cracks between her fingers, and landed on the white dress.

In an instant, all the teachers and students had surrounded her. Ye Jing knelt by her side, stroking her back.

"I was listening to the story of Saint Francis," she said, "and I was overcome by compassion for him, so I started crying. I didn't even realize."

"Oh, glory, glory," Sister Eunice said to the ceiling.

Sister Eunice drove the two girls home that afternoon, jabbering about Saint Francis and the importance of works as they walked to her car. Xiao Chun trailed some distance behind them, gazing serenely at the birds and trees. "It is because your sister works so hard," Sister Eunice said to Xiao Xue, "always helping out those around her, always thinking of the good of others, that she has been blessed in this way. I know you have it in you to be blessed too!"

"I don't want to bleed," Xiao Xue said. "It looks like it hurts."

"Not even for Jesus?"

"I said I don't want to!"

Sister Eunice looked a little saddened by this, but whatever guilt Xiao Xue might have felt disappeared when Sister Eunice insisted that Xiao Chun lie across the backseat and thereby take up most of the space. Xiao Xue practically had to paint herself onto the door. She pressed her cheek against the cold glass of the window, listening to the car's grunts. The long-nosed Buick made her a little uncomfortable. It reminded her of a beast turned inside out, bones to the weather, the tough hide of the leather seats protected, the thick stitching in the cushions like fur markings.

The missionaries had arrived in this car five years ago. It was as if they'd timed their appearance to the sunset. In the liquid red light, the pale vehicle appeared armored in gold. It nuzzled the dirt road and whinnied as it slowed to a stop.

Xiao Xue had never seen a car up close before. Four foreigners stepped out: two men in suits, strips of fabric lolling from their necks like tongues, and two women with curls that had been dragooned into orderliness by a cavalry of hairpins. Xiao Xue couldn't quite understand what she was seeing. They were people —she knew that, of course—but they were so removed from her concept of people that someone might have convinced her otherwise. They didn't look comely or hideous so much as otherworldly. If she were a powerful being, she'd thought, she would choose these people to represent her.

The missionaries built a school and next to that a chapel. No longer did the children have to walk an hour each way to get to the school a town over. The missionaries set up a food pantry where wheat flour and rice were always in supply. They spoke not only Mandarin but also Hokkien. All the villagers had to do was set aside some time on Sundays to listen to their stories.

And so they breathed in the missionaries' messages, and so they drank the wine that could, in the right hands, thicken into blood. The stories became facts, if not among the adults, then at least among the children. It was as if they'd lacked immunity.

Xiao Xue had liked the missionaries at first, even Sister Eunice, who doled out candy to any child who could perfectly recite a Bible verse or prayer in English to her. Xiao Xue had chosen the Lord's Prayer because it was relatively short and easy to read. Sister Eunice's face, normally still as a pond, had quivered into a smile, little ripples spreading near the corners of her mouth and eyes. She laid a warm, heavy hand on Xiao Xue's head, and Xiao Xue swore to herself that she would memorize every word in the Bible if this was going to be the typical response. The piece of candy, a doubloon of chocolate, she split into four pieces so she could continue to savor it until she was done memorizing the next passage.

But then, without even being asked, Xiao Chun had recited the Apostles' Creed in front of the whole assembly, in Latin. In that moment, Xiao Xue saw clearly her place in Sister Eunice's eyes (and by extension, she supposed, God's). She never recited again, even when Sister Eunice called upon her to do so. There just didn't seem to be a point.

The pilgrims began arriving on the seventh day. Bearing gifts of dried fruit, oolong tea, and ginseng shaped like dangling puppets, they arrived, tracking mud onto the freshly washed floor and clogging up the family's one outhouse. Christians and non-Christians, they arrived, spurred by the missionaries' word-of-mouth network, because a spectacle was a spectacle no matter what one believed.

Xiao Xue's father had at first railed against the idea of strangers in his home, but the other villagers begged him to reconsider. Pilgrims meant money for the restaurant and the corner store. "Maybe you can even sell some of your bamboo carvings," her mother said.

For days her mother swept and scrubbed. This put her in a bad mood, even though she had been more excited by the idea of pilgrims than anyone else in the family. Nothing was clean enough, not the low wooden table on which Xiao Xue had spilled sauce and left a stain, not the cups and bowls, which were cobwebbed with fine cracks. Whenever Xiao Xue asked for anything, be it an afternoon snack or help with sewing a truant button back onto her school uniform, she received only a scolding. The morning they were set to receive the first visitors, while Xiao Xue was playing with beanbags by herself, bothering absolutely no one, her mother said, "Am I supposed to do everything around here? Go make yourself useful!" Xiao Xue stomped out of her mother's hollering range and into the bedroom, where her sister was taking a nap. She'd been about to wake Xiao Chun up but stopped when she saw her expression. What was that English word they'd learned in school? *Rapturous*. On Xiao Chun's fair face, with its long dark lashes and brows, the expression was *enrapturing*.

She rooted around in her mother's drawer and found the sewing scissors. Xiao Chun snoozed through her haircut.

Her mother shrieked when she saw Xiao Xue's handiwork. "You told me to make myself useful," Xiao Xue said. "Her bangs were getting long."

She was locked in the closet as punishment. All day she could hear pilgrims swishing about on the floors, burbling excitedly. A few times she could hear her sister's voice, thin and shiny like a fishing line. It was dark by the time they let Xiao Xue out. Xiao Chun was the one to do it. "I forgive you," she said, her uneven bangs pulled back with a pearly headband Xiao Xue didn't recognize. It must have been a new gift from Sister Eunice.

"I don't care," Xiao Xue said.

"Well, I still forgive you. I just hope you learn the error of your ways. Envy is a dangerous sin." Xiao Chun reached out and lifted a tuft of Xiao Xue's coarse hair. Once, while playing with friends, Xiao Chun had called her over so she could practice braiding. Xiao Xue sat down, her back to the other girls, and her sister began combing roughly through the tangle. Distracted by the pain, she didn't notice the muffled giggles until it was too late. Her hand flew up—the comb was stuck in her hair. When she failed to pull it out, the giggles sharpened into gasping laughter. In the end, her mother had to snip the comb loose. "Little hen, how did you do this?" she said, gathering the newly cut strands into proper braids and tying yellow ribbons around the ends. Yet Xiao Xue didn't tattle. Maybe she believed her mother would have taken her sister's side anyway. Or maybe some part of her did feel like it was her fault, having such ugly hair. According to Sister Eunice, places like Europe and the United States were prosperous because God favored Christian nations. What if her sister was beautiful because God favored her? What did that mean about Xiao Xue?

Xiao Xue snuck into her father's work shed one evening. He'd been spending more and more time there of late, making bamboo figurines for the pilgrims, who, it turned out, were willing to buy them, if for no other reason than that he was the father of the miracle girl.

He didn't acknowledge her at first. She padded around the small space, proving her fingertips on the augers' fanged bits, sliding her palm between the jaws of the vise and cranking the handle until she felt pain. She stood on tiptoes to see what her father was working on—most of the toys in the house came from here. For their most recent birthdays, Xiao Chun had received a dove; Xiao Xue had received a fat, grumpy-looking hen.

Her father was carving a woman wearing a flowing wimple, her hands together in prayer. Xiao Xue would have guessed he was carving the Virgin Mary, except the face wasn't a foreigner's. She felt an odd revulsion at the mismatch. Mary was pure and clean, shaped from white marble, not brown bamboo.

"You usually make animals," she said.

"Does your mother know you're here?"

"Yes," she lied. "Why aren't you making animals?"

"The pilgrims are asking for Mary. Go do your homework."

"I thought you didn't like the pilgrims."

Her father put down his tools so he could toss her a carved chicken. She caught it and fiddled with the movable wings. "It doesn't matter what I think," he said.

"They're stupid." She thought about the pilgrims' loud conversations with her sister, who held court in her white dress, cradling babies, washing the feet of the old. She thought about her own feet sliding around in the shit overflowing from the outhouse. The more she thought, the more upset she felt. "You should stop letting them come. You said the only thing they're good for is tiring Xiao Chun out."

He sighed. "Who knows. The town has been doing much better since they arrived. And Wong Daifu says your sister's healthy, just a little anemic. So maybe it's fine. I still don't know whether I believe any of this miracle talk, but money is money."

He went back to his carving. She stood there. She'd hoped he would take her side on this at least, though why should she have? All the problems in her family were her fault. The clothes she ripped while running and climbing. Her mother getting tired easily since giving birth to her. The family not having a son.

A daughter was fine for a first child—a blessing, even, because eldest daughters could be relied on to take care of younger siblings, whereas eldest sons could not—but then Xiao Xue had come along, tearing her way into the world, dark and bearish even as a baby. Their mother had bled so much that the midwife warned her against ever having another child.

Her parents never talked about it, though sometimes they yelled about it. Once, an auntie from the village asked her parents to look after her newborn son. All afternoon they tickled his little feet and his round tummy. That evening Xiao Xue saw her father sneak up behind her mother as she was washing dishes and wrap his arms around her waist. He whispered something in her ear. She pushed him away. "You know we can't," she said.

"You're too cautious. Maybe that old shrew was wrong," her father said.

"What if she's not? Do you want to raise our children by yourself?"

He threw a dish on the floor. "So that's it, then," he said. "My family's name ends with me." Grabbing a new pack of cigarettes, he crashed out of the house. The next morning Xiao Xue found him dozing on a chair in the kitchen, one cigarette left in the pack. She sat down next to him to eat her breakfast, accidentally jostling the table in the process. He rolled up the steel doors of his eyelids reluctantly, as though not quite ready to open shop.

"You always come at the wrong time," he said. And then the doors rolled down again.

On the twelfth day, Xiao Chun stopped eating. At lunch she gave her food to one of the younger children. "All I need is the Eucharist," she announced. Sister Eunice practically cartwheeled to the tabernacle, where they stored the consecrated hosts.

"Won't you be hungry later?" the child asked her.

"Jesus received no food while on the cross," she said. "Even if I felt hunger, it would pale in comparison to what he experienced. There are those who need this meal more. I do not wish to be someone who simply takes and takes."

From that day forward, all of Xiao Chun's school lunches went to the other children. The boys clamored loudest, and one of them usually ended up getting her portion. One afternoon Ye Jing dropped by their house to deliver a hat his mother had woven for Xiao Chun in thanks. It was yellow-brown with thorny, unfinished ends. Near the brim she'd scarred the bamboo with a tiny cross. Xiao Chun was napping, so Xiao Xue let him into the house.

Of all the villagers, Ye Jing's family had perhaps taken to the missionaries the most. Xiao Xue's father said it was because of the revolution in China. Like the missionaries, Ye Jing's parents had narrowly escaped the Communists. They'd bartered all their valuables for a ride on an unreliable ship. The story about Moses guiding the Israelites across the Red Sea rang out to them like a clarion. Ye Jing didn't understand why she disliked the missionaries so much. "They were nice to us," he insisted whenever the topic came up. "They were the only ones my grandma could talk to about how much she missed China. Did you know that a rich man wanted to marry Sister Eunice, but she decided it was more important to serve God? She left her entire family behind to come help us."

"Do you want to see her?" Xiao Xue asked, then grabbed his hand without waiting for his response. "Come on."

They squatted on the floor next to the bed. Xiao Chun was getting paler by the day. Ye Jing lifted a hand but didn't touch her, just laid it next to her pinkie on the bedspread. "She still isn't eating?" he asked.

"Only the host."

"She doesn't look like she's getting thinner. That's good." His expression was soft like clay yet to be sculpted.

"You should kiss her," she said. "See if she wakes up."

"What?"

"Kiss her."

"That's not funny."

She grabbed his wrist to stop him from leaving. "Practice on me. Pretend I'm her."

Still gripping him, she lay down on her back and closed her eyes. First she felt his breath. Then she felt his lips. With a tug, he fell forward onto her. They lay like that for a little while, perfectly overlapped, unmoving. His body was unevenly hard. It felt like lying on pebbles but in a world where land was sky. Suddenly he whined in a pained way and pushed himself to his feet.

"This is dirty," he said, scrabbling at his lips as if they were poisonous slugs. "Bad. You're bad." He ran out of the house. She wanted to chase after him, but her legs had other ideas. On the bed, Xiao Chun stirred and curled up on her side. Her sister was the inside of a nautilus shell, bright and pure. Sometimes Xiao Xue struggled to believe they were sisters at all.

That night, before bed, she scrubbed her face until the skin split. She felt better after the minor bloodletting, as if sanctified, as if lightened.

The teachers liked to tell this story: One day God decided to draw mankind a bath. He took one group of people and cleansed them first. They, having bathed in pure water, emerged white. Then God took a second group of people and cleansed them. They, having bathed in slightly soiled water, emerged yellow. Finally God took a third group of people and cleansed them. They, having bathed in heavily soiled water, emerged black.

"I don't like this story," Xiao Xue said to her sister once, after a teacher had retold it. "It says we're dirty."

"We're not the dirtiest," Xiao Chun said.

"It says God loves the foreigners more than us."

"God has infinite love. You're misunderstanding the story."

But Xiao Xue didn't believe her. How could her sister possibly understand, the honors student, the village beauty? How could she understand the pain of imperfect love, a star delicately cut from golden paper and then roughly torn? Sometimes second-most was second-least. And sometimes second was simply last.

*

The days dragged like the foot of a cross in the dirt. If the Bible had taught Xiao Xue anything, it was that everything had a time frame. God created the world in six days. The earth flooded for forty days and forty nights. But this commotion around the stigmata was easing into a kind of permanence that she had not anticipated. The stream of pilgrims had not slowed. The presents for Xiao Chun piled up in the closet, tumbling out and whanging Xiao Xue on the head whenever she opened the door. Her parents couldn't even punish her in the usual way anymore if she misbehaved.

They started sending her to bed without dinner. One night, after Xiao Xue had kicked Ye Jing in the shin (she'd overheard him predicting Xiao Chun's canonization), her mother sat down next to her and pushed a small steamed bun into her hand. "I don't know what your school has been telling you," she said, sighing, "but some things can't be changed. We all have the *ming* we have. A man fated to be poor will always be poor. A man blessed with good fortune will never go hungry. The only thing you can do is accept. If you don't, it just leads to more suffering."

"You and Dad didn't accept going hungry," Xiao Xue said. "You joined the Church."

Her mother stood, shaking her head. "Eat your bun. And don't tell your dad."

Xiao Xue stole away to the bushes behind the school and plucked six mean red berries from them. Years ago she had accidentally eaten a few of these berries and gotten so ill that her parents stayed by her side all night. These berries were riper than those from last time, sweet but with a stimulating tartness underneath.

The convulsions started during the geography lesson: "The Mongoloids, with their wide cheekbones, weak brow ridges, and flat noses, were given dominion over East Asia and Southeast Asia. The Caucasoids, with their oval faces, thin noses, and superior courage and genius, were given dominion over all of Europe, parts of North Asia . . ."

She fell out of her chair. The bitter-gourd porridge the school had served for lunch rushed from her and puddled on the ground. A jagged pain in her side, under the ribs—was this how Saint Francis had felt? When Xiao Xue opened her eyes again, she saw only waving banners of light, the archangels soaring into battle bearing the standard of God. Children screaming, a voice urging calm. An angel with six incandescent wings gliding closer, closer.

Xiao Chun touched her on the shoulder. The angel vanished, as did the pain. Xiao Chun smiled beneficently and said, "You'll be all right now."

"What happened? Was it the stigmata?" another student asked.

Xiao Chun reached into the puddle and picked out a single red seed. "She ate the berries behind the school," she explained. "I'm sure she didn't mean to."

"You healed her," Sister Eunice whispered.

"God healed her," Xiao Chun said. "I merely prayed. When his love passed through me, I understood what I had to do."

Xiao Xue leaned back against her chair and closed her eyes, struggling in vain to call the angel back. She knew this next part. The story about Xiao Chun's actions today would spread, as all the other stories about her had. There would be more pilgrims, more presents. There would be investigators sent by the Church, all of whom would leave humbled and awed because it was true, her sister was a miracle. Xiao Xue excelled only in eating up the food.

Once more the students gathered around Xiao Chun. Even the class next door had rushed in, Ye Jing and all the other boys. They haloed her, limned her with the gold leaf of their adoration while she clasped their hands with her own bandaged ones. A perfect circle of love flowed around her, through her, so much love that she couldn't contain it and it had to bleed out her palms as if she were offering rosebuds. *Here. Take.*

Where was that love all those times Sister Eunice bent Xiao Xue over her knee and spanked her light-brown flesh until it turned purple-red? Xiao Chun never once defended her or begged Sister Eunice to stop. Instead she watched Sister Eunice mete out the punishment, the impulse of a smile at the corner of her lips.

"You ate that berry on purpose, didn't you?" Xiao Chun asked as they were walking home. "You've eaten it before. I remember."

"I saw an angel," Xiao Xue said.

"Why did you do this? I was worried, you know."

"I saw an angel!" Xiao Xue screamed. "And you made him go away because you couldn't stand me getting more attention!"

Xiao Chun actually jumped a little. When she spoke again, her voice was very soft. "Have you ever thought," she said, "that maybe I get more attention because I'm not constantly making trouble just to get it? Because I actually think about other people? All those times Mom had trouble standing after scrubbing the floor, did you once offer to help? Maybe you don't get attention because you don't deserve it."

She drew out that last sentence slowly, like a magician pulling a sword from her mouth. Then she straightened the bow on her uniform and walked off, leaving Xiao Xue in the middle of the road.

The priest from Europe arrived on day fifty-something, a trunk of scientific instruments in tow. The villagers thronged him as he passed. They tried to explain, though he showed no sign of understanding them, that Xiao Chun was truly blessed. She was their miracle, they said, Taiwan's miracle. A pure, shining thing no one could ever have imagined rising from its dusty yellow ground. Tell all the foreigners, they urged him. Tell them that God has favored us too.

The house was noisy nearly all the time now. There was talk of more visitors from Europe, of an official chapel, another school, a souvenir stand. "How many figurines do you think you can carve in a month?" Sister Eunice asked Xiao Xue's father, translating for the priest. "Oh, a lot," he answered. "However many the faithful need."

Xiao Xue slipped out of the house while they planned and made her way to her father's shed. Lined up on the workbench was a choir of little Marys. Her father was improving: Their faces had thinned to ovals, their noses were alpine peaks. But still there was something familiar about the eyes and the expression. It was Xiao Chun, she realized. He'd been carving her all along.

She wandered over to the vise and the augers. Picking up the sharpest one, she held the tip to her palm and pushed down. A single tear of blood welled up. She looked at the new addition to her hand, or rather, the subtraction, an absence to be filled with God's love. She wondered what it would feel like, and how deep the wound would have to go before she finally became holy.

Our Children

FROM *West Branch*

I WAS ONCE married to a man. He was tall and burly, with fat, heavy hands and too many calluses to count. Peter. Weekends, he worked on vintage sports cars for fun. He lifted weights in our home gym, blasting Journey or the Ramones or best-of-classic-rock mixes. You know the ones, from movies and commercials and the like. He sometimes did this naked. I'd accidentally catch him but then stay to watch, pressing myself flat on the outside of the door, peeking while he posed and flexed and turned to get a good look at himself, sometimes half hard. Sometimes more than half. He kissed his fingers in front of food. He used pet names for me. Baby Pie was one. TeeTee. Legs. Little Doh, short for Doughnut. "Doughnut Hole," he later explained during an argument. "You follow?" he said, making sure I was properly insulted. I thought this was normal. Peter made his money in construction. Licked his lips a lot. I didn't know what marriage was supposed to be. I had no idea what I was expecting. We had two children together and they both look vaguely of him but I love them regardless. And that's what's important.

I met Dan at the grocery store. In the produce section, feeling sweet potatoes. I don't know that many people think to feel sweet potatoes. But I do, and so did Dan that day, luckily enough. When I went for a plastic bag he was just right there, watching. Things I noticed: a chipped or strangely shaped cuspid, the pleat in the front of his suit pants. I must have looked down, blushing. It's something that happens to me. There was no way to ignore him. It would not have been polite. Later I thought to ask him why he was doing his own grocery shopping. *Where is your wife or your housekeeper?* This, after I knew more about him. But by then it was pointless. Inconsequential. Everything that was to happen had already begun to happen.

Peter was easy. Let go of me, just like that. Said okay to the money, the house, whichever of the cars I wanted. He must have had something else cooking by then. I refuse to believe he just hated me that much. He called Dan "Loverboy" in our emails with lawyers. He said he wanted custody split right in half. He moved to a three-bedroom condo on the water. "A magical tower," our daughter called it for the longest time.

Every other weekend our house swelled with them: a new population. They congregated. They organized. They became fresh in the breakfast nook when I said we had pancakes but not waffles. They sat for hours in the living room: bare feet leaving heat marks on the glass of the coffee table, juice pooling, crumbs everywhere you could imagine. They hooted at the chug of machine guns and grenades in the games they played. I knew they pointed their controllers at my back when I turned to walk out, arms full of plates, crumpled napkins. "Anything else, guys?" I asked over my shoulder anyway. When I sliced a thumb cutting strawberries for their sundaes and screamed "darn it," they chuckled under their breath. "What, you think I won't say *fuck*," I said, getting in their faces. "Fuck," I said, cupping the blood. I let some drip onto the table, into the sprinkles. "Fuck these sprinkles too." I upended the bowl. They stared. That got them. They were seven, seven, six, five. Three older boys. The youngest, by eight months, the girl.

When they left, when the house was empty again, even the fabric of the area rugs became cooler to the touch. I heard the high-frequency hum of electronics and the tumble of the dryer, the soft *lap, lap* of hand towels one onto the other, floors down. I stood in the doorway to the living room and it appeared to me as a glacier: cold and empty and white.

Dan's wife was basically just me with brown hair. She stayed in his five-bedroom federal colonial across town and drove the SUV he paid for. She hosted wine nights on his dime and cried to her guests, mothers of children who went to school with my children. In random text messages she needled him about leaving her. "Hope it was worth it," she wrote a lot. "Tearing our family apart."

Then she wised up and started writing *"your* family." "Tearing *your* family apart." She changed the verb here and there. She used *splitting, ripping, breaking.* Once she wrote *exploding* and it evoked something and I was impressed, for a second at least.

The things she must have said about me. What kind of wicked thing I became in her eyes. Sometimes I asked Dan.

"Nothing, hon," he would say, lifting a pot top on the stove, looking into the fridge, slicing open envelopes. "None of it matters."

"No, I'm just wondering." I'd try to make it buttoned up, but there's no way to remove the whine from that. Once I got it out of him. Threatened to withhold his favorite position, but just before. Seconds before.

"She said you're aging in the face. That you've seen better days. Rode hard and put away wet. Sagging in the ass. Okay? Is this what you want?" I swear he was panting.

"Okay," I said. Okay.

I felt bad, I did. I wouldn't have chosen it this way. The moms at school knew me as a home wrecker, but I didn't set out to wreck anything. Two people fell in love. Rings from other people can't stop that. I am not innocent, but I did not intend for this to happen. I dreamed of texting her myself. "I'm so sorry for everything. I didn't mean for you to be hurt. There was a glitch. He and I should have met years ago and then you would have been spared all of this."

"Why couldn't we have met before everything," I said to Dan in bed one night. "When we were young?" He was still inside. He liked when I was wistful, I think. I felt a change.

"Tell me about you when you were young." His face was buried somewhere near my shoulder. I had to guess that this is what he said.

"I was a cheerleader," I said. Lie. "I was on yearbook. I wore glasses and twirled my ponytail with a pencil and sat on the edge of the teacher's desk. I got in trouble for being mean," I said, and let a pout change my voice. "I stole another girl's boyfriend and I made her cry in the bathroom."

"Jesus," he said, rearing.

I did sometimes wonder. Wish. That we had met when we were young, before everything. Before we made our lives. *But the children, your children,* something always chided. This thing that chided, by

the way, was not My Best Self. Not my voice. It was choral, all altos.
The moan of disappointed mothers. *Then you would not have your
beautiful children,* the mothers said. And this is true. But I would
have made and met other children. I would have loved these other
children just the same because I am capable of so much love.

Dan's wife liked to fuck us. Late changes to the dates of his weekends, taking one of their kids instead of both, conjuring appoint-
ments and meetings that she expected us to believe. More than
once we had to cancel plans.

"Deep breath," Dan said one of these nights. She had just
dropped them off. I was wearing the dress I would have worn to
the opera. "We'll make another plan." I swear his son, one of the
sons, eyed me from behind him. His big, glassy pupils celebrating.

On this night I had had it. I took off the dress, my makeup. I
slammed and smashed so many things in our bathroom. I came
downstairs, changed. Sat on the bottom step tying and retying a
sneaker, waiting for him to see.

"So," I said when his shadow darkened me, finally. "I'm going
for a run. Need to let off some steam. This is insane."

"Okay, sweets," he said. I heard loud cartoon music from the
living room. His socks were pilled and too fuzzy. The way he stood,
I saw a gut. All decency had gone out the window.

"But it's not. It's actually not okay." I stood up and pushed past
him, my shoulder in his chest. And usually he would grab me
somewhere. My hand, my elbow. The back of my neck, if it was like
that. A handful of hair, even. He let me pass.

I did run sometimes, so it was believable. But that night I walked
to Dan's old house. Of course her car was there. Same Suburban
as mine. Same Midnight Package, even. I looked in its window. I
knew she would be filthy. Wrappers, Tic Tacs, pretzel ends, open
sodas. A splayed magazine on the passenger seat. I couldn't imagine what she had let the children do to the back.

She was on her couch, feet on an ottoman, I think. Something
I couldn't see beneath the line of the coffee table. Her hair was
up and she was eating something out of a cup, TV going in front
of her. I thought to knock on the door, start something. Why not.
Why the hell not. But I didn't. I just watched her and judged her
and savored the taste of that judgment.

Peter? Peter was still Peter. *Should I have stayed with you, Peter?* I thought when he came to pick up our children. *Then there would only be two of them and two of us; we would not be outnumbered.* He looked fitter, different clothes. He patted me on the back when I walked them to the car. Like we were old chums, classmates, colleagues. He didn't spring the kids on us to punish me. He loved our children and looked forward to them and greeted them with zest and his real smile and this made me feel very, very guilty.

We made a plan. Something fun for me and Dan, the kids. A weekend in the woods: a stream, a cabin, a tame campfire out front, its very top spinning a line of black into the evening sky, the sunset.

"We'll be on one side of the house, they'll be on the other," Dan said, showing me with his hands how much room we'd have. "It's a beautiful place. You'll love it." He said the last part like he actually believed it.

It was sweet to watch them pack their things. What they thought they'd need. My two wouldn't leave for a day, not to mention a weekend, without books. Three apiece, weighing down their backpacks. The other two brought handheld video games and charger cables, disconnected phones that they could use with Wi-Fi. What can I say. They are not mine. Nothing about them is from me.

"Wait," I said in the front hallway, the kids, their luggage sitting around my feet like an audience. "Does everyone have a toothbrush?"

I watched them all run back up. Listened to the drawers in the bathroom slide open and closed, all the things within shifting, and I thought, *This is going to be a lovely time. We are going to make a memory with our children that we will cherish forever. I am going to be calm and easy and light.* I pictured myself on a glacier, the sun warming my front, my back cool and wet. Quiet everywhere.

The cabin was smaller than I thought. But it was far from the road, and a stream ran right by it, and round white rocks lined its base like the fruit-gemmed hedge of a gingerbread house. Immediately I imagined standing in its kitchen, stirring cocoa, looking out the window at the expanse of land, the thick weave of the woods, the mountains behind everything. It was true, I did feel calm. I felt just fine.

But it turns out there was no Wi-Fi, and Dan's kids were livid.

"Let's run them ragged," Dan said. "I brought stuff. I'll play with them outside and they'll be so tired they'll collapse." He had his hand in a baseball glove and punched its palm with the other fist. "You go inside. Shave, take a bath. Get ready for me. For later."

I rolled my eyes at his wink and turned away, but I tried to walk back to the house as sexily as I could. It was not easy. The ground was uneven with rocks and roots. I couldn't roll my hips. A chipmunk, unafraid, darted just in front of my foot. Behind me, I heard them screaming, the *thwack* of a ball, the sound of the wind moving over its stitches.

And he was right. They passed out before I was able even to feed them. We left them all where they were. I covered them with blankets. His two, on the larger couch, foot to foot. One of mine on each armchair. I looked at their dirty little faces, the way the dried sweat stuck their hair to their heads. I turned off the television and the lights and left the room. Across the house moments later Dan held a hand over my mouth to keep me quiet and I was relieved. For the first time in a long time it felt like the beginning again.

But when I woke up in the night something had happened. It was that black tail of smoke from the fire. It was the rot from between the beams in the walls, seeping. It was that chipmunk being eaten, limb by limb, by a raccoon under the deck. I heard the chew and crunch. I didn't know what to do. I lifted my hands to brush back my hair, but they were heavy. Too heavy. Laden with hate, anger, sleep, something. I sat up—slow, slow—a puppet waking, someone's hand in my back.

I heard Dan breathing, his back to me. I didn't crane to see his face. My movement would wake him. It could have been anyone, anything, lying there.

"Oh," I said out loud. It was smooth and deep and greasy, this voice. It was not me and it was not the mothers chiding me. It was a dawning. It was a crack. "Dan?" I said, and put my hand on the being next to me.

"What is it?" Dan said, jumping awake. "What?" He sat up, looked around, the whites of his eyes darting, leaving streaks in my slow vision.

"Dan," I said, and patted him. Once, twice, three times in the space between his shoulders. My hand tapped like something mechanical. He didn't feel warm to the touch. "Oh," I said again then because the sludge inside me was beginning to thin and redden. I imagined effervescence. I imagined light and heat and a great sound booming. Rattling. "We have to leave these children here."

"What?" he said, and the whites shrunk as he squinted at me and the change in his voice told me he was cocking his head. "Jesus, what? You had a dream. Go back to sleep." He may have been right. I may have had a dream that pointed me in that direction. That's how it might have gotten in. He flopped back into his pillow and his hand found its way up the front of my T-shirt. He tried to push me back.

"No, we do. We have to leave them here," I said. "Not forever. Maybe we come back for them. When they've grown a little, found their way. Do you understand what our lives will be like?" This voice was a marvel. It would have sickened anyone.

Maybe he had dreamt the same thing at the same time or just after I did, the character in our minds miming deeds, synchronous. Maybe whatever it was had started in on him too. Because minutes later he sat up, slow like I had. He sighed like he was waking up for a workday. And he moved his legs over the side of the bed and started to pull his pants on.

It might have been any number of things. But I think it was the rot.

We drove home with the windows open, August air coming in, the stereo on. He held my hand pressed into his thigh and tapped the tips of my fingers with his when it was a song that had specific meaning to him. The road was damp. The grass at its median already dewed and glittering in our headlights. The moon. The sky. The smell of honeysuckle when he dipped too close to the shoulder. I wanted to say something about the stars and the night, how lucky we were. He wanted to say something too, I could see it. But we both knew what not to do to a good thing.

We drank wine at the table, smoked a bowl, made no move to hide either. Shed our clothes in the kitchen, fucked on the marble floor of the foyer, then went into the shower and did it there. We brought the wine bottle with us. It sloshed as we moved, spilling into the water we were sitting under. We were sitting at that point. We soaped each other, lubed and scrubbed and then gave up and got out, went to the bedroom, leaving wet footprints, puddles, and drips across the carpets and wood. Our hair soaked our pillows and we warmed quickly. We finished what was left in the bottle. We thought of more weed but didn't want to leave the bed. We did not touch but fell asleep separately, each breathing with a heaviness and a peace that had been at that point unknown to us.

I did not dream at all of our children. I awoke well before dawn and I envisioned them. I knew what they were going to do. Their future. They would awaken and start to work. Make paint from the juice of wild blueberries, use it to dye linens and tiny frocks for the littlest one, mine. They would make these frocks. A loom, a needle and thread. They would weave mats from grasses they collected by the stream, char fish and rodents over that very same campfire. They would ransack the kitchen. Find the cookies, the cereal in the cupboard. Try coffee for the first time. Try on for size the shoes found in the closets, the shirts in the luggage I had left in our haste to get away. They would belt those shirts around their waists using tails from pelts of animals. That raccoon: mischievous, insatiable. Dead, finally. His family too.

A band of them, these children, in size order, maybe, marching across that expanse, hands on hips, singing a song they made up. It would be warm. Even up in the mountains it would be warm. The night had been warm, the day would be hot. There was electricity and food. They would be so busy.

They would grow. Because if left alone and let to live, all things grow.

The three boys have fashioned tools from sticks and rocks. They sharpen stones on other stones and affix them with rope. At first they *ah* at the sparks flying blue and orange. Then they get back to their work. They find an ax in the garage. A BB gun. They smear their faces with dirt and lie on their fronts, waiting for the rustle of a buck in the thicket. Soon they see one. No, a doe. Sight her big black eyes and hear her breath as if she's only inches away. Those eyes, they think. The hooves and tail. How does such a thing exist with us? The eldest takes it down with an arrow. Magic shot. Magic. A set they also found in the garage. The eldest wears a bandanna around his head, red and knotted in the back. He is the pack leader. He runs to the deer and waits for it to die, watching blood pulse from the wound. Things die so slowly, he thinks. He is seven, and it takes much longer than the deaths in his game, where bodies fall and then disappear seconds later.

So they leave the deer to die. Play catch on the big lawn while the thing heaves its last breaths a hundred feet away. The girl— during all of this, the girl, mine—has stayed in the house. She is pointing her way through a picture book. She is reaching for the second shelf of the fridge for a piece of plastic-wrapped cheese. But she can't reach so she gives up and takes a small cupcake she finds on the counter. Last from a box of a hardening dozen. Lucky.

The eldest and the second eldest try to drag the dead thing back. Onto the expanse so they can prepare it. But it's too heavy, more than a hundred pounds. The weight of all of these children and then some. So the two send the third back to the house. Tell him to watch the girl. Tell him he shouldn't see this. That they are seven and he is only six and he is not mature enough to see this, any of this, all of this. He cries on his way back to the house, swearing he hates the two. That he'll never play with them again. He kicks the baseball they were all playing with the day before. Hopes it rolls into a gully or a gulch or the stream, at least, so no one has the pleasure of it again.

Its skin is so thick! It takes a few passes. But the tools they made are decent, would impress an adult, and the white of the belly, slit over and over, finally gives. An amateur cut, but it gives. Blood, more blood, the shining bend of an intestine. The puffed white of something else. A stomach, maybe. They don't know. But there are flies starting to buzz. It smells. And so, so much blood. And then they are afraid of eating the wrong thing, of getting sick and dying for such a stupid reason. The eldest calls it off and starts to walk away. But the other one stays behind for a minute. *We killed her for no reason,* he thinks. He could cry. If he starts crying, who's to say when it will stop. So then he thinks, *Things die for no reason all the time,* and he picks up a rock and smashes the doe's mouth. He takes a small front tooth that he knocks loose. He rubs it between his fingers and puts it in his pocket before he runs to meet the others.

They teach the girl to read. They allot two hours a day for the studying of something, all of them. They estimate birthdays and they celebrate with singing and games. They learn to cook, mend, make beds, become adults.

When the girl is of natural reproductive age, she pairs up with the eldest boy. Who is, after all, unrelated to her. They wed. A ceremony in a clearing. Flower crowns, a sunny day, a cake they make from woodland berries. They mate like bobcats on a flat rock in the sun. Or like humans in a room of the cabin, its door locked. They have a child, a son. They name him something earthy: Leaf, Stone, Birch, Blue. They name him something familial: Dan.

I sucked down the smell of the same honeysuckle patch as I went back up. I prepared to stop when I passed a trooper. Prepared what I would say. I was doing eighty, eighty-five. He must have been sleeping, though, because he never came up behind me.

It was just before dawn when I turned into the cabin's drive. I went slow, afraid to make noise. The gravel, the pop of a branch. The lights were off, the front door and storm door shut, all windows on the front of the house down. I could hear the hum of the central air conditioning. The door was locked, thank God, or not. But there was a key under the mat and it opened quietly enough and then I was inside. The counter was wiped clean, still stacked with snacks. Juice packs, bags and bags of chips, cupcakes, paper napkins. I put my keys down and went in toward the living room and that's when I could smell their bodies. Hot, sweet. Sleeping children have a smell. Especially when there are several of them together, in one room.

They hadn't moved much. The blanket kicked off the two boys on the couch. I fixed it. I patted their feet. I found my son, brushed his hair back from his face. His forehead was cool, cooler than what you would expect for a living thing. But he breathed and breathed and I could almost feel him ticking under my palm. My daughter was curled up, small enough to fit on the seat of the armchair. A kitten, a mouse. She was silent and clean and young and unharmed.

I sat on the floor in the middle of them, my back against the coffee table. I watched the sun come up and turn the walls blue, then pink, then gold, then dim down to the normal light of day. When they began to stir, when sleep had run its clear course, I stood up and went to the kitchen. I wanted them to find me there, bent over a cup of coffee, worrying at a crossword, the tails of my robe dragging on the floor. I had forgotten my robe, but I was still in pajamas and everything else would be right. I would look like a mother.

One of his sons was the first to come in.

"Good morning, sweetheart," I said. He was rubbing his eyes. "Can I make you something to eat?"

"Okay," he said, and sat. "A bagel, maybe? Or cereal. Anything." He picked up his handheld video game. "Thank you," he said, without looking up from it.

The rest wandered in, one at a time. I fed them. I asked them to finish their milk, almond milk for Dan's. I said yes when they asked if they could change and play outside. I washed the dishes by hand. I folded the blankets, smacked the couch cushions flat. Made the bed Dan and I had left during the night. And then I watched out the window. I watched the sun on their hair as they ran, laughing. I watched the wind catch the hems of their shirts and the dirt come off their shoes. I watched them fall and roll and push each other and yell and cry and stop and get up again. I watched the sun get higher and higher in the sky, and when it was time I opened the door and stood on the porch and I called to them.

The Rest of Us

FROM *One Story*

Love the violence that births you.
—Nabila Lovelace

WE FELL IN LOVE with *Boyz n the Hood*—José, Cristian, and me—when we were just turning ten. Instead of identifying with its morals, we saw only ourselves onscreen. When Ricky and Tre split up in the back alleys and the Bloods gunned Ricky down, we clapped and cheered as Ricky fell and his white shirt bloomed into red. We felt famous. Those houses in South Central looked just like ours, had the same trash and the same potholed streets, snapbacks with matching bandannas, malt liquor shatter across stoop steps, the pop-pop whole corner dive, the black and brown faces pressed to asphalt. And José was always something of a Doughboy, did the end-of-the-movie speech best—the one where Doughboy tells Tre the world don't know, don't show, or don't care about the hood. Became our motto every time another siren went off or another crackhead came stumbling by. We'd stay quiet, trading Flamin' Hots and Kool-Aid while we people-watched from behind my gate, trying not to roast in the awful lake-effect heat. Then Cristian would start it and get us all going: "I ain't been up this early in a long time . . ."

"We all gotta go sometime," José would conclude, and then we'd follow suit. Only they'd gang up on me so fast, because I had skipped a grade. I was the bookworm, teacher's pet, house slave. It didn't help that I could pass in the right light but they couldn't. My skin never turned dark dark, just less pale in the summer.

"You're more of a Tre, though, verdad?"

"You mean pussy," Cristian would clarify, shoving me.

"Claro, that's what I meant: a pussy."

"Fuck y'all," and I usually said this not just in my defense but also Cuba Gooding Jr.'s, and for light-skinned boys everywhere. I mean, maybe it didn't really stick with you, that breakout performance—Tre's tears as he put the gun in his father Furious's hands—but back in Chicago it meant something to the rest of us.

Ours was not a world of exploration. We knew its boundaries well. Two blocks south was Cobra's territory. Four blocks west and we'd find ourselves on a Viceroy corner. Muslims and Jews to the north. The white people all lived east, by the lakefront, they always did and they always will. The universe as we knew it extended from our respective doorways to the corner store, which our parents affectionately called el Chino, because it was run by what they thought were Chinese immigrants. We gave them points for originality. Besides, who could argue with that conditioning? *Vete pal Chino. Go to el Chino and bring me esoda. I need Wonder Bread —traémelo del Chino.* For a long time we thought the sign hanging above the entrance said just that, el Chino. But then we learned to read—me and Cristian did—and we found out what it really spelled: Food & Liquor.

We were not ambitious. We went to school because there was nowhere else to go. Five days a week we waited eagerly for the yellow bus to take us and patiently for it to bring us back. Otherwise we went wherever our parents told us to, wherever they drove us: to relatives' houses on the other side of the highway, to the Salvation Army, to ALDI for some last-minute groceries. We would have preferred to walk, just for the novelty of seeing the hood on foot. But walking was impossible; to do so, we would've had to cross multiple gang lines. Since we didn't have friends in other neighborhoods, that would have been mutually assured destruction. We had our school friends we knew only in school and at birthday parties, when the moms conspired to work miracles. But other than that, we had each other, and we had our families. Big ones, because jesucristo wanted it so and our parents had brothers and sisters in the homeland, primo after primo calling to ask about snow, its taste on the tip of the tongue. Cristian was the only boy in his family, all of the ones before him were girls. His dad had given

up, stopped wanting to know the baby's sex because it was prede-
termined, but out came Cristian and his pops shouted "¡Es niño,
es niño!" in the delivery room. José had an older brother who kept
an empty wine bottle in the backseat of his turquoise Jetta "for protection," a sister that was nothing to look at until she was, and both
his abuelas still breathing. I was an only child, and todo el mundo
kept their eye on me, parents, grandparents, even the neighbor
lady Doña Rosa who was blind as a bat but somehow always knew
when I was getting into something, could just feel it. "¿Dónde stán
lo niño, dónde?" Swallowing letters like the Caribbeans do.

Yeah, I had a lot of attention. I think that's why I got out.

But we didn't have it so bad. We went to pickup soccer games
at Montrose Field and it was like the whole city came out: Colom-
bians, Ricans, Mexicans, every inch of grass covered in folding
chairs and pastel blankets depicting La Virgen. You'd think it was
the World Cup, the way colored folk would shout "Golazo" every
time a ball swished the back of the net. Cristian's abuelas used
to illegally sell some of the best spoils from las patrias, all home-
cooked, food so good that the grease would drip down spics' hairy
forearms and still they licked it. We used to wake up at the crack of
dawn and help them get the whole mercado together, yawning as
we wrapped tamales in aluminum foil or rinsed out camp coolers
with the sweet smell of plantains worked in. Our favorite part—
mine really—was when they sent us to el Chino for ice bags. We'd
take turns hurling them against the concrete, trying to break the
cubes as the light slowly started to pour down from the lakefront
and into the ghetto. Then we'd follow their instructions: beer cans
at the bottom, a layer of ice in between, and a few bottles of pop
on top, just in case the cops came by. Foolproof.

We had my front porch, it was the tallest. We used to take turns
jumping off of it, feeling the shock in our legs as we made impact
on the grass, competing to see who would cross the railing and
then pussy out, cross back, and take the walk of shame. More often
than not it was me—I was the frailest, and that's what they called
me, Frail Boy—but sometimes it wasn't me taking that walk, and
then I'd let them have it for real. *All day talking shit, y'all soft, y'all
weak, get at my level.* Of course that's what kids do. Everything's
a competition, especially in the summer. Who got their ass beat
hardest? Who could guzzle the most Jarritos in a minute? Who

could smoke my old man's Newports fastest? I didn't get to see the boys for nearly a month after that one. It wasn't even that he was disappointed I'd stole from him. It was that me and mis estúpidos amigos had cost him a head high and a few bucks.

And we had imagination. For every intersection we could not cross, another was invented in our backyards. Cristian's dad didn't have papers for the longest time and was good with his hands so he did a little bit of everything—electrical, plumbing, painting, you name it. Then he got into landscaping and their yard went from dead to Jardín de Edén, white hydrangeas fluffy as clouds and a bird feeder, no joke, they'd be out there tweeting every morning. We spent hours, from daybreak until the lightning bugs glowed, dancing around the sprinkler as it waved across Cristian's lush lawn, pretending it was a portal to another world. We traveled to foreign nations, distant planets, even visited our extended families in the homeland. One time José started crying after we jumped the sprinkler and we didn't say nothing because we knew about his uncle getting deported before he even told us, damn near everyone did. We couldn't fix that. We wanted to, but we couldn't.

For a while we didn't have to worry about the world beyond our gated lawns. Our parents did their best to hide us from alleyways and trap houses, from the vatos with tattoos crawling up their thick necks. All of life was play life: basketball, tag, paletas, fútbol, Mario Kart, kiddie pools, scraped knees, teasing kids, wrestling moves, late-night TV when José's mom used to pass out and we'd see sexy ladies on *Sábado Gigante*. I can still remember falling asleep to the static sounds of Don Francisco and El Chacal, those trumpet blasts chasing me to my dreams. *¡Fuera! ¡Fuera!*

All our stories were play stories: how José had got a black eye when we tried to practice pile drivers, how I threw up after a Skittles-eating contest and said I could taste the rainbow because it burned, how Cristian pissed his pants when we went to see *Jurassic Park* and didn't tell nobody until my old man could smell it from the front seat. When he pulled over and got out the car, José said for sure Cristian was about to get whooped, but my dad would never hit another kid, just me. Instead he pulled Cristian out the backseat, and Cristian was so scared we were about to leave him in the street, he didn't move, not an inch. Then, after setting down

some newspaper and muttering to himself, my old man buckled
Cristian back in and lit himself a square.

"Life finds a way," he said as he put the key in the ignition.

And then there was change. Time got the best of us. We grew fuzz
above our lips, our balls dropped overnight, voice cracks morph-
ing into booming laughter until that was just how we sounded now.
I remember I looked in the mirror one morning and *poof:* those
puffy brown cheeks—*hay que liiiiiindos*—that tía fingers couldn't
resist pinching were gone. And Cristian seemed to outgrow his
clothes by the minute. He went from losing at Keep-Away to using his lanky limbs to dunk us during games of H-O-R-S-E. José
followed in his testosterone-charged brother's footsteps, putting
hours into the rusted weights in their basement. He got muscles
the earliest—didn't look like much, but then we'd go Shirts N'
Skins, and José was all veiny and toned in the sunlight. We'd always
known the boy was mixed, but it didn't show until puberty. You
could see it in his afro curls, in his flat-ass nose that looked like it
had been hit by a book. Kids got to calling him Nubarrón, the way
he'd rumble into your face, whether playfully or out of anger, we
never really knew. And at first we didn't call him that. But then he
told us he kind of liked it. Made him sound hard. So it stuck.

Suddenly we were young men. Our families started to say, "Ahí
van los jóvenes," and not "los jovencitos." The streets caught wind
too. As teenagers we got noticed by the older guys, who started
coming around our houses and courting us, like it was some kind
of draft. Guys with names like Loco or Bruto from around the way,
with blunts tucked behind their ears and the freshest clothes, Bulls
jerseys and Polo Ralph Lauren, pristine Nikes and crisp Rollies on
their wrists that cost more than my entire wardrobe. They'd stick
gifts in between the bars of my black gate and spics couldn't fight
the temptation: money clips with more bills than we'd ever seen,
gold chains and diamond earrings, dimes so strong you could
smell the flower through the bag.

"Fuck this school shit," they'd say. "Come get some work."

And we did get some work, because that was the era of Nubarrón. He'd been the closest to it through his brother, Tomás, who
was doing eight months at Cook County on a plea deal. Just before
they locked him up, Tomás left baby brother with enough bread to

get us started. So we took the 750 and we bought a lotta coca, first thing. We had never cooked a day in our lives, let alone touched a stove, but there we were, standing around the pan, watching this crackhead hold his butter knife like a whisk. Just mumbling to himself.

"Pay me in rock," he said for the third time, licking his lips. He was the landlord of a four-story spot we operated out on Kedzie. We called him Mickey-Dee, on account of how he was quick to whip it.

I remember when we packed up the crib—just a few stacks from our first sales and clean clothes—to move into Mickey-Dee's spare apartment. Of course, we couldn't go quietly. We got the guilt trip from our families. Wondering where it was we spent all our time; wondering how it was we came by those clothes; wondering why it was we had given up on school. So we made excuses, until we didn't. More than once we showed up drunk or high at Montrose Field, at the barbecue, at a Sunday dinner. One day our parents stopped asking questions and instead were just glad we showed up at all.

We had it down to a science, like steps out of a lab manual: the measuring, the mixing, the white bubbles boiling over just the right blaze, and keep tapping that, yo flatten that. Every day we woke up to the alarm of our apartment buzzer, to junkies with the jitters making their way up and down the intercom. And then we'd let them in, or start up on the next batch, or flip it, zip it, send it off. For a while we knew every sob story there is, we saw every breed of addict you could imagine. Ones with mangled teeth and hollowed eyes, bloody sores crawling across their arms. White boys, black boys, brown boys who had dropped out of school, out of work, putas y maricas caked in makeup looking for a quick fix before the lots, expensive suits with money and a problem who came back, always, sometimes twice a day. You can't imagine what some people will say just for a little escape—I'll suck your cock, wash your car, you got homework, I used to tutor math—and none of it mattered, we took dead presidents or we took nada. I thought we were doing them a favor when we told them no. But I realized time and time again, when you look at some pobre hijueputa, red-eyed and scratching at his throat, no favor is enough. He'll keep fiending till he dies.

The more we made, the better we got, the fatter the rock. Fifty here, a sawbuck there. José didn't have the patience for a cook. He would fuck up the batch while daydreaming, almost set the place on fire once, so we put him on packaging duty. Cristian, it turned out, was a natural salesman. He came up with the three-for-ten deal that got our name out. I was the one with a knack for crystal, could be in the other room and feel it popping from down the hall. We spent all day in that disgusting apartment with nothing but mattresses and the floorboards, either cold as hell or dripping sweat. We saw the seasons change from below the hum of our corner streetlight. The howling wind, the falling leaves, when the lake would freeze over and there was so much snow in the streets, not even the druggies would brave it. Until they did.

Still, we got too comfortable. In the beginning we always sold together, just in case someone ever tried to pull a fast one. We got the Glocks for the same reason. One time I got cocky and did a sale alone, while José and Cristian worked the block. I was supposed to be off-duty, but this vieja caught me on my way to the spot, and something about when she grabbed me, how she pled —*mijo mijo espéreme*—it was like I could hear the islands she'd fled flowing from her mouth. *So today's your lucky day,* I said, *Frail Boy's feeling himself.* And I remember leaving the gun on the table while she smoked it up right then and there. Just the two of us with the gun in between and the batch cracking at my back, burnt plastic floating in the air. All of a sudden she started cackling, so hard she was doubled on her knees. Best believe I grabbed the piece then.

"Hay que tene cuidao," she finally said, gasping.

So we played it more carefully. We started campaigning. Recruiting was easy, we didn't have to try. We went everywhere desperate boys gathered: the stoop, the park, the beach, anywhere they'd listen. We'd roll up on the playground in our freshest duds and cleanest cuts, flashing cash aimlessly. Kids would always congregate around Cristian, he used to pull 'em in with those long-ass arms, ask about moms, they pops, whether baby primo needed money for that school lunch. *How much? Show me that hand.* Bam. There it is.

We had a whole operation. Tomás finally got out of jail and moved in, saying it was time for adult swim, time for a new approach, because we weren't striving for that next level. Or maybe it was just me who wasn't. I hadn't even known how much we were making, I only knew that it was enough. Enough to heat weenies in the same pan we heated rock, enough to not be ashamed of the clothes on my back, enough to spend without hesitation, enough to go to el Chino and grab a bottle of something nice, just for me. As far as I could tell, we were the most successful spics we knew.

But one day José pulled up to the corner in a rusty Oldsmobile, Tomás riding shotgun and holding a Steel Reserve in his grip. They had just rented a couple of nearby apartments from Mickey-Dee. We were expanding.

"Is this that next level?" I asked.

Tomás spit out the window and brought a finger to his temple. "Can't let 'em see you coming," he said.

Nubarrón nodded along like it was gospel.

It blindsided us, the success. We developed a reputation as quickly as we developed a routine. We ran a couple different spots, a few right across from each other, all on the same turf. Sometimes we started in the hallway of one building and by the time we crossed the street to the other, we'd be dry. I mean, we made so much, we gave out credit. Like a fucking bank. We used to say, what's a twenty every now and then if you get the fiend for a hundred down the line?

Next we got raided, sometimes twice in the same week. It was like a game we played with the PD. The intercom would buzz, but not to the tune of a sale, more like someone trying to play the part. And why not? We liked to keep things interesting. We'd hear the boots rushing up the stairs, the angry shouts for us to show hands. Then we shimmied up the chimney ladder as the ram came slamming on the door—reinforced, so that always took a little time. The pigs trashed the place, naturally, and took out everything: the dressings in the fridge, the rubbers in the medicine cabinet, the blunt roaches in the ashtray. But they wouldn't find anything serious, because we weren't idiots. We were professionals. We always had the supply rotating across apartments. And when they climbed the ladder and pushed on the roof hatch, we felt it strain under our weight and tried not to laugh. Tomás, José, Cristian, and me. Just sitting there, smoking squares and casting clouds to the night sky, peeping over the rooftop and waiting for them to leave. The shit became procedural. By the time the sirens were gone, we'd have a line of volunteers outside the door begging to clean up the mess in exchange for crumbs of crack. We'd be back open for business within the hour. We didn't even sweat it, really.

Lemme address the elephant in the room: I ain't gonna say.

We didn't say so back then, and don't plan on saying so now. Ask anyone else near the corners, near the courts, near the street vendors selling mangoes on a stick—any spic who's old enough to remember Frail Boy, and they'll tell you: we didn't see nothing. We weren't *out* when Mickey-Dee got shot. We weren't *there* when his body turned up floating and bloated under the California Bridge. We weren't *around* when his ass disappeared one day. I mean, we barely noticed the guy. Who would? The man was just another fiend in the background.

But the thing is, people think just because they're not the same type of people, that people have no people. But people do. Even crackheads have people who care about them. Or at least, this one did.

We were making more money than I really knew what to do with. José, Cristian, and Tomás all seemed more cut out for it than me. We reached the point where we didn't really need to get our hands dirty, where we had enough weight being moved that we could step back and take a more managerial role. But still we stuck with it. Maybe it was that immigrant zeal we'd been instilled with from a young age. Or maybe it was just because we were good at it. We enjoyed the rush, the high of knowing it would catch up to us someday. It was only a matter of time before we didn't hustle the chimney ladder fast enough. Before the cops got wise and brought a chopper into the mix. Before some strung-out fool dug a knife in our guts and made off with the stash.

So maybe that's why they kidnapped our landlord, Mickey-Dee. I remember rolling up in the spot and we were all there, about to drink and smoke and play games, when Tomás started talking about how Mickey-Dee had been shorting us. Apparently he was making a little side money with the product, which we should have respected, given our stories. Still, Tomás took it personally, and Nubarrón was on his side. We couldn't let some druggie step on our territory. We had to address it directly. But me and Cristian, we mostly had a laugh over the whole thing. Wasn't there plenty to go around? We couldn't be losing sleep over one addict with a dream, especially one we knew.

"One is all it takes," said José.

"For what?"

"For more to get ideas."

Cristian lit a square. "What if we just, no sé, keep tabs on him? See how it plays out."

Por fin, we agreed on something.

"So it's settled," I said. "We let him be."

Tomás and José exchanged looks. "Nah, he in the closet."

Mickey-Dee, that poor son of a bitch. There we were, the same kids who'd asked him for help, now too big for their breeches, staring down at him. Just covered in his own piss while bound and gagged. Those salt-and-pepper eyebrows stained red from a gash on his forehead. Hands tied up so tight with an extension cord that his black skin turned blue. Couldn't understand a damn word he was saying through the rag, but we got the gist. You could see it in him. Why do him so dirty; we'd had a good thing, hadn't we? Did we have to ruin it?

We exchanged heated words, our fists clenched.

One of us said, "I'll end this."

And that's the story of how a bullet wound up inside Mickey-Dee.

After that night I put some distance between us. José and Tomás kept going on like it was the cost of business. Said, to be honest, it sent the right kind of message more efficiently that way. Then I went home for the first time in a long time, and I was surprised to find everything still intact: my parents' love, my childhood bedroom, even Doña Rosa, who was at death's door, was there to say "¡Coño!" from her front porch as I walked in through the gate.

For a few days we were in touch through Cristian, who also didn't like how the whole thing had gone down. I know because he told me so when we went to the barbershop that next week. But we could move past it, he'd said when he dropped me off at my crib. We could keep going without looking back. We were good at that.

I was alone when the phone rang. We used to always answer back then because you never knew. It was José's mom, in hysterics. She hadn't seen her sons in days, they hadn't even called. Through tears she begged me for answers that I still don't have:

"Good afternoon Daniel usted habla con la Mari madre de José y Tomás so sorry to call without warning es que no he hablado con mis hijos and I know—how embarrassing—it seems odd for their age pero siempre pregunto por ellos and they tend to stop by every few days porque les suplico que tengan cuidado do not misunderstand it is only God's place to judge y soy mujer de fe fe que los guardé so I try to respect His plan however han pasado varios días entonces me preocupo probably nothing but these streets this city can be so cold yan andan como hombres sin miedo but keeping in mind that you are good friends pensé que usted sabría por donde están of course you three were inseparable I am surprised que le encontré sólo yo no lo creo the chances seem so low más adultos que nada I remember it like yesterday cuando nos veíamos *Sábado Gigante* and oh Don Francisco was such a dog and a charmer y esas mujeres me imagino que no les pagaban bien but the three of you loved it and so did I como se obligaban a terminarla tan lindos like it was uncertain when we would get to watch again ay Daniel no sé que hacer we mothers are creatures of suffering se sufre por los hijos y seguiré sufriendo but Daniel are you listening please end my agony no importa como es que ganen su dinero it makes no difference to me as long as you come home que pecado dejar una madre a la incertidumbre and do you hear Daniel it is me Daniel cuénteme lo que pasó sin dudarse I will not tell anyone about what happened pero necesito saber porque quiero llamar a la policia and they will hate that if at the end of the day todo está bien no hay nada abnormal just the old lady and that is how they call me la vieja como si fueran extranjeros in their own house can you believe how bold how cheeky but please Daniel me muero sin ellos por eso le pido a Dios y a usted bring me a miracle por favor tráigame paz."

So what happened? Nothing surprising. Where we came from, people would bring their own justice because ours was not a world of due process. We didn't call narcs, we didn't file suits, we didn't hire lawyers, we didn't go to courts, we didn't testify on stands, we didn't pay restitutions, we didn't put brothers behind bars, we didn't fist-bump through bulletproof glass while cradling receivers to our ears talking about see what we did to you? We put you here.

Nah, we kept it simple.

Mickey-Dee's people did what we would have done. Textbook retaliation. They went up to the spot, struck a deal with Tomás and José, whose dumbasses probably got all excited about the score, and then they lit up the motherfucker. Took all the money, took all the rock. Burned the building down too, for good measure. Used gas from the stove, so it looked done by some fiend who had been too high to notice. For a while the neighborhood was on the map. Our block even made the six o'clock news: local spics end each others' misery.

Did me and Cristian change? Not on your life. We probably considered it. Real talk, our families begged us to. But still we stayed put. We didn't skip town, we didn't take the Oldsmobile to St. Louis, we didn't try a fresh start, we didn't change our names, we didn't connect with a friend of Cristian's dad, we didn't whack weeds and shear shrubs with the other spics down there, we didn't tell ourselves we didn't have it so bad. We probably should have, but we didn't. We said we would get it right. We knew how not to mess it up.

So we switched gears. We found a plug for weed and that was a quieter line of work. We upcharged college kids, or moms from the burbs, and finally undercovers—who eventually put us away. That was the funniest thing for us. We sold crack for years and no one batted an eye. But one time we got caught with a few ounces of grass, and that was that. We always thought it would be something glorious. Mickey-Dee's people chasing us down an alley. Or some sort of firefight, our white shirts blooming into red. But that's not how it went down. It was just another day at the office. We worked the block, because that's what we did. Handed off to the wrong man, and before we knew it, we were in the back of a van.

And then I was in a cell for a long while. We made the same mistakes. We got separated, got denied parole, got transferred to different complexes. We lost touch. And I didn't know for sure that Cristian was gone or elsewhere until I got my date. But when I finally got out and saw that his family had moved back to the homeland, I knew it was because here, there was nothing left.

Now this area is too busy to think about or remember what we went through. How twenty, thirty years ago, you wouldn't step foot in this neighborhood unless you espoke espanish, unless you could be vouched for, unless you didn't care that we were in the windows, on the front steps, beside the popped hydrant splashing and dancing, getting darker and darker in the setting sun. Can't say I'm surprised by the newcomers, but even our own people don't believe us. Kids whose folks I used to roll with—who were too young to remember what life was on this block—saying things like *Our parents used to know you, Frail Boy. They made this place better than how you left it.* Can you believe that? Like I wasn't a part of our history. Spics with no sense of roots, out here ruining it for the last of us.

Because our parents had no papers, the first thing we were taught in life was that we were the tellers of our own stories. When we were little, José, Cristian, and me knew that well. Time after time our parents gave us the talk—sometimes together—about how we had to be prepared for our world to end. Who to tell the day they disappeared, how to dial a calling card long distance, what to say to the gringos who'd come knocking at our door. We knew that before we knew how to ride a bike. And sometimes we were tested on it. What would we do first if they never came home. How would we be believed. Look: we had to get our story straight.

So we don't care if you don't believe us. To be frank, that's nothing new. You can't make it through this city without a little disbelief. If we walked around expecting to be believed, we wouldn't keep so many receipts. Matter fact, I have one on me right now for this Squirt and these Newports, because I'm not about to get stopped today, I have things to do. You see, we ain't got time like we used to. We aren't believed here now, just like we weren't believed back then. I can't say what more belief would have done for José, or Tomás, or Cristian. But I'll tell you what I can't believe: that they're gone and that time goes on; that the nine months of winter finally thaws into another summer, where the vibrant lakefront comes to life with grill meat sizzles and salsa music blasts and the laughter of the little brown children like us on playgrounds and soccer fields, learning the long way how it's not just a city, a world, but a whole life full of disbelief.

And we don't care if you wanna try to forget that it happened. Whenever the locals talk about how this part of town is changing, I think of us. Us then and us now. And all those years before, when we used to watch Jordan fly across staticky TV screens, hugging each other and cheering with our parents each time he scored. Then it was '98 and he put it over Bryon Russell with 5.2 seconds left, and suddenly we were flying too, we were soaring up and down the block with flashing sparklers, spelling our names out in

light while barefoot on the grass and sidewalk, and it didn't matter that one day soon we wouldn't be believed, that people would
think the worst of us, because we thought it would last forever: that
time spent watching the fireworks go up and knowing, for once,
we could be outside at night and not be worried because all of us
were there—the whole city making noise and putting down its fists
for just a minute—part of something only we understood.

So we're not concerned about y'all moving up in here.

Not at all.

Because you weren't there.

And you can't take that from us.

BRANDON HOBSON

Escape from the Dysphesiac People

FROM *McSweeney's*

BELOVED GRANDCHILDREN: Dr. Estep has recommended I tell the story of how, many years ago, I escaped from the Darkening Land and returned home. I escaped from the men who talked funny, the ones who removed me from my home and cut my hair and put me on a train. I expected it would happen; they had already taken all my friends from school. It occurred late one night in September in what my aunt Adele referred to as the Year of Removal, when all those men from the Darkening Land Commune arrived in our small community. I won't lie: when these men broke into our house I was so terrified I couldn't speak. They were all wearing dark jackets and holding handcuffs and claiming they were from "juvenile services." Their voices were difficult to understand—I heard in them the slurred ramblings of drunkards or southerners and feared for my life. I knew stories of how they drugged people and brainwashed them to work and act in their nonindigenous ways. My poor aunt Adele went into hysterics, cursing at them, screaming in rage, and they restrained her and pulled me away. They held me down and shaved my head. The last thing I remember was one of them saying, "It's the Boys Ranch for you." Then I blacked out.

You might know that such trauma—the removal from your home, from your family, from your own identity—causes unease even after years of talking about it, and so be it, my beloved! But

this is not so much a story of a traumatic event as it is a story of
escape. This is not a mélange of distorted events, nor is it a call
for sympathy. You must know the history of removal, and this is
my own history—my way of remembering those weeks when I was
gone. Holy hell. What was weeks felt like months. Dr. Estep told
me some years later that my entire sense of time would be mis-
placed and exaggerated as I recalled all that had happened, and
for a while it was. Beloved: I was only fifteen when they took me.

When I awoke I was on a train headed to the Darkening Land.
One of the "juvenile services" men said I needed structure. He sat
beside me and snoozed. Everyone on the train looked dead. I saw
their bodies slumped, mouths open. Outside, the world flew by. I
wasn't able to see anything except fog. In the window I noticed my
smoky reflection. I leaned against the cold glass and tried to sleep.
A man a few rows in front of me stood from his seat. His spine was
so badly crooked he was bent forward, craning his neck to look
back at me. He was coughing dust and smoke.

I could barely understand what was going on with the people
on the train. Another older man and his wife were in seats across
from me. The man's face sagged from his skull. He blew his nose
into a handkerchief. "I don't feel well," he told his wife.

"You're pale," she said. "You look tired and pitiful."

"I don't feel well," he kept saying.

By the time we pulled in to the station, I felt sick too. I had the
taste of battery acid in my mouth. I sat and waited while others
got their bags and exited. I had my own bag, which I slung over
my shoulder as I walked off the train with the "juvenile services"
officer. He led me by the arm through the lobby to a pale man
who wore glasses that magnified his eyes in a very sinister way. He
squinted at me as I approached. I realized there were people all
around, watching us.

"Ah, we'll go to the car," the man said, and led me by the arm.
Everyone led me by the arm, as if I were a small child. It was irritat-
ing and worrisome. This man talked funny. I would've made a run
for it, but my legs were heavy and sore from the long train ride,
plus there were officers all around. The pale man led me outside
to a parking lot. It was still dark out, but I knew the sun would be
coming up soon. When we reached the car, the man stopped and
turned to me.

"I was stabbed in a public toilet," he told me. He pulled up his shirt and showed me a mass of scars in his side. "I won't tell you the details, son. Ah. It happened at a restroom in a park. The guy thought I wanted to lie with him for sexual explorations or experimentations and penetrations. But I just needed to pee. Ah. He stabbed and robbed me."

I didn't know what I was supposed to say.

"Mah," he said. "Forget what I said about penetrations. It's safe on the ranch. You won't get stabbed. Ah, you'll have your own room. We're all dysphesiac, so bear with us. Ah."

He twitched as he spoke. We got into his car, a battered thing smelling of rotting food and cigarette smoke. He puckered his lips and lit a cigarette, then started the engine and asked what music I wanted to listen to. His smoke hung in the air.

I remained silent.

He pulled out of the lot and turned up the radio, but there was no music. I heard static, only static.

On the drive, the pale man told me his name was Jackson. We drove through winding streets lined with barren trees, past a tall grain elevator and empty buildings. There were deserted motels with shattered windows and broken signs. Empty parking lots, trash strewn on the streets. A dense fog hung on the horizon like smoke. The boardinghouse we arrived at was a brick two-story with a large front porch and a flickering yellow porch light. The yard was full of weeds. Like the rest of the town, the neighborhood was silent and dead. I decided right then that I wouldn't like it. In Jackson's yard I saw the ancient tree with cracked bark that resembled the faces of the dead. Insects crawled all over it, buzzing, twitching their antennae.

I followed Jackson into the rotting house and asked for water to drink. The living room was warm and bare, with a few paintings on the walls of tanks and aircraft. I noticed model airplanes around the room—on the TV, on shelves, and one in pieces on the dining room table, which Jackson silently pointed to as we walked past. He showed me my room, in the back, with a single bed and a window that looked out on the backyard. A desk fan was on and hummed quietly. I lay down on the bed.

"I'll be back with a glass of mmmwater," Jackson said.

I kicked off my shoes and closed my eyes. When I opened them he was there again, standing over me with the glass.

"Drink this," he said. He sat on the edge of the bed. "There will be work for you to do here. Ah."

I shook my head.

"Mah," he said. His face twitched. "You'll choose your name, son. How about Jim? Think about it, ah, or maybe we'll just call you Chief."

"I don't want to change my name," I said.

"Chief it is. Oh, ah, you'll need to learn to act and talk just like us."

I shook my head.

"Mah," he said. "Your hair looks good short. You're in better territory, ah, away from the dusty plains. Away from the tornadoes and the rattlesnakes. You'll be happier here. Oh. Ah."

He twitched and talked for a long time about sickness and loneliness and displacement, but I don't remember everything he said. He was a sad, angry man with a long face. I have seen cattle whose faces reminded me of this man's. When he was finished talking he told me goodnight and left. But I was unable to fall asleep, unsure of my exact location. I knew I was somewhere in the middle, maybe the Midwest, nowhere near the plains. The train went east and north, it seemed. Outside it was still dark. I tried to concentrate on something peaceful: an open field at dusk, a big sky.

I heard barking outside and got up to look out the window. I saw hounds rummaging around, tearing into garbage. One of the hounds ran off with something in its mouth. The others were fighting, growling and barking at one another. I saw dark trees with low-drooping branches. I saw black vultures hanging in the moonlit sky.

Now this happened: At some point I woke in the middle of the night, confused. It took a moment to remember where I was, my surroundings. I saw the glass of water on the nightstand beside me. My bag and my shoes were on the floor. I sat up and saw the figure of an old man standing in the doorway, an apparition. I didn't recognize him. His hair was silver and long and hung languidly.

I was too afraid to say anything, and after a moment he turned and left. I got up and followed him. He walked into the bathroom, where he looked at his reflection in the mirror. He raised his hands to touch the mirror, tilted his head, studying himself. I could see his reflection, but it was much blurrier than he appeared in the room. I reached and turned on the light, but as soon as I did he disappeared. I turned the light off and on again, but he didn't reappear. "Where are you?" I whispered. I called for him, but he never responded. I turned and walked through the quiet house, in the dark, looking for him. I peeked into a bedroom and saw Jackson asleep with his back to me, snoring. His room hummed with a fan.

I stepped quietly back to the bathroom. Again I turned the light on and off, whispered for him, then returned to my bedroom. From the window I saw a hawk resting on a fence post at the back of the yard. The hawk was still while the moon shone blue in the dark sky. I sat on the bed and glanced at the clock; it was almost four in the morning. What was I supposed to think? I wasn't able to go back to sleep, too unsettled by what I had witnessed, too afraid of whatever it meant.

Beloved: I saw many people that first night. Apparitions of women and men with blankets over their shoulders, walking down the hallway. I saw children being carried. I saw people crawling and reaching out to me for help. They kept coming and coming, walking and crawling down the hallway past my bedroom. In the dark I couldn't see their faces, but their bodies were struggling against a wind, pushing forward. My ancestors, I thought. My ancestors walking the Trail.

I stared into the dark hall. I felt compelled to watch them. They pushed forward and kept walking, falling. Soon enough I began to nod off, but all night I kept waking to images of bodies in the hall. People crying out, walking, crawling. I saw a woman approach me. She brought me a seed basket with good cause. She was very beautiful, slender with long raven hair.

"I'm planting pink cherry blossoms to swell in the gray-world," she told me. "The Seven Dancers, the Pleiades star system, is our home. Follow the road out and remember the Tsalagi is about harmony." Smoke drooled from her mouth as she walked away.

After that I drifted in and out of sleep until the room brightened. I woke horrified and knew I had to leave the place. I knew I needed to find a way to get out of that house. I lay in bed and thought of Aunt Adele back home. I missed her terribly. I thought of my dead ancestors whose spirits roamed the land, whose celestial forms moved in all different directions, who entered the bodies of bobcats and eagles or floated aimlessly with the wind. I thought of the ones sitting silent on the mountains, watching the trees sway with the blowing snow, their images disappearing into the whiteness.

I rose and went into the living room, where a man introduced himself as Andrew Jack's son, Carl. He was a giant who stood so tall his head nearly reached the ceiling. He wore a green cap and overalls and was eating a piece of chicken while reading a newspaper. He had flocculent hair and a puckered face. He spoke in a deep voice, I remember.

"You're awake, boy," he said, looking down at me.

"Who is Andrew Jack?" I asked.

"My own pa," he said. "Andrew Jack is my pa, period."

I took my hands out of my pockets and crossed my arms because Carl the giant made me nervous the way he stood there eating his piece of chicken.

"I told you a story last night, boy, while you was asleep, about the sinner who doesn't work. Period. I hope it entered your subconscious, boy."

I remained silent.

"Fah," he said. "We own the whole ranch out here, period. We own the house and the barn out there, where you'll work with the other Indians we took from that town of yours, period. My job is to supervise, period, ah, the kitchen out there while Jackson supervises the field."

He seemed to be waiting for me to say something, but I didn't speak.

"Fah," he said, chewing.

I sat down and waited as he finished his chicken leg, making disgusting chewing sounds. Finally he wiped his hands on his pants and said we'd go out to the barn to work with the others, shoveling and cleaning it up. "There's work to be done today," he said. "It's, ah, your first day here, period. Fah."

"What work?" I said.

"You'll shovel. Ah. I'm tired to the bone, but you'll shovel and also carry barrels, boy. Clean the can, period. I'll mine the kitchen for the others making calf fries or fuel our vehicles unbeknownst to furlong horse dung."

"What?"

"Fah," he said, and as he grinned sinisterly at me I noticed his blistered lip.

Listen up, grandchildren: I worked that whole day with very little food. I shoveled dirt and cow and horse shit and raked hay. I cleaned the stable with six other Indians and we weren't even allowed to talk. At the end of the afternoon I was so weak from hunger I was bowled over from stomach pains.

And this was how it was every day for a few weeks. No school, just work. Every day we loaded and moved barrels and wheelbarrows full of rocks and dirt and vegetables from a garden. I raked dirt and rocks and shoveled horse shit. At night my arms were so sore I couldn't wash my face. They fed us every evening, but the food wasn't very good. Sometimes they let us watch the black-and-white television until nine or so, then it was off to bed. At least I had my own room, though I remember every once in a while one of the other Indian boys, Thomas, I think, would ask to sleep in my room. I never agreed.

"Mine is horrible," he said. "I have to share it with two little kids who piss the bed every night. They cry and beg to go home. Last night we watched Carl catch a rat with his bare hands; then he ate it."

"A rat?" I said.

"Carl is a monster. He's cockeyed and pale. He's a ten-foot-tall beast who opens his mouth and breathes."

I kept my head down and worked. I prayed to the Great Spirit that someone would come rescue me. While the others complained so much, I mostly kept quiet. I knew if I could just stay silent and work, maybe they wouldn't push me as hard as the others. I wrote letters to Aunt Adele and told her I missed her and that I would find a way to come home. Carl said he would mail the letters, but I don't think he ever did, because I never heard back from Aunt Adele. It made me sad, especially at night when I tried to fall asleep. Jackson felt sorry for me, I suppose, because one night he invited me to help carry the beer kegs from the back of the truck to a barn dance in town. The other boys were at a different house. I was sure glad I wasn't with them, doing whatever work they had to do there. I guess Jackson must've liked me some to let me go. I was glad to go with him, which was better than staying at the house with Carl the giant and his dad.

In town I helped Jackson load the truck, even though my arms were still hurting from the work I'd done. We drove out to the southern part of town and down a gravel road where there were plenty of cars parked. I was glad to see that a couple of Jackson's friends were there to help move the beer kegs into the barn.

Already, at dusk, the barn was crowded. A band of old men with gray beards and straw hats played some type of old, sad country music, droning slide guitar and low singing. I became aware of my surroundings, the people around me wearing loose-fitting flannel shirts and boots. I saw the intensity and pain on people's faces, no laughter at all.

Jackson told me to stay put and stepped away a minute. While he was gone I overheard two pale men talking near me. "The jaw's sore," one guy said to the other. "Increased gun sales, people on edge. Fah. Fought Indians today."

The other guy rocked on his heels. "Let's all be mighty proud, Taggert."

"Fought in a public toilet," the first guy said, twitching. "Jah. Jaw soreness is worrisome. No comment."

"For me it's the throat. Damn the sheriff. I heard he left for good, rode off into the cherry blossoms."

"Open your mouth and let me look. Ah. Ah."

I found myself staring at them until they noticed. One of the guys gave a friendly nod, but I didn't nod back. No matter where I looked, I felt threatened. I couldn't take it. Jackson returned with an old man who was thin and pale, with a face like a badger's. He asked about how wildcat masks were used to stalk wild turkeys.

"Also," he said, his face twitching, "we understand there's a way Jim Thorpe dominated sports with his body, using his strength."

Jackson coughed into his fist. "Mah, that's all purely speculation. The boy's here to work on the ranch."

They both looked at me, waiting for a response.

I asked where the restroom was, and Jackson said I'd have to go outside. "I'll have to walk beside you," he said, and we wandered to the other side of the room, where I noticed a group of people huddled around a bunch of mannequins. All the mannequins were faceless and unclothed, as if the barn were storage for unused department store equipment. They were positioned in different poses. Some had their arms raised. Others were kneeling. Their faces had no eyes or mouths, only noses. I found myself staring at them.

"It's for pictures," Jackson said. "For the newspaper, nothing else. Ah. Don't just stand there, boy. Go ahead look at them or do you need to pee."

I went over to one of the mannequins. It was a man on his knees, crawling. He was wearing a headdress, and I knew then that he was supposed to be an Indian. I knew then that they were all supposed to be Indians. I leaned in and touched the mannequin's face. I looked at all of them in their poses, hunched, crawling, their hands reaching out for help. It was too similar to the apparitions that had appeared in the middle of the night. My ancestors, crawling, suffering, dying on the Trail. It was sickening. I felt a chill and then suddenly nauseated. People around me, all throughout the room, were glancing at me. When I looked at them they looked away.

I had been ill at ease since I'd arrived at the ranch, but now I felt the terror. It hit hard right then. This terror was unlike anything I had felt, and I knew I had to get out of there. I looked at Jackson and pointed to my stomach.

"Stomach pain," he said. "Vomit? You got to go outside."

I nodded, and he led me to the door near the back of the barn. I stepped outside and he pointed to a tree nearby, where I walked, looking back at him. He stood at the doorway, a shadow in the night. This was the last I ever saw of pale, foul-lipped Jackson.

Beloved: I ran. I ran from the barn as hard as I could, following the road heading south to a small field. I could see the main street on the other side of the field. Squeezing my way through a large bush and a wooden fence, I ran down a small slope of grass to the dark field, where I heard things around me grunting and croaking, like frogs in a pond, but I didn't let them startle me. I would find a train, a bus, some way to get out.

I ran and ran. Bulbous clouds assumed strange shapes. The mist hanging above the grass was dense. The road seemed to open up into a new world, and to the east I saw the sun rising. I followed the road as it wound around and downhill, walking now, until I saw it dead-end ahead, past a park. Tall trees towered over the horizon, and all around me were plum trees and peach trees and pink cherry trees. It was a land of enchantment. Suddenly a boy on a bicycle rode by. He rang his bicycle bell as he passed, and I watched him coast down the hill toward a playground, where he climbed off his bicycle and ran to a group of other kids. There

was a small pond and an old house at the end of the road. I began
to walk toward them, and as I got closer I noticed an older man
working in his yard. He wore overalls, and though I couldn't see
his face I saw he had long white hair to his shoulders. He was down
on his knees, digging through a trash bag. As I passed him, he
stood and looked at me.

"Siyo," he said.

I gave a slight wave and kept walking.

"Wait a minute," he said. "Did you hear me? I said hello."

I turned and looked at him. He waved me over and told me his
name was Tsala. His eyes held an intensity, full of pain and aban-
donment.

"There's the road with the pink cherry blossoms," he said. He
stood with a stoop. He pointed toward the woods beyond where the
road ended, and I noticed for the first time the swollen pink blossoms. In the blue-gray world, it was the brightest color I had seen.

I followed him around to the back of his house. He invited me
into his kitchen. On the walls was thick wallpaper with flowery de-
signs, and ovals and rectangles where pictures used to hang. I saw
dishes piled in the sink, spilled coffee, vials and prescription bottles of pills on the counter. There was a small kitchen table with
two chairs. He sat in one and pointed for me to sit in the other,
across from him.

He poured us coffee. I drank it black from a chipped mug. I
was glad to see another Native person. He brought his pipe and we
shared a smoke. I noticed one eye was blue and the other gray. He
got up and left the room for a few minutes, and when he returned
he had a handful of stones that he set on the table in front of
me. He took a pencil and drew a triangle on a piece of paper and
placed stones within it. He chewed on sugarcane and spoke in a
low, serious voice. "These are the stones that represent the wisdom
fire within you," he said. "Look for the fire."

I leaned in and studied the triangle and a stone within it. "Rose
quartz," Tsala said. "For overcoming grief. You can begin healing.
I want you to keep it with you. Reach into the triangle and take it."

I reached in and took the stone. I looked at it in my hand. It was
rose-colored and smooth.

"Remember your ancestors," he told me. "Remember they were
removed from their homes, and then they had no homes. They

walked the Trail, walked and crawled and died. They suffered. But you already know this. Come with me."

Tsala led me back to the trail lined with cherry blossoms. "I have the stories that heal," he said. "All stories heal. Tell me, where is your home?"

"Oklahoma."

"Go follow this trail lined with cherry blossoms," he said. "It leads westward to a place without sadness or death or men who talk funny."

He shook my hand and I told him goodbye. As I started to walk, I turned back to him and watched him turn into an eagle, spread his wings, and fly into the gray sky.

Beloved grandchildren: I followed that trail. I escaped the Darkening Land. I walked down it and was not afraid, and I felt no worry about where I was going, which I knew was west because I could see in the distance the setting sun. The sky was turning pink and yellow. Soon white feathers were falling all around me, flooding the trail like fresh winter snow. I saw my ancestors ahead, but they were not crawling and wailing; they were standing. The winding trail I walked was lined with cherry blossoms, and I did not grow tired, and the sky opened up with the language of the elders saying, *Home.*

Playing Metal Gear Solid V: The Phantom Pain

FROM *The New Yorker*

FIRST YOU HAVE to gather the cash to preorder the game at the local GameStop, where your cousin works, and even though he hooks it up with the employee discount, the game is still a bit out of your price range because you've been using your Taco Bell paychecks to help your pops, who's been out of work since you were ten, and who makes you feel unbearably guilty about spending money on useless hobbies while kids in Kabul are destroying their bodies to build compounds for white businessmen and warlords —but shit, it's Kojima, it's Metal Gear, so, after scrimping and saving (like literal dimes you're picking up off the street), you've got the cash, which you give to your cousin, who purchases the game on your behalf, and then, on the day it's released, you just have to find a way to get to the store.

But because your oldest brother has taken the Civic to Sac State, you're hauling your 260-pound ass on a bicycle you haven't touched since middle school, and thank Allah (if He's up there) that the bike is still rideable, because you're sure there'll be a line if you don't get to GameStop early, so, huffing and puffing, you're regretting all the Taco Bell you've eaten over the past two years, but you ride with such fervor that you end up being only third in line, and it's your cousin himself who hands you the game in a brown paper bag, as if it were something illegal or illicit, which it isn't, of course, it's Metal Gear, it's Kojima, it's the final game in a series so fundamentally a part of your childhood that often, when you hear the Irish Gaelic chorus from "The Best Is Yet to Come," you cannot help weeping softly into your keyboard.

For some reason, riding back home is easier.

You leave the bike behind the trash cans at the side of the house and hop the wooden fence into the backyard, and if the door to the garage is open, you slip in, and if it's not, which it isn't, you've got to take a chance on the screen door in the backyard, but lo and behold, your father is ankle-deep in the dirt, hunched over, yanking at weeds with his bare hands the way he used to as a farmer in Logar, before war and famine forced him to flee to the western coast of the American empire, where he labored for many years until it broke his body for good, and even though his doctor has forbidden him to work in the yard, owing to the torn nerves in his neck and spine—which, you know from your mother, were first damaged when he was tortured by Russians shortly after the murder of his younger brother, Watak, during the Soviet War—he is out here clawing at the earth and its spoils, as if he were digging for treasure or his own grave.

Spotting you only four feet away from the sliding glass door, he gestures for you to come over, and though you are tired and sweaty, with your feet aching and the most important game of the decade hidden inside your underwear, you approach him.

He signals for you to crouch down beside him, then he runs his dirty fingers through his hair until flakes of his scalp fall onto his shoulders and his beard.

This isn't good.

When your father runs his hands through his hair, it is because he has forgotten his terrible, flaking dandruff, which he forgets only during times of severe emotional or physical distress, which means that he is about to tell you a story that is either upsetting or horrifying or both, which isn't fair, because you are a son and not a therapist.

Your father is a dark, sturdy man, and so unlike you that as a child you were sure that one day Hagrid would come to your door and inform you of your status as a Mudblood, and then your true life—the life without the weight of your father's history, pain, guilt, hopelessness, helplessness, judgment, and shame—would begin.

Your father asks you where you were.

"The library."

"You have to study?"

You tell him you do, which isn't, technically, a lie.

"All right," he says in English, because he has given up on speaking to you in Pashto, "but after you finish, come back down. I have something I need to talk to you about."

Hurry.

When you get to your room, you lock the door and turn up MF Doom on your portable speaker to ward off mothers, fathers, grandmothers, sisters, and brothers who want to harp at you about prayer, the Quran, Pashto, Farsi, a new job, new classes, exercise, basketball, jogging, talking, guests, chores, homework help, bathroom help, family time, time, because usually "Mad-villainy" does the trick.

Open the brown paper bag and toss the kush your cousin has stashed with your game because he needs a new smoking buddy since his best friend gave up the ganja for God again, and he sees you as a prime target, probably because he thinks you've got nothing better to do with your time or you're not as religious as your brothers or you're desperate to escape the unrelenting nature of a corporeal existence, and goddamn, the physical map of Afghanistan that comes with the game is fucking beautiful.

Not that you're a patriot or a nationalist or one of those Afghans who walk around in a pakol and kameez and play the tabla and claim that their favorite singer is Ahmad Zahir, but the fact that 1980s Afghanistan is the final setting of the most legendary and artistically significant gaming franchise in the history of time made you all the more excited to get your hands on it, especially since you've been shooting at Afghans in your games (Call of Duty and Battlefield and Splinter Cell) for so long that you've become oddly immune to the self-loathing you felt when you were first massacring wave after wave of militant fighters who looked just like your father.

Now, finally, start the game.

After you escape from the hospital where Big Boss was recovering from the explosion he barely survived in the prequel to the Phantom Pain, you and Revolver Ocelot travel to the brutal scenes of northern Kabul Province—its rocky cliffs, its dirt roads, and its sunlight bleeding off into the dark mountains just the way you remember from all those years ago, when you visited Kabul as a child—and although your initial mission is to locate and extract

Kazuhira Miller, the Phantom Pain is the first Metal Gear Solid game to be set in a radically open-world environment, and you decide to postpone the rescue of Kazuhira Miller until after you get some Soviet blood on your hands, a feat you accomplish promptly by locating and massacring an entire base of Russian combatants.

Your father, you know, didn't kill a single Russian during his years as a mujahideen in Logar, but there is something in the act of slaughtering these Soviet NPCs that makes you feel connected to him and his history of warfare.

Thinking of your father and his small village, you head south to explore the outer limits of the open world in the Phantom Pain, crossing trails and deserts and mountain passes, occasionally stopping at a checkpoint or a military barracks to slaughter more Russians, and you find yourself, incredibly, skirting the city of Kabul, still dominated by the Soviets, and continuing on to Logar, to Mohammad Agha, and when you get to Wagh Jan, the roadside-market village that abuts the Kabul-Logar highway, just the way you remember it, you hitch your horse and begin to sneak along the clay compounds and the shops, climbing walls and crawling atop roofs, and whenever a local Afghan spots you, you knock him out with a tranquilizer, until you make it to the bridge that leads to the inner corridors of your parents' home village, Naw'e Kaleh, which looks so much like the photos and your own blurred memories from the trip when you were a kid that you begin to become uneasy, not yet afraid, but as if consumed by an overwhelming sense of déjà vu.

Sneaking along the dirt roads, past the golden fields and the apple orchards and the mazes of clay compounds, you come upon the house where your father used to reside, and it is there—on the road in front of your father's home—that you spot Watak, your father's sixteen-year-old brother, whom you recognize only because his picture (unsmiling, head shaved, handsome, and sixteen forever) hangs on the wall of the room in your home where your parents pray, but here he is, in your game, and you press Pause and you set down the controller, and now you are afraid.

Sweat is running down your legs in rivulets, in streams, your heart is thumping, and you are wondering if sniffing the kush as you did earlier has got you high.

You look out the window and see your brother walking toward the house in the dark and you realize that you've been playing for too long.

You're blinking a lot.

Too much.

You notice that your room is a mess and that it smells like ass and that you've become so accustomed to its smell and its mess that from the space inside your head, behind your eyes, the space in which your first-person POV is rooted, you—

Ignore the knock.

It's just your little sister.

Get back to the game.

There is a bearded, heavyset man beside Watak, who you soon realize is your father.

You pause the game again and put down the controller.

Doom spits, "His life is like a folklore legend . . . Why you so stiff, you need to smoke more, bredrin . . . Instead of trying to riff with the broke war veteran."

It seems to you a sign.

You extract the kush from the trash, and because you have no matches or lighter, you put hunks of it in your mouth and you chew and nearly vomit twice.

Return to the game.

Hiding in your grandfather's mulberry tree, you listen to your father and his brother discuss what they will eat for suhoor, thereby indicating that it is still Ramadan, that this is just days before Watak's murder.

Then it hits you.

Here is what you're going to do: Before your father is tortured and his brother murdered, you are going to tranquilize them both and you are going to carry them to your horse and cross Logar's terrain until you reach a safe spot where you can call a helicopter and fly them back to your offshore platform: Mother Base.

But just as you load your tranquilizers, your brother bangs on your door and demands that you come out, and after ignoring him for a bit, which only makes him madder and louder, you shout that you are sick, but the voice that comes out of your mouth is not your own, it is the voice of a faraway man imitating your voice, and your brother can tell.

He leaves, and you return to the game.

From the cover of the mulberry tree, you aim your tranquilizer gun, but you forget that you've got the laser scope activated, and Watak sees the red light flashing on your father's forehead and they're off, running and firing back at your tree with rifles they had hidden underneath their patus, and you are struck twice, so you need a few moments to recover your health, and by the time you do, they're gone.

Your brother is back, and this time he has brought along your oldest brother, who somehow is able to shout louder and bang harder than your second-oldest brother, and they're both asking what you're doing and why you won't come out and why you won't grow up and why you insist on worrying your mother and your father, who you know gets those terrible migraines triggered by stress, and now your oldest brother is banging so hard you're afraid the door will come off its hinges, so you lug your dresser in front of it as a barricade and then you go back to your spot in front of the TV, and you sit on the floor and press Play.

At night, under cover of darkness, you sneak toward your father's compound, and you scale the fifteen-foot-high walls of clay and crawl along the rooftops until you get to the highest point in the compound, where your father stands, on the lookout for incoming jets and firebombs, and you shoot him twice in the back with tranquilizers, and as he is falling you catch him in your arms, your father, who at this time is around the same age that you are now, and in the dark, on the roof of the compound that he will lose to this war, you hold him, his body still strong and well, his heart unbroken, and you set him down gently on the clay so that the sky does not swallow him.

Climbing down into the courtyard, you go from chamber to chamber, spotting uncles and aunts and cousins you've never met in real life, and you find Watak near the cow's shed, sleeping just behind the doorway of a room filled with women, as if to protect them, and after you aim your tranquilizer gun and send Watak into a deeper sleep, your grandmother, a lifelong insomniac, rises from her toshak and strikes you in the shoulder with a machete and calls for the men in the house, of whom there are many, to awaken and slaughter the Russian who has come to kill us all in our sleep.

The damage from the machete is significant.

Nonetheless, you still have the strength to tranquilize your grandmother, pick up Watak, and climb back onto the roof while all your uncles and cousins and even your grandfather are awakened and armed and begin to fire at your legs as you hustle along, bleeding and weary, to the spot where your father rests.

With your uncle on one shoulder and your father on the other, you leap off the roof into the shadows of an apple orchard.

The men are pouring out onto the roads and the fields, calling upon neighbors and allies, and because the orchard is soon surrounded on all sides, it seems certain that you will be captured, but you are saved by, of all things, a squadron of Spetsnaz, who begin to fire on the villagers, and in the confusion of the shootout, as the entire village is lit up by a hundred gunfights, each fight a microcosm of larger battles and wars and global conflicts strung together by the invisible wires of beloved men who will die peacefully in their sleep, you make your way out of the orchard, passing trails and streams and rivers and mulberry trees, until you reach your horse and ride out of Wagh Jan, toward an extraction point in the nearby Black Mountains.

But now, at the door, is your father.

"Zoya?" he is saying, very gently, the way he used to say it when you were a kid, when you were in Logar, when you got the flu, when the pills and the IV and the home remedies weren't working, when there was nothing to do but wait for the aching to ebb, and your father was there, maybe in the orchard, maybe on the veranda, and he was holding you in his lap, running his fingers through your hair, and saying your name, the way he is saying it now, as if it were almost a question.

"Zoya?" he says and, when you do not reply, nothing else.

Keep going.

Russians chase you on the ground and in the air, they fire and you are struck once, twice, three or four times, and there are so many Russians, but your horse is quick and nimble and manages the terrain better than their trucks can, and you make it to the extraction point, in a hollow of the Black Mountains, with enough time to summon the helicopter and to set up a perimeter of mines, and you hide your father and his brother at the mouth of a cave, behind a large boulder the shape of a believer in prostration, where you lie prone with a sniper rifle and begin to pick off Russian paratroopers in the distance, and you fire at the engines of the trucks and ignore the tanks, which will reach you last, and it is mere moments before your helicopter will arrive, and just as you think you are going to make it, your horse is slaughtered in a flurry of gunfire and your pilot is struck by a single bullet from a lone rifleman, and the helicopter falls to the earth and bursts into flames, killing many Russians and giving you just enough time to rush into the cave, into the heart of the Black Mountains.

   With your father on one shoulder and your uncle on the other, and with the lights of the Soviet gunfire dying away at the outer edges of your vision, you trudge deeper into the darkness of the cave, and though you cannot be sure that your father and his brother are still alive, that they haven't been shot in the chaos, that they are not now corpses, you feel compelled to keep moving into a darkness so complete that your reflection becomes visible on the screen of the television in front of you, and it is as if the figures in the image were journeying inside you, delving into your flesh.

   To be saved.

Switzerland

FROM *The New Yorker*

IT'S BEEN THIRTY YEARS since I saw Soraya. In that time I tried to find her only once. I think I was afraid of seeing her, afraid of trying to understand her now that I was older and maybe could, which I suppose is the same as saying that I was afraid of myself: of what I might discover beneath my understanding. The years passed and I thought of her less and less. I went to university, then graduate school, got married sooner than I'd imagined and had two daughters, only a year apart. If Soraya came to mind at all, flickering past in a mercurial chain of associations, she would recede again just as quickly.

I met Soraya when I was thirteen, the year that my family spent abroad in Switzerland. "Expect the worst" might have been the family motto, had my father not explicitly instructed us that it was "Trust no one, suspect everyone." We lived on the edge of a cliff, though our house was impressive. We were European Jews, even in America, which is to say that catastrophic things had happened, and might happen again. Our parents fought violently, their marriage forever on the verge of collapse. Financial ruin also loomed; we were warned that the house would soon have to be sold. No money had come in since our father left the family business, after years of daily screaming battles with our grandfather. When our father went back to school, I was two, my brother four, and my sister yet to be born. Premed courses were followed by medical school at Columbia, then a residency in orthopedic surgery at the Hospital for Special Surgery, though what kind of special we didn't know. During those eleven years of training, my father logged countless nights on call in the emergency room, greeting a grisly parade of victims: car crashes, motorcycle accidents, and, once, the crash of an Avianca airplane headed for Bogotá, which nose-dived into a hill in Cove Neck. At bottom, he may have clung to the superstitious belief that these nightly confrontations with horror could save his family from it. But one stormy September afternoon my grandmother was hit by a speeding van at the corner of First Avenue and Fiftieth Street, causing hemorrhaging in her brain. When my father got to Bellevue Hospital, his mother was lying on a stretcher in the emergency room. She squeezed his hand and slipped into a coma. Six weeks later, she died. Less than a year after her death, my father finished his residency and moved our family to Switzerland, where he began a fellowship in trauma.

That Switzerland—neutral, alpine, orderly—has the best institute for trauma in the world seems paradoxical. The whole country had, back then, the atmosphere of a sanatorium or an asylum. Instead of padded walls it had the snow, which muffled and softened everything, until after so many centuries the Swiss just went about instinctively muffling themselves. Or that was the point: a country singularly obsessed with controlled reserve and conformity, with engineering watches, with the promptness of trains, would, it follows, have an advantage in the emergency of a body smashed to pieces. That Switzerland is also a country of many languages was what granted my brother and me an unexpected reprieve from the familial gloom. The institute was in Basel, where the language is Schweizerdeutsch, but my mother was of the opinion that we should continue our French. Schweizerdeutsch was only a hairbreadth removed from Deutsch, and we were not allowed to touch anything even remotely Deutsch, the language of our maternal grandmother, whose entire family had been murdered by the Nazis. We were therefore enrolled in the École Internationale in Geneva. My brother lived in the dormitory on campus, but as I'd just barely turned thirteen, I wasn't old enough. To save me from the traumas associated with Deutsch, a solution was found for me on the western outskirts of Geneva, and in September 1987 I became a boarder in the home of a substitute English teacher named Mrs. Elderfield. She had hair dyed the color of straw and the rosy cheeks of someone raised in a damp climate, but she seemed old all the same.

My small bedroom had a window that looked onto an apple

tree. On the day that I arrived, red apples were fallen all around it, rotting in the autumn sun. Inside the room was a little desk, a reading chair, and a bed at whose foot was folded a gray woolen army blanket old enough to have been used in a world war. The brown carpet was worn down to the weave at the threshold.

Two other boarders, both eighteen, shared the back bedroom at the end of the hall. All three of our narrow beds had once belonged to Mrs. Elderfield's sons, who had grown up and moved away long before we girls arrived. There were no photographs of her boys, so we never knew what they looked like, but we rarely forgot that they had once slept in our beds. Between Mrs. Elderfield's absent sons and us there was a carnal link. There was never any mention of Mrs. Elderfield's husband, if she'd ever had one. She was not the sort of person who invited personal questions. When it was time to sleep, she switched off our lights without a word.

On my first evening in the house, I sat on the floor of the older girls' room, among their piles of clothes. Back home, girls sprayed themselves with a cheap men's cologne called Drakkar Noir. But the strong perfume that permeated these girls' clothes was unfamiliar to me. Mixed with the chemistry of their skin, it mellowed, but from time to time it built up so strongly in their bedsheets and tossed-off shirts that Mrs. Elderfield forced open the windows, and the cold air once again stripped everything bare.

I listened as the older girls discussed their lives in coded words I didn't understand. They laughed at my naïveté, but they were only ever kind to me. Marie had come from Bangkok via Boston, and Soraya from Tehran via the Sixteenth Arrondissement of Paris; her father had been the royal engineer to the shah before the revolution sent their family into exile, too late to pack Soraya's toys but in time to transfer most of their liquid assets. Wildness—sex, stimulants, a refusal to comply—was what had landed them both in Switzerland for an extra year of school, a thirteenth year that neither of them had ever heard of.

We used to set out for school in the dark. To get to the bus stop, we had to cross a field, which by November was covered in snow that the sheared brown stalks sworded through. We were always late. I was always the only one who'd eaten. Someone's hair was always wet, the ends frozen. We huddled in the enclosure, inhaling secondhand smoke from Soraya's cigarette. The bus took us

past the Armenian church to the orange tram. Then it was a long
ride to the school, on the other side of the city. Because of our
different schedules we rode back alone. Only on the first day, at
Mrs. Elderfield's insistence, did Marie and I meet up to travel together, but we took the tram in the wrong direction and ended up
in France. After that I learned the way, and usually I broke up the
journey by dropping in at the tobacco shop next to the tram stop,
where before catching the bus I bought myself some candy from
the open containers that, according to my mother, were crawling
with strangers' germs.

I'd never been so happy or so free. It wasn't only the difficult
and anxious atmosphere of my family that I'd got away from but
also my miserable school back home, with its petty, hormonal girls,
Olympic in their cruelty. I was too young for a driver's license,
so there was never any means of escape except through books or
walks in the woods behind our house. Now I spent the hours after school wandering the city of Geneva. I often ended up by the
lake, where I watched the tourist cruises come and go, or invented
stories about the people I saw, especially the ones who came to
make out on the benches. Sometimes I tried on clothes at H&M,
or wandered around the Old City, where I was drawn back to the
imposing monument to the Reformation, to the inscrutable faces
of towering stone Protestants of whose names I can recall only
John Calvin's. I hadn't yet heard of Borges, and yet at no other
time in my life was I closer to the Argentine writer, who had died
in Geneva the year before, and who, in a letter explaining his wish
to be buried in his adopted city, wrote that there he had always felt
"mysteriously happy." Years later, a friend gave me Borges's *Atlas,*
and I was startled to see a huge photo of those sombre giants I
used to visit, anti-Semites all, who believed in predestination and
the absolute sovereignty of God. In it John Calvin leans slightly
forward to gaze down at the blind Borges, seated on a stone ledge
holding his cane, chin tilted upward. Between John Calvin and
Borges, the photo seemed to say, there was a great attunement.
There was no attunement between John Calvin and me, but I too
had sat on that ledge looking up at him.

Sometimes in my wanderings a man would stare at me without
letting up, or come on to me in French. These brief encounters
embarrassed me and left me with a feeling of shame. Often the
men were African, with sparkling white smiles, but one time, as I

stood looking into the window of a chocolate shop, a European man in a beautiful suit came up behind me. He leaned in, his face touching my hair, and in faintly accented English whispered, "I could break you in two with one hand." Then he continued on his way, very calmly, as if he were a boat sailing on still water. I ran all the way to the tram stop, where I stood gasping for breath until the tram arrived and squeaked mercifully to a stop.

We were expected at the dinner table at six-thirty sharp. The wall behind Mrs. Elderfield's seat was hung with small oil paintings of alpine scenes, and even now an image of a chalet, or cows with bells, or some Heidi gathering berries in her checked apron, brings back the aroma of fish and boiled potatoes. Very little was said during those dinners. Or maybe it only seemed so in comparison with how much was said in the back bedroom.

Marie's father had met her mother in Bangkok while he was a GI and had brought her to America, where he set her up with a Cadillac Seville and a ranch house in Silver Spring, Maryland. When they divorced, her mother returned to Thailand, her father moved to Boston, and for the next ten years Marie was tossed and tugged between them. For the past few years she had lived exclusively with her mother in Bangkok, where she had a boyfriend with whom she was madly, jealously in love and would stay out with him all night, dancing in clubs, drunk or high. When Marie's mother, at her wit's end and busy with her own boyfriend, told Marie's father about the situation, he yanked her out of Thailand and deposited her in Switzerland, known for its "finishing" schools that polished the wild and the dark out of girls and contained them into well-mannered women. Ecolint was not such a school, but Marie, it turned out, was already too old for a proper finishing school. She was, in the estimation of those schools, already finished. And not in the good way. So instead Marie was sent to do an extra year of high school at Ecolint. Along with Mrs. Elderfield's house rules, there were strict instructions from Marie's father about her curfew, and after Marie got into Mrs. Elderfield's cooking wine those stringent regulations were tightened even further. Because of this, on the weekends that I did not take the train to Basel to see my parents, Marie and I were often home together while Soraya was out.

Unlike Marie, Soraya didn't radiate trouble. At least not the sort of trouble that comes of recklessness, of a desire to cross whatever boundaries or limits others have set for you, without consid-

eration of the consequences. If anything, Soraya radiated a sense
of authority, exquisite because it derived from an inner source.
Her outward appearance was neat and composed. She was small,
no taller than I was, and wore her dark straight hair cut in what
she called a Chanel bob. Her eyes were winged with eyeliner, and
she had a downy mustache that she made no effort to conceal, because she must have known that it added to her allure. She always
spoke in a low voice, as if she trafficked in secrets, a habit she may
have formed during her childhood in revolutionary Iran, or in her
adolescence, when her appetite for boys, and then men, quickly
outgrew what was considered acceptable by her family. On Sundays, when there wasn't much to do, the three of us would spend
the day closed up in the back bedroom listening to cassettes and,
in that low-slung voice further deepened by smoking, descriptions
of the men Soraya had been with and the things she'd done with
them. If these accounts didn't shock me, it was partly because I
didn't yet have a solid enough sense of sex, let alone the erotic,
to really know what to expect from it. But it was also because of
the coolness with which Soraya told her stories. She had about
her a kind of unassailability. And yet I suppose she felt the need
to test whatever it was at her core that had come to her, like all
natural gifts, without effort, and what might happen if it failed
her. The sex she described seemed to have little to do with pleasure. On the contrary, it was as if she were submitting herself to a
trial. Only when Tehran was woven into her discursive stories and
she recounted her memories of that city was her sense of pleasure
truly palpable.

November, after the arrival of the snow: it must have been November already when the businessman showed up in our conversations. Dutch, more than twice Soraya's age, he lived in a house with
no curtains on an Amsterdam canal, but every couple of weeks he
came to Geneva on business. A banker, as I recall. The lack of
curtains I remember because he told Soraya that he only fucked
his wife with the lights on when he was sure that people across the
Herengracht could see her. He stayed at the Hôtel Royal, and it
was in the restaurant of that hotel, where her uncle had taken her
for tea, that Soraya first met him. He was sitting a few tables away,
and while her uncle droned on in Farsi about all the money his
children spent, Soraya watched the banker delicately debone his

fish. Wielding his utensils with precision, a look of absolute calm
on his face, the man extracted the skeleton whole. He performed
the operation perfectly, slowly, with no sign of hunger. Not once,
as he proceeded to devour the fish, did he stop to remove a small
bone from his mouth, the way everyone does. He ate his fish without choking, without even making a passing grimace of displea-
sure at being speared in the throat by a tiny, errant bone. It takes
a certain kind of man to turn what is essentially an act of violence
into elegance. While Soraya's uncle was in the men's room, the
man called for his check, paid in cash, and rose to leave, button-
ing his sports jacket. But instead of going straight out the doors
that led to the lobby, he detoured past Soraya's table, on which he
dropped a five-hundred-franc note. His room number was written
in blue ink next to Albrecht von Haller's face, as if it were Albrecht
von Haller who was affording her this bit of precious information.
Later, while she was kneeling on his hotel bed, freezing in the cold
gusting in through the open terrace doors, the banker told her
that he always got a room overlooking the lake because the powerful stream of its fountain, which shot up hundreds of feet into
the air, aroused him. As she repeated this to us, lying flat on the
floor with her feet up on the twin bed of Mrs. Elderfield's son,
she laughed and couldn't stop. And yet, despite the laughter, an
arrangement had been made. From then on, if the banker wished
to let Soraya know of his impending arrival, he would call Mrs.
Elderfield's house and pretend to be her uncle. The five-hundred-
franc note Soraya put away in the drawer of her night table.

At the time Soraya was seeing other men. There was a boy her
age, the son of a diplomat, who came to pick her up in his father's
sports car, the transmission of which he destroyed on a drive they
took to Montreux. And there was an Algerian in his early twenties who worked as a waiter at a restaurant near the school. She
slept with the diplomat's son, whereas the Algerian, who was genu-
inely in love with her, she only allowed to kiss her. Because he had
grown up poor like Camus, she projected onto him a fantasy. But
when he had nothing to say about the sun he was raised under, she
began to lose feeling for him. It sounds cold, but later I experienced this myself: the sudden dissociation that comes with the fear
of realizing how intimate you have been with someone who is not
at all what you imagined but something other, entirely unknown.

So when the banker demanded that Soraya drop both the diplomat's son and the Algerian, it was not difficult for her to comply. It excused her of responsibility for the Algerian's pain.

That morning before we left for school, the telephone rang. When she cut things off with each of these lovers, the banker instructed, she was to wear a skirt with nothing underneath. She told us this as we crossed the frozen field on our way to the bus stop, and we laughed. But then Soraya stopped and cupped her lighter from the wind. In the brightness of the flame I caught her eyes, and for the first time I felt afraid for her. Or afraid of her, maybe. Afraid of what she lacked, or of what she possessed, that drove her beyond the place where others would draw the line.

Soraya had to call the banker from the pay phone at school at certain times of the day, even if it meant excusing herself in the middle of class. When she arrived at the Hôtel Royal for one of their meetings, an envelope would be waiting for her at the front desk, containing elaborate instructions for what she was to do when she entered the room. I don't know what happened if she failed to follow the banker's rules, or follow them to his exacting standards. It didn't occur to me that she might allow herself to be punished. Barely out of childhood, I think what I understood then, however simply, was that she was engaged in a game. A game that at any moment she could have refused to go on playing. That she, of all people, knew how easily rules could be broken, but that she elected in this instance to follow them—what could I have understood then about that? I don't know. Just as thirty years later I don't know if what I saw in her eyes when the flame illuminated them was perversity or recklessness or fear, or its opposite: the unyielding nature of her will.

During the Christmas break, Marie flew to Boston, I went to stay with my family in Basel, and Soraya went home to Paris. When we returned two weeks later, something had changed in Soraya. She seemed withdrawn, closed up in herself, and she spent her time in bed listening to her Walkman, reading books in French, or smoking out the window. Whenever the phone rang, she jumped up to answer it, and when it was for her she shut the door and sometimes didn't come out for hours. Marie came to my room more and more often, because, she said, being around Soraya gave her the creeps. As we lay together in my narrow bed, Marie would tell me stories about Bangkok, and however full of drama they were, she could still laugh at herself and make me laugh. Looking back, I think that she taught me something that, however many times I have forgotten and remembered it since then, has never really left me: something about the absurdity, and also the truth, of the dramas we need to feel fully alive.

From January, then, until April, what I mostly remember are the things that were happening to me. Kate, the American girl I became close with, who lived in a large house in the neighborhood of Champel, and showed me her father's collection of *Playboys*. The young daughter of Mrs. Elderfield's neighbor whom I sometimes babysat, and who one night sat up in bed screaming when she saw a praying mantis on the wall, lit by the headlights of a car. My long walks after school. The weekends in Basel, where I would entertain my little sister with games to distract her from my parents' arguments. And Shareef, a boy in my class with an easy smile, with whom I walked to the lake one afternoon and made out on a bench. It was the first time I'd kissed a boy, and when he pushed his tongue into my mouth, the feeling it ignited was both tender and violent. I dug my nails into his back, and he kissed me harder; we writhed together on the bench like the couples I'd sometimes watched from afar. On the tram ride home, I could smell him on my skin, and a feeling of horror took hold of me at the thought of having to see him again in school the next day. When I did, I looked past him as if he didn't exist, but with my gaze softly focused, so that I could still see the blur of his hurt in the corner of my eye.

Of that time I remember too how once I came home from school and found Soraya in the bathroom, doing her makeup in front of the mirror. Her eyes were shining, and she seemed happy and light again, as she hadn't been for weeks. She called me in and wanted to brush and braid my hair. Her cassette player was balanced on the edge of the bathtub, and while her fingers worked through my hair, she sang along. And then, when she turned to reach for a hairpin behind her, I saw the purple bruise on her throat.

And yet I never really doubted her strength. Never doubted that she was in control and doing what she wanted. Playing a game according to rules she had agreed to, if not invented. Only looking back do I realize how much I wanted to see her that way: strong-willed and free, invulnerable and under her own command. From my walks alone in Geneva, I already understood that the power to attract men, when it comes, arrives with a terrifying vulnerability. But I wanted to believe that the balance of power could be tipped in one's favor by strength or fearlessness or something I couldn't name. Soraya told us that soon after things began with the banker his wife had called on the hotel phone, and he'd instructed Soraya to go into the bathroom, but she'd refused and instead lay listening on the bed. The naked banker turned his back but had no choice other than to go on talking to his wife, whose call he hadn't expected. He spoke to her in Dutch, Soraya said, but in the same tone that the men in her own family spoke to their mothers: gravely, with a touch of fear. And as she listened, she knew something had been exposed that he had not wished to expose, and which shifted the balance between them. I preferred that story to trying to understand the bruise on Soraya's neck.

It was the first week of May when she didn't return home. Mrs. Elderfield woke us at dawn, demanding that we tell her whatever we knew about Soraya's whereabouts. Marie shrugged and looked at her chipped nail polish, and I tried to follow her cue until Mrs. Elderfield said that she was going to call both Soraya's parents and the police, and that if something had happened to her, if she was in danger and we were withholding any information, we wouldn't be forgiven or be able to forgive ourselves. Marie looked scared, and, seeing her face, I began to cry. A few hours later the police arrived. Alone with the detective and his partner in the kitchen, I told them everything I knew, which, I realized as I spoke—losing the thread, confusing myself—was not so much. Once they had interrogated Marie, they went to the back bedroom and combed through Soraya's things. Afterward, it looked as if the bedroom had been ransacked: everything, even her underwear, strewn across the floor and her bed with an air of violation.

That night, the second one that Soraya was missing, there was a huge storm. Marie and I lay awake in my bed, neither one of us speaking of the things we feared. In the morning the crunch of gravel under the wheels of a car woke us, and we jumped out of bed to look out the window. But when the door of the taxi opened, it was a man who emerged, his lips drawn tight below his heavy black mustache. In the familiar features of Soraya's father, some truth about her origins was revealed, exposing the illusion of her autonomy.

Mrs. Elderfield made us repeat to Mr. Sassani the things we'd already told the police. He was a tall and intimidating man, his face knotted in anger, and I think she wasn't brave enough to do it herself. In the end, Marie—emboldened by her new authority and the sensational quality of the news she had to deliver—did most of the talking. Mr. Sassani listened in silence, and it was impossible to say whether what he felt was fear or fury. Both, it must have been. He turned toward the door. He wanted to go to the Hôtel Royal immediately. Mrs. Elderfield tried to calm him. She repeated what was already known: that the banker had checked out two days before, the room had been searched, nothing had turned up. The police were doing everything they could. The banker had rented a car that they were working to track down. The only thing to do was stay here and wait until there was some news.

In the hours that followed, Mr. Sassani paced grimly in front of the windows of the living room. As the royal engineer to the shah, he must have insured against all kinds of collapse. But then the shah himself had fallen, and the vast and intricate structure of Mr. Sassani's life had crumbled, making a mockery of the physics of safety. He'd sent his daughter to Switzerland because of its promise to restore order and safety, but even Switzerland hadn't kept Soraya safe, and this betrayal appeared to be too much for him. At any moment it seemed he might shout or cry out.

In the end Soraya came home on her own. On her own—just as she had gotten into it on her own, of her own choosing. Crossing the newly green field that evening, arriving at the door disheveled but whole. Her eyes were bloodshot and the makeup around them was smeared, but she was calm. She didn't even express surprise at the sight of her father, only winced when he shouted her name, the last syllable muffled by a gasp or sob. He lunged for her, and for a moment it seemed that he was going to yell or raise his hand to her, but she didn't flinch, and instead he pulled her to him and embraced her, his eyes filled with tears. He spoke to her urgently, angrily, in Farsi, but she said little back. She was tired, she said in English, she needed to sleep. In a voice unnaturally high, Mrs. Elderfield asked if she wanted anything to eat. Soraya shook her head, as if there were nothing anymore that any of us could offer that she needed, and turned toward the long corridor that led to the back bedroom. As she passed me, she stopped, reached out her hand, and touched my hair. And then, very slowly, she continued on her way.

The next day her father took her back to Paris. I don't remember if we said goodbye. I think we thought, Marie and I, that she would come back, that she would return to finish the school year and tell us everything. But she never did. She left it to us to decide for ourselves what had happened to her, and in my mind I saw her in that moment when she'd touched my hair with a sad smile, and believed that what I'd seen was a kind of grace: the grace that comes of having pushed oneself to the brink, of having confronted some darkness or fear and won.

At the end of June my father finished his fellowship and, expert in trauma, moved us back to New York. The mean girls took an interest in me when I returned to school in September, and wanted to befriend me. At a party one of them turned a circle around me while I stood calmly, very still. She marveled at how I'd changed, and at my clothes bought abroad. I had gone out into the world and come back, and though I wasn't saying anything, they sensed that I knew things. For a while Marie sent me cassettes on which she'd recorded herself talking to me, telling me all that was happening in her life. But eventually they stopped arriving, and we lost touch too. And that was the end of Switzerland for me.

In my mind, that was also the end of Soraya. As I said, I never saw her again, and tried to look for her only once, the summer I was nineteen and living in Paris. Even then, I barely tried—calling two Sassani families who were listed in the phone book and then giving up. And yet if it hadn't been for her I don't know that I would have got on the motorcycle of the young man who washed dishes at the restaurant across the street from my apartment on the Rue de Chevreuse and ridden back with him to his apartment on the outskirts of the city, or gone to a bar with the older man who lived on the floor below me, who went on about the job I knew he would never get for me at the nightclub he managed, and then, when we got back to our building, lunged at me on the landing in front of his door, tackling me in an embrace. I watched a movie on the dishwasher's sofa, and afterward he told me it was dangerous to go home with men I didn't know and drove me back

to my apartment in silence. And somehow I broke free of the
nightclub manager and raced up another floor to the safety of my
own apartment, though for the rest of the summer I was terrified
of running into him, and listened for his comings and goings before I worked up the courage to open my door and bolt down the
stairs. I told myself that I did these things because I was in Paris
to practice my French and had resolved to speak to anyone who
would speak to me. But all summer I was aware that Soraya might
be near, somewhere in that city, that I was close to her and close
to something in myself that drew me and frightened me a little, as
she had. She had gone further than anyone I knew in a game that
was never only a game, one that was about power and fear, about
the refusal to comply with the vulnerabilities one is born into.

But I myself wasn't able to go very far with it. I didn't have the
courage, and after that summer I was never again so bold or so
reckless. I had one boyfriend after another, all of them gentle and
a little afraid of me, and then I got married and had two daughters
of my own. The older has my husband's sandy hair; if she were
walking in a field in autumn, you could lose her easily. But the
younger one stands out wherever she is. She grows and develops in
contrast with everything around her. It's wrong, dangerous even,
to imagine that a person has any choice in her looks. And yet I'd
swear that my daughter had something to do with the black hair
and green eyes that always attract attention, even when she's standing in a chorus of other children. She's only twelve, and still small,
but already men look at her when she walks in the street or rides
the subway. And she doesn't hunch, or put up her hood, or hide
away behind her headphones the way her friends do. She stands
erect and still, like a queen, which only makes her more an object
of their fascination. She has a proudness about her that refuses
to grow small, but if it were only that I might not have begun to
fear for her. It's her curiosity about her own power, its reach and
its limits, that scares me. Though maybe the truth is that when I
am not afraid for her, I envy her. One day I saw it: how she looked
back at the man in the business suit who stood across the subway car from her, burning a hole through her with his eyes. Her
stare was a challenge. If she'd been riding with a friend, she might
have turned her face slowly toward her, without taking her eyes off
the man, and said something to invoke laughter. It was then that
Soraya came back to me, and since then I have been what I can

only call haunted by her. By her, and by how a person can happen
to you and only half a lifetime later does this happening ripen,
burst, and deliver itself. Soraya with her downy mustache and her
winged eyeliner and her laugh, that deep laugh that came from
her stomach, when she told us about the Dutch banker's arousal.
He could have broken her in two with one hand, but either she
was already broken or she wasn't going to break.

DAVID MEANS

Clementine, Carmelita, Dog

FROM *Granta*

A MIDDLE-AGED DACHSHUND with a short-haired, caramel-colored coat scurried along a path, nervously veering from one side to the other, stopping to lower her nose to the ground to catch traces of human footwear, a whiff of rubber, an even fainter residue of shoe leather, smells that formed a vague pattern of hikers in the past. Some had probably walked through that part of the woods long ago. She lifted her nose and let it flare to catch the wind from the north, and in it she detected the familiar scent of river water after it had passed through trees and over rock, a delightful and—under other circumstances—soothing smell that in the past had arrived to her in the house when her person, Norman, opened the windows.

The wind was stirring the trees, mottling the sunlight, and she tweezed it apart to find his scent, or even her own scent, which she'd lost track of in her burst of freedom. But all she caught was a raccoon she knew and a whiff of bacon frying in some faraway kitchen, so she put her nose down and continued north again, following an even narrower path—invisible to the human eye—into thick weeds and brush, picking up burrs as she moved into the shadows of the cliffs to her left until the ground became hard and rocky.

Then she paused for a moment and lifted her head and twitched her ears to listen for a whistle, or the sound of her own name, Clementine, in Norman's distinctive pitch. All she heard was the rustle of leaves, the call of birds. How had she gotten into this predicament, her belly low to the ground, lost in a forest?

That morning Norman had jiggled the leash over her head, a delightful sound, and asked her if she wanted to go for a walk—as if she needed to be asked—and looked down as she danced and wagged and rushed to the back door to scratch and bark. At the door she had sniffed at the crack where the outside air slipped in and, as she had many times before, caught the smell that would never leave the house, the mix of patchouli and ginger that was Claire. She was still Claire's dog. In the scent was a memory of being lifted into arms and nuzzled and kissed—the waxy lipstick —and then other memories of being on the floor, rolling around, and then the stark, earthy smell that she'd noticed one day near Claire's armpit, a scent she knew from an old friend, a lumbering gray-furred beast who was often tied up outside the coffee shop in town. It was the smell of death. Claire got that smell seeping up through her skin. It became stronger and appeared in other places until she began sleeping downstairs in the living room, in a bed that moaned loudly when it moved, and there were days on that bed, sleeping in the sun at her feet, or in her arms, and then, in the strange way of humans, she disappeared completely.

When Claire was gone, Norman began to give off his own sad odor of metal and salt, and Clementine did everything she could to make him happy, grabbing his balled socks out of the laundry pile and tossing them in the air, rolling to expose her belly when he approached, leaning against him as he read on the couch, until she began to carry her own grief.

This morning he'd dangled the leash, and while she was waiting at the back door he'd gone to the kitchen and got a tool from a drawer, an oil and saltpeter thing that made a frightening sound, Clementine knew, because once he had taken her along to shoot it upstate. (Don't get me wrong. She knew it was a gun, but she didn't have a name for it—it was an object that had frightened her.) The thing was zipped into his bag when he came to the door. He stood with his hand on the handle, and she waited while he looked at the kitchen for a few seconds—minutes, in dog time—and then she was pulling at the leash, feeling the fresh air and the sun and the morning dew as she guided him along the road, deep in routine, barely bothering with the roadside odors, to the entrance of the park. On the main path that morning—with the water to the right and the woods to the left—there had been the usual familiar dogs, some passing with their noses to the ground, snobbishly, others barking a greeting. (Her own mode was to bark as if they were a threat—she was, after all, as she acknowledged in these moments, shorter than most dogs—while also wagging vigorously at the same time.) There had been an old Irish setter, Franklin, who had passed her with a nod, and then a fellow dachshund named Bonnie, who had also passed without much of a greeting, and then finally Piper, an elderly retired greyhound who had stopped to say hello while his person and Norman spoke in subdued voices—she got the tone of sadness, picked up on it—and then, when the talk was over, Norman had pulled her away from Piper and they continued up the path until they came upon a small, nameless, mixed-breed mutt who launched, unprovoked, into a crazy tail-chasing routine in the middle of the path, a dervish stirring up the dust in a way that made Clementine step away and pull on the leash, because it is a fact that there is just as much nonsense in the dog world as there is in the human world.

Sitting now on the rocky ground resting, she lifted her nose to the wind and caught the smell of a bear in a cloak of limestone dust from the quarry, and inside the same cloak was the raccoon she knew, the one that had rummaged around Norman's garbage cans, and then, of course, deer—they were everywhere. Lacking anything better to do, she put her nose down and began to follow deer traces along the rocks and into the grass, a single-file line of hooves that led to a grove of pines where they had scattered, broken in all directions, and at this spot she cried softly and hunched down, feeling for the first time what might (in human terms) be called fear, but was manifested instinctually as a riffle along her spine that ran through the same fibers that raised her hackles, and then, for a second, smelling pine sap, she closed her eyes and saw the basement workshop where she sometimes stood and watched Norman, until one of his machines made a sound that hurt her ears and sent her scurrying up the stairs.

Cold was falling and her ears twitched at the memory of the sound of the saw blade. Norman was upstairs in his room staring ahead and clicking plastic keys in front of a glowing screen while she lay on old towels in the sunlight, waiting for the clicking to stop, opening her eyes when it did and searching for a sign that he might get up, get her food. Sometimes his voice rose and fell while she sat at his feet and looked up attentively, raising her paws when he stopped. Since Claire had disappeared, he left the house in the morning only to return at night, in the dark, to pour dry kibble—that senseless food—into her dish and splash water into her drinking bowl. Behind his door the television droned, and maybe, on the way out of the house the next morning, he might reach down and ruffle her head and say, "I'm sorry, girl, I'm not such great company these days."

As she opened her eyes, stood up, and began walking, these memories were like wind against her fur, telling her where she should be instead of where she was at that moment, moving north through the trees. The sun had disappeared behind the cliffs and dark shadows spread across the river and the wind began to gust, bringing geese and scrub grass, tundra and stone—wrapped in a shroud from beyond the Arctic Circle, an icy underscent that foretold the brutality of missing vegetation; it was a smell that got animals foraging and eating, and it made her belly tense.

Here I should stress that dog memory is not at all like human memory, and that human memory, from a dog's point of view, would seem strange, clunky, unnatural, and deceptive. Dog memory isn't constructed along temporal lines, gridded out along a distorted timeline, but rather in an overlapping and of course deeply olfactory manner, like a fanned-out deck of cards, perhaps, except that the overlapping areas aren't hidden but are instead more intense, so that the quick flash of a squirrel in the corner of the yard, or the crisp sound of a bag of kibble being shaken, can overlap with the single recognizable bark of a schnauzer from a few blocks away on a moonlit night. In this account, as much as possible, dog has been translated into human, and like any such translation, the human version is a thin, feeble approximation of what transpired in Clementine's mind as she stood in the woods crying and hungry, old sensations overlapping with new ones, the different sounds that Norman's steps had made that morning, the odd sway of his gait, and the beautiful smell of a clump of onion grass—her favorite thing in the world!—as she'd deliriously sniffed and sneezed, storing the smell in the chambers of her nose for later examination while Norman waited with unusual patience.

That smell of onion grass was the last thing she could remember—again in that overlapping way—along with a small herd of deer, who that morning had been a few yards away in the woods, giving off a funk, and the sudden freedom around her neck when

Norman unharnessed her and took the leash and she darted up
into the woods, running past the place where the deer had been
and on the way catching sight of the rabbit for the first time, chasing it while feeling herself inside a familiar dynamic that worked
like this: he would let her go and she'd feel the freedom around
her neck, running, and then at some point he would call her name
or, if that didn't work, whistle to bring her back; each time she'd
bound and leap and tear up the hillside and then, when he called,
she'd find herself between two states: the desire to keep going and
the desire to return to Norman, and each time she'd keep running
until he called her name again, or whistled. Then she'd retrace
her own scent to find her way back to him.

It was true that since Claire had disappeared the sound of his
whistle had grown slack, lower in tone, but he always whistled, and
when she returned there was always a flash of joy at the reunion.
Not long ago he'd swept her into his arms and smothered her with
his blessing, saying, *Good girl, good girl, what did you find up there?*
Then with great ceremony he'd rolled her up into his arms, kissed
her, plucked a burr from her coat, and carried her over the stones
to the waterline, where he let her taste and smell an underworld
she would never know: eels, seagrass, fish, and even the moon.

Yes, in the morning light she'd caught sight of a cottontail
flash of white in the trees and then, giving chase, barking as she
ran, followed it into the brush until she came to it in a clearing,
brown with a white tail, ears straight up, frozen in place, offering a pure but confusing temptation. There they stood, the two
of them. His big eyes stared into her big eyes. The rabbit darted
sharply and Clementine was running with the grass thrashing her
belly and then, faster, with all four paws leaving the ground with
each stretched-out bound. There was nothing like those bounds!
Slowed down in dog time it was a sublime joy, the haunches tightening, spreading out, and then coiling—she could feel this sensation!—as the rabbit zigzagged at sharp angles and at some point
dashed over a creek while she followed, leaping over the water to
the other side, where, just as fast as it had appeared, the rabbit vanished, finding a cove, or a warren hole in the rocks at the bottom
of the palisade, leaving her with a wagging tail and a wet nose and
lost for the first time in her life.

*

Now she was alone in the dark, making a bed in the pine needles, circling a few times and then lowering her nose on her paws, doing her best to stay awake while the cool air fell onto her back. Out of habit she got up and circled again in place and then lay down, keeping her eyes open, twitching her eyebrows, closing them and then opening them until she was in the room with Norman, who was at his desk working, clicking his keys. Claire was there, reaching down and digging her thumb into a sweet spot where the fur gave around her neck.

Hearing a sound, she opened her eyes. There were patches of underworld moonlight and through them deer were moving quietly. The bear was still to the north in the wind. A skunk was spreading like ink.

In the car with Norman and Claire, her own face was at the open window, the wind lifting her ears, and her nose was thrust into a fantastic blast of beach and salt marsh and milkweed chaff while in the front seat they talked musically to each other, singing the way they used to sing.

Something rustled in the woods. In the faint starlight, the large shadow of the bear moved through the trees. She kept still and watched until it was devoured by the dark.

She was in the bed by the window in Norman's room. He was tapping the keys. Tap tap, tap, tap.

The tapping arrived in morning light. It came from a stick against the forest floor.

The man holding the stick was tall and lean with a small blue cap on his head. *Hey, good dog, good doggie, what are you doing out here, are you lost?* The flat of his palm offered something like coconut, wheat flour, hemp, and, as an underscent, the appealing smell of spicy meat.

The man picked her up gently and carried her—*How long have you been up here, what's your name, girl?*—across the ridge of stones, through the woods to a wider path under big trees and then down, over several large stones, to the beach, where he smoked and poured some water into a cup and laughed as she lapped it up, twirling her tongue into her mouth. In his hand was a piece of meat, spicy and sweet as she gulped it down, and then another, tossed lightly so that she could take it out of the air, not chewing it at all, swallowing it whole.

That was all it took. One bit of spicy meat and she reconfigured her relationship with the human. She felt this in her body, in her haunches, her tail, and the taste of the meat in the back of her throat. But again, it wasn't so simple. Again, this is only a translation, as close as one can get in human terms to her thinking at this moment, after the feeling of the cold water on her tongue and the taste of meat. One or two bits of meat aren't enough to establish a relationship. Yes, the moment the meat hit her mouth a new dynamic was established between this unknown person and herself, but, to put it in human terms, there was simply the *potential* in the taste of meat for future tastes of meat. The human concept of *trust* had in no way entered the dynamic yet, and she remained ready to snap at this strange man's hand, to growl, or even, if necessary, to growl and snap and raise her hackles and make a run for it. Human trust was careless and quick, often based on silly—in canine terms—externals, full of the folly of human emotion.

This is as good a place as any to note that through all of her adventures, from the early-morning walk on the path to the long trek through the woods and the night in the pine needles, Clementine did not once hear the loud report of a gun. Of course she wasn't anticipating the sound. Once the gun was in Norman's bag, it was gone from her mind, completely, naturally. It wasn't some kind of Chekhovian device that would have to, at some point, go off.

The man picked her up from the sand, brushed her paws clean —*It's gonna be okay. Where do you live?*—and carried her to the main trail. The sway of his arms made her eyes close. When she opened them, they were on a road and the limestone dust was strong, and there was a near-at-hand bacon smell coming from a house. He put her down and let her clamber down a small cinder-block stairway and through a door and into his house.

In a charged emotional state, Clementine poked around the strange rooms sniffing the corners, eagerly reconnoitering—a dusty stuffed seal under a crib in a room upstairs, eatable crumbs under a bed, a cinnamon candle near a side table, a long row of records—all the while missing the freedom she had experienced in the woods, bounding through the trees, the harness gone, and beneath that, a feeling that Norman somewhere outside was still calling her name, or whistling.

All day she explored the house, pausing for naps in the afternoon sun, and retraced the activities of previous dogs, a long-ago cat, and various persons. She found pill bugs and cobwebs (she hated cobwebs) in the corners, and on a chair in the dining room small plastic bags of something similar to skunk grass and spider flowers—not exactly onion grass, but still worth close attention.

That day Clementine came to understand that the man's name was Steve. Later in the afternoon, a woman named Luisa arrived and spoke a different language—no words like *sit*, or *walk*, or *good dog*, or *hungry*—to which she paid close attention, partly because Luisa had a smell similar to Claire's, gingery and floral with a faint verdant bready odor that—Clementine felt this, in her dog way—united them in a special way. There was also the way Luisa rubbed her neck, gently and then more firmly, using her thumb as she leaned down and said, *What should we call you?* And then went through many beautiful words until she settled on Carmelita. *Carmelita*, she said. *Carmelita*.

Even in her excitement over her new home, Carmelita was experiencing a form of grief particular to her species. There are fifty-seven varieties of dog grief, just as there are—from a dog's point of view—110 distinct varieties of human grief, ranging from a vague gloom of Sunday-afternoon sadness, for example, to the intense, peppery, lost-father grief, to the grief she was smelling in this new house, which was a lost child (or lost pup) type of grief, patches of which could be found in the kitchen, around the cabinets, near the sink, and all over the person named Luisa. It was on the toys upstairs too, and as she sniffed around she gathered pieces together and incorporated them into her own mood.

Resting in the moonlight that night, on an old blanket in the room with the stereo speakers, she kept her eyes open. An owl hooted outside. A faraway dog barked. A distant rumble sound, along with a high screeching sound, began and gradually grew into a high-pitched screeching and clattering, a booming roar that was worse than thunder, and then it tapered off, pulled itself away into the distance, and disappeared.

The light came on and Steve rubbed her belly—*It's just a train, sweetie, you'll have to get used to those*—and then, in the dark again, she detected a mouse in the corner, erect on two feet, holding and nibbling on something. When she growled it disappeared into the wall. The light came again and Luisa rubbed her head and belly. Then it was dark again, and to soothe herself she brought out from one of the chambers in her nose the smell of onion grass.

Days passed. Weeks passed. Carmelita settled into her new life. Some days Luisa was in the house, moving around, sitting at the table with the smell of green stuff, dangling a bag of it in front of Carmelita's nose so she could sniff and open her mouth and gently clasp—she had learned not to bite the bags.

One afternoon Steve took her into the woods, along a small trail, and through a fence to an open spot. She lay and watched as he dug with a shovel, cut down stalks, and stopped to smoke. (She liked to snap at the rings he made, to thrust her nose into the smell that tangled up and brought the sudden overlap of memory: Claire in her bed smoking, and the strange smell of the cans under the workbench in Norman's workshop.)

In the evenings they ate at the table in candlelight and talked about someone named Carmen. Each time the word appeared, the smell of grief would fill the room. The scent was all over the house, in different variations. She even found it on the thing that Steve carried when he left the house in the morning, a leather satchel with a bouquet of iron and steel, clinking when he hefted it up—*So long, Carmelita, see you after work, gotta go build something* —an object always worth examining when he came back to the house because it carried an interesting array of distant places and other humans.

Sometimes they took her for a walk to the woods, or down the road past the stone quarry to a park where children played and other dogs hung out. She became friendly with the dogs there and they exchanged scents and greetings. Her favorite, Alvy, a bulldog with a playful disposition and a scratching issue, came to the house one evening and they slept together in her bed, side by side. He snorted and sneezed and coughed in his sleep. When he sneezed —his massive nose was beautiful—he emitted a cornucopia of aromas, mint weed, leathery jerky Arctic vegetation, even a hint of caribou—essences he had drawn in from the northern wind and stored for future examination.

Winter came. Snow fell. The ice smell from the north became the smell outside. When Carmelita went out in the evening—her belly brushing the snow—she kept to the path and did her business quickly, stopping only for a moment to taste the air. Then she dashed back to Steve in the doorway, the warmth of the house pouring around him into the cold blue.

One night there were cries from the bedroom upstairs. She got up—noting the mouse—and went and saw them naked together, wrapped in the familiar bloom of salt and, somehow, a fragrance like the river underworld. When they were finished they brought her up onto the bed. There was a hint of spring in the air that night, and the next morning; the wind shifted and the ice smell from the north was replaced by southern smells—one day faint forsythia and crocus, another day Spanish moss and dogwood, magnolia, morning glories, and another the addition of redbuds, and of course cypress, all these smells drifting in a mirepoix (no other human word will do) of red clay and turned rich farm soil that told the animal world that green was coming. When the weather was good she would go out to the back deck—passing through the little door Steve had installed—and rest her chin on the wooden rail, looking out over the water, watching the birds in the sky, as she turned the wind around in her nose.

One morning there was another presence in the house, a small thump in Luisa's belly, a movement. Carmelita put her head down and listened, hearing a white liquid fury along with the thump, while her tongue—licking and licking Luisa's skin—tasted the tangy salt of new life.

That night she woke in darkness—the moon gone, no moon at all—to the sound of a raccoon crying. Through the window over her bed the strong southern wind slipstreamed, and when she fell back asleep she was free, chasing the rabbit (if you had been in the room, you'd have seen her paws twitching as she lay on her side), bounding through soft grass, inside the pursuit. The rabbit froze, ears straight and still, and offered its big, pooling eyes. They stood in the clearing for a moment, Carmelita on one side, the rabbit on the other. The air was clear and bright and the sun was warm overhead. Then the rabbit spoke in the language of dog. The rabbit spoke of the sadness Carmelita sometimes felt, a long stretched-out sense of displacement that would arrive suddenly, amid the hubbub of the house, the leather satchel fragrance, the thump in Luisa's skin—that heartbeat—and the memory of Claire. It spoke loudly of all the things that had gone into the past and all of the things that might, like a slice of meat, appear in the future, and then it dashed off to one side, heading toward a mountain, and with a bark (Carmelita did bark, giving a dreamy snap of her jaw) she was back in the chase, moving in gravity-free bounds over velvety grass until, with a start, she woke to darkness, staring around the room—a faint residual predawn marking the windows and, once again, the mouse on its hind legs, holding something as it gently nibbled.

The end of spring came and the air filled with a superabundance of local trees, grasses, flowers, and pollen. Some days the air was neither north nor south. A newborn was in the house too, gurgling and twisting, crying at night.

One afternoon, the house quiet, Carmelita went onto the deck to air and sun. At the railing, her chin on the wood, she examined the wind coming from the south and as she sniffed she caught and held Norman's smell. It was faint. In human terms it was not a smell at all—a microscopic tumbleweed of his molecules. But it was there. She caught it and held it in her nose, in one of the chambers, and turned it over like a gemstone.

That night the rabbit did not pause at the end of the glade and instead the chase went on and on, weaving around until she woke up in the darkness, and to soothe herself she sat up and examined the little bit of Norman's smell she had stored in her nose. (Again, this is just a translation. There wasn't in any of this a concept of causality, and the smell of Norman in the air alone, mixed into a billion other smells, wasn't enough to make her dream of escaping to the woods to trace her way back to her previous origin point. She was perfectly content in her life with Steve and Luisa and the baby, walks in the woods, good food, lots of fresh meat, even on occasion the spicy meat. That tiny bundle of molecules that smelled like Norman was just something to ponder, to bring back out.) Dawn was breaking and she got up and went to the bedroom, clicking her long nails, to listen to Steve and the baby.

One night in August she was chasing the rabbit again, a ball of white movement that pulled her along a stretch of the main path that she had traveled many times. As she ran she passed familiar pee-spots: picnic-bench legs, trash cans, bushes. The rabbit didn't zig or zag but was running in a straight line, undaunted, and because of this she felt a new kind of fury, an eagerness that drove her across the wide parking lot, past cars and people, with the wide river glassy and quivering to the left of her vision—everything in a dreamlike way pulled into the vortex of her singular desire, nothing at all playful this time, so that she kept her head down and plunged ahead. Then she was up the hill—completely familiar—and along a stone path to the door of the house where the rabbit had stopped and turned, twitching, standing still, as if offering itself to her. In a single fluid motion she clutched it in her rear paw, twisting hard, and then, when she had her chance, she got to the rabbit's neck, clamped down, and shook it until it stopped moving and then shook it some more, taking great pleasure in its resistance to the motion of *her* neck, and then, as she was tasting the bloody meat, gamey and warm, there was the sound of Steve speaking, and she was on her blanket, which she had pawed all the way across the room. It was morning. He was in the doorway to the kitchen with a mug of coffee in his hand. *You must've been dreaming,* he said. *Your little paws were moving.*

Did one dream foretell another? Was it possible that the dream indicated what was to come? Of course she would never think of it that way, because she wasn't bound by the logic of causality; the dream of the rabbit was as real as her waking state, so it overlapped with what happened one afternoon, a Saturday late in the summer, when Steve took her for a long hike along the path. (He never took her too far down the path, because he didn't want to give her up. He had made a halfhearted attempt to locate her owner, asking around, looking at posts on the Internet, until he was persuaded that no one in the area had reported a missing dachshund. But then one day at the Stop & Shop on Mountain Road, on the community bulletin board, he saw her photo. But by the summer the dog was part of the family, and it seemed important—in some mystical way—that she had appeared in the woods before Luisa became pregnant.)

Once again it seems important to stress that Carmelita's world is composed of fibers of sensation caught like lint in a web of her neurons, a vivid collection of tastes, luminous visions, dreams, and even, in her own ways, hopes and grief. Enter her nose, the enfolded sensors a million times more sensitive to odor than your own; imagine what it was like for her to hold, even as a clump of molecules, the distinctive smell of Norman, along with every thing she had ever encountered arrayed like a nebula swirl, spinning in a timeless location.

On the path she pulled on the leash, feeling big. It was a perfect day, with a breeze that carried not only the usual scents of the sea but of the city too: streets and car exhaust and pretzel stands and oniony salsa and baking bread.

At a turn in the path the wind funneled along the rock and narrowed, bringing together several streams. In this wind she detected Norman's smell again, just a trace. Steve often let her loose for a few minutes at this spot where the trail was quiet and the trees were sparse. Like Norman, he called and whistled her back, but he didn't wait as long, most of the time, and the dynamic was somehow different.

As she ran up through the woods, not really chasing anything —although of course the rabbit dream was still fresh—she was surprised in a wide clearing by a rabbit in the grass ahead, eating clover, unaware of her presence. She drew closer, barked, and the rabbit froze and then dashed away, making a zigzag, leaping across a creek.

With joy and fury she ran, entering freedom. It was a smart old rabbit, larger than the one in the dream. It disappeared ahead while Carmelita kept running, skirting the creek, slowing down to nose the ground.

It was here that she caught Norman's smell in the air again, stronger than before, a distinctive slice of odor coming through the woods, not just Norman but his house and yard too. It came strongly, in a clear-cut, redolent shape, so she ran toward it, tracking and triangulating as it appeared and then disappeared. A flash of brown dog through the grass and then the woods, her instincts making innumerable adjustments as she went over the rocky ground, through another grove of trees, pulling away from Steve, having passed beyond the familiar dynamic as the pull of the voice behind her was counteracted by the scent ahead.

It was a matter of chance that Steve had been on the phone with Luisa, talking about the baby, about diapers or formula. On this day the wind was just right and Clementine was fifty or so yards behind a certain boundary line, not ignoring the sound of Steve's voice, distant but clear, calling her name, but overwhelmed by the scent ahead. Simply put, the smell of Norman prevailed over the sound of Steve.

I wish I could make words *be* dog, get into her coat and paws and belly and ears as she ran, slowing down on the main trail, passing the picnic tables, the trash bins, catching now and then the familiar fragrance of home, but also, by this point, her own trace of scent on the asphalt where she had passed a hundred times long ago. If I could make words *be* dog, then perhaps I could find the way to inhabit the true dynamic, to imagine a world defined not by notions of power, or morality, or memory, or sentiment, but instead by pure instinct locked in her body, her little legs, as she trotted up the hill along the wall and, when the wall disappeared, cut across manicured grass, past the sign to the park, another great spot to pee, then up the road—staying to the side as she had been taught—to the driveway, stopping there for a moment to sniff.

Out on the back porch Norman was at a table under a wide green umbrella, working. Music was coming through the open door. His neck was stiff and he had his hand up and was trying to work out a kink. He sighed and stood to stretch when he heard her bark, once, a big bark for such a small dog. Then he had his arms out and was running and she was running too, with her body squirming around her flapping tail until he was near and then, with another yip, yip, yip, she was on her back with her belly up, bending this way and that, waiting for his hands, because that was all there was at that moment, his hands lifting her up, lifting, until, still squirming and crying, she was pushing her face into his face, licking and licking as he spoke to her, saying, *Oh girl I missed you so much, I missed you, I let you go and started missing you the second you were gone, and when you were gone I knew I had to go on,* and then there was a burst of something beyond the wind itself, beyond the taste of meat, and the two of them were *inside* reunion; even in that moment she was aware that his smell had changed, and she was still dancing on her paws as she went into the house to investigate, checking the floorboard beneath the sink, going from room to room, from one corner to the next.

One day in the fall, keeping the leash tight, he took her back along the path to the spot where she had left him. It might've been that day, or another, when she caught Steve's scent in the wind, the baby too, and then, another time, Luisa's distinctive scent. In her dreams the rabbit still appeared from time to time, and she ran and leapt and bounded between earth and sky, hovering in bliss and stillness that seemed beyond the animal kingdom. Often at the end of a long-dreamed chase she met the rabbit and they watched each other from their respective sides of the clearing, frozen inside the moment, speaking with their eyes of the tang of onion grass and the taste of spicy meat.

Paradise

FROM *The Southern Review*

"I THINK WE should go, Dad," I said, shielding my eyes from the wind. The sheriff had tweeted an evacuation order for Pulga twenty minutes before. It was quarter to eight in the morning and the sky didn't look right. Ten minutes ago it had turned from bright blue to a thick, pale orangy gray.

"I'm not going anywhere," said Wesley, my father-in-law. He looked eastward with his face crinkling up. He was a big bull of a man, about five eleven. He was white and bald and wore glasses. He had a chipped front tooth and his son's blue eyes. He wore a Cowboys T-shirt and blue nylon shorts and black flip-flops. Eighty years old.

"That sky, though," I said. I'm five two with a big ass and strong arms. I'm forty-four. My black hair frizzed all around my head. I wore black nylon shorts and a pink nylon top and no shoes.

We stood in the front yard of the house, which was on Edgewood Lane. Wes's black Yukon sat in the driveway. I'd parked my little green Prius by the curb. The winds whipped down the road. The crape myrtle bushes I planted on the sides of the house right after Mike died flattened and splayed from the hard gusts. The cottonwoods fringing the road shook like a huge hand was slapping them. Dead gold grass and dried leaves crawled along our front yard instead of a proper lawn. Back inside, Jessie still dawdled, drinking her milk in the kitchen and playing with Henrietta.

"Shelly," I said. Our neighbor, a hefty yellow-haired woman, had just walked fast out of her house wearing flowered shorts and a white T-shirt.

"Fernanda, they're evacuating Pulga," she said. Pulga's a little town maybe fifteen miles away from Paradise as the crow flies.

"I know," I said.

"You got Jessie?" Shelly asked.

"Yeah, I think we're going to go in like ten minutes," I said. Wesley shook his head.

"Wes," Shelly said, grimacing. "Sonny boy, smell that air."

Already it smelled like burning.

"Fires here every year," Wesley said, tilting his head my way. "She can go."

"She is the cat's mother," Shelly said, pulling her phone out of her shorts pocket and jabbing at it.

Ten or twelve other neighbors came hurrying out of their houses. Martin, Tillie, Babs, Fred, Nancy, I can't remember. Already Serena Hammer's Honda and Joe Tate's Chevrolet chugged down Edgewood toward Pearson and Skyway. The rest of us stood out there gawking for probably too long, making clucking noises and talking about the Carr fire in Nor Cal last August.

"Concow lines are down," Shelly said, gripping her iPhone. Concow's another town, closer to us than Pulga. "Can't get hold of my mother."

"Evacuation for Paradise," Martin suddenly hollered, from two houses down. He's another white man—but they're all white except for me on this street, so why keep saying it. His nose practically touched his iPhone's screen. "They're telling us to haul out."

Shelly hustled indoors. People started moving back and forth between their houses and their cars. They lugged clothes, water, lamps, pillows, makeup cases, books, pictures, all this unnecessary crap.

I looked at Wesley. He sniffed.

"I'm not running," he said. "I built this house in 1982."

"Wes," I said. "Look at the color of that goddamn sky."

"This is my house, you just live here," he said. "You and Jessie can go."

He started walking toward the myrtles on the left side of the house, where the hose was.

I ran inside.

Wes didn't want his son, Mike, to marry me. It wasn't a secret. I'm Pomo and Mexican and grew up in the Evergreen Mobile

Home Park with my parents, Lupita and Ben. Mike and I knew
each other from around. We'd seen each other at Paradise High,
where we graduated in '84, and then later at Butte Community.
But Mike had been raised up on Edgewood. When he was young,
he dated girls like valedictorian Renee Henson and cheerleader
Willa Miller, whose parents lived on Pentz and Mountain View.
I stuck to a crew of Native, black, and Mexican kids who played
video games and got sent to detention when they shrugged at
the white teachers. Mike was a blockhead back then anyway and I
wasn't interested. He played football and I'd seen him soaking wet
and drunk at house parties on Saturday nights.

Mike was above me because my parents worked as janitors at
Paradise's Best Western and Chico's Oxford Suites. But his pa,
Wesley Noonan, was one of the best lawyers in town. Wes set up
a three-man outfit—Noonan, Gump, & Penzer—up on Skyway,
where he did estate planning for folks from Paradise to Chico. Wes
was a big man, and not just physically. When he'd walk into Tattie's Café, where I bused and then waitressed during high school,
diners would look up at him in an eager manner. Tattie herself
(she's now dead) would run up to him, wiping her hands on her
apron and seating him, his pretty red-haired wife, Laura, and Mike
right away.

"I'll have the steak and a Scotch," Wes would say to me on the
nights when I took his order. He looked me over once and then
never again.

"Would you like that rare, sir?" I'd ask him, though I knew.

He'd sit there and sniff, like he was mad that the Scotch wasn't
in front of him already.

"He likes it well," Laura said, smiling. Mike would gawk at me a
little bit and then blush and look down.

The twentieth time I pretended to forget that Wes liked his
meat scorched, he set his jaw and smacked at a water glass so that
it went flying.

"How many times do I have to tell you the same thing?" he
snapped, while the water dripped.

"Dad," Mike had said.

Laura had begun to mop up the spill with her napkin.

"What's my name?" I asked him then.

Wes's face twisted. "What?"

"What's my name?" I asked again. I pointed to my name tag,

FERNANDA. "Come on, I've been getting you steak for a year, you must know it by now." I just didn't like the way he did business.

Tattie came running over, wailing, "We've got this covered, the bill for tonight's taken care of, Wesley."

To do penance, Tattie made me keep bringing the table complimentary olives and fried cheese bites that came out of my check. But even though I fed that mope to the gills, I still got fired later that night.

Mike and I started dating eight years ago. I'd gotten a divorce and come back home from Dublin, Georgia, where my first husband, Scott, lived. Mike hadn't gone to law school like his father wanted but instead became a police officer. He did K-9 patrol first, with a German shepherd named Logan and then with Henrietta. We were both in our midthirties around this time and so more free from our parents. My folks had moved back to Sonoma, where my dad's people were, and so I could stretch my legs a little. And Mike had become a grown man a world away from the drunk dummy who blushed and stammered at restaurants with his pop. He'd learned CPR, community policing. He was married for seven years and then divorced Willa in '99. He rented a little red house with Logan on Magalia Street, and kept it as tidy as a teakettle.

I lived back in the mobile home park in Evergreen where my parents had raised me, so we were still in two different worlds. But once I returned from Dublin, I joined a Facebook page, "Life in Paradise, Ca.," and I guess he saw me on it. We messaged back and forth about the good old days in PHS as if we'd known each other better than we had. After a while he asked me out.

"I always had a crush on you," he said on our fourth date. Jesus, had he grown up into a strapping son of a bitch, with these biceps on him and thick, hard thighs. He hadn't turned my head back in the day, but now I got wild for him.

"Do you remember that night at Tattie's with your dad?"

"Yes," he said, and cracked up. "Hot diggity, I thought, watch out."

"I'll bet he was mad," I said.

Mike had green eyes with long lashes. He nudged up onto me and I felt the sweet heat coming off his mouth and his face. "He's always mad," he said.

*

The reason why I know that Wes didn't want Mike to marry me was because on our wedding day he sat in the front pew just shaking his head. I didn't care. I was the happiest I'd ever been. Mike and I had our baby, Jessie, a year and a half later. The first German shepherd, Logan, died, but then we got smart-as-a-wizard Henrietta. We four lived like queens and a prince in that ugly little red house. Laura would come over Sundays to see the baby, but Wes kept himself to himself except on Jessie's birthday and on the holidays.

The second Thanksgiving we were married, Laura hosted the meal. I remember how I got Jessie dressed up in blue velvet with a little Peter Pan collar. I wore a white lace dress, which I'd found at the Goodwill on East Avenue and spruced up by bleaching it and mending the torn slip. Mike wore green sweatpants and a brown sweatshirt and said that belts weren't for turkey. We all bustled into Wes and Laura's huge house, admiring the figurines and the Chinese whatnots. I worried that Jessie would totter around screaming and break something, but when Laura kissed her all over and Wes started laughing at her antics I let myself relax a little bit.

After the main course but before dessert, Mike took my hand and led me through the house's hallway and down a short flight of steps. He brought me to Wes's bonus room/basement, which was lined in knotty pinewood and carpeted with dark brown fluff.

"The pirate's cave," Mike said, snuggling his face in my neck. Here, Wes kept a collection of Chinese vases, wrapped in bubble plastic, and framed jerseys from the Cowboys and the 49ers. On a shelf Wes had stored a big bronze General Custer in more of that bubble plastic. In another cabinet I saw geodes and fancy autographed baseballs, a stuffed boar, and in the corner he'd lumped some white supremacy survivalist hooey like expensive bottled water and boxes of freeze-dried chicken strips. Also, on the west side of the room, there was a big wall safe, which was all steel and had a *Mission Impossible* code box.

"What's in here?" I whispered.

"Oh, a fuck ton of euros and dollars and gold bars, like for the End of Days or I don't know what," Mike said, wrinkling his nose at the contraption. He looked at me and started playing with the lace on my dress. "One of these days I'm going to break into this damn safe and then take you to Bermuda."

We started making out like a pair of wolves while in the dining room Laura clattered the silverware and yelled out, "Pie!"

Mike never did take me to Bermuda. He died in '16. Heart attack. Laura had passed the year before, from cancer.

At Mike's funeral, Wes didn't hug me or pat my hand, and I wouldn't have wanted him to anyway. We sat there next to each other, stiff, while the police department marched up and down the aisles, offering me condolences. Wes didn't say anything then, but apparently he was already thinking about bailing us out. It was pretty plain that I'd go broke without the policeman's paycheck, what with Mike's miniature pension and my having to take care of Jessie.

A week after the service, Wes sent me an e-mail: "You 2 can live in the back room if you want."

Wes had more money for Jessie and me than my parents would ever have been able to scrape up. So I brought Jess and Henrietta to live with Wes at his ancestral manor. The house was a massive six-bedroom, way more than him and Laura had ever needed. It was just too big, layered with cream-colored acrylic carpet and Persian rugs. Wes had an L.A. architect build it to his specifications back in the '80s, though I don't know where all the cash went. Scattered around the salon and his office were the better examples of his Chinese vase collection. Also, Laura had collected a gang of Lladró figurines, which she'd stored in a huge hutch in the living room. There was Limoges china in the kitchen and a squad of expensive books on Winston Churchill in the library. All that old-fashioned mahogany furniture of his looked as filthy to me as a family of warthogs. And then, of course, there was his man cave filled with baseballs, jerseys, bronze statues of Indian killers, the extra supplies, and his big wall safe with I guess enough money to start a new society after the sun exploded and the zombies rose.

At the little red house, I packed a few boxes and threw a lot of things away. Jessie and I drove our Prius to Edgewood and moved into a back bedroom. Laura's old sewing station became my daughter's play space. Right away I started doing all the cleaning and cooking and gardening. At night I'd hold Jessie and try not to scream into my pillow over the loss of Mike.

"The baby's a keeper, but I know what you are," Wes said the day we arrived. He marched me down to the bonus room and showed me the bubble-wrapped extra vases and the bronze fucking Custer. He gestured at the wall safe. "I ever see you trying to get into this thing, you're out." He took the time to point a finger at me, and I wasn't carrying Jessie in my arms, but if he'd gestured at my kid like that I would have smacked him until his lip split. I didn't burn any calories on him insulting me, though. Mike's death had changed the girl who had once taunted Wes about knowing her name. I knew I had to eat the grits he gave me.

I nodded and said, "I get it."

His face shifted a little then, because he saw I wasn't interested in his junk.

"Now, I don't mean any ill feelings about it, understand," he said.

"It's okay," I said, just feeling like kicking that man until he grunted. "You're all right."

Still, Wes stopped being quite such a shit by the time the fire came. He adored Jessie, who'd just turned six. Every once in a while he'd even thank me for my chicken dinners and also my vegetarian experiments with the increased fiber. And last year on my birthday he took me to a new French restaurant that some Oregonians set up in the venue that used to be Tattie's. Wes had sat with me in a corner booth, silent and awkward, while I ate a steak and felt weird.

I left Wes fiddling with the hose in the front yard and bolted into the kitchen. Jessie sat at the breakfast nook finishing her milk and petting Henrietta with her feet. As soon as I came in, Henrietta sat up, stiff and staring. But my daughter did not even notice the color of the sky because she's always daisying about like a Princess Petunia. I think she got her personality from her father, who was a lallygagger when he was a kid."

"Mom, Henrietta won't drink my milk," she yelled at me. Jessie's a gorgeous little creature with bronze skin and long legs. She has sleek black hair and incomprehensible green eyes that must mean that I have some white in me.

"Honey, just sit there, don't move," I said. Henrietta jumped up and padded over, standing next to me and looking around and breathing with her mouth open.

We had a little white plastic television on the counter. I searched

frantically for the remote and found it by the coffeepot. While
Henrietta pawed me, I grabbed it and started pressing. I flipped
past bright, screamy cartoons to a black newscaster wearing a blue
suit and red lipstick. The lady looked as serious as the pope while
jabbering something. The screen suddenly split to show a white
woman with a pert, upturned nose who wore a big black jacket
and had her brown hair flipping around her head from the wind.
The white woman looked to be standing on traffic-jammed Skyway,
which is the main road through Paradise and cuts all the way to
Chico. The sky on the screen was a darkening bronze, and when I
looked out the window I saw that it was that color here too.

"Bobbie, I think there's an alert out for your region now," the
black lady said.

The white lady with the wind-whipped hair nodded. "There's
an evacuation alert for the community of Paradise, and there's already traffic on the road. So we recommend—"

From behind the white lady, I could see a bloom of gold and
red suddenly shooting up through the brassy sky.

"Oh," said somebody offscreen, maybe a cameraman.

"What?" the white lady said. I snapped off the television. Henrietta and I ran from the kitchen to the hall and then to my bedroom, which I shared with Jessie. I lunged toward our green bu-
reau and opened the drawers. From the top drawer I grabbed her
clothes, and from the bottom one I snatched mine, but all just
randomly. I had jeans and nightgowns lumped in my arms, and
did I need sneakers? I dropped the clothes and ran to the closet
and tore the door open and found my Kivas there. I put them on.
I grabbed Jessie's little Mary Janes and put them in my shirt, in my
sports bra. Then I ran out the room. Henrietta came flying out
after me.

With the dog whining at my heels, I dashed down the hall again,
making my way across the living room and then another hallway
and then to a little carpeted stairway that went down to a basement. The big safe gleamed from the west wall, all steel and with
its nuclear code box where I just probably had to type in *LAURA* to
get to Wes's treasure. Beneath the safe, next to the bubble-wrapped
Custer, there were three big boxes of Arrowhead water and some
cartons of chicken strips. I had no idea what to take, but water
seemed like a good idea. I could pour it on Jessie if there was fire. I

lifted one of the water boxes up, using my back and hurting it, and then jostled with it up the stairs. I almost tripped over Henrietta but somehow stayed on my feet. I ran through the kitchen with my load as fast as I could and then out to the front yard.

Wes sprayed Henrietta and me as soon as I hit the lawn. He had turned on the hose full-force and thumbed the nozzle so that it jetted out with a big white fan of water, and the wind sent it shooting crazily everywhere.

I took the blast in the face and kept going. "Help, help," I said.

"Just go," Wes said. "This is my house and Laura's. I'm not leaving it to burn."

I blinked. My eyes were watering even without the help of the hose. The sky had turned a bright, bright gold. I could smell smoke, thick smoke, like acid. Everybody on the street was racing around and loading their cars.

"You could lose everything, Wes," I said. "Tell me the code for the safe, and if I can, I'll get your stuff and we'll pack it out of here," I said.

He looked at me funny. "I don't think so."

"Okay," I said. He could have called me Pocahontas right then and started dancing around in a Klan hood and I would not have given a single tiny shit. I turned from him and ran straight to my Prius—the Prius instead of his giant Yukon in the driveway. It was a stupid move, but like his weirdness with the safe, I'd learned not to mess with Wes's things and I was just operating on habit. I dashed to the curb in my Kivas and put the box of water down in front of my car. I grabbed at the Prius's back door, but it was locked. I started crying. I ran back into the house and raced around looking for my keys.

"Mom, Mom," Jessie yelled from the kitchen.

I swear to the Lord Almighty that goblins must have took my keys and hid them under the Dora the Explorer sweatshirt in the second bathroom, on the floor, by the shower stall. I'd had to stand in the hall with Henrietta growling at my feet and piece my actions of last night and this morning back together. I wasn't thinking straight. I shouldn't have been focusing on those keys. It was a waste of time. I finally figured it out, ran to the bathroom, and thrashed around until I found them under the sweatshirt. Henrietta tried to help me by digging at the clothes. I jangled the keys into my hand and we ran back out to the kitchen. I snatched up Jessie from the kitchen table, gripping her in both arms so that one of her shoes fell out of my bra. I ran back with her and Henrietta out to the front yard.

I think it might have been eight forty-five by that time, maybe nine or even nine-fifteen. I could hear sirens. I could see towers of smoke from far off. I looked at the cars fleeing down Edgewood. Wes remained standing on the soaking lawn with a tsunami of water pouring out of his hose onto the myrtles, the cottonwoods, the dry grass, the house windows, the whole facade. Jessie had her face in my neck and started screaming. I looked at the Prius, and then I looked at the black Yukon shining in the driveway. If fire swept over the car, we'd have a better chance of barreling through in that monstrosity than in my flimsy eco compact.

I ran back to the house with Jessie bouncing up and down on my shoulder. I dashed into the foyer. There was a big mahogany secretary set up on the wall with little porcelain Chinese dishes that held keys and coins. I saw Wes's Yukon keys on their thick plastic key chain in a little red dish. I balanced Jessie on one hip and grabbed them. Henrietta started barking. I ran back out to the front yard and dashed for the Yukon and clicked it open. I tossed Jessie into the beige leather backseat and Henrietta jumped in after her.

Then I ran back to Wesley.

"Dude, listen," I said.

Wesley's face was folded up like a wallet. He stayed on the lawn pouring water on the house where he'd lived with his wife, and seemed like he was ready to die there.

"Wes," I said.

"Oh, God," he said.

"Wes, Jessie and I need you in our lives to protect us and be with us as a family," I said, insanely saying any hokum that I thought he'd listen to. "You have to come with us. We can't make it without you."

He turned and looked at me with real, tender, human eyes, for maybe the first time.

"Okay," he said.

"Okay," I said. I was already running to the Yukon.

"I'm driving," he said, dropping the hose.

"You're an old man," I yelled. "And you have to protect the baby from the fire with your body."

"Okay," he said.

We got into the car, slammed the doors. We left the Arrowhead water on the curb. Jessie began screaming again. I started the Yukon and jammed it down the driveway and almost crashed into a Camry that was speeding down Edgewood. Wes gripped on to Jessie in the backseat and didn't say anything about my freak driving. I screeched onto the street and pushed the gas so we zipped toward the end of Edgewood, where we'd turn the corner onto Pearson.

There was a traffic jam, right at the stop sign. Pearson was one long clog of cars. Our Yukon idled four back from the intersection. I recognized Martin's brown Dodge in front of me and Nancy's gray something, I don't know, a four-door. Somebody else I couldn't make out had taken the front of the line, ahead of Nancy. Big, fluffy pieces of ash fell down from the sky, like snowflakes. I had to turn on the wipers just to push the crud off the windshield.

"No problem," I said in a calm, normal voice, like I was at Starbucks and they'd accidentally put oat milk in my frappuccino. "Just need this to clear and then we'll be off."

In the backseat, Wes held on to Jessie, who sobbed herself hoarse. He kissed her many times on the cheek. "You're a very good baby," he said.

"I'm not a baby," Jessie cried. She didn't know what was going on.

Henrietta sat quivering next to Wes. The dog began to nudge her way up past Wes and Jessie, then slid up in the space between my seat and the Yukon's big console where you keep your Big Gulps in its handy holes. She slipped through and lumbered onto the front seat next to me. Then she just sat there, looking out of the windshield like a person.

I reached out and petted Henrietta on the nose and flashed on Mike. He used to roll around with Logan and Henrietta, and the pups had opened up their mouths soft and pretended to bite him while he laughed.

"Yup, yup, yup," I said, rolling up all the automatic windows because the smoke and ash came flowing in. "We're going to be okay. We're going to be good. We're going to be fine."

We sat there. We sat there. The cars didn't move. We sat there. More ash flakes fell. I don't know how much time passed. The sky began to change again. Black smoke started to stream into the gold sky, like the design on a Chinese vase.

"Come on, come on," I said.

"Move your ass!" I could hear a man screaming, I don't know from where.

The car at the intersection moved onto Pearson. Maybe ten minutes passed, maybe more. A full, thick stream of cars waited behind me. Ahead of me, Nancy switched on her turn signal, which flickered at me like a sign from another, normal world.

"Do you think it'll all burn down?" Wes asked.

"Yes," I said.

"My safe's fireproof, but I don't know to what degree," he said.

"All I care about's that child you're holding on to now," I said.

Maybe ten, twelve, twenty, I don't know how many more minutes crawled by.

"I'm never going to make back what I lose," Wes said. "I'm too old."

"Insurance'll cover you and then Trump'll make you a rich man with one of those disaster packages," I rattled on. The sky was really starting to darken, and I could see a thick haze of smoke coming in fast on a current.

Nancy moved onto Pearson. I inched the Yukon to the stoplight. I turned on my turn signal like she had because we had all become robots.

"That asshole will leave us stranded," Wes said. "He'll piss on some more hookers and burn it all on golf."

I started laughing. Tears were streaming down my face. "You liked him, I thought."

"Only on Mexicans and Puerto Ricans," Wes said.

"Right." I laughed some more.

"Not you," Wes said.

"I don't care, it's okay," I said. "Because if we get out of this alive I'm going to punch you till you sneeze teeth, you old son of a bitch."

"Okay," Wes said.

I turned my head over my shoulder to look at my daughter tucking her nose into Wes's armpit. "But everything's good, right, Jessie? Everything's good."

Next to me, Henrietta's jaws were working strange, like she was nibbling something. I saw froth on her lips.

"Everything's good," Jessie said. She clung to Grandpa but had stopped crying, I think.

"Here we go," I said. I got an open spot and moved onto Pearson. Pearson was filled with traffic. We sat there like on Edgewood, watching the known sky disappear. The wind whipped through the world. The pine trees standing tall above us thrashed and tottered against heavens that quickly crowded in with orange-pewter clouds. We still had to move from Pearson, past the elementary school, past the Gold Nugget Museum, past the park, and onto Skyway. From Skyway we'd flee southeast to Chico, about forty minutes out.

We barely moved, just little bits, while it got hotter in the car. The sky got swallowed by busy blackness. The earth burned fast. The people used both lanes, of course. I didn't like to see the people in the lane to our left. Women and men bent over their wheels, mumbling to themselves, kids scrambling in the backseats. At one point I saw Shelly in her Dodge Caravan, which was strange, because I thought she had been long gone. She saw me and we smiled at each other, our faces both shuddering. We looked away from each other. We looked toward the road ahead, which got worse as the minutes ticked away.

"Don't let her look out the window," I said to Wes.

At both sides of the road, the landscape turned into what looked I swear to holy Jesus like molten lava. Black-brown clouds streamed down through a bloody sky and onto a swell of hills that had fried deep black and were streaked through with flame. It was getting furnace hot in the car. It was close, like you couldn't inhale right.

Wes put his T-shirt over Jessie's mouth and said, "Breathe, baby, breathe."

"No! No! No! No! No! No!" Jessie started screaming.

Henrietta started moving back and forth on the seat, as if she wanted to pace but there wasn't enough room.

"No! No! No! No! No! No!" my daughter shrieked.

"You're all right! You're all right!" I yelled.

"Here you go, oh, my sweet sugar," Wes crooned. "Oh, my sweet sugar."

Crack! Crack!

"What was that?" I asked.

"Maybe some tires going, exploding," Wes said.

"I don't think they're ours," I said. I had no idea. Maybe they were.

We moved up Pearson, slow, slow. We got onto Skyway. The whole universe had turned into a place of red sky and pine trees swaying like demons dancing. Through the hot, hot windshield —the heat blew off the dashboard in waves, and threw itself off the side windows—we could see walls of flames tearing up from Tacos El Paraiso and Bill's Auto Repair. We crossed Vista Way and saw that Noonan, Gump, & Penzer had long orange rockets of fire shooting up from its roof and out its windows.

Wes turned his head to look at his old office burning. Then he looked forward again.

Jessie went quiet. Henrietta crouched down and did not move. We were all of us silent, but breathing like animals.

"I'm sorry about the safe," Wes said. He started crying.

"Just make sure my kid doesn't get dead, you old buzzard," I said.

"Of course it's all for you, you're my dear son's wife," he sobbed while clutching my daughter. "Everything I have is for you and Jessie. The money, the gold, the stocks, the car, the house—"

I kept my eyes on the road ahead. A wave of red-gold flame and sparks curled across the sky and earth ahead of us. *Any minute now it'll be clearing,* I told myself. *Any minute, we can get away.* Far off, I *did* see the sky brighten briefly, and then go dark again. It brightened once more, then darkened out. Dark, then darker. Then bright once more. Then dark.

"It's going to be good, don't worry, don't scare her," I said, my whole mouth like sandpaper.

"Tell me you forgive me," he wept.

I watched the hellfire sweep across the trees to our right and kept my foot steady on the gas.

"Tell me," he said.

"I forgive you, you Custer-loving bastard," I lied.

I could hear the howling, eating sound of the fire. On the horizon, that tiny pale clear spot opened in the sky again, and flickered. The red underworld rose up to heaven, exploded in the pines, and whirled above us like naked stars. The pale spot of clear sky continued glimmering ahead, though, and I aimed for it, without praying, and filled with something less like faith than a blind keeping-on. And what I hoped was not my last thought was *What a Native woman's got to put up with in this goddamned life doesn't stop until the minute that she dies.*

Good Boy

FROM *The Paris Review*

I'VE ALWAYS HAD a problem with introductions. To me, they don't matter. It's either you know me or you don't—you get? If you don't, the main thing you need to know is that I am a hustler through and through. I'm that guy that gets shit done. Simple. Kick me out of the house at fifteen—a barged-in-on secret behind me, a heartbreak falling into my shin as I walk—and watch me grow some real useful muscles. Watch me learn how to play all the necessary games, good and ungood; watch me learn how to notice red eyes, how to figure out when to squat and bite the road's shoulder with all my might. Watch me learn why a *good* knife (and not just any type of good, but the moral-less kind, the fatherlike kind) is necessary when you're sleeping under a bridge. Just a week after that, watch me swear on my own destiny and insist to the God who made me that I'm bigger than that lesson now; then watch my ori align. Watch me walk from that cursed bridge a free man and learn how to really make money between age damaged and age twenty-two; watch me pay the streets what I owe in blood and notes (up front, no installments); watch me never lack where to sleep again. Second thing to know about me: I know how to make the crucial handshakes. Third thing: I no dey make the same mistake twice. Almost evict me from my place in Surulere at age x and watch rage stab me forward. Watch how in three weeks I treat my own fuckup with not just a room but an apartment four times as big in Gbagada. The how is irrelevant. Fourth thing: I am serious about being alive. Because of this, there is nothing I can't survive. Anybody who knows me knows that; the rest na breeze. It is my God-given right to be here. This life? Me, I must chop am, and it must be on my own terms. What makes all this worth it, otherwise? Nothing. Someone I know joked just two days ago sef, that even if I end up in hell at the end of the day, I won't stop kicking, I won't stop reaching for something, I will insist on my space. In reality, I'm not the kind of guy who ends up in a place like that because fifth thing: I'm not the kind of guy who believes in hell, or in a god who imagines a lake of fire. I just can't see it—you have a mind that's wider than the sky and that is what you use it to picture? To me, that sounds too petty, too human, too undivine to be real. People sell all kinds of gods all the time. I know the One that moves me and it's not the one I was raised on. To me, you can't say you're love, choose to roast people for eternity, and then pretend it breaks your heart. Pick a side. Anyhow, the guy said the hell thing to make a point and it's true—luck finds my head, business competes with my blood on who keeps me best, and either might fail depending on the day. So now I always wonder: What do people want to use my name for? It will not buy you anything. Name-drop me and they'll still redirect you to me. In that sense, it's irrelevant to know. I answer a first name only and it's for the people I know. But my story? Ah damn. Now, that? That, many people can do a whole lot with.

Start here: I'm not inspiring. When I first moved to Lagos, I didn't come here with good mind. I came here with one mission and one mission only: to get a lot of money, so as to prove my popsy wrong. That's all. For me, blood family doesn't mean shit. Family is your spine dividing into four, hot metal in your back, red life shooting out of you in a geyser. It's you falling forward in slow motion, a yelp in your neck, whole outfit ruined in the air. You, reading this, you're here, alive, because your parents synced and you showed up. That's it. Even if they planned for a child, it was still a raffle draw. A hand went in a bowl and picked you. The tree shook and a fruit fell down. If it pains you to read, then cry. It's deeper for your mum because she probably pushed so hard her body gasped, only for your ungrateful head to come out of it. But your father? Half the time, all he did was grunt and drop some bands. And on the way to where I am, what I learned is that anybody with money can drop money. And most men, ehn? Can drop money. Even poor men. That's something I wish my mother had known so she wouldn't have *but-at-least*ed herself into the ground. Money loves circles and men run in circles stinking, adrenaline pumping. Money hardly goes to lone dots, unless you threaten it. And even then, believe me when I tell you it probably took a hundred-person team to execute that threat, most of them unnamed. The face of a thing is not the body of it. Even women with serious money—few and far between dots—have to pretend they don't have. There's a reason, you know? It's in the code; it'll take a new world for that to stop being true. Men with small money will still impress each other over beer, men with medium money will find ways to barter, and men with large money will slice this country like cake if they get sad enough, bored enough. Dropping money is all tied to pride and they taught us that we need pride. So for many of us, that act alone—of rescuing someone, of fulfilling a duty, of settling a debt—pumps blood somewhere specific.

When I lost home, my goal was simple. All those insults that my father used to be casual about, I wanted to erase them. I wanted to outdo him, so that when people called our family name there would be more to say about me than about the man who picked me up as a boy and stretched me into a man in the space of an afternoon. I was on the streets so fast it felt like I dreamed those memories of the Man reading a newspaper, the Head of the House watching the news, the Father petting the koboko like something safe. He beat the sound out of all of them, so those days when I used to play my mind back wondering if things could have been different, I met more bite than bark. But he hardly talked anyway, except to say things like *You won't amount to anything,* so it's not like I was missing much. He was furious a lot, which makes sense. People are like that when they hate themselves.

He was wrong about what he said, though. Embarrassingly wrong. What I have amounted to can buy who he was, at least twice. My father was a well-educated man, a man who had a *should-be-so* for everything. The table *should be* set so, all family members *should be* at home by seven p.m., breakfast *should* always include eggs, a wife *should be* this way, a husband *should be* that. Dutiful, he never excused himself from his own hand. The one time he was unable to pay our school fees and our mother offered, the house did a headstand and blood rushed into our brains, I swear. We sat at home that term. That's what *should* can do. About me, he believed I should be grateful he still chose to raise me, having noticed my *softness* from early; he believed I owed him something and feared that if I didn't love the way he prescribed for me, I'd ruin my life. Funny, because his love tied his hands often; his love made an army out of us. That day when he walked in on me and my classmate, I saw him fight himself to the ground. What followed was what he thought he *had* to do. He questioned every feeling, tested it for fitness. If he didn't think it would suit a man his size, he'd treat it like a son, send it away with its head bowed. Rage was good, rage was a feeling with a hard core and some biceps. So, a beautiful rainfall of blows. What kind of weak father would have no problem with what he saw? What kind of weak man would see such a thing and let his son go free? *Look at yourself,* he kept saying, staring me down. *Look at yourself. You've destroyed the family name.* I dropped the family name after four years away. They can keep it. It stopped meaning anything to me. Any weight put on my name since then comes straight to me. Is for me. Just me.

He used to say, *It's as you make your bed that you lie in it.* I sleep in a made bed every night. King size. It's someone else's job to make it. He also loved to say, *Any man who comes back home after seven p.m. is a thief.* Some days I leave home to work at seven p.m. because I can. Na me get my life. I'm many things but a thief is not one of them. The easiest way to put what I do in context is to quote Jay-Z: *I'm not a businessman. I'm a business, man.* Everywhere you look around you, there are gaps in markets. I see them and fill them. That's what I do. I did some shady things in my earlier days, I can't front, but those ones are not for the books. When Popsy first kicked me out, I went to my uncle's house—a pastor, and he housed me. I don't discuss those years for good reason. Let's just put it like this: everything that was "holy" in me left me there. Na there my eye first tear. So when I left, I worked with churches, supplying actors for dramatic miracles. I trained them from experience—taught them how to faint, how to roll their eyes into their heads, when and through where exactly the spirit should flee. Pastors rushed it. Me and my guys got our first place in Opebi with the money we made. We paid two years' rent, cash down. I'm sure the land-lord thought we were Yahoo boys, but why question cold cheese when you can just shut up and feed your family? After that, as a side thing, me and my guys used to move shrooms in on a steady. People went crazy for that. We opened a barbershop in VI briefly, but they shut it down when the queues became too long. They said we were doing illegal shit, but really, one of us was a therapist and many men needed somewhere to talk on a low. After that I used to organize people for VIPs. My friend was a sitting politician's son, so he plugged it. As for how we run things, Wizkid don already talk am: *I know bad guys that know real bad guys, that know some other guys.* We made a low-key app with photos and specifications—twins, triplets, dark-skinned, mixed-race, BBW, gay men, drag queens, lesbians, kinksters, all sorts. All our clients needed to do was tap the screen and a fee would appear. Whoever they chose would be on the next flight in. It's not mouth I'll use to tell you how much money we pulled from that. It's not a small job to guard a tall gate. If you know, you know. But over time it became too heavy, because secret yato si secret, kink yato si kink, and if you know anything about underbellies and darkness, you know their everlastingness. The deeper you go underground, the darker it gets, because the more they trust you with. And you know what? In life you have to be careful who you allow to trust you; you have to know where to stop before life stops you.

Now I run a souvenir shop. I sell fridge magnets from all sorts of countries, for people who lie to their partners about traveling abroad for work. If you lie like that, you need supporting gifts. I woke up one day, saw the gap, and did quick maths. We fly things in from all over, daily. We have our own duty-free—everything from perfumes to whiskey to Montblanc to Swarovski to Crème de la Mer and La Prairie dem—you name it. Now, it's not just husbands and wives who use us. It's people who lie to their parents about what they do and how much they earn and how much they travel (and dem plenty). We found a guy who's a wizard with Photoshop, hooked him up. Now we also have a photography studio to complete the whole deal. We work with low-key hotels too, for those who need where to hide until the lie expires. Just last week we sorted out an influencer who wanted to turn her Instagram around but didn't have the funds for it. After she filled the forms, our photographer took the pictures and placed her in multiple locations in all the countries she said she wanted to travel to. From this Lagos here, she was posting photos of herself on the plane, at the airport, in the cities themselves. Our plugs do the legwork and get their cut. In the photo I like the most, the babe is sitting in the Rock Zanzibar and there are prawns inside her mouth that she never tasted. In the next grid, her Internet self is in Sandton Skye with a friend, eating risotto and drinking sauvignon blanc at the Codfather. They posted it from 1004 here. The week after, we dipped her Insta self in Lac Rose in Senegal. Come and see comments. Her leg has never touched there, the water doesn't know her skin, but who must know? She gained thousands of followers from that move, because image. Everything in this life is what? Image. These days, people always talk about getting a seat at the table, putting a foot in the door. Me? I make doors out of thin air.

In my life I have never put on long-sleeve shirt, lined my own collar with a tie, knotted it and pulled it up to my neck. I've never worn suit in this Lagos heat or carried briefcase to any office, and since I turned twenty, not once has landlord knocked on my door for rent. I know I'm lucky, trust me, but when people look down on me for being me I just know their brains are small. If you think it's only hard work, and not smart work, that will keep your life together in this country, then you're a fool now. Are you not? You're a fool. We started this thing last year. So far I've seen over two hundred clients and we don't charge chicken change. Why does it work? Because there's always a market for lies. It's the demand that makes the supply necessary. The other day somebody asked me what I'll do after this and I told him I don't know. I always know; I just don't discuss my moves before I move. My next target market is already set. Never forget: wherever there are people, there are opportunities, and anything can be doctored so far you know who to call doctor.

Me and my partner live in a six-bedroom house in Lekki, except for when we're at our beach house in Ilashe. We got this place when he moved from Jozi to come and be with me. He's half from there and half from here. When we got tired of the distance, we had to choose. In that his old apartment in Maboneng, all it took was one look at each other and K. laughed because he already knew. We didn't even table the question twice; his bags were here a month from then. Between me and K. we can afford to live nice on some expat shit because he has never not earned in dollars and for him work is a drug. If you step outside our front door, we have two Mercedes-Benzes parked in a line. Behind the Benzes a Bentley, behind the Bentley a Lexus convertible that was just delivered last month. We bought it together, tear rubber. All this and thirty is not that far behind me. Next is a G-Wag. K. doesn't know yet, I'm surprising him with it for his thirty-eighth and I know he'll cry. We like cars, both of us, but his own is different. He knows everything about engines and wiring and all. Me, I collect them because I can. In a way, your car is like a second outfit. My wardrobe is full of casual things, but I'm always making statements. Short, memorable statements. Clothes are just one way to tension streets. But a mad whip is a great way to say *Don't fuck with me,* and here the streets need to hear that in pidgin, Yoruba, Igbo, Hausa, plus many other languages. For everyday things we ride either Benz. Both are tinted, with customized plates. Police have not checked our license or car papers in years. To them, our names are *Chairman,* and why wouldn't it be when we're more government than their governor. *Here, this one for you. This one for the kids.* We keep them happy and they save us stress. For parties where there will be VIPs, we use the Bentley and leave with the right business cards. Me and K. wear rings, but people don't ask personal questions when they see what you've come out of. We bought that right to go unchallenged. It was not cheap. When I'm going somewhere chilled with K., we take the Lexus and drop the top. Still so new, it gives me what they call . . . endorphins. Me and K. love watching sunsets like that. When he falls into his dark moods, I take him on long drives and he blasts the music until the mirror starts beating and we can't hear our heads. King of the aux, give him two songs max and he'll reset us both. I love those drives. Some nights when we're bored, after playing FIFA, me and my guys race each other down the Link Bridge at two a.m. with some Formula One energy. Whoever loses has to buy the next stash of loud. Sometimes K. stays home and watches Netflix; other times he comes with us, and I see how happy he gets with his head outside the window, wind beating against his face. That's an answered prayer right there. Before K., I'd never been with a guy who gelled with my friends.

Years ago we couldn't have imagined half the shit we have now, but it's real. To me, the joy of having money is in sharing it. Life of my dreams with the people of my dreams. Even though we all have our places, my closest friends have keys to my house, and I have keys to theirs. Sometimes you need a break from your normal. Right from day one, they didn't waste time at all—rascals, all of them—they claimed their rooms sharp-sharp. Maro picked the room downstairs that opens into the garden. Akin likes the guest chalet. You should've seen the rest fighting. It's their house too at this point, so they cycle in and out as they like. Some of them drive my cars out on dates. There used to be another car years ago—our first one—but for May's thirtieth, K. said we should give her the Hummer. It suits her, and babes love a dyke with a big car. Gives off the right message. Plus we'd outgrown our love for it and she was obsessed. Simple maths. Life is about give and take. I tell people all the time: streets na electric, anybody fit shock you. So when you find your people, the ones wey go ride for you till this world fold, commit to them like it's a religion. We live our lives like it is. Every other Friday one of us will host games night. We rotate houses. Lagos Island this week, Ikoyi next week, Magodo upper week. We show up unless we can't.

Speaking of my guys? I'd put a bullet in any body for them if it comes to that. I always pray it never comes to it. But check this, some weeks back, one of them came to my house crying his eyes out. Way over three decades into his life. He has seen heartbreak, stabbings, jungle justice that involved fire with a body smoking, and this was the third time I'd ever seen him cry. The whys of the first two will follow me to my grave. But that day I had to hold him until he could breathe again. His father had died, and when he got the news, he said he could feel himself spinning. The last of all of us to become fatherless, he was on the street outside a restaurant where they'd been eating, and his person hugged him after he got the call, held him as he tried not to break down. My guy said he felt so much sadness mixed with fear mixed with relief mixed with shame; that instead of relaxing, he scanned the street and pulled out of the hug, but not before thumping his person on the back three times, code for No Homo, Bro. *Who does that,* he wanted to know, *no one was even there, just like two kids passing; I'm not even that kind of guy.* Me and Maro laughed out loud, then told him the truth. Maro and I have been friends for twelve years. Before we got free, you know how many times we made someone we love feel crazy in public, just to save our own face? It's enough to flood Yaba

Left. But if you catch it, you can fix it. That's another thing about my life: Without my friends, I'd be dead. Without my friends, I wouldn't have words for things that need names to shift, I wouldn't have ever faced things you need safety to confess. I know what else he was feeling, what he was saying under what he was saying: there's something about losing a dad whose life killed you, you know? There's no way to explain it. You either know the feeling or you don't, you get? You feel like you can finally breathe.

At some point I asked Maro, who knew his father was one of us, if he thought he'd be himself if his father had not died. He said, *No. He hated himself for it, so no. And you know what? If my popsy had as much as opened his mouth to say he needed me to correct it, or to say that I could solve his depression by marrying that Efua babe I was seeing, best believe I'd be on baby number three with her today. So as free as I am now, I'm only free to date whoever the fuck I like, fuck whoever the hell I want, because he never asked that of me.* I could see it. Maro's father never married, but he had a *best friend* who sometimes showed up to the house for weekends. Uncle H. had a wife he couldn't stop telling about business trips. Maro's father would set the table, shave his head in anticipation, and then act surprised at the knock. Many times they cooked dinner from scratch. *My friend, go and play with your own friends,* Uncle H. used to say to Maro, laughing. *Let me catch up with my own.* But Maro has a memory he talks about often, of his father looking at his skinny jeans with disgust and asking him, *Is that what you want to be?* They never talked about it again. He was drunk then. Maro's story is not as simple as mine—how can it be when there was a noose involved—but I sat there thinking, *My god, one less death and my boy would not exist. My guy, my best friend whose love saved my life, would not exist.* You know what I did? I hid behind my teeth and thanked God for it. Terrible, but I thought, *We are fatherless boys now and sure there are big griefs in us, but at least we get to be us. At least we get to be us.* At the end of that conversation, when we got drunk-drunk, we sang along to the song Akin wrote in five minutes while we were smoking. Genius man, that one. We sang:

If you know where people go
when they die
pardon me for assuming

for assuming you'll reach there before me
before us
tell our fathers they tried
tell them they made some good boys
made some good boys, in the end, out of us.

We all cried for real then. Whether it was the happy or sad kind, till now, nobody knows.

Last last, all of us go still die. But if we must live, then shey it only makes sense to love? At different times we were terrified that we wouldn't find our tribe, we wouldn't find our people who would see us for us because of what we'd been told to hide. But here we are, all flavors of free. One of my guys has a boyfriend and a girlfriend. They live together. They said it's called a throuple. Me I cannot wrap my head around it. May dates multiple women at once and they all know. Some of the people she dates even date each other too. They say that one is polyamory. Me do I understand it? No. Another one of my friends does not want anything to do with sex. He has never tried it and he's not moved by it. I can't relate, but I've learned that you don't have to relate to give people the space to be. Me I'm in love and safe — imagine? I'm safe. So I confessed too that I don't think both my father and I could have stayed alive, in each other's lives, as our individual selves. Someone needed to become something else. So I did. I didn't fully become me until he was gone. I never thought I could voice those words. But you know what I like the most about all of us? Before we met each other, we all had lies we needed to tell ourselves and others if we were going to live well. Maro says there's already a term for that type of lie: necessary fictions. Looking at each other and saying, *This is my own lie, this is my own truth. No, that other part was a mask, this part here is my face.* It's a survival thing. If you know this country, then you know not to walk maskless. But let me tell you something, this love shit is holy. When it's pure and patient, the thing just bends your knees. It's scary — I shook so much the first time Maro told me he loved me. I didn't even know friends could say that without it turning into something else, so I thought he wanted something and I tried to reply with my body, just out of reflex, out of gratitude. He saw where I was going, stopped me, and said, *It's me.* I remember that moment clearly: it was one tear at a time until I couldn't stop. He didn't run; he held me. When you meet real care, it changes you, it remakes you as you. It lets you take a deep breath; it turns your friend into your brother. It took me time, but I say it back to all of them now.

Any way, you want to know what I said when I was at work one day and got a call to come back home because my father was sick—after years of not hearing from him? I said yes. And I stayed there for two months. I took care of him and paid all the hospital bills. When he got well enough to say hello to me, my father followed the greeting with a request. *You're doing well for yourself,* he said, *and my life is going. There's only one more thing remaining. Won't you let me meet the woman you will marry? Won't you let me see you whole?* Now the difference between Maro's story and my own is that my father looked at me, even knowing I owed him nothing, and he still asked that of me. I held his hand, my heart capsizing slowly, and said, *Yes sir, you will see me whole.*

When? he asked.

Tomorrow just here, I said. For the anxiety that request dragged out of me, I planned to walk out of there and never return. Still I said, *If you're ready, then I'm ready. Tomorrow.*

Good, he said, and closed his eyes. He believed he needed to bless my heart for love to work for me. Imagine that. A man I lived without for over a decade. A man who didn't know if I still had a beating heart wanted to meet the person I would love enough to start a life with.

I went home and cried on K.'s shoulder. It was both of us who pooled resources together to do what we could for my dad. For months K. had been dipping his hand into his pocket for the man who almost made us impossible, the man who would hate him on sight. It was somewhere in that breakdown that I changed my mind. The next day I took K. to my father's bedside. My person stood by me, watching us. *Where is she?* my father asked, ignoring the obvious. I stared back my response, no words involved, just eye to eye, man to man. I saw it click. He swallowed and then opened his mouth to talk. Nothing came out. I repeated myself with a closed mouth, hands in my pockets, staring him down. I felt K. turn to stone in fear. The money we'd both spent bullied my father in front of me, its knuckles ready for his teeth. *Do you under-*

stand? the money asked him. He shrank and I almost pitied him. I reached for K.'s hand, and feeling how much it had been sweating, I lifted his hand to my mouth and pressed my lips to it before holding his palm to my chest. *Are you sure you understand, Dad?* I asked. By then my voice was hot iron. No one, I decided there and then, is allowed to kill me twice. Using my child-voice he said, *Yes sir,* and using his dad-voice, I said, *Good boy.*

Portrait of Two Young Ladies in White and Green Robes (Unidentified Artist, circa Sixteenth Century)

FROM *Conjunctions*

I.

A FEW HOURS AGO your last descendant died. She held only a whisper of your essence—or, as one would say in this scientifically rigorous present, only a minuscule percentage of her genetic material was derived from yours—but of them all, she was the one who reminded me most of you.

She was a documentary filmmaker, the third generation of your descendants to be born and raised in America. Her work examined ways in which the technologies of her era shaped people's lives. In her twenties and thirties she lived in China, where she made a series of films about the state's electronic surveillance system, the tools used by the government to monitor its population, the balance to be struck between security and personal freedom. Her documentaries were as fair as they could be, in my view, taking into account the inherent biases of her Western upbringing and education. The Chinese government, which after all this time remains deficient at accepting criticism, disagreed. After they revoked her visa she returned to America and settled in San Francisco.

You would have enjoyed San Francisco, I think. Its pastel hues and precipitous slopes, its anarchic spirit, the lapping glitter of water all around.

I befriended her later in her life, when it became clear she would have no children. I presented myself as an admirer of her work and a student of Chinese history; also, an immigrant from Hangzhou, where I knew her own family was originally from. We grew close. I made myself indispensable to her. At the end of her life, I was in the hospital room when the lines jagging up and down across the screen of the vital-signs monitor subsided. Humans have developed the custom of measuring the distance a person stands from the border between the living and the dead. They watch each step their loved ones take toward that one-way crossing, count down every last breath.

I suggested to your descendant once that the technologies highlighted in her films were really no different from what people living during the Ming dynasty or any other historical period of China would have called magic. Then, they had been watched by ghosts and demons and deities, their sins recorded, their actions influenced; now it was the turn of facial-recognition software, online-history tracking apps, predictive algorithms. She smiled and said that I was in the company of brilliant minds: a famous writer and futurist had proposed a similar idea many years ago.

I didn't tell her that I'd met this writer on a beach in Trincomalee, Sri Lanka, even more years ago, or that he and I had struck up a conversation while sipping lukewarm beers and waiting for the waves to settle. At one point he was describing his vision of the future to me, space elevators and communication satellites and personal devices that contained near-infinite reserves of information, and I said all that sounded much the same as the way things had always been, Chang-er floating to the moon, texts charmed to display whatever knowledge the reader sought, an enduring invisible world overlaid upon the physical one.

"Magic, you mean?" he said.

"That's one word for it," I said.

Mostly we had talked about what we were both there for, which was to go diving. He asked why I had chosen this relatively obscure beach. I told him I had heard that the remnants of a medieval

Hindu temple lay submerged in the vicinity (the work of Portu-
guese colonial forces, which, after looting the complex and killing
its priests and pilgrims, had gone above and beyond to lever it
over the cliff edge into the bay). Later, when the sea had calmed,
I swam between broken columns and poised bronze goddesses,
over inscriptions of faith splintered across the rocks. Now and
then I still search for such relics, even if I don't bother document-
ing them. Nostalgia, I suppose. In the green silence of the water
I could sense the shimmer of the eternal. I hoped that when the
writer found these ruins—I might as well have drawn him a map,
with all the hints I provided—he would as well.

II.

The night before your wedding, the last night I would have with
you, I surrendered my pride on the altar of desperation and asked
you why in all eighteen hells you were doing this.

"I want to have a child," you said.

"Wait," I said, "seriously? Since when?"

"Since Xiangyang, maybe," you said. "It's hard to tell, these
things."

Back then we didn't think in terms of time. Our references were
geography and action, places we had been, things we had done.
In Xiangyang we had talked a jilted, impoverished artist out of
jumping into the Hanshui River, and spun a pretext to give him a
hundred taels of silver: we would ask him to paint our portrait. We
wore our best dresses for it, you in white and I in green, tinted our
cheeks and lips, put pins in our hair. We never collected the painting from him. We prided ourselves on traveling light, and anyway,
we saw no use for it, a record of things that would never change.

Xiangyang was several Ming emperors past, a hundred stops
ago in our travels through China. We looked for enchanted ar-
tifacts, analyzed and catalogued them, sought to understand the
wondrous within the human realm. Until we stopped in at West
Lake to follow up on rumors of a jade bracelet that could heal its
wearer (a fake, it turned out) and you met the man you decided
would do for a husband, I had never considered that we might not
live like this always. For a moment I thought that I must not know
you at all.

You had been hoping it would pass, you said, like a thunder-storm, or an inept dynasty. "Also, children frighten me. They need so much, and they are so easy to lose."

I placed my palm on your stomach, between the twin ridges of your hips. "All right," I said. "A child." I imagined your belly swelling the way those of human women did, the creature that would tear its way out. Yours; and not yours. "You don't have to marry him for that."

"It wouldn't be fair to him. Or to the child."

"What about to me?" This was why I hadn't wanted to ask. I'd known I would succumb to self-pity, and that it would make no difference.

You told me you had calculated the fate of the man who would be your husband based on the ten stems and twelve branches of his birth. He had a delicate constitution. He would pass in twenty-four years, before his fiftieth birthday.

I didn't say anything.

You said, "What is twenty-four years to you?"

I said, "What will twenty-four years be to *you?*" I wasn't thinking twenty-four. I was thinking fifty, sixty, your skin drying to parchment, your hair thinning and graying, your frame stooping ever closer to the ground in which you would—if you did this—some-day rot.

You touched my face. I waited for you to ask if I would give up my own immortality, if I was willing to step with you out of the wilderness of myth and into the terraced rice fields and tiled roofs of history.

"You don't have to stay," you said.

I told some version of this story to a man I met in a tavern in rural Shandong. A spirit trading in her immortality to have a child with a human, asking her companion to wait twenty-four years until they could be together again. I was on my way north to Beijing, to bring your son back home following his placement as top scholar in the imperial examination; the boy might have excelled at composing eloquent Confucian nonsense, but he would have been picked apart by bandits the moment his horse trotted beyond the city walls. This man was traveling south, returning to Suzhou after visiting a friend. The tavern was empty except for the two of us. We ended up drinking together, probably for much longer than we should have, talking over the noise of the torn paper windows flapping in the wind.

When I was done, the man said, "But so . . . what happened? When the twenty-four years were up?"

I laughed. "Nothing." Seen in a certain light, now, I could appreciate the glinting, mocking edges of our story. The wine probably helped. It felt potent and tasted foul. "She died within two years. The birth was difficult for her and she never recovered." Neither of us had thought to calculate your fate, in addition to your husband's. After all, we had walked through fires and dived off waterfalls, dismembered demons, batted away the assorted Buddhist monks determined to save us by destroying us so we could reincarnate as lovely, pliant daughters and wives and mothers. What could possibly happen to you while ensconced in domesticity, running a medicine shop with your constitutionally challenged husband? It turned out you were fucking terrible at being a human.

My fellow traveler poured me another cup of wine from the jar we were sharing and told me a story as well, of a young man who had been in love with a prostitute but lacked the wealth to redeem her from the brothel. Instead she was acquired by a textiles merchant and he took her away with him to another province. The young man expressed his sorrow through any number of histrionic poems. Twenty-four years later, no longer young, he was visiting a friend in a town in that province and found out, by chance, that the no-longer prostitute lived close by, and also that the merchant had died and she was now a widow.

"Twenty-four years!" I said. "Really?"

He smiled. "Don't you think that's why we met today?"

"What did"—I almost said *you,* since it was obvious he was talking about himself—"he do?"

"Nothing."

I said, "He no longer loved her?"

"He did," said the man. "He chose his love over her."

Nine days after your son and I arrived back in Zhenjiang, your husband collapsed while in his shop. At the funeral I heard your voice beneath the drone of the Taoist priest reciting his interminable scriptures, asking, *What is twenty-four years to you?*

Quite a while later I read a story about two snake spirits in human guise. The white maiden and the green maiden, they were called. It's part of a collection of folktales by a late-Ming writer and poet from Suzhou. In this story the white maiden lives in the depths of West Lake and attains immortality from ingesting some magical pills that a human boy accidentally swallowed and then vomited out again. The green maiden's equally immortal state is never explained. The boy grows up to become the white maiden's husband, their early sharing of bodily fluids a portent of compatibility. A turtle spirit in the form of a Buddhist monk has it out for the white maiden—he was also in that lake, and wanted those pills for himself—and traps her in a pagoda. The green maiden, her faithful companion, hones her skills for twenty-four years and succeeds in breaking the white maiden out of her prison. After which, the white maiden returns to her husband and her son, their medicine shop, her bucolic life. Nothing further is said of the green maiden.

III.

At some point between your death and your husband's, I returned to Xiangyang to look for our artist. Age had petrified him; I barely recognized him beneath its encrustation. When he saw me he told me I bore a remarkable resemblance to someone he had met long ago. "I painted their portrait," he said. "That girl and her sister."

I imagined how you would have smirked at that, the notion of us as sisters, and for an instant it was like I was standing at the bottom of a very deep well, its lid skewed to expose a hallucinatory glimmer of sky. "That's so funny," I said, "because that's why I'm here." I explained that I worked for an art collector who had heard of the painting and was interested in acquiring it.

"You're sixty years too late," he said. "I gave it away. Couldn't stand to look at it."

I said, as calmly as I could, "Why?"

"I couldn't get it right." His arthritic hands curled open and then closed again. "There was something about the two of them. The way they were. I couldn't get that into the portrait." He stopped painting altogether shortly afterward.

"I'm so sorry," I said.

He shook his head. He told me his friend—the same one he

had given the painting to—got him a position at a trading house, and within ten years he had made enough money for ten lifetimes. "Best decision I ever made," he said, "after not drowning myself over a whore."

It took me almost three hundred years to find that damn painting. From Xiangyang I followed the mercantile route that the cotton trader who had taken the painting would have, floating south and east on overladen barges down the Hanshui. By the time I located a branch of the man's family he had been dead for decades, his possessions scattered across his three concubines and fourteen children. Meanwhile, your son sold the medicine shop, returned to Beijing, rose to become a senior official in the Ministry of Justice, and—in what he must have thought of as a personal political coup, but with less-than-ideal timing—married your granddaughter into Ming nobility right before the Jurchens stampeded into the capital. I was in Changsha, checking on a lead from an art dealer, and I had to hustle to Beijing to extract her and her newborn from that shitshow. (I left her husband behind, which was better for all concerned.) I parked them in Hangzhou, the last place we had lived before I lost you, and there your family remained until the final act of the Qing dynasty, a modest clan of tea growers on the slopes surrounding West Lake, safely hidden in the undergrowth of history.

My search led me, eventually, to Guangzhou, the port city on the Pearl River where the Qing had consolidated all maritime trade. There I learned of an English missionary who fancied himself a guardian of Chinese culture and how he had convinced the painting's erstwhile owner, a recent convert to Christianity, to give it to him for safekeeping. *In our great capital of London,* he said, *we have a special building that stores treasures from all over the world, to make sure they won't be lost, or ruined, or stolen.* He had fled for England on the last clipper ship out of Guangzhou before the British navy began bombing the city during the Second Opium War.

And that's where our portrait is. Room 33 of the British Museum, in the company of a red lacquer box depicting a spring landscape and a commendable forgery of a Jingdezhen porcelain vase. The placard beneath the painting highlights the delicacy of its brushstrokes and the insights it provides into female friendship during the Ming era. Our artist was too harsh on himself. He might not have understood us, but he did manage to set down what he saw. You are smiling at me. It was something I said, I don't remember what. I used to think that as long as I could make you smile, the world would be a fine place. The colors of our dresses glow against the dun background, and behind us the clouds swirl like at any moment they could lift us away.

There's something I must confess. When I finally saw the painting, I might have—sort of—cried. I never had, previously. They took you away in the bridal sedan, and again in the coffin, and both times I watched you become the centerpiece of their human rituals, composed and costumed, almost unrecognizable to me. So then, three hundred years later, to be undone by patterns of ink on silk, swatches of white and green paint, a memory of an unmemorable day: it was quite alarming, actually. Thankfully, the man standing a few feet away from me in the gallery said, no doubt after observing me sniffle for far too long, "You seem like you could use a drink."

He could have suggested a dagger through my eye and I would have taken it. "Do you know a place?" I said.

He looked startled, which might have been for any number of reasons: my forwardness, my speaking English—I had picked it up from the sailors on the long voyage over—or the accent with which I was doing it, which must have made me sound as if I had grown up scuffling for survival on the docks of London. Then he laughed, and offered me both his arm and his handkerchief.

The establishment where he took me was gold-trimmed and gaudy, with mirrored walls and fat, winged babies painted across the ceiling. He salvaged my opinion of him by ordering me an enchanting drink. It was a translucent green, as if lit by a hidden flame, and when I sipped it I could taste anise and fennel. After the first glass, he told me, I would see things as I wished they were; after the second glass, as they were not; and, finally, as they truly were.

As we drank he asked me what I had seen, looking at that painting. Beauty, I said, and how it passed.

"Young people are supposed to defer such dour thoughts to the old," he said.

"Oh," I said, "I just look young for my age."

"The ephemerality of beauty is indeed a tragedy," he said, "but surely not in art. The painting will preserve those women's beauty forever."

"While they grew old and died," I said. "That's even worse. It should have been the other way around."

He and I were both well past our third glasses by then, so I told him the story of the hermit on Taishi Mountain who would remain alive for as long as his portrait was intact. The version I told was the one you and I had followed from village to village throughout Henan Province, seeking to determine its authenticity: a scholar official, fallen out of favor with the first Ming court, who begged his portrait to assume the burden of aging for him so he could serve as a historian of the dynasty from its founding to its fall.

"Fascinating," said my drinking companion. "The Ming dynasty ended in . . . what was it, the seventeenth century? What happened to him then?"

"I don't know," I said. "The story doesn't get that far."

We had found him, this hermit, and you coaxed him into showing us the painting. The person depicted in it looked like some ill-tempered ancestor of his who at the time of the portrait sitting was still alive solely to spite all expectations to the contrary. Once he was done with this history of the Ming, the hermit told us, he would burn the portrait. He had no wish to live forever. On our way down from Taishi Mountain I said to you that I was sure he would come up with another reason for living before he laid down his ink brush. *You don't think being eternal can start to feel tiring after a while?* you said. *It hasn't yet,* I said, *and we have several hundred years on him.* We made a wager: the loser would procure a water dragon's pearl for the winner. But then you died, long before the last Ming emperor did, and I never went back to Taishi to check.

I spent the rest of that day walking through London, admiring, despite myself, its gardens, its cathedrals, its prosperity, its purpose. It reminded me of the grandest days of the Ming, when lantern displays ignited entire mountainsides and Zheng He's treasure fleet measured the breadth of the oceans. In King's Cross Station I saw the twentieth century roaring toward us, all steel and smoke, insatiable, and I thought of how the Summer Palace had burned for days after British troops set it ablaze to punish the Qing government for outlawing the import of opium. When I returned to Hangzhou I put your great-great-grandson on a ship that landed in California shortly before the Chinese Exclusion Act was signed into law. He hated America, the vast and relentless otherness of it, but he never once tried to go back to China.

Quite a while later I read a story about an Englishman and a magical portrait, written by an author as noted for a controversial lifestyle as for his literary skill. This Englishman's wish to remain young and beautiful is granted: his portrait will age in his place. He spends his days and nights seeking pleasures and indulging them. While his physical appearance remains unchanged, his painted likeness grows increasingly old and hideous. The Englishman believes this reflects a cosmic judgment being levied on his personal moral choices. He doesn't consider the possibility that the painting is simply showing him, as such a magical artifact does, what he would have become had he continued to age in typical mortal fashion, or that even his most callous acts are nothing out of the ordinary for a person of his breeding and his means, or that the cosmos has never noticed what humans do to themselves or to each other.

Imagine a *qilin*—you were always partial to those annoyingly pious creatures—which lives in an enchanted garden. The keepers mandated to care for this *qilin* feed it delicacies, brush its mane, polish its rainbowed scales, and all the while, these keepers, they're also secretly siphoning away the *qilin*'s magic for themselves, because they can. Visitors from beyond the garden are permitted in so they can gaze upon the splendor of the *qilin* and applaud the keepers for how well they are tending to their charge. The visitors bring stories of the *qilin* back with them, and that's how, over time, poachers come to learn about this remarkable animal, the grace of its antlers and its jeweled brilliance, an irresistible challenge.

When the first poachers scale the wall of the garden, the *qilin* is outraged. It puffs up its chest to scorch them with its righteous breath of fire, and . . . nothing. Nothing at all, except the emptiest, most embarrassing wheeze; and the rest of the poachers, waiting outside the walls, hear that sound as well, and they understand what it means. They overrun the garden, wound the *qilin* with their arrows, entangle it in their nets. The *qilin*'s keepers try to stop them and are either killed or persuaded to acquiesce. Once the *qilin* is on the ground, the poachers carve away its ornamentation with their knives. There's something for each of them to take away and sell: the antlers, the mane, the dragon scales, the cloven hooves. They leave the *qilin* alive, though. This way the *qilin*'s ornamentation can grow back and they can return and cut it away again, and again, until this arrangement settles into normalcy, until the *qilin*'s purpose becomes, in the very first place, to bring the poachers wealth.

Now a horde of children crowd in. They see the garden as their playground, the *qilin* as their amusement. It will be fun, they think, to play at being keepers. They dress up in the uniforms they have stripped off the keepers' corpses and argue over what they should do with the *qilin*, flopping about in its own blood and excrement, until someone gets the idea of opening it up, because who knows what treasures it might hold? The children rush to rip open the *qilin*'s belly and start grabbing at what's inside. The kidneys, the entrails, the liver, the heart. Because they can.

So you can see how what I did to your great-great-grandson, for him, seemed the obvious choice. Certain exile versus probable extinction. But I've come to suspect that all I did was stretch the thread of your lineage tighter, and thinner, and in the end it broke anyway.

IV.

You know, I used to think about all the questions I would ask you if I could. Whether you had indeed run the numbers on your own fate but decided not to share, and if so whether it was to spare me or because you thought I would try to stop you. (Of course I would have.) Whether, if you could have seen how this would go down, one brief fuse of a human life lighting another until everything went dark, you would still think it was worth it. (You'd probably have said yes regardless of what you truly thought; you could never bear to be wrong.) Whether you didn't ask me to join you because you were afraid I would say no, or maybe that I would say yes. (I still don't know what I would have said. But you should have asked, you should have.)

This morning, though, I have no questions left. I leave the hospital and take a walk through the city. Up and down its hills, past the swaddled homeless on its sidewalks, along the reclaimed curve of its bay, under its gray-scale sky. The fog drifting in across the water is the Pacific Ocean's marine layer cooled to dew point, and also all the ghosts waiting to be remembered before the morning sun burns them away. You're gone now, six hundred years gone, but guess what: I did stay after all.

The Last Days of Rodney

FROM *American Short Fiction*

HE WAS KNOWN most everywhere—a face, a caption, a grainy video clip—but it had been over twenty years now, and he was still trying to forge a new chapter unconnected to the first. Wishful thinking, he knew. It would always be connected. No one would ever bring up his name without mentioning the past, without talking about the public spectacle of a private beating that almost killed him, but didn't. And when his heart slowed and breath filled his lungs, he was someone else.

It wasn't amnesia. He knew he was the man on the tape. He could piece together the jumbled happenings of how things spiraled out of hand. How he misheard the first officer and moved away when he was ordered to stay put. Police didn't understand things like reflexes, how the body rises up on its own to stave off danger. For years after, he practiced forgetting. Cough syrups that made sleep blacker than night. Pills with complicated names he got from therapists, which he crushed and chased with liquor until every memory was as distant as a picture show.

That was what his dad called the movies—picture shows. And by the time a home movie changed Rodney's life, his father couldn't see too good or hear much either. They hadn't been close. They were a family of deserters. Of runners, of folks who took long absences when things got hard or heated, which was often. But now that the old man was small and sickly and senile, now that he couldn't do much more than drink a bit of whiskey and talk trash over a game of dominoes, Rodney had seen more of him than he ever had as a child. He had given up on completing the family photo album in his mind long ago, ramming some shiny, youthful version of the man into memories of backyard barbecues or parent-teacher conferences. No, what made Dad comforting now was that he didn't ask about the case or what had happened that night. The dementia had settled so far in that he couldn't hold on to the telling. Only the distant past was accessible. New things were drops on the skin, felt for a second and then wiped away. And Rodney needed that forgetting.

Mornings like this one, he realized he still hadn't gotten it down. He rolled out of bed while Vera was sleeping. Picked his pants up off the floor and stepped into them. Stuck his wallet in his back pocket and pulled a shirt off the chair. At the front door, he slid his feet into his flip-flops and stepped outside. The sun was weak at this hour. The cul-de-sac deserted, an unnatural sight at almost any time of day. There was always a bit of noise in the air, though. A car driving by spraying the street with bass or some sing-song refrain. The chatter of kids on their way to school. The neighboring couple, waking the whole block up with their quarreling or fucking.

He headed down the street to the corner store. He wanted a cigarette, a cup of coffee, and a newspaper. The parking lot was empty, no sign of life but a stray beer can rolling downhill. Inside, he shuffled past the clerk, a graying head bent over a spreadsheet. "Sup, Rajeev," Rodney said. The man grunted in reply. It wasn't Rajeev but someone new. "Oh sorry, my bad."

The Lotto machine loomed in the corner. He moved toward it without stopping. He had told Vera he wasn't going to play anymore. This wasn't a lie. He wasn't playing. He was *winning*. Lotto just needed to say the same. And until it did, he folded the cards into thin strips and slid them into the last pocket in his wallet, as guilty as an illicit phone number. It felt like cheating almost, but Vera didn't understand. He was looking for a sign. He had been looking all over for them ever since the incident. People said he was lucky. Not for what happened, but because there was video, because he won the civil suit (after the clusterfuck of the criminal), but mostly because he was still alive. Cracked skull and eleven fractures be damned. He had lived. A still-sentient being, aware of the needs of every single cell and muscle calling for comfort, rest, or Vicodin.

He wasn't sure what he expected Lotto to tell him. He had

seen enough in his life to know there were some problems money couldn't solve. And let's face it, Lotto was not the best tool for divination. He had tried all the usual routes, the velvet pews of storefront Pentecostal churches, head-wrapped psychics in glass cases peering into palms or playing cards. He even went way across town to the botanica, where he bought some tall white candles adorned with the faces of spooky-looking saints. He burned them for a while, but clarity never came. He tried therapy. First the real kind and then the reality-show kind, but the latter was for money, and by then he was so close to the edge, the wide eye of those cameras gave him something to focus on long enough to get through the minutes and hours that squeezed the air out of his chest and throat. It hadn't helped with the anonymity he hoped for, but he figured that ship had long sailed anyway.

On the lottery form, he colored in the numbers. The same sequence every time. The day of his birth, but not the year. The birth year of his firstborn, Jermaine, who was now grown and not speaking to him. The number of separate fractures inflicted that day. Each time he penned it in, he felt a twinge of some dark feeling he couldn't name and thought to himself he wouldn't play that number anymore. It had been in the newspaper with the rest of the details, a string of disembodied facts that read like a rap sheet.

Sticking the form under his arm, he walked up to the coffee machine and slid a paper cup under the spout. The streaming, dark liquid sloshed violently as it approached the rim. One cream, two sugars. He slapped a lid on.

"A pack of Newports," he said to the clerk at the counter as he reached over and grabbed a newspaper from the stack and set it down along with his lottery form.

He scanned the front-page headline and tried to turn it over before it could register. But even the safety of the sports page, with a Dodger in midswing, didn't erase the previous image or the large blocks of black text. Another police shooting. An unarmed thirty-six-year-old father of two shot seven times, five of them in the back, the coroner reported.

"Twelve dollars and forty cents," the clerk said, interrupting his thoughts.

Rodney fished out his wallet. Shit. Only a ten. He put the ten-dollar bill on the counter. "I'm short two dollars. Let me bring it tomorrow."

The clerk shook his gray head and scrunched up his face. "No, you pay now."

"C'mon, man. Y'all see me almost every day."

"I don't see you. You pay now." The man's face was as brown as his own, but the clerk's skin had a greenish tinge to it, no doubt obtained from a steady diet of honey buns and long shifts spent under fluorescent lights. But this likeness didn't matter, he knew. Country mattered. Culture mattered. Similar concentrations of melanin, not so much.

"Where you from, man?" Rodney said, taking a sip from the coffee cup. "Where's Rajeev?"

The man shot Rodney a sideways look but didn't say anything. "You never mind where I'm from. You gon' pay?" One hand fluttered on the counter, the fingers drumming an odd rhythm on the red laminate surface, the universal language for "Hurry the fuck up." The other hand remained hidden, though, underneath, and Rodney could see the clerk's mind slowly calculating the odds. Was this towering, broad-shouldered dark figure a threat? Was he trying to walk out with more than the ten dollars sitting on the counter could pay for?

He almost laughed out loud. The only people who ever considered him a threat were those who didn't recognize him. Anyone who remembered his story from the papers knew the person he was most in danger of harming was himself. After years of being recognized, he was damn near out of practice with this particular performance of being big and black and male in a public space. Don't pick up a lot of items, especially anything you don't plan on buying. Make a performance of placing any unwanted merchandise back on the shelves. Slowly and solidly. Make noise when you're behind people. Cross the street first. And so on. He practiced fading into the background, trying to return to anonymity, but he had a body that was hard to hide in. His size made him conspicuous in public. This was typically true for white spaces, but black spaces were hard too. Oakland was hard. Any place where people knew his face was hard. People kept wanting to talk to him. Not because they wanted to hear from him, but because they had things to say, things to wrestle with, that seeing him brought up. And sometimes that was harder than being an object everyone orbits. Who could take on all that, really? Jesus couldn't.

"Fine, man. That should cover these," Rodney said as he picked up the lottery form and crumpled it in his pocket. He'd have to play those numbers another day. He tucked the folded newspaper under his armpit, pocketed the pack of cigarettes, and left. He hadn't lied to Vera after all. That was a plus, right?

Outside, he sat down on the curb facing the parking lot and spread out his purchases. Coffee on the right, cigs on the left, paper in the middle. He lit a cigarette and turned his attention to the front page, but he couldn't make himself read past the first sentence. All of a sudden his head was throbbing, an insistent knocking at the base of his skull. He put the paper down and inhaled a drag of his cigarette. He was sitting too low on the ground. The whole parking lot was tilted. He hadn't eaten anything. Shit, he shouldn't have left his change in there. He could have gotten a doughnut or a candy bar. Something that could right his blood sugar. He felt tingly now, in his head, his fingers.

He looked down at the paper to turn the page, but the picture kept him frozen. The man was relaxed and smiling, a posed photo with friends or family cropped out of it, an anonymous, lazy arm draped around his neck. Rodney couldn't help feeling that the man was interrogating him somehow, looking deep into his head, lacing a singular question in his mind—why me and not you?

He kicked the paper away from him and reached for the coffee. The rush of heat singed him, and he swallowed quickly to get the liquid off his tongue. He felt it burning a path down to his stomach. He shook his head and stood up, grabbing the pack of cigarettes. No paper today. No Lotto either. Maybe this was the sign he had been waiting for.

He didn't pay much attention to dreams and hated when people bothered him with theirs, but he had a recurring one he couldn't shake. He could stave it off if the sleep was deep enough, if he tipped off with a cap or two of NyQuil, but now even that wasn't working, and he couldn't talk about it.

Just yesterday he tried. He woke up, chest heaving, covered with sweat, and stumbled down to the kitchen. Everything was still there as he'd left it the day before, the black spindly chairs, the glass table, the dingy vertical blinds. Vera was standing over the stove, scrambling eggs, when she saw him. "You look awful. Sit, let me get you some water. You feeling okay?"

He nodded as he sat down, his breath still coming out jagged. "You ever have that feeling you're going to die?" he blurted out.

"Honey, we're all going to die," she said, sitting a glass of water in front of him.

"Not someday, I mean like soon. Like today."

Vera looked at him, confused. She leaned over and put the back of her hand against his forehead, checking for fever.

He pulled away from her. "Like Jesus, you know, or MLK, or Malcolm. They all knew it was coming. They could feel it."

Her brown eyes widened and her mouth twisted up. "Are *you* comparing yourself to Jesus or MLK?"

"Course not. I'm just saying . . . I feel it coming on, that's all. Like it's already here. If it was a blood clot heading toward the heart, it'd be over here already," he said, pointing to his chest, close to the shoulder.

Vera froze for a second, without answering him. Then, she stepped backward, muttering to herself, "Now, where did I put Dr. Morgan's new number?"

She began foraging through the kitchen drawers, drifting over to the loose papers and stacks of mail sitting in a corner of the kitchen counter. He knew she was looking for a reality other than the one he was presenting her with. And he knew then, he couldn't make her deal with this too. The cost of being with him was already too much.

Outside the convenience store, Rodney drifted back home in a stupor. The days were taking shape in a way that meant something, even if he couldn't discern their meaning. He walked into the house just as Vera and the boys were preparing to leave. Eleven-year-old Reggie was clattering around in the kitchen while Vera wrestled with their youngest. With her trench coat and purse on, she was kneeling in front of four-year-old Marlon, trying to get him to allow her to tie his shoes.

"Stop," the boy whined. "Let me do it," he said as he pushed her hands away.

Vera sighed. "Fine, you have two minutes." She looked up at Rodney standing in the doorway. "Where you been?"

"Out of smokes," he said, closing the door behind him.

She eyed the convenience-store coffee cup in his hand. "Don't know why you insist on wasting good money when there's a perfectly decent coffeemaker in the kitchen."

"It doesn't taste as good when I make it."

Vera rolled her eyes before turning back to sleepy-eyed Marlon, still trying to form the loops with his tiny hands. "See, if you went to sleep when I told you to, you wouldn't be tired. Now, let me tie your shoes or we're going to be late."

The boy's mouth contracted into a frown. His hands flew up to his face to rub his eyes. Vera tied Marlon's shoes and pulled him to his feet.

"Is Reggie dressed?" Rodney asked.

"Should be. He's eating now."

Vera moved toward the door, guiding Marlon by his shoulder. Rodney reached down and kissed Marlon's forehead. "Have a good day. Be good."

He turned to Vera, putting one arm around her, but she jerked forward, and his mouth just grazed the side of her face. "Love you," he said, whispering low into her neck.

She mumbled something indistinguishable back.

"No sugar?" He stepped closer, tightening his arm around her.

"Move. We can't be late again. I don't have time for this."

"You don't have time for me? You don't have time to kiss your husband?"

She groaned and gave him a dry, heartless peck on the lips.

"Really? Ugh, next time, don't kiss me," he said, putting his hand over his mouth.

She laughed in spite of herself. She kissed him. "You make me sick, you know that."

He nodded and grinned at her. "Y'all have a good day," he said, opening the door for her and Marlon. He then headed to the kitchen, where he found Reggie standing over the sink, slurping milk from a cereal bowl.

Reggie drained it of all the syrupy sweet milk and placed it in the bottom of the sink with a resounding clank. "Hi, Dad. Bye, Dad," he said and rushed past his father, his sneakers squeaking on the linoleum. Reggie grabbed his jacket and threw his book bag over his shoulder.

"You need some money?" Rodney said, standing at the counter, fingering the ripped envelope of an unpaid bill.

Reggie paused and turned to face him. "Yeah."

Rodney pulled out his wallet and then remembered he didn't have any more cash. Shit. "I need to go to the ATM. Hold on, I think I got some cash upstairs."

Reggie shook his head and opened the front door. "It's okay. Mom gave me some."

The sound of a long mechanical hiss filled the room. "Shit, the bus!" Reggie took off, sprinting toward the bus stop before Rodney could say anything about the cursing.

An uneasy quiet settled over the house. He hated a quiet house. When he was a kid, moments alone were so rare, they were like cherished jewels. Now they were something else entirely. Proof of his wrongs. The latitude and longitude of his errors could be tracked in this way, by the duration of quiet. This moment right now, set to last between eight and ten hours, was proof too. He was between jobs again. That he was home with no foreseeable place to go was another piece of mounting evidence.

Just then Reggie opened the screen door and stepped back inside.

"I missed the bus. Can you give me a ride?"

He tried to look irritated, but he was grateful. "Again? You're getting too old for this. You have to start getting out of here on time." He reached for his keys and grabbed a sweater, and they both headed outside to the car.

The light in the sky was still weak, hidden by gray clouds. He sank down into the seat, feeling his weight upon the tires. It was a Cadillac, but not wide and boatlike the way he wished. They didn't make those cars anymore, those long Buicks and Cadillacs that seemed to stretch out like a city block, the kind that he had wanted when he was Reggie's age, the kind that men in his neighborhood steered around corners and Sunday drivers using one graceful, lazy hand. The few days he spent with his dad as a kid were in those kinds of cars, running errands across town, the metal shining in the sunlight and the radio dial too sacred to be fiddled with.

Rodney drove slowly, humming along with the radio, his foot easing up and down on the gas as they moved through one intersection after another. When they pulled up to the school, he had a thought. "Reg, how about playing hooky today? We can drive around, go get hot dogs at the pier, maybe go to the aquarium. What do you say?"

Reggie looked pensive. "Isn't Mom gon' be mad?"

"Yeah, but we ain't got to tell her. I'll call the school myself. It'll be just between us."

Reggie cocked his head to the side. "I don't know, Dad. Today's the last day to turn in permission slips for dodgeball, and if I don't, I can't play. And," he lowered his voice conspiratorially, "Kia is going to be *my* lab partner today. Kia, Dad!"

Rodney nodded and laughed. "That *is* major."

"Can we do it next Tuesday? Mr. Milton is giving a test."

"We'll see. Go on now. You're gonna be late."

Reggie popped open the door and hopped out. "Bye, Dad," he said as he slammed the door.

Rodney watched as the kid raced toward the building, his camouflage book bag bouncing up and down as he ran.

It was still early. He debated whether to go home and take a nap, but he didn't feel quite ready to face the house, the silent judgment of the couch, the dirty dishes, the laundry sitting in piles. He drove to the old folks' home instead, but the staff had just tried to feed his father, and it seemed the man couldn't stay awake.

"Did he eat much?" he asked Ms. Russell, the nursing assistant on duty.

"Not much, just some grits, but he slept through most of breakfast," the woman said, reaching for the tray sitting in front of the old man propped up in a wheelchair.

"Just leave it," Rodney said. The food was largely untouched, a bowl of grits three-quarters full, one piece of buttered toast, and some dry, hard eggs. Only the plastic container of applesauce was empty, the lid curling backward over the rim. "Have y'all been messing with his meds again? Why he so tired? It's nine in the morning."

The woman gave him a stony look. "I don't believe there's been a change in his medication," she said. "But if you want to check, you can go down to the nurses' station." She cleared the other trays from the table and walked away.

"Pop, you still hungry?" he said, shaking the man's shoulder.

His father stirred but didn't open his eyes.

"C'mon, Pop, you need to eat a little more, and then you can lie down."

The man opened his eyes for a moment. A slit of gray iris struck the light as he peered at Rodney. A chill came over him. It felt like all of creation was looking at him through that eye. He had been seen, caught, and it was only a matter of time before he was taken whole.

Rodney stood up from the table and backed out of the room,

trying to escape that eye. He hurried down the hallway, ignoring Ms. Russell calling after him, and slid into his car. He sped out of the parking lot, driving fast, until he hit the last of morning traffic merging off the expressway. He headed north, just driving, stretches of concrete speeding toward him. The sun dipped down, brighter now, but still hidden behind the clouds. Another gray eye.

He decided to go see a picture. He wanted to hide somewhere dark and closed in. But after the flick was over, he wasn't ready to go home, so he snuck into another. There were only a few other people in the theater this early, and he wondered what they too were avoiding.

A couple was making out in the right corner a few rows over. They clearly weren't teenagers. A pale woman in a wrinkled blazer, a blond man with a receding, thinning hairline. Was this an affair or the bored and joyless seeking a thrill? He tried not to watch them, but he was curious how far they would go. Their pawing wasn't laden with the desire of the young but the sweaty desperation of the fallen. He knew it well, could recognize it anywhere. He tried to watch the movie, a silly slapstick comedy. The acting was bad, and most of the jokes were well worn. He wanted to laugh but found he couldn't. Even when the shiny-suited Wall Street dude fell in shit, couldn't get up out of it, and it was all over his back, his front, smeared across his forehead and lips, he could do no more than chuckle and watch the couple out of the corner of his eye, the woman then mounting the guy, the two jerking in succession as the score broke into song.

It took him a minute to notice the usher in his crisp white shirt and gold name tag, a flashlight dangling in hand and two cops at his heels. They stood in the aisle, squinting, their eyes not yet accustomed to the dark. He felt their gaze rove over him and hold a moment before turning toward the grunting couple. The employee flashed his light on and off, on and off, as the cops approached them. Rodney's breath caught. He wanted to run but felt frozen. He let the frozen part take over, knowing it was better to remain still until the couple left. He tried to concentrate on the silly movie, but he heard the woman protesting, her shrieking pitch rising above the sound coming from the speakers. "This is a mistake!" she yelled as she and her lover were shuffled past him. He didn't look their way. He just waited for their voices to recede, focusing on his body—his feet sticking to the floor, his fingers gripping the hand rests, a bone in his leg aching suddenly, an itch over his ear he wouldn't raise an arm to scratch. He was here, and if he was here, he couldn't be there, those many nights ago, under a clear night sky, rolling over on the concrete with blood in his eye, his mouth tasting of metal. When the credits began, he didn't move. He didn't even get up when the soundtrack listing scrolled past. Only after the lights went up, the screen went white, and the employees moved in with trash cans and brooms did he rise and stagger toward the exit. He drove home in a daze.

The house was still too quiet. He turned on some music. Something loud with a hard beat that made it difficult for his mind to wander. It was still light out. He stood with the refrigerator door open, searching for something to eat. On the bottom shelf sat a raw pot roast, red and thick, water beading underneath the plastic wrap. He could be useful, he thought. He pulled out the meat and set it on the counter. He put the oven on preheat and got to work. When it was in the oven, the meat seasoned and surrounded by peeled potatoes, he was proud of himself. He had turned it around, but now what? He wasn't one for washing dishes, but he could do some laundry. He went upstairs and dragged the dirty clothes hampers down to the basement. He threw a load in the washer. When he reached for the detergent, his eye caught a glint of something down on the shelf below. Buried beneath old cleaning rags was a small bottle of dark liquor. He held it up to the light. Did he hide this, or was this Vera's? She never drank around him, for obvious reasons, but he knew she enjoyed good liquor from time to time. He slipped the bottle in his pocket and finished adding the soap to the clothes. He wanted to be mad but wasn't sure whom to be mad at. He went upstairs to the kitchen, opened the sliding door, and stepped into the backyard.

The yard wasn't huge, but it did have a patio and a pool. He hated the pool. Maintenance was a bitch and he couldn't even swim that well. He bought it as a big *fuck you* after the settlement. Well, that's not true entirely. He blew most of the settlement money, but the reality show that he did after rehab, that's what he used to buy this house. Sure, he heard what people said about him back then. How they laughed at him, in his face and behind his back, on television, and in grocery stores. Idiots at the mall who'd stop him, saying, "Can't we all just get along?" Or worse, asking him to say it, like he was a sitcom star with a catchphrase they couldn't go without hearing. What better revenge was there than a big, stupid house with a pool? Granted, it wasn't that big. Not MC Hammer big, *MTV Cribs* big, or even gated-community big, but it was larger than anything he had ever lived in. Now he was just trying his best to hang on to it.

He could see the water level in the pool was a foot lower than it should be. He pulled down the child-protective gate and stepped closer to the edge. He kept the pool filled to the minimum level, just high enough to stop the pump from running dry, but the water had evaporated and was getting dangerously close to the skimmer. He unraveled the hose and turned the spigot. The pool took forever to fill the inches he needed. He knew he had to talk with Vera about getting rid of it, filling it in with dirt or concrete. As frugal as she was, she was reluctant to let it go. The symbol meant something to her. And on the few occasions when they invited family over for barbecues and watched the kids splash around in the water with their cousins, he knew it felt like they had won something, stolen something they were never meant to have. Only an ungrateful asshole would give it back.

When he popped back into the house, it was nearly dusk. He now remembered the pot roast, the smell of burnt meat filling his nose. He opened the mouth of the oven and the roast stared back at him, dry, all the water cooked away, the potatoes shrunken and hard. He pulled it out and put it on the top of the stove. He hadn't been outside that long, he thought, but he had no way of knowing. The sun had been up and now it wasn't. Maybe he forgot a step. As he stared at it, he did remember that Vera often used those clear roasting bags; maybe that was the missing piece.

He heard the lock turn in the front door. A cacophony of sound rose up behind him as Vera and the boys came in the house, leaving a trail of the day behind them, the boys immediately separating themselves from shoes, jackets, book bags right there in the hallway. Vera stepped out of her heels and went upstairs to peel off her bra and girdle.

"What's that smell?" she asked, returning to the kitchen in blue sweats.

"Delicious pot roast? Can't you tell?"

"You cooked?" Her eyes widened. He knew what she was thinking. Work or no work, she usually had to be flat on her back with fever for him to cook anything. "What did you do to it?" she asked, drifting over to the stove and peering down at the roast like it was a strange and foul creature he had dragged into the house.

"I cooked it. What do you mean what did I do to it?"

She walked away, went back to putting the kids' things in their proper places. A few minutes later he heard her on the phone in the living room. "Yes, that's right. Okay, thanks."

Then she was standing next to him again, staring at the pot roast. "Put it in the fridge. I'll see if I can make a soup out of it tomorrow."

"What about tonight?" he asked sheepishly.

"I ordered Chinese," she said with a toothy grin. "Would you mind going to get it?"

When he settled into the car, he felt the bottle poke his hip. He pulled it out and stuck it underneath the passenger seat and tried to forget he had ever seen it.

Later that night, after they'd eaten and put the kids to sleep, he climbed into bed beside Vera. She yawned and pulled the covers up to her neck, turning to face the wall. He listened to her breathing, but he couldn't fall asleep. Instead he felt the air compressing, the ceiling lowering, the streak of moonlight growing dimmer and dimmer. A tomb, it was. Everything led back to that. Vera coughed. He eased over to her side of the bed, pressed his body against her back, and shifted himself so she could feel his hardness. She didn't respond. He grazed his hands over her body, kissing her neck. Her fingers reached out and grabbed ahold of his, tightening around his hand. "Hon, I'm really tired," she said.

He sighed and pulled away from her. He wanted to say something more, something that would make her see that he needed her right then. That her arms, her kisses, might be the only thing that would keep his thoughts from returning to that shiny bottle outside in the car, underneath the seat. But she had saved his life so many times already, did he have any right to ask her to do it again? Besides, he knew she was tired. Not just in her body, but in all the other parts too. How long before she washed her hands of him altogether?

He crept downstairs and out to the car, where he retrieved the bottle and put it into his jacket pocket. He returned to the house and wandered into the backyard. He kept the overhead lights off but turned the pool lights on. Most of the bulbs were blown, but two were still working, and they caused the water to glow in this way he found mesmerizing. He removed his flip-flops and rolled his pants up to his knees. He stepped down into the shallow end and sat at the edge, dipping his feet into the water. It felt cold at first, and he realized he hadn't brought a towel or anything.

He pulled the bottle from his jacket and set it in his lap. It gleamed in the dim light. He twisted off the cap and put his nose to it. The familiar smell rushed inside him. It had been almost two years since he had been this close to it. He poured some out on the pavement. "For the brothers who ain't here," he muttered. When he was a young man, sharing a bottle and shooting the shit with his father and the rest of the old heads, he found this ritual upsetting—the waste of good hooch on pavement that couldn't enjoy it nor put a few dollars in on the next—but once he got older, he understood, observed it religiously, even when he was drinking alone.

His thoughts returned to the morning, the moments in the convenience-store parking lot and the face of the man he saw in the paper. He poured out a little more liquor before taking a long deep swig. He stared at the water. He did a talk show once where he heard someone say water is always remembering, always trying to get back to itself. It was funny to think of water with memories. "Can we trade?" But he knew he didn't want water's memories, he just wanted to give his up, have them disappear like those people on soap operas who get amnesia like most folks get the flu. He wanted amnesia for himself, for others. Isn't that a baptism? The washing away of sins. That whatever happened before is no longer.

He turned the bottle upside down, felt the warm medicinal liquid ripping down his throat, searing his chest. *A baptism is all I need.* He stepped down so his feet were on the pool floor, the water rising up to his thighs. *Make me clean. Make me new.* He drifted toward the deep, darker end of the pool and the water climbed higher and higher. He lowered himself into it, first his shoulders, then his head. Just a moment now, and then one moment more. When he came up, it would all be different.

CHRISTA ROMANOSKY

In This Sort of World, the Asshole Wins

FROM *The Cincinnati Review*

WHEN THE FATIGUE finally hit, her sleep brought dreams of Don before he overdosed, and in these dreams his skin was made of colorful crepe paper that kept tearing off when she reached for him, until all that was left was a tumbleweed frame, a hollow yellow bouquet of him. And when she woke in the afternoon with her aching unbearable, Tiff finally gave up and called up some bitch who'd known Don and had a car and owed her and would take her to Grubber John.

When Some Bitch pulled up, late as usual, Tiff loaded her son, Bucky, into the backseat, and they rode to the gas-station ATM while Tiff smoked out the passenger-side window. They rolled through the McDonald's drive-through, muffler rattling, Bucky trilling "Lu lu lu lu lu" until Tiff finally said, "Quit!" and then, "Eat your nuggets, baby." She took a bite from her steaming burger and threw the rest of it out the window. Then she was hungry again; it branched through her like rivers, like a burrowing, aching pulse.

"Stop smoking around your kid," Some Bitch hollered, which Tiff ignored, because who the fuck was she? The hairs of her legs hurt. Her teeth ached. Bright plumes of exhaust moved around them like they were hauling a dragon. Tiff shoved the twenty in her bra. "I'll pay you back," she said. That bitch was known for holding things over your head when you least expected it.

"Keep it," Some Bitch said. "Then neither of us are liars."

The small things, the ways people tried to demean Tiff, she'd learned, carried no weight. She'd heard it all. She imagined rain. Imagined those roly-poly bugs, armadillos, Magic 8-Balls, hail— everything moving downhill and disappearing for good, straight off her back, into the abyss. They were all assholes. The only way for them to win was for her to lose, and she refused.

"I'm tired," Some Bitch exhaled. "The neighbor's dog barked all night. I'm putting antifreeze in its water, I swear to god."

"The whole world is tired," Tiff said. "Get over it."

Grubber John lived above Rust Creek, where the mines had tunneled through and left, collapsing the field at the edge of the hills in rough divots. Trees had grown back sickly and anemic— hawthorns, crab apples. Tiff stepped over tarp. There was more in the bed of his truck, rolled and fastened with rope around a human-sized object. "Christmas tree," John explained. "Just now getting around to dumping it."

This was no-man's land. Pokeweed rose up from broken porch boards, stacks of newspapers. A few rusted torsos of trucks on cinder blocks. In his garage John analyzed Tiff like a dog in a kennel, sniffling, sighing before handing off the crisp baggie, saying, "I got you, girl." Her body flooded with relief just having relief so close. "If you want to earn," he added, "hit me up sometime. Don was good people." On the concrete step someone had arranged cigarette butts in the shape of a smiley face.

"My boy's got the insanity fleas inside," he added. "Want to kick it with me out here?" But Some Bitch had to work a late shift, was already back in the car, already singing "Itsy Bitchy Spider" to Bucky, who was losing his shit over spilled chicken nuggets.

The foothills fumed with the fog of a hot evening, like ghosts rising from the dead, all at once, up into the uninterrupted sky. Somewhere in the hills, dozens of abandoned mine shafts, half sealed and filled with bats—an exit wound that had no entrance.

Don loved it out in the boondocks, which is what he'd always called it—he'd grown up deer hunting, rabbit hunting. "You can eat anything with a pulse," he once told Tiff, when he shot and skinned a raccoon.

"Where should I drop you?" Some Bitch said, elbowing her. "I've got things to do." She was all bones, this bitch, like a Halloween prop, half inflated.

"You don't have diddly-squat to do," Tiff said, because the only thing she could think of was to push back.

At Tiff's parents' house, the canaries didn't sing, and the tropical fish made tiny unplanned laps around the tank. The television filled the room with a nervous blue light. Tiff switched on cartoons for Bucky before locking herself in the bathroom with the tiny china dolls her mother loved so much, the dolls she had once accused her mother of loving more than she loved Tiff, to which her mother replied, "Those dolls aren't constantly misbehaving, so." Her mother never loved her yet somehow extended her love for the canaries, the tropical fish. She loved the eleven o'clock news. She loved bacon bits. It was pathetic how many inanimate things Tiff's mother loved.

Tiff lit and inhaled quickly, imagined herself a crab pulled out of its shell, spindly and legless—and when she began to feel the deluge, she fit right back into the shell like a thimble, a silver soldered thing. When her mother pounded on the door forty minutes later, Tiff shouted, "Jesus, I'm constipated!" And when Tiff finally emerged, Bucky was standing in front of the door in sweatpants too large for his body, and she lifted him to her. "How's my brave little man?" she said, kissing his face, tickling his arms. "Let's find a cartoon that you like. Did you miss me, buddy?" She kissed his smooth face. This feeling, this love for him, there was nothing like it.

At night there was no anxiety, no expectations to be doing day work. Tiff felt nocturnal, like her world did not depend on the daylight. No one had bothered to put the window screens back in, and mayflies charged the TV, the aquarium lights, tapping like dog nails, and night beetles hammered into the kitchen light. Tiff flipped through TV programming no one cared about—world's best avocado slicer, the incredible pillow refresher—her stash gaping and unused like a minnow on the coffee table, didn't hear her father come into the room, had no idea how long he'd been standing there when he said, "What is going on here?" and she bolted upright to grab it away, to tuck it into her waistband, a place her father couldn't reach. Minutes, seconds—she imagined herself becoming liquid, leaking through the couch into the carpet, evaporating upward.

"Someone gave it to me," she finally said, crossing her arms.

"I don't even know what it is. I was trying to figure that out." The infomercials had shifted to the two-step pet-fur remover. Happy yellow dogs flashed across the screen. They leached into the walls. Everything about this place was godawful and decaying, with a glittering veneer.

"Do you think we're idiots?" her father said. "Don died from that shit, and you're bringing it into our house?" His voice was loud, but his body sagged in its beater, and everything carried the cadence of someone acting a role. "How could you do this to us, after everything we've done?"

And Tiff felt that flooding hot knot in her body, huffed, "After everything you've done, I fucking hate you," feeling suddenly fifteen again, then twelve, as though she was devolving, melting right there in the living room. Like she was roadkill sloughing off layers, until all that was left was a scattering of bones that could not be reassembled. The whole place stunk of dog piss, creek water.

"We enable you. That's what it is," her father said, as if he was delivering sad news, a death, a stroke, something unrecoverable. "If I called CPS right now, you'd be out of here, and you'd never see Bucky again. I don't know, should I do it?" He picked up the phone. "You tell me what I should do."

And Tiff said, "Go ahead. Then everyone will know what a fucked-up parent you are." She felt her love drain, hurled the candle off the coffee table, the magazines into the wall. She could lose Bucky. Her father could finally hold true to his word. "Funny how you never called CPS when that other thing happened," Tiff shot back, because she would call every bluff that ever existed.

When he reached to grab her arm, she bolted, out of the house, barefoot, down to the creek with the dead fish, dead trees from the fracking water, thinking maybe it'd be best if she were dead too. But as the sadness dredged out her insides, mutated and emptied the hurt and desperation, she began to refill with rage.

She would leave in the night. She would start a new life and they would never see her again. She would make sure that Bucky hated them, those hypocrites who never did a thing about that thing she refused to talk about, and now it was too late to fix it. Her brothers lived three states away, and Tiff was stuck—a bruised thing no one wanted and no one could make better. And somewhere, someone who should be locked up was free.

*

Tiff's father moved through the rooms of the house like a heavy wind, a silent nebula, a heavy, distant tide. "Tell *that girl*," he'd say to her mother, "to take Bucky outside for a change." And her mother would say, "You tell her," while Tiff stood six feet away, organizing fish sticks on a tray, bending the aluminum around them like a mass grave. Bucky played computer games. Bucky learned to use a remote. Days passed where Tiff refused to get out of bed altogether. There was no point. Without the dope, she ached and itched and shivered uncontrollably. Some Bitch refused to take her anywhere when Bucky was with her, so she was left in captivity, pacing the trailer. She was balled up on the couch. She was constipated, not eating. "Excavator," Bucky kept repeating, pressing the toy against her legs. "Dump truck!"

"You need to get a job," her mother said after work, ripping the covers off her wilted, rippling body. "Turn in applications."

"Get out of my room!" Tiff yelled, pulling the covers back. "I'm not even dressed, you fucking pervert!" Her posters from high school were curling on the walls: P.O.D., Linkin Park, hiding the holes made by hairbrushes, jewelry boxes, fists. She might as well still be sixteen.

"Are you depressed?" her mother accused. "Do you need to be medicated again?"

Every joint ached, every fiber. Even her underwear hurt.

"You're the one who needs to be medicated, crazy woman," she huffed.

Her mother switched gears. "You used to be so different," her mother said. "I don't understand what happened." But Tiff recognized this tactic too.

"You know exactly what happened," she said.

And when her mother tried once more to pull the covers away, Tiff growled, "You are a fucking terrible mother."

"And you'll be one too. Then you'll know how it feels," her mother snapped before exiting, blanket trailing like a parachute. And down the hall she heard her mother exhale: "We should have sent her away when she was in high school." And her father reply, "I told you then we should have done it." And Tiff began to feel that familiar buzzing, her skin itching, on fire, like rocks skipping on a lake above her bones. She touched her arm where the cut marks made a tiny fence line above her elbow, piano keys. She dug her nail in. "I'm getting up now. Are you happy?" she shouted,

locking the door and smoking a cigarette to help settle the aching. She pulled on a dress—something striped and faded that she
hadn't worn since she was fourteen, before she'd begun covering
her arms.

But her parents had discovered the marks anyway, had forced
her to attend exactly one therapy session. "You think the cutting
is the problem," the therapist had said during the evaluation, "but
it's a symptom."

"You're a symptom," Tiff said, crossing her legs. The walls were
decorated with scenes of sailboats, periwinkle wildflowers. "Is that
supposed to make me feel better?" She curled into herself, away
from this woman who knew nothing about her life and after she
left would never think of her again.

"You're going to find," the therapist continued, unfazed, "that
in this life, you are pushing everyone away from you, forcefully
repelling people—but really, at the core, all you want is someone close."

"I've never been repelling," Tiff said. "I have a fear of heights."

It had gone like that for the rest of the session. "Without vulnerability," the therapist finally said, closing her notebook, "you can
never really heal."

Whatever the therapist had reported to her parents, they had
never taken her back there.

Don was the reason she had finally stopped cutting, not the
therapist, not her parents. "That's rage being put inside you," he
explained to her. "You got to let that rage out." She'd beaten on
him until she really felt each hit, turned his brown chest red as
radishes, then cried into his own hurt body.

"See?" he said, kissing her head, unscathed. "You just needed
somewhere to put it." He had smelled like pepper and wild ber-
gamot. Like sun-hot fields. Sometimes she still dreamed of waking
up next to him, in the house they lost, on a mattress that Tiff had
since dragged to the curb, left in the rain to rot along with the rest
of the possessions she could not take with her.

By the time she was dressed, Bucky was the only one left in the
house. Her mother had put sticky notes on the TV, the remote,
the screen, the bathroom door: FEED PETS. But for the amount
of time it took for her to write that out, she could have fed them
herself. Tiff felt the biting, prickling anger stirring up, climbing
her throat.

"Shark?" Bucky was saying, thrusting the toy in her face. "Shark?" His diaper had leaked onto his pants, which her mother had not cleaned up before leaving. Tiff's lips ached. Her teeth ached. She couldn't find any clean diapers, stuck Bucky's feet through a plastic grocery bag, tied it in the front, which made him wail. "Don't you dare rip it off," she said. The broke remote kept freezing the TV, and the canaries began rattling their cage, pecking and scratching for food. Her entire body was buzzing, vibrating, crawling inside of itself. She threw the remote onto the couch, shook the wire birdcage, which only caused more ruckus. The air conditioner rattled in the window. Tiff grabbed the cage from the counter, lugged it out to the front porch, and hurled it into the driveway. The door popped open on impact. And before Tiff could rush to it, the birds were gone, into the wide white sky, toward the gas site that had scalped the hillside.

Tiff tried to determine how her mother was really to blame for this. She should have clipped their wings. She should have known better than to ask Tiff to feed them. Those birds never sang anyway. They were prisoners, and Tiff had done them a favor, even if they died by sundown tonight. That, Tiff decided, was the godawful truth.

She packed a suitcase. Her back hurt. Her toes hurt, her fingernails. She checked the mail again, saw a birthday card for her father, slit it and pocketed the twenty bucks, tucking the card and envelope into the side of the kitchen trash.

She texted Some Bitch about getting something. After thirty minutes and no response, Tiff moved on to a guy she'd met at the bar a few months back, had met up with a few times since—an oil-and-gas man, here from Texas for nine months, just long enough to collect a hefty paycheck and retreat from this shithole town, taking anything of value with him. When he didn't respond, she called five times in a row. Then she texted once more: "My son's sick and I need twenty bucks for a copay."

At the Red Roof Inn off the highway, she let that man come on her stomach on one of the yellowed double beds while she stared at the ashy wall. "Oh oh oh," she cried out as she finished him off in her hands, because these men always felt better believing Tiff got pleasure too. His belly heaved with relief. Then they both snorted some shit, and she felt like a person taking her first breath after falling into a cold river.

After exiting the building, she chucked her hoodie into the dumpster next to the empty outdoor pool. She couldn't stand the smell of bodies, their emissions—the rotten, sweet fragrance of them. The stucco siding looked like one of those sugar eggs that you could lick until you created a dent, a hole, like she could crawl through and keep going, into the innards of some other person's life—a businessperson, a car salesman, a cashier.

A maintenance worker carrying a few trash bags to the dumpster stopped and stared at Tiff before finally saying, "You can't loiter here."

She eyed him over. "I was visiting a friend, Jesus."

"Jesus would never be your friend," he said shortly. He looked like a toothless mannequin, a blow-up-doll version of a man. She could have crumpled him in her own two hands. "You better get on your way now."

She threw her candy wrapper onto the concrete. "Do this earth a favor and fuck off." The buzz was wearing off, and she began feeling deflated too.

He followed her through the lot. When they got to her car, she whirled to face him, raised her key between her knuckles. "I am afraid for my safety. I am going to report you to your manager."

"I see you have a car seat in there, you piece-of-shit mother," he replied. "For the record, CPS will hear from me."

"For the record, I'm a babysitter," she exclaimed. "I haven't even babysat in years, so you're the piece of shit, for assuming things you don't know shit about. And besides, this isn't even my car."

There weren't any sidewalks, so she cut through the grass. When she got around the corner by the McDonald's, her heart was chugging like an old washing machine, and between dumpsters she snorted a little of the crank she'd stolen from the guy at the motel, the stuff she'd sworn she would save for later, some cheap trucker amphetamine to keep her moving. She decided that everything could happen. Everything was a possibility. She hooted a few times like a siren into the open air. It felt good. She would make something of her life. It was true that years were lost, ruined—but there was still so much time.

Three days passed like freight cars, maybe more. Some Bitch finally called her back, but Tiff was rambling about possible futures, audio waves. She began to see cockroaches coming out of every hole, every orifice. Sleep was for the weak, and days passed in a fever. The sycamore leaves were green and flapping like condor wings, everywhere she went. The creek seemed to be inching closer to her, no matter what part of town she wandered into. Friends came and went. "They're making meth in the old mine shafts," someone was saying. "They're actually making it from nail polish remover, Jesus."

"That's bullshit," Tiff said. "They'll burn up."

But the next time she looked for that guy, there was only the peeling earth in front of her, covered by pavement, and cars on top of that. Time was a funny thing, the way it stretched and recoiled.

Her car was still in the motel lot, and once it was dark, she followed the highway home—just her and the water trucks heading toward the gas wells that speckled the hillsides. She put on Bach, a CD her father had given her as a high school graduation gift. "Thank god one of you has brains," he'd said that day. The windshield wipers swayed in B-flat minor. She felt their pain, her pain, every pain that ever existed. She saw a naked woman standing in the horse field, but when she glanced back, it was just empty floodplains.

At home she shut a window, slammed a door. Turned on the radio, the AC. When Bucky finally woke up crying, she cuddled him to her chest. "I got you, baby," she said, rocking him. "Something woke you up, huh? Something scared you." He smelled like mint and vinegar, baby powder. Her mouth emitted the heat of her sore bottom teeth, and she inhaled him like a fugue.

When things got dire again, when her mother was bitching about the lost canaries, lack of rent, threatening to kick Tiff out, Tiff called Grubber John, who said he could probably think of some ways they could help each other, and by the time Some Bitch dropped her off, Grubber John was already on the porch in a beater and Steelers cap, planting petunias with a shotgun stuffed into the earth like a sapling. "My cane!" he said. "And my widow-maker." He cleared his throat, glanced down. "Hell, I don't shoot that thing. Sorry again about your loss."

The screen door was ripped at the bottom, and a hound walked through it onto the porch, barking. "Is he friendly?" Tiff asked as Some Bitch pulled away.

"Come on and see," Grubber John said, shifting weight, and

when she did, he grabbed her in by the arm and pushed a hand-gun into her rib cage. "If you ever run your mouth or steal from me, this is what's going to get you. I want you to remember that. If you tell anyone about where we're headed, you will be buried there. I am trying to help you out because I know you got a kid. But if your loyalty wanes, your kid will no longer have a mother. Understood?"

His eyes were wide and brown and empty. He reminded Tiff of one of those alien television creatures Bucky liked to watch, like, you could fall down the rabbit hole of his eyes—while it sang and chirped and pretended to be having a wonderful day.

"I am not going to run my mouth," Tiff replied, shaking him free. "Jesus."

"Don told me if something happened to take care of you. So that's what this is. Business." He paused. "Maybe pleasure."

She followed him to the Chevy. The cornfield out front wavered like desert air. Tiff regretted not having Some Bitch along. Her bottom incisor hurt. She put some lidocaine on her gums. By the time they drove over the creek, he was slowly pressing his finger-tips against her leg, down the length of her, as though there'd been some unspoken agreement.

"You think Don meant this sort of taking care?" Tiff asked, and John replied, "In fact, he did not specify," which made Tiff want to laugh and sob and rip something to shreds. Don was a sweetheart. He would have befriended Saddam Hussein.

The hillside was eroding, shale crackled like mangy dog skin, road cut out and rocky, but between two ravines about a half a mile back, Grubber John turned off the engine. Below the heavy ridge of rock and clay, a pit entrance, shaded by crab-apple trees, sumac, milkweed, thistle. "Here we are," Grubber John said, handing her a flashlight. "We are the forgotten people, owner of the forgotten things. And this is my humble abode."

Inside, Tiff was startled by a hunched woman who looked like a hologram of a person, wavering beneath the fluorescent light fastened above her, clutching empty soda bottles. "I have paper cuts on all of my fingers," she was explaining. "I don't know why this always happens to me."

"Okay," Tiff said. "She's nuts. And this place is going to cave in on us." She'd read about the runoff. How it killed off an entire river.

"Greta works for me. She's my mom's best friend's sister and a hell of a lady," John said, redirecting her to an area of the mine that widened around the bend, where gray tarp sat beneath medicine bottles, bagged fertilizer, Tupperware, empty soda bottles. "I want you to work with me too. I know you need it."

The old shaft was damp and smelled of rotten eggs, was held up by propped railroad ties, old metal machinery that looked like the abandoned jaws of a gator. Somehow Grubber John had gotten a sofa inside the shaft, a folding table and chairs, a battery-powered radio, a few large plastic bins.

He smoked her up quickly, and Tiff felt completely, utterly alone, like time was stretching her like a rubber band, warping her into an unrecognizable thing. A hound slunk by as if it was guilty of some terrible crime, eyes glowing in the lantern light, and a caged cat in heat kept rubbing against the bars, howling. "That's my coyote bait," he said, leaning in. "I put her in that cage in a field and shoot what comes to eat her."

"That's fucked up," Tiff said.

He pressed his fingers into her wrist. "You're fucked up," he said. He let his finger trail along her collarbone, down her rib cage.

Tiff could not remember the last time someone touched her who wasn't taking something from her. The cavern was achy, and the single light shivered, like Tiff was seeing it from the bottom of a pool, and Grubber John leaned in and said, "You act all tough and mighty, but I know who you really are. You're small. You're so small, you'd fit into the palm of my hand and there'd be room to spare." He moved his knee between her unshaven legs. "I always know how to spot a girl like you."

He was right. And he was not right. Her head was cramped against the cushion, and he clutched her wrist. The woman with the bottles had disappeared. And when she closed her eyes, Grubber John smelled like a far-off campfire, the burning hot engine of a car. Like she was in the backyard of Don's and her house, grilling up burgers. When she opened them again, he was at her waist, pulling off her shorts. "You have the body of a ten-year-old child," Grubber John said, shaking his head, pulling off her underwear. The couch reeked of BO and vomit.

He didn't use a condom, moved against her roughly, saying, "Is this okay?" and Tiff focused on the glossy bituminous walls of the mine, the way the shadows pulsed like oceans, the flaking layers

of mud and stone. "The crazy ones are always wild in bed," he was
saying. And Tiff simply let her brain unplug from her body. She
did it all the time: Waiting in a long line at the Walmart. Getting
a tooth pulled. For some reason she kept seeing trees—long fans
of sumac and walnut, and weather vanes, all whirling in the same
direction. She slapped him hard in the face, in the chest, and listened to his response echo through the chambers. She thought
about bats, those canaries. How saving it would be to have wings.

"I want you here every day," John said. "Don was my boy, and
you're the mother of his child. And that means we've got to get
you right." But no one in this world was right, and then he gave
her some dope and cash—for one last spin, he explained—drove
her back to the road past his house, said, "You should probably
call someone."

Tiff walked through other people's lawns, blank as daylight, two
miles like that. She made a call to Some Bitch. Pissed in a gas-station bathroom. An hour later Some Bitch picked her up along
the road in an unfamiliar beat-up truck, foam falling from the
seat where it had been rat-chewed, split open. "Why can't you ever
come to me?" she said, hair knotted into one frayed rope.

"Do you have any Plan B?" Tiff asked. "Or Plan C?"

"You stink," Some Bitch said, rolling the windows down. "God,
you reek." She was wearing pink plastic barrettes that probably belonged to one of her daughters, and had a scab across her cheek.

"Tonight I sent Billy to his dad's," Some Bitch confessed. "I
said I'd never choose my boyfriend over my kid, but then I went
and did it, what the fuck." Tiff offered up some of her stash. They
smoked up in the Walmart lot, beneath the shivering lot lights.
Then Some Bitch eyeballed Tiff, exhaled. "At a certain point, what
is the point of going on like this?"

"The point is the sharpest part of the knife," Tiff said. "The
stabbing part."

But Some Bitch was already gone off on a tangent. "The thing
about John," she was saying, "is that he will fix your glasses and
then rob you blind. You watch him. He is never looking out for
you, I'm telling you what. I went to county for him."

"People want to pretend they're all noble and generous, but
guess what? They're not. Life is all about figuring out how to get
yours. It's your own fault you went to county, bitch."

Some Bitch tried to argue with her, but it was like taking your

car to the shop. They were always going to tell you that you needed
to buy something, to fix something that didn't need fixed. It was
all about making a buck off your back. And the government was
the biggest crook of them all. They were probably putting something in the water to rot out her teeth, cause cancer. Send out
computer viruses to sell the antidote.

The flags at the car lot across the street rippled and retracted.
Tiff inhaled and felt her entire body widen. "Better?" Some Bitch
said, driving her back. "That shit is in its prime." In the driveway of
Tiff's parents' place, Some Bitch gave her something to calm her
nerves, snorting some herself. "Valium-type shit. But now you owe
me again," she said, gaping, giggling, widening before Tiff's very
eyes. "How do you want to pay me, bitch?"

"I'll fucking pay you," Tiff said. But after that hit, time was fuzzy,
passing like a train in both directions. Tiff sank into the truck, the
world like a drill bit. It was possible that Some Bitch was her only
friend in the world. Her body felt lifted, carried, helium on a warm
night. It reminded her of the balloons released at Don's funeral.
She'd written a note in black Sharpie. Her name and number, an
outline of Bucky's hand, *I'll see you soon,* and since she never got
a call, she figured the balloons had just kept ascending, all the
way up.

When she finally woke, it was dark, and she was in her parents'
driveway covered in mosquitoes, dew. She slammed the door going
in, causing the dogs to stir and grumble. "Can it," she said, kicking
her shoes off at them. Bucky was asleep in his bedroom, cupping
the head of a ratty stuffed dog. He looked smaller in the hallway
light. The first time she'd held him, he was only two pounds, five
ounces, a month early and tubes out the wazoo. They had named
him Buckingham Prince Morris—Don thought it should be something with royalty, in case he wanted to be an actor someday. "He
would have the name for it," Don had insisted.

The hallway echoed with orange light, carpet worn down in the
center. On the door to her room, a sticky note: FEED FISH OR
MOVE OUT. When she reached into her purse for her pen to write
back, *You feed the fish,* she saw that the cash from Grubber John was
gone. The baggies were gone. Everything was gone.

The swarming, crawling heat beneath her skin returned, and
the anger beneath that. She would cut Some Bitch. She would take
her out with a shovel, like a rabid animal. She would grind her

face into the road. She slammed the door, over and over, until her mother, from her bedroom, yelled, "People are sleeping! Knock it off!"

"You assholes think you can fuck my shit up," Tiff yelled into the walls, the doorways. "The joke is on you. Everything is already fucked up. Everything is ruined, you ruined it, and nothing I can do will ruin it any further. You think I'm the asshole—but let me tell you something. You are the real assholes, you phony, ludicrous people! I will ruin everything you love. I will rip you to shreds."

She stormed into the living room and scooped one of the aquarium fish in her hand, then another, hurling them into the kitchen sink. "I'm a maniac! Is that what you want to hear?" she shouted. "I'm psychotic." With each fish, the noise they made hitting the metal, she felt a small surge of relief. And when all nine were dead and smeared across the sink bottom, Tiff began to subside, the way an ocean wave eventually reels itself back in.

She imagined her parents awake and welded together in bed, comforting each other, confirming what they'd always believed: Tiff was no good. There was something wrong with her. Tiff was a thing that had happened to them. It wasn't that she was cursed; she *was* the curse. But nothing stirred, and she used the toilet, wiped her face, shuddered like a night insect. Then she climbed into Bucky's bed, pressed her forehead against his shoulder, his tiny arm. Her wet sleeves left marks on his clothes.

"Hey, little man," she sang softly. "Who do you love more than anyone else in this world?" She cooed, "Your mama loves you, no matter what those assholes do. You know that?" She felt warm, lighter. She would go back to the mines. She would do whatever Grubber John wanted. She would work with that nut Greta, whatever it took to get right, get out of this house, get her own place, and take Bucky with her.

Tonight Bucky smelled like mint, old sweet milk. She pressed her mouth to his lip, as though he held the source to the only oxygen in the room. And when Bucky finally stirred, she said, "You having a bad dream, baby?" but he slept on, oblivious to how much Tiff loved him. Enough to consume him, she thought. What a funny way to feel about a thing you love.

Love Letter

FROM *The New Yorker*

FEBRUARY 22, 202_.

Dear Robbie,

Got your email, kid. Sorry for handwriting in reply. Not sure email-ing is the best move, considering the topic, but of course (you be-ing nearly six foot now, your mother says?) that's up to you, dear, although, you know: strange times.

Beautiful day here. A flock of geese just now came in low over the deck, and your grandmother and I, holding the bright-blue mugs you kindly sent at Christmas, did simultaneous hip swivels as they zinged off toward Rosley and, I expect, an easy meal on the golf course there.

Forgive my use of initials in what follows. Would not wish to cause further difficulties for G., M., or J. (good folks all, we very much enjoyed meeting them when you stopped by last Easter), should this get sidetracked and read by someone other than you.

I think you are right regarding G. That ship has sailed. Best to let that go. M., per your explanation, does not lack proper pa-perwork but did know, all the while, that G. did lack it, yes? And did nothing about that? Am not suggesting, of course, that she should have. But, putting ourselves into "their" heads—as I think, these days, it is prudent to try to do—we might ask, why didn't M. (again, according to them, to their way of thinking) do what she "should" have done, by letting someone in authority know about G.? Since being here is "a privilege and not a right." Are we or are we not (as I have grown sick of hearing) "a nation of laws"?

Even as they change the laws constantly to suit their own beliefs!

Believe me, I am as disgusted as you are with all this.

But the world, in my (ancient) experience, sometimes moves off in a certain direction and, having moved, being so large and inscrutable, cannot be recalled to its previous, better state, and so, in this current situation, it behooves us, I would say, to think as they think, as well as we can manage, to avoid as much unpleasantness and future harm as possible.

But of course you were writing, really, to ask about J. Yes, am still in touch with the lawyer you mentioned. Don't feel he would be much help. At this point. In his prime, he was, yes, a prince of a guy striding into a courthouse, but he is not now the man he was. He opposed, perhaps too energetically, the DOJ review/ouster of sitting judges and endured much abuse in the press and his property was defaced and he was briefly detained and these days, from what I have heard, is mostly just puttering around his yard, keeping his views to himself.

Where is J. now? Do you know? State facility or fed? That may matter. I expect "they" (loyalists) would (with the power of the courts now behind them) say that although J. is a citizen, she forfeited certain rights and privileges by declining to offer the requested info on G. & M. You may recall R. & K., friends of ours, who gave you, for your fifth (sixth?) birthday, that bronze Lincoln bank? They are loyalists, still in touch, and that is the sort of logic they follow. A guy over in Bremerton befriended a guy at the gym and they would go on runs together and so forth, and the first guy, after declining to comment on what he knew of his friend's voting past, suddenly found he could no longer register his work vehicle (he was a florist, so this proved problematic). R. & K.'s take on this: a person is "no patriot" if he refuses to answer a "simple question" from his "own homeland government."

That is where we find ourselves.

You asked if you are supposed to stand by and watch your friend's life be ruined.

Two answers: one as a citizen, the other as a grandfather.

(You have turned to me in what must be a difficult time and I am trying to be frank.)

As a citizen: I can, of course, understand why a young (intelligent, good-looking) person (perpetual delight to know, I might add) would feel that it is his duty to "do something" on behalf of his friend J.

But what, exactly?

That is the question.

When you reach a certain age, you see that time is all we have. By which I mean, moments like those overhead geese this morning, and watching your mother be born, and sitting at the dining-room table here waiting for the phone to ring and announce that a certain baby (you) had been born, or that day when all of us hiked out at Point Lobos. Those baby deer, the extremely loud seal, your sister's scarf drifting down, down to that black, briny boulder, the replacement you so generously bought her in Monterey, how pleased you made her with your kindness. Those things were real. That is what (that is all) one gets. This other stuff is real only to the extent that it interferes with those moments.

Now, you may say (I can hear you saying it and see the look on your face as you do) that this incident with J. *is* an interference. I respect that. But as your grandfather, I beg you not to underestimate the power/danger of this moment. Perhaps I haven't told you this yet: in the early days I wrote two letters to the editor of the local rag, one overwrought, the other comic. Neither had any effect. Those who agreed with me agreed with me; those who did not remained unpersuaded. After a third attempt was rejected, I found myself pulled over, up near the house, for no reason I could discern. The cop (nice guy, just a kid, really, from my perspective) asked what I did all day. Did I have any hobbies? I said no. He said, *Some of us heard you like to type.* I sat in my car, looking over at his large, pale arm. His face was the face of a kid. His arm, though, was the arm of a man.

How would you know about that? I said.

Have a good night, sir, he said. *Stay off the computer.*

Good Lord, his stupidity and bulk there in the darkness, the metallic clanking from his belt area, the palpable certainty he seemed to feel regarding his cause, a cause I cannot begin, even at this late date, to get my head around, or view from within, so to speak.

I do not want you anywhere near, or under the sway of, that sort of person, ever.

I feel here a need to address the last part of your email, which (I want to assure you) did not upset me or "hurt my feelings." No. When you reach my age, and if you are lucky enough to have a grandson like you (stellar), you will know that nothing that that grandson could say could ever hurt your feelings, and in fact I am so touched that you thought to write me in your time of need and be so direct and even (I admit it) somewhat rough with me.

Seen in retrospect, yes: I have regrets. There was a certain critical period. I see that now. During that period your grandmother and I were doing, every night, a jigsaw puzzle each, at that dining-room table I know you know well, we were planning to have the kitchen redone, were in the midst of having the walls out in the yard rebuilt at great expense, I was experiencing the first intimations of the dental issues I know you have heard so much (too much?) about. Every night, as we sat across from each other, doing those puzzles, from the TV in the next room blared this litany of things that had never before happened, that we could never have imagined happening, that were now happening, and the only response from the TV pundits was a wry, satirical smugness that assumed, as we assumed, that those things could and would soon be undone and that all would return to normal—that some adult or adults would arrive, as they had always arrived in the past, to set things right. It did not seem (and please destroy this letter after you have read it) that someone so clownish could disrupt something so noble and time-tested and seemingly strong, that had been with us literally every day of our lives. We had taken, in other words, a profound gift for granted. Did not know the gift was a fluke, a chimera, a wonderful accident of consensus and mutual understanding.

Because this destruction was emanating from such an inept source, who seemed (at that time) merely comically thuggish, who seemed to know so little about what he was disrupting, and because life was going on, and because every day he/they burst through some new gate of propriety, we soon found that no genuine outrage was available to us anymore. If you'll allow me a crude metaphor (as I'm sure you, the King of las Bromas de Fartos, will): A guy comes into a dinner party, takes a dump on the rug in the living room. The guests get all excited, yell in protest. He takes a second dump. The guests feel, Well, yelling didn't help. (While some of them applaud his audacity.) He takes a third dump, on the table, and still no one throws him out. At that point the sky has become the limit in terms of future dumps.

So although your grandmother and I, during this critical period, often said, you know, "Someone should arrange a march" or "Those f___ing Republican senators," we soon grew weary of hearing ourselves saying those things and, to avoid being old people emptily repeating ourselves, stopped saying those things, and did our puzzles and so forth, waiting for the election.

I'm speaking here of the second, not the third (of the son), which, being a total sham, didn't hurt (surprise) as much.

Post-election, doing new puzzles (mine a difficult sort of Catskills summer scene), noting those early pardons (which, by the time they were granted, we'd been well prepared to expect, and tolerate), and then that deluge of pardons (each making way for the next), and the celebratory verbal nonsense accompanying the pardons (to which, again, we were by this time somewhat inured), and the targeting of judges, and the incidents in Reno and Lowell, and the investigations into pundits, and the casting aside of term limits, we still did not really believe in the thing that was happening. Birds still burst out of the trees and so forth.

I feel I am disappointing you.

I just want to say that history, when it arrives, may not look as you expect, based on the reading of history books. Things in there are always so clear. One knows exactly what one would have done.

Your grandmother and I (and many others) would have had to be more extreme people than we were, during that critical period, to have done whatever it was we should have been doing. And our lives had not prepared us for extremity, to mobilize or to be as focused and energized as I can see, in retrospect, we would have needed to be. We were not prepared to drop everything in defense of a system that was, to us, like oxygen: used constantly, never noted. We were spoiled, I think I am trying to say. As were those on the other side: willing to tear it all down because they had been so thoroughly nourished by the vacuous plenty in which we all lived, a bountiful condition that allowed people to thrive and opine and swagger around like kings and queens while remaining ignorant of their own history.

What would you have had me do? What would you have done? I know what you will say: you would have fought. But how? How would you have fought? Would you have called your senator? (In those days you could still at least record your feeble message on a senator's answering machine without reprisal, but you might as well have been singing or whistling or passing wind into it for all the good it did.) Well, we did that. We called, we wrote letters. Would you have given money to certain people running for office? We did that as well. Would you have marched? For some reason there were suddenly no marches. Organized a march? Then and now, I did not and do not know how to arrange a march. I was still working full-time. This dental thing had just begun. That rather occupies the mind. You know where we live: Would you have had me go down to Waterville and harangue the officials there? They were all in agreement with us. At that time. Would you have armed yourself? I would not and will not, and I do not believe you would either. I hope not. By that, all is lost.

Let me, at the end, return to the beginning. I advise and implore you: stay out of this business with J. Your involvement will not help (especially if you don't know where they have taken her, fed or state) and may in fact hurt. I hope I do not offend if I here use the phrase "empty gesture." Not only would J.'s situation be made worse, so might that of your mother, father, sister, grandmother, grandfather, etc., etc. Part of the complication is that you are not alone in this.

I want you well. I want you someday to be an old fart yourself, writing a (too) long letter to a (beloved) grandson. In this world we speak much of courage and not, I feel, enough about discretion and caution. I know how that will sound to you. Let it be. I have lived this long and have the right.

It occurs to me only now that you and J. may be more than just friends.

That, if the case, would, I know, (must) complicate the matter.

I had, last night, a vivid dream of those days, of that critical pre-election period. I was sitting across from your grandmother, she at work on her puzzle (puppies and kittens), I on mine (gnomes in trees), and suddenly we saw, in a flash, things as they were, that is, we realized that this was the critical moment. We looked at each other across the table with such freshness, if I may say it that way, such love for each other and for our country, the country in which we had lived our whole lives, the many roads, hills, lakes, malls, byways, villages we had known and moved about and around in so freely.

How precious and dear it all seemed.

Your grandmother stood, with that decisiveness I know you know.

"Let us think of what we must do," she said.

Then I woke. There in bed I felt, for a brief instant, that it was *that* time again and not *this* time. Lying there, I found myself wondering, for the first time in a long while, not *What should I have done?* but *What might I yet do?*

I came back to myself, gradually. It was sad. A sad moment. To be once again in a time and place where action was not possible.

I wish with all my heart that we could have passed it on to you intact. I do. That is, now, not to be. That regret I will take to my grave. Wisdom, now, amounts to making such intelligent accommodations as we can. I am not saying stick your head in the sand. J. made a choice. I respect her for it. And yet. No one is calling on you to do anything. You are, in my view, doing much good simply by rising in the morning, being as present and kind as possible, keeping sanity alive in the world, so that someday, when (if) this thing passes, the country may find its way back to normalcy, with your help and the help of those like you.

In this, you are, and I am, I hope, like cave people, sheltering a small, remaining trace of fire through a dark period.

But please know that I understand how hard it must be to stay silent and inactive if in fact J. was more than just a friend. She is a lovely person and I recall her crossing our yard with her particular grace and brio, swinging your car keys on that long silver chain, her dog (Whiskey?) running there beside her.

I feel I have made my preference clear, above. I say what follows not to encourage. But: we have money (not much, but some) set aside. Should push come to shove. I am finding it hard to advise you. Please let us know what you are inclined to do, as we find that this (you) is all that we now can think of.

With much love, more than you can know,

GPa.

A Way with Bea

FROM *The Paris Review*

BEA WALKS INTO the classroom wearing the clothes she had on the day before. The Teacher understands that this is going to be a bad day. Bea's hair is uncombed, face unwashed. She arrives precisely twelve seconds late. Not so late that the Teacher *has* to make a big deal about it. But not on time. Bea walks like a prisoner forcibly escorted, snatching herself along, step by step, then pouring her thin body into the seat. She has no books, no pencil or paper. She drapes herself over the desk and waits for the Teacher to continue or challenge.

The Teacher rides the L two stops from the school and into an entirely different country. Chicago pieces itself together that way. The platform at her station offers a clear view of the rear deck of her condo and she always looks. Sometimes she hopes to catch her husband there with a woman, a stranger or a friend, his hand invading the buttons of this woman's shirt, taking a fistful of her breast. This has never happened. She is relieved and disappointed. Occasionally she catches him grilling in the brown sandals she hates. She feels like a spy trying to decipher her own life.

The Teacher grew up in the country and has seen things die the right way. You can't die right in the city. There's no place to take yourself off to be alone with your thoughts and the last wind you will ever feel. In the living room, her husband reads a magazine with his ancient cat on his lap. She has told him that it is far past

time for that cat. He was disgusted by her cruelty. She shouldn't
have married a man from the city.

The Teacher dissects Bea as the girl walks toward her classroom.
*She looks like a doll made for tea parties that was thrown outside to fend
for itself.* A nobility lives in Bea's bones, an ancient, undiluted
beauty that most eyes have forgotten. She grows in angles. The
broadness of her nose and the wide, sculpted divot leading down
to her lips and the deep, delicate hollows behind her collarbone.
The disorder of her swarming hair, misshapen and dusty, but still
a laurel.

The Teacher raises a glass to her friend the Engineer, who has
been promoted. The Teacher can't afford this restaurant, but the
Advertising Executive will pay. She always pays. They crowd around
a laptop, perfumes mingling, to watch her latest car commercial.
The waiters weave around the obstruction. Someone asks about
the Lawyer's big case that has not been decided yet. The Other
Lawyer handles lucrative but ethically disgusting cases that no one
asks about. The Teacher knows how her friends imagine her in
class, as sure as a mother goose, with students trailing obediently
behind. Every gathering, she is sainted anew for her work. She
regains a bit of purpose and savors it as long as she can, until it
evaporates, processed into the air of the school.

Bea announces that the endoplasmic reticulum has been drawn
in the wrong place. She walks up to the board, showing the class
her fearless back, and wipes at the drawing of a cell. She rakes
the chalk across the blackboard with the concentration of a doctor repairing a beating heart. This happens with these children.
Every now and again, their bellies are full enough, a lesson hits
them in the right way, or they have paused their channel-surfing
to learn about it in a documentary. The Teacher knows better
than to get too excited. Next week Bea will be hungry and falli-
ble.

Bea's brother is Aldous. Which means her mother is Flora. Flora is
regarded less as a person than as a familiar, chaotic fixture of the
neighborhood. A tiny woman singing in a drunken chorus with
men or a scabby statue sleeping soundly in empty lots. Bea doesn't

have to take home a report card. Ever. No one will make generic
parental demands for better grades. The Teacher returns to herself at Bea's age and begins crafting infinite versions of her life.
She wonders what terrible things such freedom would have done
to her.

The Teacher considers asking Bea if she can comb her hair for
her. *Girl, sit down and let me give you some twists.* The Teacher thinks
of Bea arriving early in the morning. She will bring her own count-
er-sized vats and silos of grease and gel. She will give her archi-
tect-straight parts. She will oil the girl's scalp, her finger pointing
down each tender row. And then the girl will go to Stanford and
then Flora will get off drugs. No. Too much, even for fantasy. The
ask curdles on her tongue.

The Teacher stands in the laundry closet and fishes the net bag
containing her bras out of the washing machine. Her gaze falls
on the domed hood of the litter box and she starts. She has not
seen the cat for days. In fact, she forgot that they even had a cat.
Her husband jumps when she races into the bedroom. "Where's
the cat?" she pants. He holds the information for a beat as her
punishment, then points to his closet. Did this man put a dead
cat in the closet? The fact that she has to wonder makes her feel
such embarrassment for him that she turns away. She walks to the
closet and unfolds the fan doors slowly, so as to not disturb sleep
or death. On the bottom of the shallow closet the cat seems flat
and shapeless like the discarded clothes surrounding it, an abandoned vessel that life no longer occupies. But the cat has looked
this way for months now, so the Teacher reaches out to gently,
gently rub an ear.

Lately when the Teacher receives her most cherished compliment,
a toneless voice in her mind responds with such swiftness that the
words feel like facts. You're a great teacher. *Not as great as your
grandmother, your great-aunt, or your cousin.* You're a great teacher.
Not as great as the National Teacher of the Year. You're a great teacher.
You aren't even the best in this shitty little school. You're a great teacher.
*There is absolutely no proof of that. You teach science. There has to be proof
or it can't be true.*

*

Bea does not walk into the classroom and the Teacher is afraid. Bea only comes to school because it is a relatively safe place to be during the day. Girls who find other safe places for the day usually return multiplied into two people in one way or another.

The Teacher walks into her empty classroom, and the urge to throw a tantrum is so strong her arms shoot up from her sides before she stops them. She had been so proud that she had made her classroom pleasing to the eye. She had been just *biblically* prideful that she had found a modern design that organized the chaos of the body into three colors and three harmonious fonts. Against Bea's empty seat, Bea's crisped edges, every lesson the Teacher has to teach seems trivial. The bell rings. The Teacher allows her arms to soften.

The Teacher puts down her fork and stares at her husband. A worn white tablecloth edged in lace tries to put her in the spirit of their honeymoon. But it is hard to remember the man who grinned at her across lopsided wooden tables in tiny restaurants in the Caribbean while looking at him here with his mouth only half lifted in a smirk. She leans back, withdrawing from him. "I am aware that teaching is not going to be like a made-for-TV movie or an after-school special, and fuck you," says the Teacher.

The next morning the Teacher feels a little better about herself because Bea has never brought her to tears. The English Teacher is getting out of her Jetta. Bea has wrung tears out of her, twice. As expected, the tears improved nothing for anyone. The Teacher's Blackness has given her the gift of mastery over her tear ducts. In her entire life there has been no benefit to expressing sorrow or anger or frustration or pain, so the Teacher offers Bea none. She understands that Bea cannot offer her any. They will have to find something else to exchange.

Bea walks into class without a look in the Teacher's direction. She wears clothes from the emergency closet. A pair of purple corduroy pants cut in a reasonably popular fashion. A white sweater that has lost all its comforting softness. The Teacher wonders if Bea knows what it is like to find comfort in the things wrapped around your body.

*

The next day Bea walks into class in a dress a size too small, with tiny yellow and green flowers on a bright blue background. It is a strange juxtaposition with her feline face. The impatience of her eyes. If other students do not answer questions to her liking, she raises her hand. She has the right answer or a sullen question that shows that she understands the complex interactions of the brain. When Bea's arm climbs into the air, the Teacher worries that the too-small dress will give and she will burst in the classroom, petals everywhere.

On the way to the train the Teacher speed-walks through the corner store to buy a certain thick, grape-flavored drink her husband loves. When her friends call it Ghetto Grape, the Teacher feels her face tighten. She moves through the store so fast that she almost misses Aldous, Bea's brother. Slow and ponderous in front of the Hostess cupcakes. He stares at the selection, brand-new in their packages and already stale.

The Teacher and her husband wander Home Depot. Her husband loves Home Depot, but she has no idea why. He is limited to sections he can choose completed items from, like plants, appliances, or grills. He buys nothing here that has to come from here. The Teacher walks away from him and into the aisles of more challenging equipment. The Teacher eavesdrops on the men around her, agreeing and disagreeing with their assessments of the best tool for the job. She touches the soft splinters in lumber, rattles a bin of nails, cups her palm around pipes. Her father and great-aunts taught her how to fix things. She finds her husband, tall and handsome, carrying a box of light bulbs and looking for her.

Bea has been confined in the Principal's conference room. The Teacher considers sneaking in but watches through the glass panel instead. The girl carefully unwraps a Hershey's Kiss. She uses a dirty nail with streaks of mucus-green polish to scrape the foil away, then tugs lightly at the branded ribbon still stuck to the chocolate. The Teacher feels a soul-deep respect for this girl's calm.

Down the hall, the faculty lounge crackles with some new sin. The English Teacher says, "Did you hear about Bea? She cut up a bird with scissors." The Teacher pauses. Imagines a bird. Imagines Bea.

Imagines scissors. Silver with lightly pockmarked black handles. She hears the metal open and close. She tries to turn it into a weapon. She can't put these pieces together. But she can feel the teachers' fear under the hissing indignation. She is embarrassed for them.

The clump of skin and tissue and organs smeared across a paper plate on the desk seems to demand that everyone in the Principal's office remain standing as they discuss what to do about Bea. The Teacher pushes hard against people a teacher isn't supposed to push against. "This thing has been dead for days," she says. She pounds her fist on the desk and sends shame vibrating through them all. The featherless oddity bounces in agreement. "Did anyone see her kill it? Send that girl back to class."

Bea is snapping her gum. The powerful cracks echo off the smooth surfaces in the classroom, incorrectly punctuating the Teacher's lesson. For a while Bea entertains herself by leaving the air empty and then firing off a round, making the girl next to her jump. This is a direct challenge, and the Teacher gets angry. She has an unspoken agreement with Bea, built on respect that she is not at all sure is mutual. She is supposed to have a way with Bea.

Bea does not walk into the classroom and has not walked into the classroom for four days now. The Teacher closes her eyes, feeling her worth orbiting that one empty seat. She knows she shouldn't be thinking this way.

The Teacher attempts to be honest with herself about why she sent Bea to the office five days ago. When she examines the moment, she hears the sound of Bea's final snap of gum, as sharp as clapping hands. When she examines her anger, she detects the unprofessional residue of feeling betrayed. She assumes that Bea will not come walking into her classroom for a fifth day, but she does. Bea is so attentive in class that the Teacher is afraid the girl is setting her up.

For three weeks straight, Bea arrives on time. Her supplies are in a black canvas satchel with a flap over the top. It is the first

time the Teacher has seen her hold anything close and carefully. It sits on her lap the entire class. She is clean underneath
a new, age-inappropriate veneer. Her hair has been seized and
shaped into a stiff box of weave on her head, and cheap, bright
pink lipstick streaks across her mouth. She has been cared for.
The Teacher unearths another thought: she wishes that the
girl's caretakers were classier. That evening on the L she brings
that thought out again and again and lets it sit, stinking, beside
her.

Bea waits for the Teacher in the classroom. The Teacher is shocked,
shocked. Thudding heart. She has not thought out a play. She bus-
ies herself at her desk after a short greeting. They are alone for
thirty long seconds. It occurs to the Teacher that maybe Bea has
something to say, and she lifts her head and raises her eyebrows,
ready to receive. The moment is gone.

The Gym Teacher does not shake easily but she is shaken. She
says, "I think that girl has an eyeball in her book bag. An *eyeball.*" A
laugh rises from the Teacher's throat before she can stop it.

Bea walks into class thirty seconds early without her prized black
canvas satchel. Instead she has a plastic grocery bag with a chorus of *thank yous* printed on the side. She comes to the Teacher's
desk like a doe to a fence. Today she wears clean clothes and the
Teacher's wish has been granted. Bea's face is washed. There is no
ridiculous weave.

The Teacher's husband has flown to the other side of the planet
on business. His cat chooses four days after his departure as the
day to leak shit on the carpet and die.

The Teacher knows of two ways to get animal bones so smooth
and glossy they seem unreal, almost manufactured. She remem-
bers her great-aunts, the unsentimental efficiency of their land,
soft denim coveralls, and a summertime discovery of luminous
little skulls. The life in good Alabama soil can do all the work,
reclaiming the meat and polishing the bones. That's one way. The
other is to boil them.

*

Aldous cups his hands under the brown running water and over
and over he pours water into Bea's hair. He has placed a slightly
sour towel across her shoulders. He adds a gummy, clear hair gel
that was abandoned in the bathroom by a girl who doesn't come
over anymore. Most of the hairbrush's milky-blue plastic handle
has broken off, but he clutches the stump in an underhand fist.
He brushes until her hair goes limp across his wide fingers. He
loops a rubber band around the handful of hair, suspicious of
his work, wondering if it will hold. He steps away. Bea does not
smile, but she does not take it down. Both children slink into
the morning.

The Teacher had offered Bea a window of time to pick up irresistible contraband, a biology textbook from a better school dis-
trict. In preparation for the girl's visit, she has manufactured a
number of coincidences. Inside her refrigerator ten sandwiches
in wax paper form a sacred tower. The oaty fullness of good wheat
bread, the sharp tang of mustard, the smooth paper with creases
like gifts, all carefully conjured from her own childhood. She is
practicing a casual *I made too many for my nephew, you wanna try
one? Take a few home?* A plump yellow timer on the stove will ting at
the end of the lesson. *Would you like to stay for dinner?* In the closet
is an almost-new denim satchel with a flap over the top. *Oh, you
need something to carry all this stuff.* She gives last looks around her
home, her classroom, the set. Everything is pulled taut and ready
to snare.

The Teacher will tell her husband that she took care of his cat.

Haguillory

FROM *Zoetrope: All-Story*

WHEN HAGUILLORY WOKE at four-thirty and went to the kitchen in his shorts and slippers, Dot was already there at the table, tanked up on coffee. He poured himself a cup without much looking at his wife. Outside the kitchen window, his tomatoes blushed in the moonlight. The blue crabs down in the Sabine marshes would have been gorging all night under that bright full moon, and this morning Haguillory planned to catch some.

He fixed his coffee and pretended there was nothing strange about Dot sitting up before dawn, when she was usually in bed until nine or ten. Her joints kept her awake late, and on top of that, she'd get herself all agitated watching the nightly news or reading the paper. How she could stand it, he didn't know; it was always the same thing: New Orleans this, Katrina that, like those people were the only ones who'd been hit by a storm.

In the wee hours she would finally bump down the hall to sleep in the extra room, the one that used to be for the kids, and wake Haguillory on the way, dropping her dishes in the sink, closing doors harder than she needed to. Lord, did she make some racket moving around the house. Then she'd stay in that room, with the door shut, until long after sunrise. Maybe she was sleeping, or maybe she was sick of his face. He was sick of hers too, most days.

Never mind, though. At least Haguillory could, in the quiet solitude, wholly inhabit the kitchen: coffeepot, preserves, dainty demitasse cups and silverware Dot saved for company. He played house in the morning dark. He even cleaned up after himself.

But it was different with her sitting there. He had learned, in his five years of retirement, that if he helped with housework, she yelled, whereas if he left a trail of dirt and crumbs as he went about his day, she rewarded him with a petulant silence. So now he spilled some sugar on the counter, stirred and sloshed coffee out of the cup, then left the spoon on top of the pot. For good measure, he swept the spilled sugar to the floor.

She spoke anyway. "I'm going with you this morning. I done put some Cokes in the cooler, and I had my bath. Go get your clothes on."

"Tide don't come in till nine," he lied.

"I want to see how things are down there."

"About the same as last time. No point looking at it again."

"How could it be the same? That was months ago." She grabbed hold of the table's edge, rocked a couple of times, and pulled herself creaking and popping out of the chair. "Let's beat the crowd," she said.

"We don't got to go *now*."

But she was already out the door.

This early, the August day was an oven set to *warm*. By midmorning they'd be back up to *broil*, and Dot would be spitting mean —mean as a cat with its tail on fire.

Haguillory stalled in the garden, picking a few nearly ripe tomatoes and unloading a vine of dewy string beans. The lawn beyond was littered with wilted leaves and pecans, still in their green husks, all fallen into his yard from the neighbor's tree, just across the property line. He gathered the nuts in a flap of untucked shirt. The moon hanging in the dark sky shone through the bare branches. It was dying, that tree, no question. Well, good.

For all old Matherne had to know, the storm could have done that. Haguillory's own trees hadn't been the same since Rita hit last year. They were gaunt and crooked. There was sun in the yard where there used to be shade. One of the oaks had dropped its thickest limb through his roof, right over the living room. When he and Dot had come home, almost a week after the storm, he found his favorite chair soaked and growing black paisleys of mildew; it had to be put to the street, along with the end table he'd built, and the TV remote control, and his fishing magazines, and his lamp, and the vibrating pad for his back. All ruined.

On his way to the garage, Haguillory dumped the pecans noisily into the garbage can. Then he loaded the nets, twine, cooler, tackle box, fishing rod, and a couple of lawn chairs into the bed of the truck.

Dot, in the cab, had twisted her head around to watch him. She was saying something through the glass. When he opened the driver's door, she said, "I was trying to tell you to grab me a hat."

He slunk his hand behind the bench seat and pulled out the lopsided, sweat-stained straw contraption that their son, Danny, used to wear when Haguillory took him fishing, just the two of them, father and son. But they didn't do that anymore. His son didn't come around much at all—not since Haguillory spoke his mind about that child Danny and his wife adopted two years ago out of some country he'd never heard of. They already had a kid of their own. Why did they need another one? The hat was dry-rotted and raveling at the rim and too big for Dot's head, but she had the good sense to keep her mouth shut about it.

He had planned to pick up a package of melt at the grocery around the corner before heading south into the marsh, but after parking outside the store, he saw that it didn't open until six.

"*Mais,* I could have told you that," Dot said. "We can stop in Hackberry."

"They won't have melt."

"What you think? Sulphur is the only town with melt? They have melt in Hackberry."

"I don't know if that store is still standing."

"It is. It was on the news."

Her and her news.

In the truck cab, they were as close as they had been, physically speaking, in a very long time. They did not sleep in the same bed anymore. They did not eat together at the same table. They did not visit the same friends; or rather, Dot visited the same friends, and Haguillory visited no one at all. She'd been especially prickly after that week of evacuation last fall at Danny's house up in De-Ridder. Well, that hadn't been fun for anyone. Air mattresses on the floor. Fighting for the television or, when the power went out, for the lanterns and battery-powered fans, or, days later, for the better MREs. Their daughter, Carol, with that good-for-nothing boyfriend of hers, sharing a mattress in front of everybody. And the adopted child, not quite right, with her foreign lisp and feline eyes. She was about ten, just a few years older than Danny's natural son, and you could see the little boy tense up whenever she got too close, like a dog expecting a kick. There was that screaming fit she'd thrown, with a fork in her hand, when she got the ham-slice MRE instead of the chili and macaroni. Haguillory said, so she could hear, that they ought to send her back to where she came from, if it was so bad here. The girl had to learn. Dot hadn't liked that at all. But what? Did she think he had fun saying that kind of truth?

Now here they were, in the truck, with nothing to listen to but AM radio and each other coughing, snuffling, and throat-clearing. Between Lake Charles and Hackberry they spoke only once, about a quarter of an hour into the drive. With the light coming up, they could see a storm building in the west, and a few vanguard clouds above. From time to time the sky spat on their windshield. They drove by a pasture that held a herd of red cows.

"Look at them cows," Haguillory said. "They all in a clump. Gonna get some rain today."

Dot clucked her tongue. "Them cows are scattered."

"Aw!" said Haguillory.

The Hackberry store was indeed standing, although a third of its roof was draped in blue plastic. Across the street, a house that had been neatly halved by a fallen oak tree was fronted by a FEMA trailer. The pasture beside the store had been turned into an appliance graveyard, filled with row upon row of taped-up refrigerators and freezers, ruined washers, dryers, and stoves. A fridge on the outer row said, in red, spray-painted letters, *Do not open! Insurance adjuster inside!*

Haguillory laughed.

The store, which was the last stop before you got to the oil reserve, was busy, even this early, with young men in their industrial blues getting fried chicken and pizza slices from the hot bar for their lunch. Dot waddled along beside Haguillory, then stopped, picked up a package of boudin on sale, and took out her glasses to read the label. He didn't wait for her.

Behind the meat counter, a sleepy teenager was wrapping up a pound of shrimp for an old man in sagging khaki coveralls and a cap. When it came his turn, Haguillory tapped the glass and asked the boy how much the night crawlers were.

"What we need night crawlers for?" Dot said, pulling up next to him. "We don't need no night crawlers."

"If I want to fish!" Haguillory snapped. "How much you asking for them?"

"Two dollars," the boy said.

"Shoo! Two dollars for some worms?"

The teenager said nothing.

Haguillory hovered for a while, then finally slid the glass back and reached down to pluck one of the little Styrofoam boxes from the stack. He opened the lid and peered into the dirt. A thick pink segment of worm throbbed on the surface.

"You just looking to *lamentation*," Dot said.

"How many they got in here?" Haguillory asked.

"I don't know. A bunch." The teenager looked around for another customer.

"Two pounds of melt," Dot said, stepping past her husband.

"No melt today."

"Aw!" said Haguillory.

"We'll get us some chicken necks instead," Dot said.

"You think the crabs don't know the difference?"

"The crabs *don't* know the difference."

It was almost full daylight when Haguillory and Dot at last got themselves established in the lawn chairs on the footbridge that crossed the canal. From each of four pilings they dangled a chicken neck on a length of twine. The marsh grass shivered in a little bit of a breeze. Dense, iron-blue clouds were mustering to the west, but they had a few good hours before the storm would break here. The truck was parked nearby, on the highway median, and they could get to it fast.

Every few minutes Haguillory, restless, would rise from his chair and take one of the lines in hand, ever so gently easing the bait up from the depths of the brackish water until it appeared just below the surface. If he felt a tug or spied a dogged claw, he'd say, "Pass me that net! Quick! Quick!"

But Dot was seldom quick. Sometimes she was distracted, fussing in her purse for a hankie or for aspirin, which she was taking in handfuls, or for whatever else was knocking around in that apparently bottomless sack. But when she was quick, she was too quick, and her passing shadow would send the crab skittering back into the murk.

"What, you never caught a crab before?" he said.

They had been out there a little more than two hours and had netted exactly five crabs when another car pulled in behind their truck. Before the brake lights had even gone off, a woman threw open the passenger door and charged down the gravel shoulder toward the footbridge, shaking her head and mouthing what could only be curses. Two boys, maybe eight and ten, emerged, sheepish, from the backseat and trailed after her. The smaller one wore a huge T-shirt that swallowed his shoulders and reached to his knees. They were all of them in white rubber shrimping boots many sizes too big. The driver killed the motor and opened his door. He leaned against the car, resting his crossed arms on the roof and looking after the woman and the boys. A baseball cap cut a shadow across his eyes and cheeks.

The woman stopped suddenly, turned around. She flung her arms over her head and dropped them to her sides. "Are you sure this is where?" she yelled back at the man. The man half nodded, half shrugged, and a frustrated growl came from the woman's chest. She set off again for the bridge. "Perkins!" she called out. "Mr. Perks!"

The boys started too—a chirping chorus of "Perkins! Perkins!" —the older one louder and more zealous.

"Lord have mercy," Haguillory said.

Dot reached into the cooler, past the clattering crabs, for an RC Cola and a root beer. "Here," she said. "Drink your root beer." She took off her shoes and wriggled her toes. She was red-faced and sweating. The church bulletin she'd folded into a fan wasn't doing her much good.

The woman was now before them. The two boys clomped up in their big white boots and hung on the railing, one casting his eyes out across the marsh, the other down into the water.

"Y'all seen a cat around here?" the woman said. She looked like a shriveled little monkey, Haguillory thought, with a sharp little monkey face and angry, clasping monkey hands. Her bristly peroxide hair stood up straight and square, like a fez.

"We ain't seen no cat out here," Haguillory said.

"What does it look like?" Dot asked.

"That son of a bitch back there," the woman said, jerking her head back toward the car in the median; and the younger boy's shoulders hunched up to his ears.

That son of a bitch, presumably the boys' father, was now mounting the bridge, hands in pockets, toothpick in teeth. "Any luck?" he said, looking at no one, and he could have meant the crabs or the cat.

"He don't have any *claws,*" the woman said, and stalked off, over the bridge and into the grass. "Perkins!" she yelled.

The older boy followed her, and the younger one hung back, still gazing down into the water. Their father leaned against the bridge railing next to him. Behind them, the woman and the older boy were fanning out into the marsh in lurching, sloshing steps, parting the cordgrass with their hands as they went and calling the cat.

"Y'all catching any?" the man said.

"Just enough to make you mad," Haguillory said.

"Really?" the man said. "I'm surprised. The crabs been going nuts since the storm knocked out those flood weirs. Still pretty high salt, even into Sweet Lake."

"It ain't for lack of crabs," Haguillory said.

Dot cut him a pair of eyes, and he took up his fishing rod. He opened the container he'd bought at the store and tugged a night crawler out of the dirt. He pinched it in two, tossed half back in, and threaded the other half onto the hook. About three feet up the line, he attached a plastic cork, then wiped his gooey fingers on his coveralls. He scooted his chair closer to the water and dropped the line in. He'd see what else was there to be caught.

"*Mais,* what?" Dot said to the man. "You dumped her cat in the marsh?"

"He kept peeing on my bunk," the younger one said quietly, then squatted, stretched the T-shirt over his knees, and tucked it under the toes of his boots. He pulled on one of the crab lines, hand over hand, as slowly as if he were creeping up on a rabbit. After a while he reached out an arm, fluttered his fingers. "There's a big one on here. Gimme the net. I'll pull it in for you." But nobody gave him the net. "There it goes," he said, sighing.

"Y'all can't imagine what it's like," the boy's father said. "Three adults, two kids, and a incontinent cat. In a ten-by-thirty-foot box? Nobody can live like that. It's been almost a year!" He stripped off his hat and beat it against his thigh.

"*Ç'est un bonrien,* that FEMA," Haguillory said. He spat into the canal. This young fella and his family, that little boy with his shirt too big—they'd never show *that* on the news. It was sad, how they forgot about some people, not about others. He himself was still waiting on payment for the damage Rita had done to his roof. "I'm sick to death of Katrina," he said. "You don't hear about nothing else!"

He was fixing to say more—about all the people in this world, like those looters in flooded New Orleans or that little adopted girl at Danny's, who seemed to think their suffering entitled them to inflict suffering on others—when the cork on his fishing line dipped below the surface. He jerked the rod to the right, stood up from his chair, and began reeling in the line, the tip of the rod arching and quivering with the weight of whatever was down there tugging. What was down there was a little garfish, about a foot and a half long, maybe two pounds.

Haguillory grabbed it behind the gills. "Reach me those pliers," he said to Dot, and she did. "Young man," he said, "you know what that is?"

The boy came closer, eyed the fish. "That's a gar."

"That's one ugly fish," Haguillory said, and he felt the ugliness in a frisson down his spine. The eel-like body, the long jaws opening and closing, the needle teeth and staring eyes, the blood pooling around the hook in its cheek. He yanked out the bare hook; then he wrapped the pliers around the base of the gar's snout. Those night crawlers didn't come cheap. "Watch what I do with that fish," he said, and he squeezed until, with a crunch, the snout snapped off and fell to the planks at his feet. The little fish thrashed in his hand, working what was left of its jaw. Haguillory leaned over the railing and dropped the fish back into the water. He wiped his hands on his coveralls and sat. "Now," he said to the boy. "You see?"

"Yes, sir," the boy said, and looked up at his father.

"Those are trash fish," the man said. He jammed his hat backward onto the boy's head and gave the brim a little tug. "I never could eat those, myself."

Dot made that noise with her tongue. *"T'a pas honte!"* she said. She got up, wobbly, and crossed the bridge, following the path to the marsh. Out there in the grass, the woman was shouting something at the older boy. Dot reached the end of the path, held out one arm for balance, and tested the mucky ground with her foot.

"You going to fall over if you try that," Haguillory said, but she didn't listen. Fine. Let her break a hip. Was it his fault the gar was an ugly fish?

He lifted his tackle box onto his lap and dug around until he found a multitool that he'd won as a door prize at one of the gumbo luncheons the painters' union put on. It had pliers, a screwdriver, a knife, a toothpick: a good little tool. He never used it. He held it out to the boy. "You want that?"

The boy shrugged. "Sure," he said, and took it. The tool disappeared under his T-shirt.

"Tell the man thank you," the boy's father said.

"Thank you."

"I'm sorry for y'all," Haguillory said.

The sky had gone dark in the time since this family had arrived, the storm nearly upon them. To the west, a single, stunning bolt of lightning touched the marsh, chased by a whipcrack of thunder.

The boy ducked and cringed like a little animal, then glanced at his father and smiled, embarrassed.

"We better get going," the man said. He called out to the woman and the older boy, but they were already coming back.

Dot was talking with the woman, who was moving her hands, excited. She pointed, back toward Hackberry and the direction from which they had come, then swung her finger around to the man on the bridge and jabbed the air. Dot wagged her head violently and talked for a while too, pointing occasionally at Haguillory.

The older boy reached the bridge first.

"Well?" the man said, and the boy said nothing. He bumped the shoulder of the younger one as he passed.

Then came Dot and the woman. The woman scooped the younger boy to her side, held him against her hip. "We'll come back tomorrow," she said, and eyed a second flash of lightning.

The deep hum of thunder buzzed in Haguillory's chest.

"It's been a week," the man said. "That cat is probably long gone."

"Maybe if you'd said something earlier," the woman said, "instead of letting us think he ran away. And after all that."

It looked to Haguillory like she was going to cry. Over a cat.

"Y'all have no idea what we went through to keep that cat with us."

"Oh, *chère*," Dot said.

"I'm going to leave you my phone number," the woman said. She patted herself down, like she might actually have a pen and paper stashed in those cutoffs. "Y'all have something to write with?"

"Just tell me the number," Haguillory said. "I'll remember."

"He won't remember. Here, I've got a pen in my purse." Dot dug in her purse, forever. Once the woman had the pen, there was the problem of something to write on, but Dot held out her palm. "Write it here."

The woman wrote the number and called out to the cat a few more times before turning abruptly away.

"Y'all stay dry," the man said.

The boy in the big T-shirt gave Haguillory a quick, down-at-the-hip wave. His older brother was already waiting at the car, staring down the highway, arms stiff at his sides, hands clenched into fists, like he was trying to see clear to the Gulf. The man went to him, laid a palm on the nape of his neck, steered him gently into the backseat, and shut the door. They all settled in and drove away.

"Over a cat," Haguillory said, and started to gather their things. He cut the crab lines off the pilings and let the loose ends of twine slide into the canal. He secured the fishhook to a guide and reeled the line in tight, then folded the chairs and propped them and the net and the rod against the cooler. A fat drop of rain tapped his arm. Another one, his neck.

Dot just stood there, watching.

Haguillory knelt and closed his tackle box.

"You think I don't know what you did to Matherne's tree?" Dot said.

He pressed tight the lid on the container of worms. "What tree?"

"That pecan tree. You think I don't know?"

"The storm killed that tree!"

"Or to the Landrys' dog?"

"Aw!"

She raised a finger in the air. "The next time Carol calls, you're not going to hang up. You're going to talk. And if somebody tells you that somebody died, you know what you're going to say? You're going to tell them, 'I'm sorry to hear that.' You're not going to say, '*Mais*, so?' And," she said, shaking so hard her cheeks jiggled, "you're going to quit calling Zareena 'that girl Danny adopted.' She's your granddaughter. You just call her 'my granddaughter' from now on. You hear me?"

"I don't have to do nothing," Haguillory said. He looked down at Dot's bare feet, her legs muddy to the calves. He wanted to say, *You going to get in my truck like that?* But it wasn't worth it.

"You're a spiteful man, and why?" she said. "*À la tête dure,* yeah. I should have known that from the beginning."

That part was true, he thought. She should have. From the very first time they met at the dance hall in Basile, when he told her—just for the hell of it—that his name was Herman, and for months, even after things had gone past dancing, she had called him Herman, and all his friends had gone along with it, snickering behind her back, until one day she asked a visiting cousin, "Where's Herman?" and he said, "Who?" and she said, "Herman! He was just standing right here," and he said, "There isn't any Herman, you must mean Haguillory," and the jig was finally up. She should have known then. Fair warning. But she had married him anyhow.

"I've had just about enough," she said. She picked up her shoes, and nothing else, and turned toward the truck, flapping one hand at her side like she was shaking off a punch.

Inside the cooler, the crabs rattled around. When Haguillory opened the lid, three of them lifted their claws, furious, cursing God. Five crabs weren't even enough to bother with. He dumped them out on the bridge and kicked them, one by one, over the edge, into the water.

He carried the cooler and the rod and the chairs to the truck. Dot was sitting in the cab, staring past the beads of rain sliding down the windshield, as if searching for something far down the road, the same way the boy had done. Well, what did they think they would find? He snuck up to her window and tapped on the glass to see if he could scare her. She didn't flinch.

When he went back to collect his tackle box and the last odds and ends from the bridge, he said, "Well, I'll be damned."

There was the cat. It crouched in the gravel path and mewled.

Haguillory wiped the rain from his forehead and arms. He bent over and wriggled his fingers. "Come here, you," he said.

The cat hesitated, meowed, tensed as if it was about to dart off into the marsh, then lifted its tail in the air and came to Haguillory. It shoved its cheek against his shin.

He cast a glance over his shoulder at the truck. Dot was leaning across the seat, reaching for the key, which he'd left in the ignition. She started the engine, adjusted the air-conditioning vents, and rested her head against the window, eyes closed.

Haguillory slipped a hand under the cat's belly and lifted it, held it against his chest. It was light and limp, purring in deep, relieved breaths. All down its sides, the fur was matted in clumps, and at the base of its tail was a solid, tangled carpet of hair and grass and shit. It smelled disgusting.

"You need a bath, you," Haguillory said.

The rain was seeping through his clothes and through the cat's fur. Its thick ruff seemed to melt away; underneath was a skinny little neck. Haguillory smoothed his hand over the cat's forehead, flattened its ears back and held them.

"You had to pee on that little boy's bed?" he said.

Its big eyes stared, yellow and bright. He felt sorry for it, he really did, but in the end it was just a cat, wasn't it? He wrapped his fingers around a paw and pressed on the soft pads to spread the impotent toes. Then, as smooth and easy as he would throw a fishing line, Haguillory tossed out his arm and flung the cat, pinwheeling, over the rail and into the canal, thinking, as it splashed, *We'll see how spiteful I am.* Thinking, *There's all kinds of meanness, and all kinds of mercy too.*

You Are My Dear Friend

FROM *The New Yorker*

THE BAKERS HELD a party in their flat, and Mrs. Baker told Geeta that she was to bring the children in to say goodnight to the guests. So just before eight-thirty she made the girls undress and pulled their purple nightgowns down over their heads. Sally, nine years old, stretched her chubby fingers skyward. Emma, seven, was less cooperative, but together they managed it. The girls smiled sleepily at Geeta through veils of blond hair. Holding each by the hand, she walked them up the corridor toward the smell of rum and cigarettes.

The guests were scattered across the living room, most of them reclining on the Bakers' couches with the spent aspect of runners at the end of a race. Geeta paused with the girls at the entrance.

From an armchair by the window, Mrs. Baker surfaced. Tall and thin, she wore her yellow hair in a plumb-line ponytail down her black turtleneck sweater.

"There they are," she said. "Come here, my bumblebees."

Two small hands left Geeta's, and then the girls were in their mother's arms. She heard Mr. Baker's voice from over by the bar. "Geeta has saved our lives, ladies and gentlemen. Take my advice. Don't try to go it alone in this country. Get an au pair." Now she could see him, one elbow on the bar's burnished surface. He raised his glass in her direction. "Just don't steal ours, because you'll have to fight us to the bloody death."

Laughter dribbled its way across the room. Mrs. Baker was crouching between her daughters, arms around their shoulders. She was drunk, but Geeta knew that those gray-green eyes could snap to attention at any moment. She was not afraid of Mrs. Baker, because she knew that Mrs. Baker liked her. She was not afraid of Mr. Baker either, because in matters of child-rearing, as in most others, he deferred to his wife.

"All right, little misses, say goodnight to this debauched lot," Mrs. Baker said. Emma giggled and said, "G'night." Sally stared at the lounging figures, something imperious in her expression. But when she spoke it was a plaintive whisper. "Goodnight."

"And goodnight to you, Geeta," Mrs. Baker said. "We'll try to be quiet, but if we disturb you—"

"I will call the police. Goodnight, Mrs. Baker," Geeta said.

There was more laughter. The girls' mother gave them one last squeeze and then stood, looking wistful. As the children were walking toward her, Geeta glanced around. Most of the Bakers' guests were British expatriates like them, but there were a few Indians, one of whom was sitting in a chair at her elbow, away from the rest. There wasn't supposed to be a chair in that corner. He must have dragged it over. He had his forearms on his knees and was watching her. She glanced away immediately but retained the impression of a puffy face, tired eyes behind glasses.

Then she felt the children tugging at her hands, and she marched them back to their bedroom, where she locked the windows, turned down their beds, pushed their dolls to the side, switched on the frog-shaped night-light, and stroked their foreheads before leaving them to sleep.

Her own bedroom was small but well appointed. The Bakers had told her that they were aware of how domestic help was treated in India, and that they would sooner drown themselves than treat another human being that way. So Geeta had sheets and pillows from England and a cupboard that was much too large for her few clothes. She had her own bathroom, and a cell phone, whose bill, for the past eighteen months, the Bakers had paid.

On weekdays her mornings were hers. The children went to an international school, and as long as she was at the gate by one-fifteen, the Bakers didn't care what she did. Besides Geeta, they employed a maidservant, a cook, and two drivers. The cook was old and beyond the nip of jealousy, and Geeta barely saw the drivers, but it was possible that the maidservant resented her for her relative freedom. To ward off any ill feeling, every so often Geeta brought home a trinket for the girl, who was a chatty, dimpled creature from Jharkhand. Geeta was from Odisha and had nothing in common with her, except the fact that people in Bangalore knew almost nothing about where either of them came from.

At various times Geeta had bought the girl an alarm clock, a pair of leaf-shaped earrings, and a fake-silver pendant engraved with the words "You Are My Dear Friend." She worried that she might have overdone it a bit with the pendant, but the girl loved it and loved Geeta for it.

A few days after the party, Geeta was walking in the Shivajinagar market. She needed nothing but enjoyed the hustle and the abundance of the place, the carts of folded handkerchiefs with crimped edges, the stacks of unbranded jeans, the enormous steel cooking pots meant for weddings. She'd paused at a stationery stall and was examining a fake-gold-nib pen when she heard her name.

Looking up, she saw a vaguely familiar man approaching her with a smile. She did not smile back but waited for him to clarify in her memory.

The Bakers', the smoke, the chair by the corner.

"You walk fast," he said. He wore a polyester checkered shirt over his trousers, and on his feet were rubber chappals. He didn't, in this outfit, look like someone the Bakers would know.

"You don't remember me," he said, sounding disappointed.

"You were in Mr. and Mrs. Baker's house on"—she paused to count back—"Saturday."

"That's right," he said. His face was less puffy than she remembered, but his eyes were just as tired. His name, he told her, was Srikanth. "How long have you been working for those people?" he asked. "What did they call you—an au pair?"

Sensing the delicate contempt behind the question, she answered, "For some time."

"And before that?"

"I was working somewhere else."

Srikanth eyed her with amusement. "Are all au pairs as talkative as you?"

By now she was thoroughly wary, which, paradoxically, made her appear serene. When he told her that he was looking for a new frying pan, she nodded. When he asked if she wanted to help him choose one, she looked him full in the face and lied. "Sorry, they will be angry with me if I don't go home."

But, just before she was out of earshot, some instinct made her turn back and say, "Frying pans are this way. I can show you if you want."

During one of their walks in the market, which became routine over the next several months, Srikanth told Geeta that a colleague had invited him to the Bakers' party, and that he had hated it. "Not one person said anything interesting," he said. "Except for you. My little au pair."

He spoke English, Tamil, and atrocious Hindi. She spoke Hindi, Odia, and passable English. So they made English their language, though she learned a few Tamil words, flattening her tongue in her mouth to speak them. *Veetu,* house. *Mazhai,* rain. *Ponnu,* girl.

When she told the Bakers that she was leaving to get married, they did not try to dissuade her.

"I don't remember him," Mrs. Baker said. "Do you, Charlie?"

"Not well. Someone brought him along, I think. How old are you, Geeta?"

"Twenty-nine," she said.

He nodded. "Older than I thought. But he's quite a bit older than that?"

"He is fifty-three years old," she said.

"Not a child," Mrs. Baker said, and there was a warning there, but whether it was addressed to Geeta or to Mr. Baker was unclear, as was whether it was meant to refer to Srikanth or to Geeta herself. "Emma and Sally are going to hate this, you know," she added.

Mr. Baker said, "Are we at least invited to the wedding, then?"

Geeta smiled. He sighed a little sadly, as if he'd never expected that they would be.

She called to tell Sister Stella, who took some time to remember her. Geeta could see the wide rosewood desk in the dark-paneled office. Three ballpoint pens: red, green, black. The old Bible bound in brown leather, as big as a briefcase. The wooden cross on its stand. The ruler that stretched the breadth of the desk. Sister Stella said, "And he is a Christian?"

"No," Geeta said. "But he is willing to convert."

"Oh? In that case," Sister Stella said, "this is a joyful day indeed."

They got married in March. Srikanth left for the office around nine o'clock, and Geeta spent most mornings wandering around the large house. She loved to sit in the vast garden at noon, when trees throttled the sunlight and she could hear the hectic buzzing of heat above the canopy. The house had belonged to Srikanth's father, who had, of all things, won the lottery and bought this fan-shaped slice of land in the heart of Bangalore. Now it was worth a fortune.

"He was a miser," Srikanth told her. "If he could have taken this house with him when he died, he would have. Nothing made him suffer more than giving it to me. But the only other option was Swati, and he would have burned it down before giving it to a girl."

She had met Srikanth's sister, Swati, a tall, officious woman, who arrived on the express from Chennai for the wedding. It was a registry wedding and was over before Geeta knew it. She heard Srikanth say, "Geeta, you have to sign," and she blushed, knowing that Swati was watching.

There had been a brother too, but he had died in childhood.

The morning after the wedding, before taking the express back to Chennai, Swati invited them to visit her. She made the offer with cool professionalism, and her eyes betrayed no emotion.

"She is not married?" Geeta asked after Swati left in a taxi, refusing to allow them to drive her to Cantonment Station.

"Why would you think that?" Srikanth asked. "She's got two children, a boy and a girl." He touched her lower back. "Not everyone stays alone for as long as you."

She knew that he had been married before, that his first wife was still alive. She knew that he had a daughter, who was grown. She did not ask for pictures or details, because early on in their meetings he had joked that he was an old man, and that by the time he'd told her everything about himself, she too would be old. She sensed the warning and was discreet. She thought of the word *divorce*, mentally pronouncing it *DIE-vorce*, but the one time he said it he bit off the first syllable like a hiccup: *di-VORCE*. And somehow that dampened her desire to hear more, as if it could only be further proof of her ignorance. Srikanth had a commerce degree; she had her tenth-standard pass certificate, which Sister Stella had handed over as dispassionately as if it were a ration card.

They had sex the night Swati left. After he climaxed, he hovered above her for another second before letting himself drop
onto her body. Then he rolled off and flipped her on her side and
drew her back against him. The bed they lay on was his parents', a
high, antique frame with carved posts and a thin, pitiless mattress.
Part of her longed for her room at the Bakers', her foreign sheets,
and her too-soft pillows.

"And what about you?" he asked in a drowsy voice, after they'd
lain in silence for a while.

"Me?"

"Yes, you. My little au pair from Odisha. You're not going to tell
me more about yourself? Where you went to school, what you were
like as a child?"

"It is boring," she said.

"No," he said. "You're not boring."

It was not what she meant, and she began to correct him, but
his hand twitched, and she knew he was asleep. She knew too that
he had been relieved by her nonanswer. It was natural, she told
herself. No man at his stage in life could possibly be interested in
childhood stories.

In July it started to rain. Like clockwork, for two hours each afternoon. The ground in the garden turned swampy. Sitting beneath
the terra-cotta overhang of the roof, she watched the toads with
their lustrous jumping throats, and the fat brown sparrows that sat
impassive and then quaked themselves dry.

She heard Srikanth come back from work, calling her name.
She lifted her body and brought herself inside. The house was full
of dark, heavy furniture, his parents' furniture.

"You haven't started making dinner," he said.

"I'll start now," she said, moving toward the kitchen.

"It's almost eight."

There was a grandfather clock next to a hatstand whose arms
were antlers. She blinked.

"You've been dreaming all day?"

"Maybe we can go out?"

"I have been out. I just want to stay quietly at home."

She went into the kitchen to start dinner. He followed her.

He said, "What did you do today?"

She poured a cup of rice into a pot and ran her fingers through it, feeling for stones.

"Nothing."

"Did you read?"

There was a library, full of stiff-spined books he claimed his father had bought to make himself appear more intimidating to visitors.

"A little," she said. She had taken down one of the books, but its leather binding had reminded her of Sister Stella's Bible, and she had spent the rest of the afternoon thinking about the hot convent-school courtyard and the dreary, soothing presence of the nuns.

"I don't understand," he said finally.

"Understand what?"

"You! What is it that you want? In this world?"

"Nothing," she said.

"Nothing?" he echoed. "Not even a child?"

She looked up at him. He was smiling in a way that made her, for a moment, furious. Then the fury was gone. She picked out a stone from the rice, flicking it away.

"That's it, isn't it?" he pressed. "You want to have a child?"

She didn't answer. He took the pot from her hands and set it down.

He said, "I'm not a young man anymore."

"I know."

"You know everything," he said, teasing her now. "My genius little au pair."

And he led her by the hand to the antique bed with the four carved posters and that punishing mattress.

Five months later, on Christmas Eve, they went to midnight Mass. Srikanth had still not converted, but he promised to do it soon. He fell asleep during the hymns, and Geeta had to wake him when the choir began to file out. He drove them home and fell asleep again right away, while she lay awake, trying to think of how to phrase what she had to say to him.

The next morning she said, "I think we should go to a doctor."

He frowned at her. "I've already had a child, remember."

"I know," she said. "It is me."

The doctor at Baptist Hospital confirmed this. That week Geeta caught a bus and rang the bell at the Bakers' door. The maidservant answered and hugged Geeta.

They discussed her problem. The maidservant was of the opinion that Geeta's sterility was a good thing, but when she saw Geeta's expression she leaned in conspiratorially.

"You can do adoption, you know," she whispered.

Geeta shook her head. "It takes many years, and it is very expensive. And those adoption people will see how old Srikanth is, and they will say no."

"But that's only if you do it here. In Jharkhand, babies are being adopted all the time. I know a place where no one checks. You can do it fast, and they will give you any baby you want. Old, young, boy, girl." She sat back and scrutinized Geeta's face. "You should get an older child. Otherwise your husband will be dead before it has started walking."

The first thing that surprised Geeta was the girl's height. Rani was eight but nearly as tall as she was. Her brown eyes took in the house with a single glance. On the train she had been silent, eating very little but doing it obediently. Now she stood still, staring at the mossy steps leading to the veranda and the flowerpots that held only ancient gray dirt. Srikanth had already gone inside with Rani's bag.

In Ranchi, the orphanage director, a scraggy woman with a coal miner's cough, had given them Rani's background, which amounted to no more than a blur of prejudices. She was supposedly from a tribal village deep in the forests of eastern Jharkhand. She had come to the orphanage a year before, deposited by an older girl who claimed to be her sister but could as easily have been her mother. The father was not in the picture, and everyone was almost certainly better off that way; there was the lurking stink of criminality, possibly even Naxalism, around him. Rani was not intelligent, the orphanage director went on, tribal girls rarely were, but she was strong and could help with the house. While all this was being conveyed to them, Geeta glanced at Srikanth, who was nodding seriously, as though he'd expected no less. With a chill, she wondered if he was listening to anything the orphanage director was saying. At the end, when he turned to her and asked, "Are you sure you're ready?," she was tempted to shake her head, but then she thought of the empty house waiting for her and said, "Yes."

"Come inside?" Geeta murmured now. Rani stiffened, then ran up the steps and into the hall. She drew abreast of the grandfather clock just as it lurched to four. Her thin frame flinched with each gong, but when it was over and she turned to look at Geeta, her face was blank.

"This is where you'll sleep," Geeta said.

She had chosen the room with the best view of the garden. It had been a storeroom, Srikanth had told her, in the days when he was a child and his family had four Brahmin cooks working for them. All four had slept in here. The soft wood of the door still smelled of grain and hemp. She had put in a cot and an almirah and placed a chair by the window. Because the rooms of her own life had never contained more, she had left it at that. It was, she told herself, the view that would count. A jackfruit tree stood outside, with elegant, tortured branches and fruit that looked like fat, milk-bloated babies. She might have liked the room for herself, but she knew that Srikanth would have found the idea of sleeping in a storeroom outrageous.

She was disappointed, therefore, when Rani barely seemed to notice. She resisted the urge to point out the room's advantages and instead asked, "Do you need anything?"

Rani's thick black hair had been shorn and was growing back unevenly over her ears. She wore a frilly peacock-blue frock that draggled at the hem, the same one she'd been wearing when they first saw her. Her upper lip protruded; it was possible that she was bucktoothed.

"Do I need anything?" the girl repeated. Her voice had an anesthetized quality, but within it twitched a slippery, mocking thing. Then she smiled. It was an unnerving smile to see on an eight-year-old face, somehow innocent, cunning, and flirtatious at the same time, and Geeta, to her shame, panicked.

"Then I'll leave you to rest," she said, turning her back on both the girl and the view. Her first failure, as she would later come to think of it.

She had resolved to be unshakable with Rani, but almost immediately she found herself swept up in a soft tangle of mitigation and half-lies. Each morning she lay in bed worrying about the things

the girl was going to do and say that day. They had decided that
she would stay at home until the new academic year began, that
it was important for her to feel accepted into their family before
shouldering the challenges of school. But the truth was that Geeta
felt like the one on trial. Rani loped around the house and had a
tendency to sneak up on Geeta.

"The pictures are dusty," Rani would say, and Geeta would run
for a cloth to wipe the frames.

"There is hair in the bathroom," she would observe clinically,
and Geeta would run to lift the knob of knotted hair from the
drain, dropping it into the trash with a shudder.

"You don't know how to cook," she whispered one night to
Geeta, when Srikanth had left a little rice on his plate. "Even he
hates your food."

At other times she would say nothing, merely watching Geeta
at whatever she was doing. As a way to compensate, Geeta found
herself talking. Avoiding her own history, she babbled on about
her husband's life at great length.

"This house is very old," she said. "Your grandfather won the
lottery. Your father has one sister, Swati. You'll meet her. She has
two children, a boy and a girl. Your cousins." She glanced at Rani,
then continued as though she had doted on these children for
years. "Lovely children, very well behaved. One day you'll meet
them. When your father was small, he used to think there were a
hundred rooms in this house. You know how, when you are small,
you think everything is so big? Your father's family is vegetarian.
His mother allowed only Brahmins to cook their food. She kept
four cooks." She halted, hating the sound of what she'd said. "Your
father had a brother," she said, concluding, "but he died when he
was small."

"How did he die?" the girl asked, perking up.

"I don't know," Geeta said. "He was sick, I think."

"Did he have tuberculosis?"

"No."

"Cancer?"

"I don't think so."

"Pneumonia?"

"No!" Geeta exclaimed. "I mean, I don't know."

"You didn't ask?" Rani asked slyly. "You're so stupid, you didn't
even ask?"

Geeta shrank back. "Your father and I got married only one year ago," she heard herself say slowly. "But he was married before."

"He is very old, isn't he?"

"Not so old."

"He is an old cocksucking bastard," Rani declared. And Geeta was shocked, less by the profanity than by the girl's matter-of-fact tone, though she could not deny that there was something slightly comical about it too, the bald innocence of the pronouncement.

"Rani!" she said, making an attempt to sound authoritative. "That's enough! Don't say such things about your father!"

"He's not my father," the girl replied scornfully. "My father went to jail."

Geeta felt slightly dizzy. "I didn't know."

"And you're not my mother. My mother is a poor woman," Rani said. She stepped close to Geeta, her chin tilted up, her eyes dark and powerful, albeit with a detached kind of intensity. "You are a rich woman. You can help my mother."

"What do you mean?"

Rani smiled. She had a million different smiles, and this one was regretful, benevolent, nearly tender. "Where is your jewelry?" she whispered.

It took almost a month for Geeta to tell Srikanth about any of this. In that time Rani proved herself a master of single-mindedness. At times she was wheedling, at other times forceful. Always it was the same demand. She wanted Geeta to send jewelry to her mother. Geeta lived in this big house, she was rich, so there had to be jewelry. Where was it?

Then one afternoon she found Rani going through her cupboard. It was kept locked, the key under a lace doily on the dressing table, but Rani must have seen her retrieve it. Now the door stood wide open. One of Geeta's saris had slipped to the floor. Her piles of nighties and petticoats lay slumped against one another.

"What are you doing?" Geeta asked.

"It was like this already," Rani said. She sounded bored with her own lie.

"If you're looking for jewelry, you won't find it there."

A scowl creased the girl's forehead.

"Bitch," she said.

"I may be a bitch," Geeta said, struggling to remain calm. "But

I adopted you. Even if I give you jewelry one day, it would be for you, not for your mother."

Rani turned and thrust her hand into the cupboard. Another sari fell to the ground.

"Rani!"

Drawing a breath, Geeta stepped forward and grasped the thin shoulders. The touch seemed to inflame Rani, for she began thrashing, but Geeta kept her hold until they were both outside the room. Then she let go, breathing hard. Rani stood still for a second, then leaped for Geeta, giving her arm a painful pinch before fleeing to her room and slamming the door.

That night, when they were in bed, Geeta described the incident to Srikanth. After she finished, he lay silent for a long time. Just as she began to wonder if he'd fallen asleep, he said, "This is what you wanted."

She didn't reply. Her arm where Rani had pinched it was black and yellow.

"You said you were ready," he continued. "I asked you, and you said you were ready."

She said nothing.

"I go to work every day," he said. "I sit in an office and earn money for you. Now the girl is my responsibility also? I've already finished raising my daughter, my little au pair." His voice sounded far off. "You'll have to find your way with this one."

Rani began making startling pronouncements. One afternoon she threw her arms around Geeta's waist and said, "I love you, I love you, I love you." She said this fiercely. Her voice tore into Geeta like hooks. Two hours later she told Geeta that she was ugly. "You look like a black rat," she said. "Black like shit."

"My mother fell," she said on another occasion. "She fell into a hole and then she tried to pull me inside. It was very deep." And on another day: "I saw my father. He was not wearing any clothes. He is very happy and he likes his food." And on still another day: "There were many people hiding in the jungle around my house."

From these sinister fragments, Geeta pieced together the mosaic of a short and terrifying life. She saw a weak, protective mother, an absent, unpredictable father, poverty, the looming threat of outsiders, the fear of corrupt authorities. She recalled her own parents, who, despite their curtailed presence in her life, had at least encased her in the solid outline of their love. Her father, a timid and cooperative tenant farmer, was given to breaking into soft, worried monologues that no one was allowed to hear, whispering it all to himself so that he wouldn't burden his wife and daughter. Her mother, grave and hilarious, could change her voice at will, now putting on the staid airs of a village elder, now the coarse twang of a city dweller. And those voices had remained with Geeta, even after the accident that had killed both of her parents. The convent-school years, the stone courtyard, her work for the Bakers, even her marriage—they all felt to Geeta like manifestations of her mother's never-ending repertoire.

It occurred to her, of course, that Rani could be lying, but Geeta had the suspicion that what she said was more or less accurate. Rani's lies were obvious and lazy; these baroque narratives suggested a more insidious truth. It could not be prodded from her. She could not be asked to explicate. So Geeta listened and tried to make sense of it, of this strong, mad child.

By April, Rani seemed calmer, and her proclamations had cooled, no longer burning with the terrible heat of prophecy. She seemed more prone to conversation, one day even asking Geeta to comb her hair, which Geeta did as gently as she knew how. Midway through, Rani leaned back into her chest and made a small, unconscious grunt of pleasure. The sound brought tears to Geeta's eyes, and in that moment she allowed herself the hope that maybe the worst of it was over. In front of Srikanth, however, Rani was mute, and he in turn passed over them both with the distracted benevolence of a politician taking a pause from state matters.

Only once more did she attempt to talk to him about the girl. She suggested that Rani might be lonely without the company of other children and wondered if they might visit his sister in Chennai. He said, "I know children better than you. There's nothing wrong with her. Let her learn how to entertain herself. If you spoil her now, she will never be satisfied later." His tone was so darkly bitter that she imagined he was speaking from experience, and she thought about the daughter he never saw or mentioned.

"These types of girls," he went on, "they try to get everything from you. If you give them one thing, they will ask for five the next time. Let her learn to be happy with whatever she has."

She didn't ask what he meant by "these types of girls." Tribal girls, girls from the north, rural girls, girls with shady pasts, low-caste girls, girls without money, Adivasi girls, girls clawing their way up, nonvegetarian girls, girls without morals, hardened girls, orphaned girls, ungrateful girls, or simply girls—it might have been any one of these.

The Bakers' maidservant came to visit at a time when Geeta knew Srikanth wouldn't be at home. Rani was introduced, the maidservant given a cup of tea and shown around the house. They wandered from room to room, and the maidservant was extravagant with her praise. At one point the maidservant turned and Geeta saw that she was wearing the pendant she'd given her, with the engraving that read "You Are My Dear Friend." She commented on it, saying how nice the maidservant looked.

"I never take it off," the maidservant declared, fishing it out from the neckline of her kurta and holding it dramatically up to her lips.

Geeta saw Rani's gaze fix briefly on the pendant and then drift away. When the maidservant had gone, Geeta took the teacups into the kitchen and started to wash them. She heard Rani come in, but she did not turn. Then a dazzling pain shot through her back, and she whirled around, knocking Rani to the floor. The knife skittered away, still dotted with pieces of the onion Geeta had been chopping earlier. The cut was low down and alarmingly near her spine, but she could tell at once that it was not deep. She touched it and felt warm blood. From the ground, Rani looked up at her, and there was nothing in her face to suggest that anything momentous had taken place.

"Why did you do that?" Geeta asked, voice trembling.

"You gave that bitch your jewelry."

"That wasn't jewelry!" Geeta cried. "It was just a cheap necklace I bought in the market. It's not even real. It's worth nothing."

She took two quick steps and picked up the knife. Before she could think twice, she'd washed it and put it back in the drawer.

"Stand up," she told Rani. "We're going to the doctor."

Her wound was dressed, but thankfully no stitches were needed. She did not tell Srikanth what had happened. She kept an eye on his shirt buttons, she cooked his meals with care, but she no longer thought of them as married.

Instead she focused her energy on Rani. They had settled on

Sophia Girls' School, run by Catholic nuns of a devout strain, of whom Srikanth approved because they were rumored to be strict, and whom Geeta liked because they reminded her of her own schooling. Rani would begin in June. She had taken an oral aptitude test and had proved, notwithstanding the orphanage director's bigotry, to be extremely intelligent.

The first day of school would be the fifth of June, a date that acquired for Geeta a kind of shimmer. All she had to do was make it to the fifth, she thought. If she could take Rani safely to the shoals of that bright morning, then it would be the end of the trial period; she would have succeeded; they would have won.

After the incident with the knife, Rani was subdued. She woke early and made her bed. She folded her few clothes and kept them in the cupboard. She never left her wet towel on the bathroom floor, as Srikanth did. She ate whatever breakfast Geeta gave her, then walked out to the long concrete driveway, which had once been gravel raked every morning, according to Srikanth, by a man in a white uniform. The first time Geeta worried that Rani might climb the gate and disappear. At noon she pretended to wander by the front door. She saw Rani marching from one gatepost to the other, then back again, a dark shape crossing a river of concrete. Geeta shouted that lunch was ready and Rani responded immediately. From that day on, she was inside before Geeta had to call.

Until the day she wasn't. Geeta put the food on the table and waited for ten minutes. Then she went to the door. Rani was speaking with a man who stood on the other side of the gate. He had a wispy mustache and his hair was locked in place by glinting gel. He was dressed in the uniform of youth—a red shirt tucked into tight jeans. As Geeta walked toward them, his eyes flickered to her; he said something to Rani, ducking his head. Then he strode off, tipping an invisible hat to Geeta.

"Who was that?" Geeta asked. "Rani, who was that?"

Rani turned with a radiant smile. "My father is not in jail anymore."

"What?"

"He said my father sent him. He's going to take me back to my father."

"Rani, listen to me. What did he say? Did he tell you his name?"

Rani shook her head. Her smile grew still more radiant. Geeta thought of the man's insolent hat tip and felt weak with fear.

"Rani, does he come every day? Has he talked to you before?"

"He told me my father has come out of jail. My mother is calling for me. He said if I go with him he will take me back to my village."

In one swift motion Geeta leaped at the gate and flung it open. She ran out into the street and saw the red shirt, as small as a stamp.

"I'll kill you!" she screamed. "Don't come back again! Are you listening? I'll kill you if you come back! I'll kill you!"

When Srikanth came home, she described the young man to him, the terrifying promises he'd made to Rani. This time Srikanth stood up and came unnecessarily close to her.

"She's too much for you," he said. His breath smelled of onions and filter coffee. "Admit it," he pressed her. "You can't do this. You are not capable. Look at you. Your hair is a mess. You don't take care of the house anymore. You hardly look at me. You only think of her."

A month ago she might have protested, but it no longer mattered what was and wasn't true. The threats had become too many, too nebulous. Later she would think of this as her final failure. The first and the last, the only two clear in her mind.

"You may have been an au pair," he said, drawing himself up, "but I am the one who has actually raised a child."

"Please," she whispered. "Talk to her."

Rani was in her room, where Geeta had instructed her to stay. She had not told Srikanth what had happened after she screamed at the young man: the way Rani had attacked her, the scratches even now blossoming on her neck, the girl's terrible moans.

Rani was, Geeta noticed with a pang, sitting by the window, on the chair Geeta had placed there months before, looking at the garden. She did not turn around when they came in.

"Young lady, you are not allowed to go near the gate again, do you understand?" Srikanth said in a sonorous voice, and Geeta wondered for whom he was performing. Partly for her, but partly, she suspected, for his vanished first wife. "I give you the money for your food. I paid for that chair you're sitting on. As long as you are under my roof, you will listen to me. And you are not allowed to speak to strangers."

Rani turned her head and smiled.

It was a smile that Geeta had never seen before. Beautiful and powerless, it robbed Geeta of breath. She wanted to run over and hug the girl, but she could feel Srikanth puffing up beside her, working himself into a fury with all the mechanical purpose of the clock in the hall.

"Are you laughing at me?" he asked softly.

At that, the girl's smile became even more helpless. Geeta closed her eyes, and at the moment she opened them she saw a strange thing—a gray-green blur shooting down outside the window. It took her a moment to realize that it was a jackfruit.

"You think you can disrespect me?" Srikanth was saying. "Just because my wife lets you disrespect her," he continued grandly, "you think you can disrespect me? Eh? I know how girls like you think. Sly, that's what you are, sly. Fine, if my wife can't do it, I'll teach you to behave. I'll teach you to be scared."

He lifted a finger in Rani's direction.

"Pack your clothes," he ordered.

Father, mother, child, suitcase. It was a parody of the family trip Geeta had suggested months ago. Srikanth, still swept up in his own theater of punishment, carried Rani's battered bag all the way to the gate, then set it down in the dust. Rani and Geeta followed, walking a foot apart, not touching.

"Go," he told Rani, holding the gate open. "Pick it up and go."

Rani picked up the bag. She slipped under his outstretched arm and past the gate. On the other side, she rolled her shoulders back, as if warming up for a marathon. She was much healthier than when she had first arrived, her face and figure fuller, her hair more lustrous, long enough now to touch her neck.

"You want to find your father and mother?" Srikanth demanded. "Go find them and don't come back here."

Rani began to walk. She walked in the direction the young man had taken earlier.

Srikanth stepped out onto the pavement and Geeta followed. Now they could see Rani's back, her shuffle more pronounced because of the weight of the suitcase.

"She won't go far," Srikanth grunted. "She'll stop."

But Rani did not falter. She passed under a streetlamp, and light raked her hair.

"She'll turn around," Srikanth said. "She'll turn and start crying at any moment."

The girl walked. On and on and on, without the slightest shift in her stride. Unaccountably, Geeta felt laughter bubbling from inside her.

"Quiet!" Srikanth snapped.

Rani had arrived at the last streetlamp. She passed under it only as a shadow, and then she was out of sight. Geeta could not tell which way she had gone.

She turned to Srikanth, who seemed to be in shock. For a moment they looked at each other, and she saw what ugliness could be released when the bloated complacence of a man like him was ruptured.

"She's playing with us," he said. "She won't really leave. Where can she go?"

"Why doesn't your daughter call you?" Geeta asked suddenly, speaking in her normal voice. "In a whole year, she hasn't called you. And you haven't called her."

He turned slowly to face her.

"You know what I think?" Geeta continued. "I think you don't know where she is."

He froze. Then, as if it were intolerable to remain even a moment longer with her, he took off running in the direction that Rani had gone.

Geeta stayed where she was. A young couple came past, walking their small dog, and she smiled at them. A breeze picked up, bringing the smell of grilled chicken from the hotel next door, and she felt a quick pang of hunger for meat.

After a long while she saw two figures coming back up the road. Rani was still carrying her own suitcase, her walk as unhurried as ever.

The girl did not look at Geeta as she stood holding the gate open. Srikanth too avoided looking at her. He was huffing, his face shining with sweat. Geeta waited a moment longer, then padlocked the gate and followed them in.

That night he pulled her to him in the old way, the two of them on their sides, his chin at her shoulder. Her eyes were closed, but she could see clearly enough. Their strange bodies, made stranger together, perched on the raft of the mattress.

"We can't do anything for her," he was saying, his voice a murmur, as dry as paper at her collarbone. The girl was damaged, he said, had been damaged from the day she was born. They would never be able to control her, they would never be able to love her enough; the older she grew, the more uncontrollable she would become, and who knew how she might hurt them, which shady characters from the streets she would invite inside the house. And once they were inside they would rape Rani, they would steal, they would murder Srikanth and Geeta in bed. And suppose Rani did manage to track down her father and mother, or they managed to find her? They might hold the child as ransom, use her as leverage to extort money. Perhaps this had been the idea all along. Softly, he whispered his insinuations into Geeta's shoulder, her ear, as tender as a man making love. It would be better for the girl to be with people who understood her, he said, people used to dealing with girls like her. It would be better for everybody, Geeta included, Geeta especially, to let her go. Wasn't Geeta tired? Wasn't she ready to go back to her life, to reading or wandering in the market, to things as they had been before? Why take on the extra burden? The girl would be fine. She had lived in their house for less than six months. She would forget soon enough. If they saw her again, she would barely remember them.

"So, my little au pair? What do you say?"

She thought of her mother's voices, blurring and shifting, already on to the next thing, the next impression. Her father mumbling his worries to himself. Sister Stella's Bible and multicolored pens. The hard ridges of the healed cut on her back. All these things she would never tell Srikanth about, but the fault was only partly his. She had lost the habit of speaking of herself, and now it was impossible to recover the details that could have made her permanent.

She heard herself say to her husband, "Yes."

Over the years they have sold off pieces of land. The hotel next door bought some, wanting to build a forested restaurant, where guests could eat dinner under softly lit trees. They sold some to a developer, who promptly built a twenty-story residential tower boasting "Unparalleled Views! Beauty Redefined!"

The residential tower has its own grocery store, where Geeta now does her shopping. This is not allowed, strictly speaking—the store is meant for residents only—but the security guard lets her in, nodding at her in a way that suggests that he believes they are in collusion against some higher authority, possibly his supervisor. The staff in the grocery store have no idea that she is not a resident, and they sometimes offer to carry her bags up to her apartment, which she politely declines. She has developed a dignified way of walking, has learned how to use her smallness to her advantage. That, coupled with the fact that she is quiet and aware of the people behind the counters—the thin boys, the young girls —makes them solicitous.

There is one girl she particularly notices. The girl works in the cosmetics section of the store, her hair pulled back in some elaborate way Geeta can't figure out, pimples powdered out of recognition, her lips a shocking magenta or pink. She wears the same uniform as the rest of them, a blue T-shirt tucked into black pants, but there is an air about her, lusciously indolent yet vicious, that Geeta finds attractive. She wanders over to try products she can never imagine using—"That is face serum," the girl tells her with shining derision when Geeta absently tries to dab something from a little bottle on her wrist—merely for the feeling that the girl produces in her. She would never go so far as to say that the girl —whose name is Ruby—reminds her of Rani. No, that would be too easy, cowardly, as if all girls who have come from unknowable places to stand in front of her were somehow the same. It is the relationship that is the same: Geeta and Rani, Geeta and Ruby. The girl stands there blazing and exposed, and Geeta circles her, unable to look away.

Palaver

FROM *McSweeney's*

HE MADE HIS MOTHER a deal: for every story he told, she'd give him one of her own.

That's hardly fair, she said.

Bullshit, he said.

It was the first time he'd used the word with her. And she let it slide, the first of many firsts between them.

He'd been living in Shin-Ōkubo for the better part of three years. She'd flown from Houston to Los Angeles to Taipei to Tokyo to see him. Or at least that's what she'd said on the phone. He knew that she and his father were going through it. This was one of the reasons he'd left, although he hadn't thought about that at the time.

Now his mom sat on the sofa, snacking on a bag of chips, holding a magazine neither of them could read. Her son stood beside a broom. His place was mostly plants and some shoes. He had this balcony overlooking a bus stop, next to a convenience store and a stairwell for the train station.

You go first, said the son.

Absolutely not, said his mother.

Fine. I'll start.

Jesus.

Once upon a time, said the son, I fell in love with a married man.

I don't need to hear this, said his mother.

We met in a bar one night, said the son. He bought me a drink. Then he asked me to come home with him.

The mother looked at her son's face before she turned to the

wall, and then to the window beside them. The one thing his apartment had going for it was the view. It'd drizzled her first morning
in the country, and she'd watched sheets of rain paint a gaggle of
grade schoolers by the stoplight.

You're serious, she asked.

No joke.

You aren't serious.

Why would I lie now?

Unbelievable. Were you safe?

I'll only tell if you play.

This isn't a fucking game.

Is that a yes?

God, said his mother.

Good, said her son, sweeping in what passed for his kitchen. We
were safe. We're safe.

Is this a thing that's still happening? asked his mother. Are you
still seeing him?

It's your turn, said the son. You give me one of yours first.

I'll make it easy for you, said the son a little later. Just tell me how
you met Dad.

It was his day off. His mother sat beside him on a bench in the
train station. They were waiting for the local line, just after rush
hour, and he figured they must've made a funny picture, as his
mom groaned with her arms crossed and he tapped away at his
phone, leaping between a volley of apps.

Who the hell are you talking to? his mother said. How long
were you living here before you lost your mind?

I only asked a question.

You're being fucking disrespectful.

Hardly.

Who are you texting?

My students.

Is that appropriate here? asked the mother.

It's fine, said the son. And it's your turn.

Gradually the platform filled beside them. Every other occu-
pant was a businessman of some sort. Every now and again they'd
chance a glance at the mother and her son, but at some point a
lady rolled two twins in a stroller onto the platform.

The kids wouldn't stop crying. Everyone turned to glare at them. Eventually, gradually, the children settled down.

When the train arrived, tinkling a three-tone melody, the son and his mother waited a moment. Then they both stood, trailing the woman with the stroller, leaning into a pair of seats by the conductor's booth.

The woman with the twins turned their way, sighing. Both of her kids waved. So the mother and her son waved back.

Once upon a time, the mother didn't tell her son, I thought I'd take you back to Toronto. We'd live with my sister. The two of us would leave Texas, in the middle of the night. We wouldn't say a word to your father and we'd never come back.

Once upon a time, the mother didn't tell her son, I thought I'd become an opera singer.

Once upon a time, the mother didn't tell her son, I wrote poetry. I scribbled the words in a notebook and hid it in the guest room. But one day—you wouldn't remember this—I found you crying underneath the bed, and the pages were spread open, right at your feet. I think you were nine. I never wrote a poem again.

The son taught English at a juvenile detention center in Yanaka. His pay could've been better, but it was more than enough to live on. Most of his students would never have a reason to use the language, or at least that's what the son told his mom, but the teens still let him teach them, falling asleep only occasionally. They thought he was interesting. Every hour or so he gave them breaks to use their phones.

That sounds depressing, said the mother.

Sometimes it is, said her son. But I like it.

You couldn't just have been depressed in Texas?

I was.

And whose fault is that?

The son opened his mouth, and then he closed it.

My students are funny, said the son. And they don't take any shit.

Impossible, said his mother.

How so?

They put up with *you.*

That isn't cute, said the son.

Anyway, said the mother. I thought you were an accountant or something.

Thanks for caring, said her son.

Don't act like you've ever kept me in the loop.

Whatever, said the son. I had another job the first few months.

And how'd that go?

It was fine. But one of the clients complained.

Because you're Black, said his mother.

No, said the son, but then he didn't say anything else.

Some nights the son stayed out a bit later. His mother would walk to the convenience store for dinner, nodding at the cashier when he bowed. Sometimes her husband texted her, and she'd think about how to reply. But she never sent anything. It was enough, for now, for him to know she'd read it.

Then one evening, smoking on her son's balcony, the mother found, folded under her chair's leg, a crumpled Polaroid of two men. One of the men was her son. The other guy looked a little older. They both smiled, holding inflatable numbers on each other's shoulders, and the mother thought, briefly, that her son looked better unshaven, after all.

So she took a photo of the photo with her phone, and then she refolded it, slipping it under the seat. The mother started to light another cigarette, but then she thought better of it, and she stepped inside instead, kicking off her son's flip-flops, leaving a window open for the breeze.

The next evening the son and his mother sat in a bar, one of the tiny enclaves lining the alleys of Ni-chōme. Posters and flyers showing men fucking in various positions were splayed across the walls, while a pulsing techno track thrummed from above. The son watched his mother eye each picture, and he winced at her, just a bit. But she didn't say anything about them.

The room was mostly empty. Two dudes fingered their drinks in the corner, whispering in each other's ears. The bartender, a bearish man, napped by the register. The son drank a frothy beer, calling out for a second, and his mother shocked him by raising her finger for one too.

The bartender said something in Japanese. It made the son

laugh. He replied with something that made the bartender shake his head.

He thinks I'm charging you, said the son.

Don't lie, said the mother. I know where we are.

You didn't say anything.

It didn't need to be said.

Is this your first time in a gay bar?

Tell me about your married man, said the mother.

This made the son wince again. He fidgeted in his seat.

Once upon a time, he said, a boy met a man.

Here we go, said the mother.

The man promised this boy a kingdom, said the son. Or at least a house in the suburbs. And the boy thought this man was lying, but he wasn't. Which made the boy happy. Except the man maybe hadn't told the entire truth.

That he had a wife, said the mother.

And a child, said the son.

Jesus.

On the way.

That doesn't make a difference!

She hadn't meant to raise her voice. The son and his mother looked around the bar. But the two men in the corner only grinned, raising their beers.

I know you don't have any morals, said the mother, but do you think home-wrecking is a game?

You're asking the wrong question, said her son.

Does his wife know?

It's your turn, said the son, sipping his beer.

A little later, on the train home, the mother exhaled in her seat. Their car was packed with drunken businessmen patting one another's backs, and couples nosing each other's ears, and stragglers tapping at screens.

Fine, she said. Your father stole me from a tower.

We can't talk on here, said the son.

You asked me a question and this is your answer.

The game's no fun if you lie.

Your father plucked me from the top floor, said the mother. Carried me all the way down. Slayed a dragon and all of the towns-people.

You're being sore, said the son. You didn't fly all this way to be sore.

I didn't fucking fly all this way to play games with you, said the mother. And how would you know, anyway?

Dad's not that kind of guy, said the son, and his mother started to say something else, but the train slowed to a stop, and his mom shifted in her seat, and he reached for the rail, steadying them both.

Most days the son went to work. The mother followed him to the train station, where they diverged—and she rode from Shinjuku to Akihabara to Shibuya, funneling change into vending machines, walking in and out of shops, snapping photo after photo in Yoyogi Park. In front of the park's shrine, some women asked the mother to take their photo, so she did. When they asked the mother if she wanted one of herself, she smiled as they snapped about forty.

Some evenings, when the mother knew her son was finally asleep, she slipped on her sneakers, hopped down the stairs, and walked the strip lining the road by the station. Even on weeknights the streetlights were always on. Traffic slowed to a trickle. The mother made bets with herself—she'd walk to the next intersection, and then she'd turn right back around, but when she actually reached said intersection, it became the *next* intersection, and *that* one became the intersection that *followed*.

When the mother made it back to the apartment, she'd stand in the doorway, waiting to hear her son's snores. Once they returned, the mother settled back into bed, flipping her phone onto its side. There was a night when her husband texted her a single emoji, and she responded immediately, without even thinking about it, just as a reaction. She thought about how there are some things we simply can't shake.

Once upon a time, said the son, I spent the night on a bench in Montrose.

Once upon a time, said the son, I woke up in an entirely different part of Houston, in someone else's clothes.

Once upon a time, said the son, I brought a boy to the house. In high school, I think.

You didn't, said the mother.

This is a thing that happened.

Liar. When?

You were at work. Or something.

What? Where did he come from?

Who?

This boy.

Where they all come from. We met on an app.

Did you have sex? In the house?

Shit, said the son. Are you really asking me that?

You're the one who brought this up, said his mother. I'm asking because I'm worried about you.

You weren't worried then, detective.

I said I *am* worried, said the mother, you little shit.

Then don't be, said her son.

And anyway, said the son, Dad caught us. He told the guy to go home.

This made the mother open her mouth, but she didn't say anything. Her son waited for the words, but they just didn't come. So they both moved on.

Once upon a time, the mother didn't tell her son, my own mother tried to marry me off.

Once upon a time, the mother didn't tell her son, I couldn't have possibly made her life any more difficult: I broke every rule she ever put in front of me.

Once upon a time, the mother didn't tell her son, I introduced your grandmother to your father, and she told me she'd never approve. I laughed right in her face. And once I started, I simply never stopped. I laughed for weeks and weeks and weeks, until I ran out of breath, and then I started again.

Sometimes, in the evenings, they walked—usually in silence. They let the city do the talking between them. But this night was dimmer than most, and they'd chosen another club in Ni-chōme, and jazz drifted from the speakers, and the son looked entirely too distracted, flipping his phone on the bar counter.

Eventually the soundtrack changed. When the mother said the singer's name aloud, her son made a face.

What? she asked.

Nothing, said the son. You're just full of surprises. Flying here. Listening to city pop.

Children are the least surprising parts of their parents' lives.
Also, said the mother, does your married man have a name?
This again, said the son.
You brought it up.
He does, said the son.
You don't have to tell me what it is, said the mother.
I wasn't going to.
What do you even do together?
Do I need to spell it out?
You know exactly what I'm asking you.
Well, said the son, once upon a time—
Enough with that.
He takes me to baseball games, said the son. He likes baseball.
And we go for walks.
That's it?
Are you saying there should be more? Do you think we're aliens?
No, said the mother, but her son couldn't read her tone—it had
a tenor he'd never heard her use before.
The son picked up his phone again. He tossed it back onto
the counter.
Fine, said the mother. Then tell me a story about your students.
You don't want to hear about them, said the son.
Of course I do. And you clearly need something else to
talk about.
They don't take me seriously, he said. It's like they know the
whole thing's just an act. But they've taught me a lot.
The mother was about to ask what, specifically, the teens had
taught him—but the son raised a finger, grabbing at his cell.
He spoke quickly and quietly. His tone reminded her of his
father's. And then the son stepped across the room, down the
stairs, and out of sight, whispering into his phone, leaving his
mother alone.
He didn't come back for a while. Eventually the mother realized
that the bartender had been watching her. They made eye contact,
and the bartender nodded, reaching for another glass.

That night they walked back to the apartment in silence, and
they'd nearly made it to the complex when the son sat on the
bench out front, hiding his head in his hands. The mother eyed

him, blinking. She thought about rubbing his back. She wasn't sure if she should.

Listen, said the mother. I won't claim to know what it's like. But I do know that disrupting a marriage could be the death of you. You have to trust me.

Is that why you flew here? asked the son. To lecture me?

I'm only telling you what I see. You have to take care of yourself.

You don't know anything about it.

I know that it's eating you up.

You don't know shit.

I know that it's got you crying at midnight halfway across the world.

What if I told you that everyone knows? said the son. Him and his wife? What if I told you that she doesn't mind? That she's got her own thing going on too? What if I told you that that's just the way it is, and I'm fine with that?

The son found himself breathing heavily, and the mother took a second to catch her own breath. A group of guys walked around them, smoking, and one of them looked their way, whistling. When the son stood up, the mother put her palm on his shoulder. He sat back down.

Maybe I should just go back, said his mother.

Maybe you should, said the son.

I left because you made me, he said.

No one made you do anything, said his mother.

No, said the son, you made me. I would've died. So you made me.

The mother wasn't sure if they were talking about the same thing, and before she could ask, the son shook his head. He stepped into the complex alone.

Once upon a time, the mother didn't tell her son, I caught you with a boy. You never knew that I knew.

Once upon a time, the mother didn't tell her son, I watched the way you looked out the window afterward, and I thought about cupping your cheeks in my palm, telling you to go where you wanted.

Once upon a time, the mother told her son, I flew halfway around the world to find you, and you were doing mostly fine. Or as fine as could be expected. I didn't know if I preferred that to finding you in a mess. I didn't know if one was better than the other. Wasn't sure if I should stay to find out.

His mother had planned to stay a week, but on her last morning she extended her ticket.

The airline didn't give her a hard time. Her son didn't say anything about it either. That evening he didn't come back to the apartment, and she walked up the road to sit in a bar by herself. She ordered a glass of wine, watching the couples sitting across from each other. Another woman sitting alone made eye contact, and the mother nodded, and she nodded too.

The next morning the son returned. He was brighter than when he'd left.

You weren't wearing those clothes yesterday, said the mother.

Another case closed, said the son.

I just don't think it's right.

Which part of it?

You know what I mean.

I don't think I do.

Then that's your problem, said the mother. It's your problem for not trusting me. It's your life. But you have to trust me to know that, at least.

And before her son could say anything else, the mother added, It wasn't my first time.

Your first time what? said the son, wiping at his face.

At one of those bars. At a bar like that.

Oh.

I'd been with my sister.

Oh.

She took me a few times, said the mother. Once she took me and your father. We had a nice time.

The mother and her son stood across from each other. She glanced outside, through the window, at some kids hopscotching on the sidewalk.

Okay, said the son.

Okay, said the mother.

Well, said the son. That would've been nice to know. Before, I mean.

The son was still standing in the doorway, and when a man in the hallway passed behind him, he turned around, nodding and saying something his mother couldn't understand. Then the son turned to his mother. He stepped back outside and closed the door.

On the weekend they went to the park. The mother watched her son pick up snack after snack in the convenience store, tossing them into his basket, bantering with the man behind the register. Neither of them said much as they took one train and then another, filtering from her son's part of Tokyo, before walking through a handful of alleys that sprawled into an open field. A soccer game went on to their right, while a group of students danced to hip-hop in the foreground. What looked like the beginnings of a wedding photo session played out just beside the blanket they'd unfolded onto the grass.

The son spread the food across their blanket, opening boxes and shuffling silverware.

I forgot to bring a fork, he said.

I'll be fine, said the mother.

I meant for me.

Of course you did.

So, said the mother. What do you and your boyfriend eat together?

This was enough for the son to look up.

I've never heard you use that word, he said.

Well, said the mother.

The son grinned. His mother didn't.

He has a name, though, said the son. You can call him that.

Baby steps, said the mother.

The son watched the students as they made their way through their dance.

We go to bars, he said. We eat at stalls. Sometimes he cooks for me.

Do you ever cook for him?

Sure.

Often?

Often enough.

You should cook for the ones you love, said the mother.

Is there a story behind that?

The mother looked at her son, squinting. For the longest time she'd thought he looked like his father, before deciding that she wasn't exactly sure *whom* he looked like. It would be a few years before she decided this was because of their own similarities.

Once upon a time, said the mother, I met your father in a library. He loved poetry. That was his thing. He saw that I loved it too. And that's when I knew—him seeing what I saw. That's what tipped me off.

Listen, said the mother. If you're ever in a relationship as long as the one I've been in with your father, you'll know what to look for. And you should trust yourself to know. Whatever that means to you. Whatever that looks like.

The son turned away from his mother. He wiped at his face. The married couple beside them stumbled around in front of the photographer.

That sounds sentimental, he said.

I didn't say it wasn't.

His mother looked over the top of his head at the newlyweds taking photos. When the woman looked up, they made eye contact. The mother smiled at her, and the woman smiled back.

Anyway, said the mother. I thought we were taking turns.

So now you want to play?

The son looked at his mother and then at the group of students, chanting and dancing. It felt like the temperature had fallen just a bit. The song sounded a little like one the mother knew, some tune she hadn't heard in a very long time, but as soon as the thought occurred to her, she cast it away, and she knew it couldn't have been possible.

Hey, he said. I'm sorry.

Yeah, she said. You should be.

No, he said. I meant for the other thing. For everything. You probably think I'm an idiot.

The teens in front of them slowed their dancing, falling all over one another. It was enough for the mother to grin despite herself. The world was bigger than anyone could ever know. Maybe that was hardly a bad thing.

You are an idiot, she said.

Thanks, said the son.

You're welcome.

Maybe you *should* leave, after all.

I don't think so, said his mother, grabbing another rice roll from the basket. Tell me something else.

KEVIN WILSON

Biology

FROM *The Southern Review*

LAST NIGHT SOMEONE from my hometown posted on Facebook to say that our eighth-grade biology teacher, Mr. Reynolds, had died. There was a link to the local funeral home's memorial page, where I stared at a picture of Mr. Reynolds as I remembered him twenty-five years previous, his thick, black-rimmed glasses and buzz cut, his hair so blond it looked white. He had gray eyes. His face was always red, not like a rash but like a tint to his skin.

My boyfriend asked me why I was crying, though he didn't look up from his book. I was someone who cried a lot, over the slightest things, but what was strange was that I didn't realize that I had been crying. And once I noticed it, I thought more about Mr. Reynolds. His first name was Franklin, and there was a time when I would call him by that name. And I cried and I cried, and finally Bobby said, "Oh, God, what's wrong? What is going on, Patrick?" and he held me, and I put down the tablet, and I didn't say a word because I didn't know what to say. Because nothing I said would have made sense to him. It wouldn't have made sense to anyone else in the world. The only person who would have understood was dead.

In eighth grade, like every single grade leading up to that year, I was unpopular. I was too fat for sports and I had all these weird habits, little tics, that, even though everyone in our town had grown used to them, kept me from getting close to anyone. I cried sometimes if people smiled at me too long. I grunted a lot when I was reading to myself. I was an island, but not far enough away from this huge body of land that was the rest of my town, so I could easily feel the separation.

Since I was about eight or nine, I'd been updating and revising this card game I'd invented called Death Cards. It was this big stack of index cards, and most of the cards had interesting life events like graduating high school or winning an astronaut scholarship or having sex for the first time. But there were also death cards that featured people dying in horrific, graphic ways. Nobody would play the game with me, so I just played against myself. By eighth grade there were more than four hundred cards in the game. I couldn't stop playing, finding my way to whatever kind of life I could have before I died violently.

And, whatever, but it was clear to most kids that I was effeminate, too sensitive, which suggested something was deficient in my makeup.

And Mr. Reynolds was famously weird. He lived with his mother. He'd been in Vietnam, which wasn't weird, really, but there was a long-standing story that one time a car in the school parking lot had backfired and Mr. Reynolds had immediately sprawled on the floor, his face radiating panic, and the principal had to come convince him to get back up and keep teaching. My cousin, who was eight years older than me, said he'd been in the class when it happened, but he was such a fucking liar, so who knew. Mr. Reynolds was very shy and quiet, and students often talked over him when he was teaching. He drove this tiny little foreign car, and the driver's side door was a completely different color from the rest of the car, and he'd duct-taped the rear bumper, but sometimes it would loosen and drag across the asphalt parking lot. Every day he wore short-sleeved shirts, weird plaid, and olive-green chinos, and ugly brown loafers. He was freakishly tall, which seemed to embarrass him, and he didn't take advantage of it in order to make himself seem imposing. He just looked stretched out, like a cartoon character.

But I liked listening to him, the way he talked about this kind of bird where the babies fight each other to the death in order to be the one who gets the food from the mother. One time he brought in this weird slug and told us about how its mouth was like sandpaper and it could tear out the eyes of a baby bird, or something like that. He talked about egg wars, where different bird species tried to fuck each other over. Maybe eighth grade was the bird year, or maybe Mr. Reynolds just really loved birds, but he seemed embarrassed by the sections that talked about human biology, our own weird bodies, and so he focused on animals, the natural world, the horrific shit that all living things did just to keep themselves alive.

I made straight As in his class, sometimes even drew pictures of dead animals to support my short-essay answers. And he would mark each one with a very detailed drawing of a thumbs-up symbol. "Good job," he'd whisper to me as he passed by my desk, handing back tests. He would stoop down and gently place the test right in front of me, and I'd feel dizzy a little. His class preceded the pep rallies or assemblies that happened every Thursday afternoon, and he said that if I wanted, I could stay in his classroom, that I had his permission to skip the pep rally. I thought maybe he'd heard about the fact that in seventh grade someone tripped me, or probably I just tripped on my own, and I fell down the bleachers and fractured my wrist. But I was happy for the respite.

He'd pull out weird taxidermy from the cabinets in his classroom, rodents and reptiles that looked so shabby that I wanted to set them on fire. I asked if he made them, and he said he'd bought them out of a catalogue. "I had high hopes for myself when I started teaching," he told me, his voice so soft and deep at the same time. He never had stubble, the smoothest face I'd ever seen. "I knew I wasn't an academic," he continued, "and I wouldn't be a scientist or anything like that. I barely passed college. But I thought I'd be a good teacher."

"You are a good teacher," I told him.

"I don't think I am," he said.

"You're my favorite teacher," I said.

He just smiled and then showed me some bones that he said he thought were a raccoon's.

There were these girls in my class, badasses, and they played basketball and dipped and wore these huge earrings that looked painful as shit. And they burned Mr. Reynolds alive if he gave them an opening. They talked about his car, how ugly it was, how slow it was. They said sometimes they saw it parked out in front of their houses and they figured he was spying on them, trying to see them naked. They said he looked like a giraffe.

"C'mon now," he'd say, getting flustered.

If I'd had a gun, if I knew how to get a gun, I would have murdered everyone in the classroom.

I guess he'd been a pretty great basketball player in high school, had led the team to a state championship, but the girls asserted that he couldn't keep up with them. They talked about this all the time, how they'd wear his ass out on the court. And he'd shake his head and talk about how sharp an eagle's talons were, the violence they could do to a human body.

Pretty soon I started eating my lunch in Mr. Reynolds's classroom. I'd sit at my desk, and he'd sit at his, and we'd eat in silence, me chewing on some rubbery ham sandwich. He always brought a thermos of soup and a package of peanut butter crackers. Afterward, he'd drop an Alka-Seltzer into a cup and drink that, because he said his stomach wasn't great. I asked him about his car, and he chuckled. "The kids hate that car, don't they?" he said.

"Why don't you get a new one?" I said.

"They cost a lot of money," he said. "And I like that car. It's a kind of science project, I guess, just seeing how long I can keep it running."

I kind of understood him, and then he said, "This might help you, Patrick. If people think you are strange, different, they can be cruel. They look for instability, an opening. My car, it's not me, is it? It's just this piece of metal that I drive to work every day. But people can look at it and laugh, and they think it hurts me, but it doesn't. Because it's not me. If you give people something easy, they'll take it. And sometimes that's all they need."

I thought about how there were so many other things about Mr. Reynolds that the kids made fun of, but I still knew what he meant. I reached into my backpack and pulled out my huge bricks of index cards.

"Now what is this?" he asked, curious.

"Death Cards," I told him.

"Is this maybe your thing?" he asked, a little smile on his face.

"I think it could be," I said.

I showed him how it worked. There were four stacks: Childhood, Young Adult, Adulthood, Old Age. For each stack there were life events, with death cards mixed in. The object was to draw four cards from each stack without getting a death card. If you got a death card during Young Adult, then you looked at the life events up to that point and that was the sum total of your life.

"What happens if you make it all the way through the game without getting a death card?" he asked. I couldn't believe he was taking it seriously. I was shaking a little.

"You still die, but you die in your sleep," I told him. "Peacefully."

He seemed to like this possibility. And so we played. Mr. Reynolds won a spelling bee, and escaped from a kidnapper, and rescued a puppy, and got a dirt bike for Christmas, an amazing childhood. He made it all the way to his second card of Adulthood before a business rival poisoned him. This seemed to please him. "This is a good game," he said.

"I play it all the time," I told him.

He reached into his desk and pulled out a blank index card. He drew a sketch of a man, a cartoony version of himself, standing in front of a chalkboard. He wrote "Become a junior high science teacher" at the top, and then he slipped it into the middle of the Adulthood deck.

"I hope I never get that one," he said.

"Maybe that's like your own secret death card," I said, and this made him smile and turn a brighter shade of red.

In the section on evolution, things got a little weird. Our town wasn't that far away from where the Scopes Trial had been, which always embarrassed me. Mr. Reynolds outlined the details of evolution, how it worked. Kima Walker, one of the most beautiful girls in the school, said softly, kind of sad, "I know that I did not come from some monkey," and I waited for Mr. Reynolds to destroy her. My parents both worked factory jobs, my mom had dropped out of high school and my dad never went to college. But they were smart people. They told me about evolution when I was so little, and they told it to me with such happiness. I think they liked the idea that you could be something but turn into something else. Around that same time I asked them about the Bible, and my mom just shrugged. "Just stories," she said.

"Do you think we evolved from monkeys?" Jeff Jeffcoat asked Mr. Reynolds, who seemed to think about it.

"Well," he said softly, "evolution takes place over thousands of

years, these slow incremental changes. For us to evolve from monkeys, the world would have to be much older than we suspect that
it is. So I'm not sure that evolution is fully proven. There are certainly verifiable instances of it, but I think it requires more analysis, maybe more than we can do in the lifespan of human beings."

I felt like someone had punched me in the stomach. Kima
Walker looked so happy. The whole class seemed to take Mr. Reynolds and place him in a better part of their consciousness. The rest
of class that day went so smoothly. I barely listened. I took out an
index card and drew a picture of a gorilla stabbing a human being
with a huge spear. I wrote "Mishap at the Zoo" at the top.

My disappointment with Mr. Reynolds, and the other students'
truce with him, ended a week later when Marigold Timmins, who
played power forward on the girls' basketball team, told Mr. Reynolds, after she'd made a D on a quiz, that she could destroy him in
a game of one-on-one. Mr. Reynolds had been writing some notes
on the chalkboard, and I watched his body stiffen, his hand just
hovering there.

"You think you could beat me?" he asked, and it looked like he
was talking to the chalkboard, about to fight it.

"I could," she said.

Mr. Reynolds turned around. "How much do you wanna bet?"
and the class went "Ooooohhhhh," and Marigold said, "Twenty dollars."

"Let me see the twenty dollars," he said, and Marigold said,
"Let me see if you have twenty dollars," and the class went
"Ooooohhhhh" again. Mr. Reynolds reached into his wallet, fucking Velcro, and slammed a twenty on his desk. Marigold reached
into her purse and counted out ten ones and a five. "That's all I
have," she said, and Mr. Reynolds said that was just fine.

"Patrick," he said, and I got scared. "You hold the money," and
so I got up and waddled around the room to get the money.

"Let's go," Mr. Reynolds said, and he walked into the hallway. It
took a few seconds, some giggling, but soon we all followed him,
down the hall, out of the main building, and into the gym.

The gym teacher, Coach Billings, seemed perturbed to have us
in there. His class was playing badminton on one half of the gym.

"Franklin?" he asked Mr. Reynolds. "You doing a science project
in here or something?"

"Jimmy, I need to use that half of the court for a demonstration. It's all about"—he paused, trying to think of something—"physics and whatnot."

Mr. Reynolds went to get a basketball, and Marigold was stretching.

"Can't have those shoes on the court, Franklin," Coach Billings said apologetically, and Mr. Reynolds just kicked off his loafers, peeled off his socks, and walked onto the court. "We'll play to five," he said, "one point per basket. Make it, take it."

I know for a fact, one hundred percent, that I was the only person in that gym who wanted Mr. Reynolds to win. Marigold's boyfriend had called me a queer one day when he saw that I had a handkerchief that had little roses embroidered on it.

Marigold took the ball from Mr. Reynolds and started dribbling to her right, looking to blow past Mr. Reynolds, but he stayed with her, and when she went for a layup, he swatted it away so easily that the whole class seemed to groan at the same time. In his bare feet, toes as long as fingers, he ran down the bouncing ball and immediately put up a weird set shot that came from his hip, and he buried it easily. "One-zero," he said, and Marigold looked puffy and angry.

Mr. Reynolds scored three points as easily as possible, even hitting a skyhook over Marigold's ineffective defense. When he got the ball back, Marigold dug in, scuffed her sneakers on the squeaky floor, and Mr. Reynolds faked a shot. In that second he dribbled past her, wide open, and he leapt into the air. It looked like he was going to dunk it, but he just didn't quite have the height, and so he bounced it off the backboard at the last second and the shot fell through.

The class hooted and hollered, and Marigold was crying. Mr. Reynolds came over to me, and I handed him the money, and he put it all in his wallet. I could not believe that he was taking Marigold's money; I thought that would be illegal. Mr. Reynolds calmly put on his socks and loafers, and we all marched back into our classroom and sat in silence until the bell rang a few minutes later.

"That was amazing," I told him, the last one out the door.

"I've not been that scared in a long time," he said, huffing a little, his teeth chattering.

I thought about what kind of life card that would be, but it seemed too complicated, too much text to write to explain it.

We were playing Death Cards in his classroom one day during lunch, and I made it all the way through the game without drawing a death card. Mr. Reynolds had fallen into a pool and drowned as a child, but he seemed happy to watch me accumulate experiences on my way to a quiet death.

When I was done, I shuffled the cards again, but Mr. Reynolds said, "Not a bad life."

"I didn't have sex, though," I said. There were sex cards interspersed through the decks, though the pictures I drew were just fancy hearts.

"It isn't necessary for a good life," he said. I felt like we were friends, and I wondered if Mr. Reynolds had any other friends. I knew that I didn't.

"Have you ever had sex?" I asked, and he blushed, but he didn't seem angry with me.

"Yeah," he said finally. "In Vietnam. It was awful."

"It was?" I asked, and he nodded.

"It was a kind of, like, a payment situation," he said. "All the guys did it, and they really wouldn't leave me alone until I did it too. I hated it so much."

"But never again?" I asked, feeling so sad.

"Nope," he said. "Never came up again. Never went looking for it again. Never felt like I needed it."

"And you feel like you've had a good life without it?" I asked. I needed to know what my life could be like.

"I haven't had a good life," he said, looking right at me, his eyes kind of watery. "But it wasn't because of sex. It's like your card game, Patrick. You just pick cards and you can't really control it."

"But you only get to play the game once," I said.

"Yeah," he said, "that's true."

"Maybe that's why we like this game," I offered.

"Maybe," he replied.

"Do you believe in heaven?" I asked.

"It doesn't seem scientifically possible," he said. "I don't even know if I'd want there to be one. Whoever made earth made heaven too, right? So who's to say that heaven would be any better?" He seemed to not even register that I was there, that I had a body and was right next to him. He seemed like he was staring into some black hole.

I reached over and touched his hand. "You're a great teacher, Franklin," I said.

He smiled. "Thanks, Patrick."

The next part of the story, I don't even want to tell it. It's not the important thing, but it's necessary. Latisha Gordon, who was the star player on the girls' basketball team, a point guard who could score in waves, was impossible to shake off when she played defense, could dribble like a playground legend, challenged Mr. Reynolds to another game of one-on-one for twenty bucks. And Mr. Reynolds said no. Latisha wasn't even in our class; she had study hall that period and just came in because she was friends with Marigold. I imagine that they had been planning this for weeks and weeks.

Finally Mr. Reynolds said okay, and I gathered up the money, and we all marched into the gym. And Latisha scored two quick baskets, but then Mr. Reynolds came back with two of his own, and then he went for a layup and came down weird and his ankle just snapped.

He didn't even make a noise in reaction. We heard that snapping sound, like a tree branch breaking off, and then it was just silence. And then we all saw Mr. Reynolds's ankle, turned the absolute wrong way, and he was holding his leg with both hands, kind of elevating it. And then kids started screaming, so loud, so sustained, and one boy threw up in the bleachers, this soupy vomit running down and dripping to the wooden floor under the bleachers.

Latisha didn't even look at Mr. Reynolds, just jogged out of the gym, afraid of getting into trouble. I wanted to run to Mr. Reynolds, to hold him, but I was paralyzed. Mr. Reynolds had drawn a death card, such a bad one, at just the wrong time. The money was in my hands, getting sweaty and warm, and I ripped it up into tiny little pieces, and I threw it down, and a few pieces fluttered around and got stuck in the vomit.

Coach Billings finally went over to Mr. Reynolds, and then an ambulance came, and they carried him out of the gym, and the principal was standing there, looking so confused and so angry, and Marigold was trying to explain what had happened. The bell rang for the next class, and I still didn't move. I just sat in the bleachers, and I stayed there the rest of the day, and I was so invisible in that school that no one even noticed. I just sat in the bleachers and cried.

That night, back at home, I drew about forty new death cards, just awful, awful scenarios. I surprised even myself. I didn't put them into the decks. I just made it a single deck, all on its own, and I turned them over one after the other, nothing but death, nothing but humiliation. I did that all night, didn't even sleep, and when I went to school the next morning, Mr. Reynolds wasn't there, and this old lady was our substitute. When we asked about Mr. Reynolds, she said he was on medical leave and would be gone for the rest of the year.

"Was he fired?" Marigold asked, and she seemed sheepish, a little guilty.

"Heavens no," the woman said. "He'll be back next year."

I found Mr. Reynolds's address in the phone book, and on Saturday I rode my bike the nearly six miles to his house, my body covered in sweat even though it was still cold out, the last bit of winter. My thighs hurt so bad and my stomach was cramping. The bike was something I'd outgrown and then shown so little interest in that my parents never bought me a new one. But I made it to Mr. Reynolds's house, his car parked in the driveway, and there was no going back now.

His mom answered the door, ancient but surprisingly sturdy, really tall, even though she was hunched over from age. She had been a teacher at the same middle school, English, but that was way before my time. My mom didn't even remember her.

"Yes?" she asked, a little afraid of this fat kid with long eyelashes. I wondered if anyone besides the two of them had been in the house in years.

"Is Mr. Reynolds here?" I asked. I reached into my backpack and showed her a box of Russell Stover chocolates that I'd bought with my allowance. "I have a get-well present for him."

"Oh, how sweet," she said. She turned around and walked back to her recliner and picked up this big book, which I remember was a biography of Sammy Davis Jr., and simply said, "He's in his room at the end of the hall."

The house smelled clean, like lemon, and everything was in its proper place. I had imagined mold and cat piss and mounted deer heads everywhere. But this was an ordinary house, a little nicer, actually, than the house I shared with my parents and younger sister. I knocked on the door, and Mr. Reynolds said, "Mom?"

"It's Patrick," I said. There was a long pause, and then he finally said, "Okay, come in."

He was sitting up in his bed, a mystery novel on his lap. There was a big desk in the room that had all these science books neatly arranged on it, lots of notes. He had a framed, signed poster of Kareem Abdul-Jabbar on his wall, and some Audubon prints that were really beautiful and looked expensive. On the nightstand was a plate with peanut butter crackers and a glass of tomato juice.

"Patrick," he said. "What are you doing here?" He seemed embarrassed to see me. He was wearing old-fashioned pajamas and a knit cap for the cold.

"I brought you this," I said, handing him the chocolates.

"Oh, that's really nice of you," he said. He looked at me for a second and then back at the chocolates. "Would you like to eat some?" he asked, and I nodded. He ripped off the plastic film and we each ate about four chocolates, chewing the nougat in silence.

"Are you okay?" I asked.

"I will be in a while," he said. "No permanent damage, surprisingly enough. The doctor says the bone will actually be stronger at the break than it was before once it heals." I tried to look at his legs, but they were under the blankets.

"And you're not in trouble?" I asked, and he blushed.

"The principal says that I can't play basketball against my students for money." He paused, thinking about things. "I can't play basketball with them even not for money," he then said. "And I'm on a kind of probationary period. But no, not really. It's hard to get fired, I think."

"That's good," I told him. "I miss you in class."

"Well, I miss you too," he said, and then I just started weeping. I don't even know why, but the sight of him there, broken, so accepting of his sad life, it made me want to die.

"Patrick," he said, reaching out for me. He touched my face, which made me feel better.

"I don't know what to do," I said, hiccuping, "I'm a freak. I hate my life."

"You are not a freak," he said.

"I'm gay, I think," I told him, the first time I'd told anyone, "but

I don't even know if I'm gay, really. How would I know? There are only about three other boys in the school who are gay, and I don't even know if they know that they are gay. And I'm just stuck here."

"If you're gay," Mr. Reynolds said, "it is not a bad thing. Okay, Patrick? It's not."

And then I looked up at him, still crying. "Are you gay?" I asked.

He looked pained but seemed to consider the question. "I don't think so," he finally said. "At one point I might have been, but I kind of missed that window. I don't think I'm anything, Patrick."

"Could I kiss you?" I asked, fumbling for something, trying to figure my way into my own life.

"No," he said. "You do not want your first kiss to be with me. It will be something you think about every single time you kiss another person."

"Please, Franklin?" I asked. Was this the reason that I'd even come here? I had no idea. I didn't know exactly what I was doing or saying.

"Life does not always have to be bad, Patrick, but maybe right now it has to be for you. But get out of here, go to college, a college in a big city or with a lot of students, and then maybe you can figure this out. Maybe you can find happiness."

"But maybe I never will," I said. "Maybe this is it."

"Maybe," he admitted, "but just try, okay? Just try."

I sniffled, trying to gain some composure. "Okay," I told him, and he smiled.

"Do you want another chocolate?" he asked me, but I said that I thought my stomach was hurting. He put the chocolates away and regarded me with tenderness.

"Did you bring your Death Cards?" he asked, and I nodded because I never went anywhere without them. I reached into my backpack and produced the stacks, held together with rubber bands.

"Could we try something?" he asked me. He took the first stack of cards, and he went through them, removing every single death card from the deck. He took the next stack and did the same, and I took a stack and removed the death cards. I finished removing all the cards from the last stack, and we stared at them, spread out over the quilt on his bed. There were so many ways to die, I realized, so many ways that things would just stop and never start again.

Then Mr. Reynolds drew a card, and he held it up for me, and it made me smile. He had won a baby beauty pageant. And then I drew. And then he did. And we did that all afternoon, without the possibility of death, an entire life, and then a life stacked on top of that, and then another life stacked on top of that, until there was nothing but life, always happening, never stopping. And I held his hand at one point, and I thanked him again, and he just nodded.

I never saw him again after that. I moved to the high school the next year, and I nearly killed myself, but I held on to the part of me that I wanted to keep. And I made it out of that place, which wasn't even a bad place really, or no worse than any other place for someone like me. And I got to somewhere good. I didn't evolve, nothing like that. I just held on to myself and found a place where I could keep living. And eventually I stopped thinking so much about Mr. Reynolds, because thinking about him meant thinking about that time in my life. And he just sat there, in this tiny little part of my heart. And he never changed either.

And now he was dead. And there was no way that I could explain it to my boyfriend. He would not know how those cards worked, the sensation of drawing them, each time wondering what awful thing might appear, and how much of a relief it was, even if it was ordinary, that you were still here, still in this world.

Little Beast

FROM *BOMB*

AT THIRTEEN, I felt my body slopping. Though I sat in the middle of the nurse's height-weight chart, though I'd memorized the textbook diagram with its cakelike cross section of flesh (epidermis, dermis, hypodermis stippled yellow with fat), my problem went deeper than biology. Mine was a more fundamental failure. My posture was liquid and my spine nonexistent despite containing the requisite thirty-three vertebrae. I spilled into conversations and overshared the banal. My words manifested as spit on listeners' cheeks. Even teachers wore expressions of disgust when my hand shot up—expressions blotted away by sympathy like a napkin blots grease.

Of course, no one at Alta said a thing. Alta was an all-girls' school built on progressive principles. Marble halls. Uniforms androgynous and ethically sourced. Conceived by third-wave feminists, Alta wasn't named after some saint. It stood for the Academy for the Literacy and Tutelage of Aspirants.

Aspirants were bright young women who would one day found a nonprofit or direct quiet, critically reviewed films that didn't sell, a fact that wouldn't matter because Alta believed in Riches Above Money, a slogan displayed without irony atop the annual list of donors. Aspirants included senators' daughters, screenwriters' daughters, celebrities' daughters, the ethnically exotic daughters of parents so undiscussed it was clear they were heir to secret dynasties.

And me. Janitor's daughter. Scholarship kid.

*

My father said, *Quit your fretting, girlie.* My father said, *They'll like you if you act yourself.* When this proved futile, my father said, *You'll only grow into yourself.* But what did he know? My father bought our jeans from Walmart bargain bins, our dinners from Grocery Outlet. He laughed too loud. In public, he was fond of asking what had clogged our toilet, what size training bra I wore. In the dusk hours between the end of my day and the beginning of his, as our Lean Cuisines orbited in the microwave's glow, my father asked endless questions. About my wins in the Biology Olympiad. About my homeroom teacher. About the girls he insisted on calling my friends. I mumbled, which made him bend closer. In his soft spine, in his supplicant's pose, I saw and despised myself.

My father had it wrong. I didn't care about the girls who asked me, so kindly, *How are you? Did you change your hair? Doing anything fun this weekend?* Girls who smiled at my answers and then drifted back to discussing tennis coaches and ski trips, the afterglow of their charity making them even more resplendent. And I didn't care about the frizzy, sharp-voiced girls who sat with me at the Olympiad and debated their horses with glee. I didn't care about the girls who volunteered for senators on weekends and cornered me with petitions, describing themselves as Future Leaders. Oh, there were aspirants of every kind at Alta, girls so golden you had to sort them into further shades of bronze and lemon and amber, gorgeous girls and kind girls and smart girls and nervy girls and charming girls and, most of all, wealthy girls. At another school I might have dreamed of befriending any one of them. But because my father was Alta's night janitor, he knew their secrets by way of secretaries and cafeteria ladies, by way of lockers and trash cans. He told me whose birthday was coming up, who passed notes to whom, and who loved Hot Cheetos or chess. His disclosures scrubbed those aspirants as clean of interest as the floors he mopped at night.

Alta's motto was *Self-expression, Open Dialogue, Open Heart,* and my father warped those words to excess—an excess I'd inherited. His DNA ran riot through my cells, spattered from my voice, his shamefulness breaking out, like acne, over me. The girls I yearned to know were the ones wrapped in silence. Even teachers didn't bother calling on them. Not glowing but shadowed girls, skinny wraiths with bitten nails, dark circles, dry hair. An exhaustion that made them seem older and wiser. Such girls had no hobbies or

sports teams that I knew of—though participation was manda-
tory at Alta. It was as if whatever drained them was extracurricu-
lar enough.

A *bit strange* was the strongest thing I heard said about the silent
girls, thanks to Alta's rampant kindness. Mostly those girls were
buffered in silence as they passed through the halls. There were
maybe five of them, though the precise number was slippery; they
disappeared or reappeared from class at will, reinforcing the sense
that they belonged not to Alta's world but to a different one. A
world my father couldn't see into. Under Alta's bright lights, these
girls' lashes drew vertical bars over their eyes. More than anything,
I wanted to know what inside them needed caging.

That summer I suffered pains in my shinbones. I gnashed my teeth
at night and dreamed of foxes nipping and gnawing. In July I woke
up six inches taller, wrists and ankles rawly exposed. *Come, girlie,*
my father would say, blowing on a breakfast Hot Pocket. *Put some
meat on yourself.* My jaw was sore from clenching. For once I turned
breakfast away.

I fled from the kitchen, the single bedroom, the bathroom with
walls so thin I heard every effort of my father's body, the living
room where each morning my father became a lump on the pull-
out couch. I spent my days in the library periodical room, which
smelled of mildew; to inhale was to imagine the green of the
smoothies aspirants drank in flavors like wheatgrass and kale. I
flipped through books my biology teacher had recommended, but
my head was as queerly hollow as my stomach. I found myself at
the rack of magazines, their colors candy-loud.

At home my father limited my TV time. He wouldn't buy magazine subscriptions. *Seventeen magazine?* he joked. *You have four years!
What's your hurry, trying to grow up so fast?*

I waded out past diet tips and relationship advice, past starlets
smiling their aspirant smiles, until I was swimming in large-sheaf
tabloids that featured stories of girls missing and found, girls taken
and stolen, girls held ransom and girls held till whatever wet and
vital thing inside them dried out. Was it that particular summer
that kept violence close to its heart like a dark clot, or was it me? I
didn't ask. The two questions were one.

I left for school that fall with my hems high above my ankles.

Aren't you cold, then? my father said as he tried to give me his jacket. But the cold just pushed me upright. Pushed me straighter.

It was a new season.

The less I ate, the heavier I felt. I dozed through class and dreamed of chewing, woke with blood in my mouth and my tongue wedged between my teeth. My body grew dense with meaning, every shrinking inch significant. A fine fur grew over my arms and stomach, warming me in place of food. The bones of my face pushed out, but they weren't the ones I'd known; they seemed of another creature. The girls who asked, so kindly, *How are you?* soon asked, *Are you okay?*, soon asked, *Don't you want to join us for lunch?*, and soon asked nothing at all. I overhead whispers from the bathroom stall: *She's a bit off, yeah? Like . . . them.*

For the first time, silence gathered around me.

And then a girl approached. I felt her before I saw her. I'd read about pheromones, those scentless, invisible particles that drew like animal to like through the deepest thickets.

Can I bum a cig? she said.

I told her I didn't smoke.

Oh. I figured you did. Her pause felt approving. *It's good, you know. For the weight and all.*

I learned that day that even these girls weren't born with nothing behind their eyes. They had ways of inviting it in.

In our home, our four hundred square feet of garden-level space where the light through the landlord's elms was forever crepuscular, my father and I shared one bathroom. Its sink had one broken drawer and one working drawer. Again and again my father forgot my new rules for privacy. Again and again he exposed my tampons and razors to the light. As I raged, he laughed. *Ahh, what do I care, girlie?* My father still cleaned my room and folded my laundry, still dusted the shoebox that held my diary. *I've seen you inside and out. Remember who cleaned your diapers, girlie?* My father moved to press his forehead to mine, as he'd done since I was small. I jerked away. In a flash of inspiration, I drew my lashes down to hide my eyes from the hurt in his.

It was, first, an accident. I was cutting a head of celery, pushing the knife through cell walls, thinking of empty calories and a particu-

lar, shimmering nothing I'd seen slide behind the eyes of a girl on
the late-night news. The knife slipped.

My father, my father. Four long strides from couch to kitchen
and he was there, bent over my bleeding wrist. He blocked my
view. His wailing hurt my ears. I pulled free and locked myself in
the bathroom.

Let me help, my father said as he pounded the door. *What's come
over you, girlie?* His voice swelled and subsided, like the pulse in my
wrist, like the warped wood between us, something like how the
pupils of the girl on TV had jumped from small to big, small to big
as a line of text flashed: RESCUED AFTER 8 MONTHS. VICTIM: HE LIKED
TO WATCH ME BREATHE. A girl in a room. A man entrapping.
The suffocation I felt at night as my shins ached with growing, as
my father snored through the wall. The bleeding made me feel
weaker, then stronger, just as the food I didn't eat made me weaker
and stronger.

I yelled in a voice not mine, *STAY OUT, YOU PERVERT.*

For once my father had nothing to say. He fled from the thing
inside me.

The next day the silence widened. Three feet, then five, a moat
till I had half the hall to myself and my bloody wrist. I picked at
the loose end of the bandage as all Alta watched. I dripped on the
floors my father would have to mop.

Once again a girl appeared, summoned by my blood as a shark
is summoned across murky waters. It wasn't the one who'd asked
for a smoke. This girl took my wrist. Her hand, like mine, was
wrapped, but in fabric and not gauze. She wore her shirt several
sizes too big, defying the Alta fashion of cuffed sleeves. She was
armored in cloth as she turned my wrist. My heart beat beneath
her fingers.

Her lashes lifted, those cage bars opened. Her teeth showed,
shockingly yellow and jagged, and what smiled at me wasn't pretty
or sweet, wasn't girl so much as beast.

And then the biology teacher called my name and rushed me
into a room.

The biology teacher leaned forward in a listening pose reminis-
cent of my father: elbows on knees, spine convex, a cave at her
center I was meant to fill with words.

I've noticed some changes in your performance this year. Is everything okay here? At home?

I conjured the nothing over my eyes.

My dear, if you won't talk I'm going to have to call your father in.

My father by day was even more slovenly than by night. If called, he'd lurch through the halls in rumpled undershirt and sagging pajamas. He had no shame. Two years ago, when he had to fetch me home for running a temperature, he hailed the lunch ladies, clapped the groundskeeper's shoulder so hard girls heard it across the lawn, addressed the dean by a nickname. My father's voice was a brassy trumpet, loud, off-pitch, a dissonance he was deaf to. He asked after girls' famous fathers; he made jokes and collected tolerant smiles. He winked as I in my fever burned with embarrassment. For weeks after, Alta was particularly kind, the questions about my father more charitable than ever.

If he came today, Alta would look at me and see only him. He'd undo everything.

No, I said, standing. *Not him. Please. Anything but that.*

The teacher flicked her tongue against her wet teeth. She nodded. I must have imagined the click then, as if I'd just given the right answer in Olympiad.

Very well, she said, writing on her pad. *But starting today Alta will be monitoring you. You're excused from all extracurriculars. Go here at two o'clock. Just show this note to your teacher.*

I entered the territory of the girls.

A strange room, down a half-flight of stairs I'd never seen. Subterranean light, the ceiling dusty and low. One barred window. A cage.

It was run by a woman who resembled a mouse, whose trembling voice bid the others to welcome me. *Into our fold,* the mouse said, as if they were four sheep instead of something else. The four ignored her—half a mouthful of a woman, not worth the effort. It was me they watched.

Seen up close, their differences became clear. A tall, dark one with shivering pupils. A freckled one with sunken cheeks and fat ankles. An elfin one with unwashed hair and skin, emitting a faint mushroomy smell. And the one who'd taken my wrist, who armored herself with a too-big uniform, who wasn't beautiful but sat as if she were.

And me.

We formed a circle. The elf spoke first. Her voice was faint. Her arms were furred like mine, more peach than pelt. Her wrists bowed like uncooked spaghetti. She was the thinnest. She was the one who'd asked for a cigarette.

Yesterday would have been . . . she said.

The mouse prompted, *What?*

Her birthday . . .

Do you mean your sister's?

Her twentieth . . . or twenty-first? I think?

How did that make you feel? said the mouse.

Not much, the elf said. God, how I envied her. She made *sister* a nothing in her mouth as we girls clotted around her.

The mouse moved on.

The tall one had a mother at whom she hurled adjectives like sharp rocks.

The freckled one spoke of food—how it went down and how it came up—with evangelical thunder, pausing to circle her tongue around her lips.

The armored one alone held the mouse's gaze. The clot shifted toward her as she spoke. She twirled her hair, slick and dark, her pale fingers darting indecently through. She was the leader. She described her older lover's tattoos and needles, his hands. *I get visiting rights after the trial,* she said—to us, but especially to the mouse, who grew stiller and stiller, as certain prey did on the nature documentaries my father preferred to the news.

What did my father know? He scrubbed Alta's halls while news about rescued dogs, civic buildings, small-time robberies, and politics washed out as the witching hour washed in. Late at night the coverage gave way to the faces of girls and what was done to their bodies. Staticky clips from dispatcher calls. Teary interviews. But loudest of all, the silence. Newscasters resorted to euphemisms even as the screen showed photo after bloody photo. When I fell asleep at three or four, it was those unspoken acts I dreamed of, more terrifying than gun or rope. The armored girl knew that same secret. She controlled her body, kept it skinny like ours, but curved in the right places. Sex came off her, which was better than beauty, stronger than the stink of the elf's unwashed hair or the freckled one's vomity breath. She was the kind of girl who scared reporters, scared my father, and scared the mouse, who cut her off and turned to me.

This is a safe space, the mouse said. *You can speak without fear of repercussion — save facts that might compromise your immediate safety. Do you understand?*

I tuned her out. I'd fooled her already. These girls were my true test. *My father,* I said to the four of them. *He watches me breathe at night.*

My father said, *Aren't you a busy one these days?* My father said, *What keeps you so long after school?* My father said, with hope a whine in his voice, *Have you made new friends, girlie?* I erected silence around me.

Later that night, as I pretended to sleep, I heard the door to my room open. My father rummaged in my shoebox. Inside he'd find the diary I no longer wrote in, the mascara I now wore, a list of negative-calorie foods, a stack of glossy magazines from my new friends. And he'd find the X-Acto knife. The armored one had handed it to me, showing as she did the parallel scars beneath her overlong shirt sleeves, scars as neat as my celery sticks.

I heard my father stand, his breath quickening. I remembered leaning, sodden, against his chest when he pulled me out of public pools where I liked to sink to the bottom for the pleasure of having him rescue me, for the feel of his love beating hard, whipped into a panic.

I studied the armored one's wrist, the elf's trailing sentences, how the freckled one worried her bottom lip until it bled, and how the tall one shivered with rage. I memorized them as I'd once memorized phylum and genus, the intricacies of the digestive system and sodium-potassium pumps, as I'd once memorized the shapes of all forty-six chromosomes, trying to decipher in their angles the language of my inheritance.

Nimbly, I answered the mouse's prompts:

I don't feel anything unless I cut myself.

Sometimes I can't get out of bed in the morning.

For a time it worked. For a time I walked the halls with the four and sat with them at lunch. We never ate; we only listed what we'd eaten. All my life I'd been good at beginnings: the promising student, the scholarship case with potential, the desired daughter eagerly anticipated in the baby book my mother filled before she died in birth. But as the weeks passed, there grew between me and the four of them a distance: a pause after I spoke, a narrowing of eyes, a cigarette they passed stopping just before it got to me.

He comes into my room at night.

He said he's seen me inside and out.

The colder they grew, the louder I became to convince them. My voice was cheap and tinny, like the imitation charm bracelet I had begged my father to buy me in my first month at Alta. I lost it after the cheap clasp rusted clean through.

I thought I'd found my place at Alta in this cage where girls traded in a currency other than money. But I was still poor. Not in charms and yachts and horses this time—I was poor in neglect, in that cold, instructive pain. I hadn't had tongues or pills or communion wafers forced into my mouth. Instead I'd had dinners of chicken and mashed potatoes, dutifully stirred halfway through heating so that they neither burnt nor froze my tongue. I'd had pillows under my cheek as I slept in my father's truck, waiting for him to finish his shift; I'd had, every hour, the shadow of his return to check on me.

I abandoned my schoolwork to study the news. Breaking news, late-night news, old news from library records. I memorized captions and quotes. The mouse commended me for my honesty. Called it progress. But I knew I was regressing. I spoke from the edge of my seat, spit flying, my spine curving toward my audience of four. Back to my invertebrate state. One day I leaned in so far while reciting a headline from 1973 that I fell from my chair.

The four watched me sprawl as the mouse ran over, squeaking. She palpated my twisted wrist and rushed from the room to get a nurse.

Only then did they descend on me. The armored one grabbed my arm and pushed back my sleeve. Her tongue emerged, neither pink nor red but mossed white like some ancient artifact. She licked my wrist and the ink of my false scars smeared.

You lie.

The other three stood behind her. Someone switched off the light so that the only illumination came from the half-window. The girls were vague shapes with flat, bright eyes.

No, I said. I said the ink was practice. I said I was drawing schematics for the real cuts. I said I'd lost the real blade. I said I'd broken the real blade. I said everything I could think of in the face of that silence. I even said—my voice soggy with desperation—that I was too poor to buy a replacement blade, that I'd do it, I would, if they would buy me another. *Please,* I said, offering my poverty for them to laugh at, and even this wasn't enough to feed those four sets of eyes, such as you find staring from the brush in wildlife photography. The elf recoiled. She was the first to leave.

When I was a small thing, before my father shifted my cot to storage and himself to the fold-up couch, before he taught me to close the door to the single bedroom at night, my father didn't call me *girlie*. He called me *Inch*. As in, *You don't need more than an inch of space, do you?* As in, *Scooch over, Inch* when we watched cartoons together. As in, *Eat up, Inch.* When he carried me, my father had a way of crooking his arm stiff against his chest so that I could perch safely, my torso pressing against his. Till the age of eight I saw the world this way. *There now, Inch, what's it like to be grown?* At night my father tucked me to sleep singing my only lullaby, the Nesquik jingle. Probably he did watch me breathe.

That night, I knew I would watch my father breathe.

Long and deep as he inhaled. *What's cooking, girlie?*

Quick snorts as he dug into the shepherd's pie. *Now that's more like it,* he said as he watched me eat a forkful of potato.

Slower as he lowered his own fork onto his plate.

Slower still as he grunted, eyelids drooping. *Delicious,* he said, half a pea falling from his mouth.

A rumbling, snagging, stalling snore as he fell dead asleep from the pills I'd layered between potatoes and beef. I prodded him. He didn't wake up; I'd given him an extra dose to be safe, because he was a fat man.

I ran to the bathroom and stuck two fingers down my throat. Up came the potatoes; out came the tears. I imagined starches and lipids untwining from my intestines. On the couch, my father was a pale lump of dough. Those same compounds ran through his blood—the glucose, the cholesterol, the hormones from the farmed beef he so loved—his blood like mine but not, as his loudness and his fat deposits were like mine but not. I had the discipline to shape myself differently.

That night, I slept beside my father.

In the morning I left him still asleep on my bed, his breath so slowed by pills that, for the first time, I couldn't hear it. My father had snored for years, a cacophony that startled me awake. I thought of shaking him, but—he seemed so peaceful. Today he'd see the daughter he wanted ripped apart by the one I'd become. Let him dream of when I was small enough to hold.

At two o'clock, after the other four had spoken, I raised my phone and showed the pictures.

My father lay on my bed, chest exposed and shirt bunched under his armpits. A streak of stomach hair trailed out of the frame, inviting the mind to complete its path. I lay beside him, staring into the camera, my eyes holding as much nothing as I could summon. Our skins were bluish white. The only color came from the bruises around my neck. Circles the size of my father's fat fingers.

The four leaned close. I didn't speak. Me, janitor's daughter. I didn't need to.

I hadn't been able to show my father beside me without also showing my room, my faded floral sheets, my taped-up photos of lynxes and penguins torn from the used *National Geographic*s my father brought home after I'd told him I wanted to be a zoologist. To distract from those details, I stood and peeled the scarf from my purpled neck.

The girls clotted around me, close enough that I could have reached out and clutched my triumph. The mouse began to squeak—but she was only a mouse. I ignored her. I watched the girls. The nothing in their eyes slipped away.

Behind it—was that awe?

The armored one leaned over to rub my bruise. This time it didn't come away under her fingers. My wounds were tender and I snarled. She flinched. She inclined her head, the signal of the pack leader's submission to a new alpha.

I snarled again when the mouse touched me. But the small woman didn't flinch. Strange. She didn't fear me, either. The look in her eyes was what I thought I'd outgrown: pity.

You poor thing. You poor, poor baby. I'm so sorry—I should have intervened sooner. They'll proceed quickly now.

I looked at her in scorn. The four did the same. But for once the mouse didn't quail.

Who will? I asked.

The authorities, the mouse said, stroking my arm so tenderly the hairs lifted one by one. *We'll call the police this moment, you poor child. Rest assured, Alta will rally around you. We'll set up a fund. You'll never have to go back.*

I could only repeat, *Child?*

The armored one began to clap the polite Alta clap, fingers against palm. The other girls took it up.

Out, the mouse said, and ushered the girls from the room. *Out, leave her alone, the lot of you are behaving like little beasts.*

Dusk came into the room, stretching the bars on the window till they threw stripes across the floor. I'd never stayed so late. Alta after-hours was my father's domain. I turned the knob and found it locked from outside. Somewhere the mouse was squeaking into a phone. I pulled and kicked, but the door was heavy, expensively made. My arms ached from last night's work.

I'd dragged my father from couch to bed for the picture. Sleep made him even sloppier: his arms floppy bolsters, his head at a loll. Friction dragged up his shirt and displayed his love handles. When I heaved him onto the bed, I rested a moment with my head on his chest. What did we look like then? Would anyone have squinted over that photo? I lifted my father's hand, which smelled of lemon-scented cleaner, and put it around my neck. I squeezed, my vision blurred. I rested, began again. Again. It was easier than any X-Acto knife. Nothing to fear; only the hands I'd known all my life.

I gave up on the door. I slid to the floor to await my punishment. Sunset painted my cage yellow and then a deep, lasting orange. And I remembered the day I'd grown from *Inch* to *Girlie.*

The dusk had been this color. I was eight, waiting for my father to return bearing Wendy's, as he did on those rare weekends he left to perform extra jobs at the houses of Alta girls. Shadows skittered around the apartment; as Inch, I was fearful. The room shrank, the dark crept closer, and as I hid my face in my arms, I felt the dark reach *inside me.* With each minute something within unfurled its limbs, put its arms through my arms, flexed my fingers to claws. I dug ridges in the meat of my thighs, and when that wasn't enough I turned to my father's prized race-car book, its glossy photos of sleek European machines so different from his truck I could almost believe he had taste. My father had promised to return to watch a documentary on big cats. Alone that night I watched animals prowl the savanna as I tore race cars into strips, scattering a pattern onto the floor. When my father arrived with two bags of Wendy's, a Frosty sitting in my spot on his arm, he saw the paper lion I'd constructed roaring up at him.

My father didn't punish me. He pushed aside the empty book, pressed his forehead to mine. *Girlie,* he said, as if unaware of the danger curled inside me, *you've grown a mind of your own, haven't you?* That night he left the single bedroom. He left me the Frosty. He forgave me and never again entered without knocking.

How had I forgotten? It wasn't triumph I'd felt when the door to the bedroom clicked closed five years ago. It was despair.

I would buy him a Frosty when I got out, I decided. I would buy two. I could almost taste the sweet, cold ache.

When the door began to open, I slopped into the breach, pleading, my mouth wide with explanations, never mind how I looked or what I spattered. But it wasn't my father on the other side. It was the mouse, and the biology teacher, and the dean, and a man I recognized as a cop only by the hat he held.

My dear girl, the mouse said, and she shook, shook, as if something stalked behind her down the unclean hall. *Your father—*

In the dusk, the beast twitched its claw against my heart.

Contributors' Notes

Other Distinguished Stories of 2020

American and Canadian Magazines
Publishing Short Stories

Contributors' Notes

GABRIEL BUMP grew up in South Shore, Chicago. His work has appeared in *The Best American Short Stories*, the *New York Times*, *McSweeney's*, *Guernica*, and elsewhere. *Everywhere You Don't Belong*, his debut novel, won the Ernest J. Gaines Award for Literary Excellence, the Heartland Booksellers Award for Fiction, and the Great Lakes Colleges Association Award for New Writers. His second novel is forthcoming. He received his MFA in fiction from the University of Massachusetts Amherst. Gabriel is an associate professor at the University of North Carolina at Chapel Hill. He lives in Durham.

• A few summers ago, during an intense mental crisis, I moved to Buffalo to sort myself out, get grounded. That was a summer of long drives. On one trip I went on vacation with my dad to the Upper Peninsula. Throughout my childhood we'd drive up from Chicago as a family. Sitting in the backseat, I'd usually read my books, play video games, sleep, or complain. Now, as an adult, making the drive alone, I soaked in each tree and town and lake. I was feeling better about myself and the world. I remember getting to the Mackinac Bridge, pulling off the highway, taking a picture of the water and huge sky. It's hard to explain what I felt. Rebirth, I guess; drowned in natural splendor. I wrote this piece, which I hope turns into a novel, based off that feeling.

RITA CHANG-EPPIG received her MFA in fiction from New York University. Her stories have appeared in *McSweeney's*, *Conjunctions*, *Clarkesworld*, *Kenyon Review Online*, *The Rumpus*, *Santa Monica Review*, *Virginia Quarterly Review*, and elsewhere. She has received fellowships from the Vermont Studio Center, the Writers Grotto, and the Martha Heasley Cox Center for

Steinbeck Studies at San José State University. She is currently working on her first novel.

• "The Miracle Girl" started as a class prompt: write the beginning of a fairy tale. Instead of turning to knights and princesses, I recalled the stories my mother told when I was a child, especially those about her early years of poverty in Taiwan and her creatively vicious fights with her sisters. But the stories that always made the deepest impression on me were those about the missionaries, specifically the stories they told her, one of which made it into the final draft. Even as a child I perceived a fundamental problem with them, despite not understanding the concept of racism or, for that matter, knowing the word. What it must have been like for her to grow up believing that God ranked people by race and that she would never be the best-loved! Some of their messages remained with her well into adulthood and, as these things often go, got passed on to me. I'm so thankful to Jesmyn Ward and Heidi Pitlor for choosing this story, which, for all its oddness, is actually an intensely personal piece about isolation, feelings of inadequacy, and the very human desire to be unconditionally loved.

VANESSA CUTI's fiction has appeared in *The Kenyon Review, AGNI, West Branch, Indiana Review, Cimarron Review, The Rumpus, Shenandoah,* and others. She received her MFA from Stony Brook Southampton and lives in the suburbs of New York.

• "Our Children" came to be when I was thinking of my own shortcomings as a mother. I arrived at the idea of a woman who yields to the urge to essentially just quit motherhood, as though spurred by some force out of her control. I wanted to explore and exaggerate the idea of a flawed parent and how it becomes especially unacceptable to be flawed if the parent in question happens to be a mother. From the start, from the way the very first line appeared to me, the story had the feeling of a fairy tale. So I kind of leaned into that as I went through it—cold stepfamily, little cabin, survival in the woods. Even though there is this heavy sense of the magical, I wanted the reader to feel like this scenario was only just outside of reality. If that.

JENZO DUQUE was born into a Colombian community in Chicago but currently lives in Brooklyn with his partner, Alicia, and their cat, Lulo. He received his MFA from Brooklyn College, where he served as an editor of *The Brooklyn Review.* Jenzo, whose work has appeared in *BOMB Magazine,*

One Story, Joyland, and *Glimmer Train,* is a 2021 Periplus Fellow and 2021 Shenandoah Editorial Fellow. He is writing his debut short story collection and novel. Read more at jenzoduque.com.

▪ Winter 2017, I was a lowly MFA student still adjusting to the hustle of New York City life and how when the snow would fall it wasn't quite so pretty (or clean) like back home. In between shifts spent as a waiter crawling in the darkness of a dine-in movie theater, I was toiling with stories and taking classes, and one day our professor assigned us "We," by Mary Grimm. The story floored me. I had never read a collective POV quite like the one in "We," and I knew I'd aspire to write my own version of it someday—a story by a bilingual collective that would showcase the community, language, and experiences I rarely saw on the page as a reader and lover of writing.

Cut to summer 2017, a roommate and I were sitting in the basement of our illegally converted duplex—which also contained my bedroom, a glorified and expensive cubby without an actual door—and watching TV. My roommate was a chain-smoking filmmaker who insisted we all split a cable Internet package because he preferred diving into rewatchable movies at odd hours and for some strange reason didn't believe in streaming. I too indulged in the chain smoking and random screenings, which was for the best, because on that particular day he had *Boyz n the Hood* on. I sat through most of it but immediately got up after telling my roommate, "We loved this movie growing up," because I could hear Frail Boy's voice in my head, and I needed to sit down to materialize his story before I lost it forever. It started there, and I revisited the piece for years until *One Story* saw it and believed.

As a first-generation citizen, a lot of my life has been spent hearing people tell me about things I couldn't do. I could never be American enough, I could never be Colombian enough, and I could never force the literary industry to value my bilingual experience on my terms. Likewise, a lot of my identity as an artist has been forged in resistance to convention, and I've produced works in an effort to reject the supposed rules of writing. To my bilingual brain, language is music. And it's not that I was cognizant of shifting between English and Spanish as an adolescent, so much as there was a song we could all sing that wasn't concerned with what words meant but rather with the feelings they evoked. Meaning it was never about either/or so much as both, interchangeably, at once.

"The Rest of Us" is the accumulation of all of that. It's a love letter to my city, my people, and the hood from which none of us come out unscathed: childhood. It was an ambition of mine to have it out in the world one day. And it's even more dreamlike to see it among the best contemporary stories our field has to offer.

BRANDON HOBSON is the author of the novels *The Removed,* recently released in 2021, *Where the Dead Sit Talking,* which was a finalist for the 2018 National Book Award and winner of the Reading the West Book Award, and other books. His fiction has won a Pushcart Prize and has appeared in *McSweeney's, Conjunctions, NOON,* and elsewhere. He teaches creative writing at New Mexico State University and at the Institute of American Indian Arts. He is an enrolled citizen of the Cherokee Nation of Oklahoma and lives in New Mexico.

 • Like a lot of my recent writing, "Escape from the Dysphesiac People" came out of thinking about the years I spent as a social worker. In this story I was especially thinking about colloquial language and the way certain authorities talked with a common acerbic aggression, exaggerated in this story, of course. For a while I worked in juvenile services and had to make referrals for kids to go to placement at boys' ranches and other long-term facilities. I was also thinking about how Natives were once removed from their homes and placed in boarding schools, where they were forced to cut their hair and change their speech in an attempt to rid them of their identity.

JAMIL JAN KOCHAI is the author of *99 Nights in Logar* (2019), a finalist for the Pen/Hemingway Award for Debut Novel and the DSC Prize for South Asian Literature. He was born in an Afghan refugee camp in Peshawar, Pakistan, but he originally hails from Logar, Afghanistan. His short stories and essays have appeared in *The New Yorker,* the *New York Times,* the *Los Angeles Times, Ploughshares,* and *The O. Henry Prize Stories 2018.* Currently he is a Stegner Fellow at Stanford University.

 • This story largely started out as a joke. While I was playing the video game Metal Gear Solid V: The Phantom Pain, the first third of which is set in Kabul, Afghanistan, I joked to my brothers that I should have Big Boss journey south to Logar in the video game and see if he could help our father and his family fight the Soviets in their village. We laughed at the idea, but it stuck with me. I thought to myself, *What if, while playing Metal Gear Solid, an Afghan gamer did discover his family inside the video game? How might he react? What might he do? And how might this experience change him and his relationship to his family and their history?* Once I figured out the point of view (second person seemed most appropriate for a story about a video game) and the central characters (I drew upon material from my novel, *99 Nights in Logar*), I wrote the whole story in a mad blaze, one of those blessed writing sessions where you feel like the story is almost writing itself, and I ended up finishing the first draft within a week or two (which is insanely fast for me). Then, after a few more rounds of revision, I sent it out.

NICOLE KRAUSS is the author of the novels *Forest Dark, Great House, The History of Love,* and *Man Walks Into a Room* and the short story collection *To Be a Man.* Her books have received many awards, and she has been called "one of America's most important novelists and an international literary sensation" by the *New York Times,* "a contemporary master" by *Esquire,* and "one of America's greatest writers" by the *Financial Times.* Her work has been published in *The New Yorker, Harper's Magazine, Esquire,* the *Atlantic,* the *New York Times,* and previous editions of *The Best American Short Stories,* and her books have been translated into thirty-seven languages.

• "Switzerland" began with my own experiences as a thirteen-year-old at boarding school in Geneva. In fact, I'd just turned thirteen a couple of weeks before moving into the boardinghouse. Not long ago I found a photograph of myself from that fall, taken in a photo booth on one of my after-school wanderings in the city. I was still a child, and no longer a child, depending on which way I looked at it. Both, really. That liminal time is interesting to me, and I wanted to go back and inhabit it again, to see what I found there.

I was interested in trying to capture the way a young woman tests her strength and will against the realities of her life: among them, that she is physically vulnerable to men, that to comply with the expectations of others requires containing herself or making herself small, that her sexuality comes with inherent dangers. The Dutch banker doesn't lead or determine this story—on the contrary, the story centers on Soraya's struggle with her sense of her own power, and he, at least as he is seen by the narrator, is only an accessory to that. He is merely the arena in which her performance of self plays out. Writing "Switzerland" depended on my ability to believe in that version of Soraya's "game," even as it is thrown into doubt by the narrator's perspective thirty years on, which encompasses a fuller sense of the tremendous fragility of the older girl's position. But if I was able to believe in her insistence on self-determination, it's because I've felt it in myself and the lives of young women I've been close to, despite everything working against it.

DAVID MEANS is the author of five short story collections, including *Assorted Fire Events, The Secret Goldfish,* and, most recently, *Instructions for a Funeral.* His novel, *Hystopia,* was longlisted for the 2016 Man Booker Prize. "Clementine, Carmelita, Dog" will appear in his next story collection, which is forthcoming .

• For fourteen years I lived with a dog, Bartleby, a miniature dachshund, and observed him as he observed me, paying an incredible amount of attention—because I loved him in the same unconditional way that he seemed to love me—to all of his gestures, his witty and humorous patterns of behavior, the way he nuzzled the ground when he picked up a particular scent and the way he lifted it to the sky to test the wind. That's the beauty of living alongside an animal, forming a complex communication beyond language, or perhaps a different kind of language. In any case, when Bartleby died, I waited a few years and then, on an impulse during the summer began to write a story about a lost dog. It's really that simple. The complexity of writing the story came from trying to locate and maintain a dog's point of view, focusing on the olfactory as much as possible, while also realizing that no matter what, I'd be writing a projection onto the animal mind and that the story would ultimately be about the human world. Writing from an animal perspective, as far away from the human as I could go, was a relief—to be eased of the burden of the political social upheaval during that time.

YXTA MAYA MURRAY is a novelist, art critic, playwright, and law professor. She has written nine books, the most recent being the story collection *The World Doesn't Work That Way, But It Could* (2020) and the novel *Art Is Everything* (2021). She has won a Whiting Award and an Arts Writers Grant and has been named a fellow at the Huntington Library for her work on radionuclide contamination in Simi Valley, California.

  • The 2017–18 California wildfire season caused more than $45 billion in damage and killed approximately 150 people. Paradise suffered one of the most violent of these conflagrations in 2018, when its citizens saw 85 percent of their town consumed. Five months later, President Donald Trump refused to sign a bill that would provide relief for these victims, as well as for those of the recent hurricane and flooding disasters. His reason? Puerto Rico would get too much money. "I don't want another single dollar going to the island," he said. That summer found me at Ucross, in Wyoming, watching videos of the hell-red passage that Paradise residents drove through while escaping certain death. It occurred to me that white supremacy is the worst strategy western civilization ever concocted. It does not even help its constituents. Fernanda, Wesley, and Jessie showed up in the midst of these musings, on a bad afternoon that found me fearful and perplexed in equal measure.

ELOGHOSA OSUNDE is a writer and multidisciplinary artist. Her writing has been published by several publications, including *Paris Review, Guernica, Gulf Coast, Catapult, and Berlin Quarterly*. Eloghosa's visual art has appeared in *Vogue*, the *New York Times*, and *Paper Magazine*. She is a 2019 Lambda Literary Fellow, a 2020 MacDowell Colony Fellow, and the 2021 prose judge of *Fugue Journal*'s annual writing contest. Her debut novel, *VAGABONDS!*, will be published in spring 2022.

• When people talk about queerness and queer people's lives in countries where our relationships are forbidden, I find that they tend to imagine the obvious and sing the same chorus. I push back against that. The law says what the law says, but I've made a separate pronouncement upon my head: I am free, and so are the people I love. No matter what they say, we are free. So many terrifying things are true at the same time—state violence, imprisonment, lynchings, etc.—yes. But so are other things. There are enough stories that focus their imagination on the scale of that violence. But for this story, it mattered to me to keep my character's agency intact. We don't choose what happens to us, but we can change our minds about what we are willing to tolerate. Power is a large part of how stories are shaped and stories present us with questions. Some ask, *If you come out, will your parents disown you?* I'm interested in more interesting questions. One of the things that breaks my heart very often is watching grown adults continue to make certain choices because they feel indebted to their families: what they study, where they live, who they marry, if they will have kids. Before writing this story, I'd been thinking a lot about how many people stay stuck in these cycles because they haven't been asked—and therefore can't ask—better questions.

Again, there's too much: What do your parents think about who you love? Not enough: Is this a part of yourself you can/would like to trust your parents with, or are you rehearsing this moment for a person who has already come out to you as being completely incapable of processing your full humanity? And if your parents can't do the necessary work of accepting you as you are, who else is holding you fully? Who else sees you completely? And how do you deepen your relationship to the people who do see you? This story asks those questions and answers some of them. So, "Good Boy" was important for me to write for many reasons, but the main one was tied to the forbiddenness of being my full self on this land and the ways in which I resist that in my daily choices, and through the people whom I refer to as family. That has little to do with blood and genetics, more to do with choice. The law doesn't affect everyone equally, and that's so important to note. "Good Boy" is situated in the world that surrounds my debut novel and focuses on queer characters who make a new world for themselves fashioned out of love and tenderness. They're people who are honest about the systems that benefit them—such as beauty, or class, or intellect, or perceived gender, or, or, or—and make those exceptions possible. My whole book is pretty much a collection of stories that occur when characters are in charge of their own lives in an unruly place like

Lagos. "Good Boy" came through that vein. It's a story about boundaries, a story in which a queer character in a lawfully homophobic country says: 1) I will love whom I want, you won't stop me, and 2) I choose me over you. It matters that such a thing exists.

JANE PEK was born and grew up in Singapore. Her short fiction has appeared or is forthcoming in the *Brooklyn Review, Witness, Conjunctions,* and *Literary Hub* and has been anthologized in *The Best American Short Stories 2020.* Her debut novel, *The Verifiers,* is forthcoming in spring 2022. She currently lives in New York, where she works as a lawyer at a global investment company.

• *The Legend of the White Snake* is one of those folktales that I feel like I was just always familiar with, growing up in Singapore, probably from cultural osmosis. There are multiple versions of the story, but the ones I am aware of all focus on the titular immortal female snake spirit (the white snake) falling in love with a human man, and the trials and tribulations they have to undergo before they can be together happily ever after. But before any of that takes place, the white snake's companion is the green snake, another female spirit, and I wanted to imagine that (to me) much more intriguing relationship.

My story is in one respect the story of a breakup, and of someone who is really quite bad at dealing with that breakup. At the same time, while I was writing it I was reading up on various periods of Chinese history as research for a novel and getting very upset at both the corrupt Qing government and the colonial powers that took advantage of such weakness, and this story also became a way for me to express some of those sentiments.

TRACEY ROSE PEYTON hails from Chicago, Illinois. She received her MFA from the Michener Center for Writers at the University of Texas at Austin. Her work has appeared in *American Short Fiction, Prairie Schooner, Guernica,* and elsewhere.

• The seed of the story began sometime around 2014, when the steady circulation of video clips of black people being murdered by police seemed to be on a continuous loop. It made me think about the first time I had seen images like that circulated—the 1991 video of the brutal beating of Rodney King. I was immediately struck by how little humanity King was afforded at the time, and I grew curious about the afterlife of such a horrific event. How might it have felt to survive what so many hadn't, what so many wouldn't?

I wrote the first two pages and set it aside. I wasn't sure how to continue, let alone whether it was a story I should even try to tell. I still worry about it, even though the story being told is a fictional one. Lest there be any confusion, I should say up front that the portrait of the protagonist is a fabrication, one that utilizes a few major details in the public record and no more. No attempts were made to utilize the true names, stories, or recollections of King's actual kin. I believe their memories are their own and aren't tchotchkes to be made available for public consumption.

What feels apt for exploration instead is public memory. "The past that is not past reappears, always to rupture the present," writes Christina Sharpe in her brilliant book *In the Wake*. I wanted to explore that rupture and its afterlife, in hopes of seeing what it might reveal.

CHRISTA ROMANOSKY'S recent fiction and poetry has been included in *Glimmer Train*, *The Cincinnati Review*, *The Missouri Review*, *Alaska Quarterly Review*, and elsewhere. She has held fellowships at the Fine Arts Work Center, James Merrill House, and Tulsa Artist Fellowship. Her writing focuses on rural spaces, extraction, and trauma. She currently works for the Virginia Department of Health in response to the COVID-19 pandemic.

• Many of the stories I write take place in an area of Appalachia similar to where I grew up, where there are few jobs and high levels of opiate and meth use and hydraulic fracturing has poisoned the water. This is where the story takes place, but that's just the husk. When I began writing this piece, I wanted to explore how people love and how people survive. And the more I explored this, the more I was sure I wanted to write about how people hate too, and how vital hatred can be for survival.

This story started out rough. A friend who read the piece suggested providing more compassion for Tiff, who at the time was fulfilling just a small role in the story. I rewrote many times over a two-year period, setting it aside for monthlong stretches, and finally I realized that this story needed to focus on Tiff, not the other character, whom I ended up removing altogether. The more I worked to get into Tiff's head, the more I began to again consider the many connections between addiction, mental health, and trauma, and how, without intervention, trauma continues to be passed along through generations and families continue to do the best they can, often with significant damage and dysfunctional patterns of behavior and coping styles.

For Tiff, survival was all she ever knew, and I wanted to explore what it was like for Tiff to be stuck in high voltage, a constant fight or flight, so that even when there was calm in the household, such as when the parents were asleep and not physically present, Tiff was stuck in the same patterns and emotional state as when she was younger—as though time stopped when her abuse began. It was really important to me that Tiff was resilient, as most survivors are. She suffered incredible losses. After losing her husband, her home, and the life she imagined for herself, it was hatred and anger that drove her. I needed the reader to see Tiff at her worst—destroying her parents' things, stealing, lying, killing small animals— so that they could understand how much her hatred was protective, how this behavior had allowed Tiff to survive and had shielded her from who and what hurt her the most. And it's heartbreaking to know that within Tiff there was still a very loving and well-meaning part that had been compartmentalized and preserved, shown only to her toddler son, because from Tiff's perspective, he was the only one in her life who hadn't harmed her, the only one deserving of love.

I never know how a story will end—I begin with a few ideas of things that will happen, but not how the characters will get from event to event and how these events will shift as more of the story is created and detailed. As this story progressed, I got to know Tiff well. I made decisions about the story based on who she was. And so by the last scene I knew what Tiff was going to do. It was inevitable that the story ends this way, because the same pattern of behavior was orbiting faster and closer from beginning to end, like a penny down a coin drop, a vortex. Something had to be destroyed in order for Tiff to survive.

GEORGE SAUNDERS is the author of eleven books, including *Lincoln in the Bardo,* which won the 2017 Man Booker Prize for best work of fiction in English. His most recent book, *A Swim in a Pond in the Rain,* is an exploration of four great Russian writers, the short story form, and the writing process. He teaches at Syracuse University.

• I'd been having some spirited political discussions with family members and some young friends, and these felt very much to me like expressions of love—all of us worrying, in our own way, about the country we love. I was also feeling that old dilemma a fiction writer feels in the middle of a crisis: how to write something that honors that which a short story is designed to do (show the reader how hard it is to live correctly in a fallen world by putting her on the horns of a true dilemma) while not somehow, via its neutrality and its focus on the long view, serving as a sort of enabler for evil. In particular, I was wondering what I personally should be doing at this moment of crisis and was noticing that I wasn't doing much. And since writing is the only thing I've ever been able to do that has the slightest whiff of power about it, I decided to write a story "about" (that is "out of") the moment I found myself in.

SHANTEKA SIGERS lives in Austin, Texas. She is a graduate of Northwestern University and New York University's MFA Writers Workshop in Paris. She has published several stories in the *Chicago Reader*'s Pure Fiction issue.

    * I was in grad school and my adviser, Hari Kunzru, wanted a brand-new story in a little less than two weeks. Bea was the little sister of the protagonist of another story I'd published. I knew her well, so off the shelf she came.

    I was never sure about what might happen to the other children in that story, but Bea was a survivor. I knew she was going to live a different life than the one that appeared to be unfolding for her. But how?

    I gave Bea a teacher. Teachers change kids' lives all the time.

    I started writing observations of Bea's presence or absence in class in chunks of barely connected narrative. But the teacher was flat, less of a character and more of a device. Right away, Hari (and several other wise readers, both advisers and students) wanted more. So over time the teacher grew a real marriage. And a legacy to live up to. And a desire to teach with her full self.

    You should also know that my family has two cats, Meyoncé and Principal Nelson. Somewhere in this timeline I'd invited our vet to participate in a Jack and Jill Career Day event. She is a delicate, bright-eyed Black woman, passionate about animals and science. I had watched her table from afar, noting a clear delineation between kids who leaned into her display of bones and organs and kids who recoiled in disgust. Later I visited her table and examined tiny parts in jars.

    "Where'd you get that cat skull?" I asked.

STEPHANIE SOILEAU's debut collection of stories, *Last One Out Shut Off the Lights,* was published in July 2020. Her work has also appeared in *Glimmer Train, Oxford American, Ecotone, Tin House, New Stories from the South,* and other journals and anthologies, and has been supported by fellowships from the Wallace Stegner Fellowship Program at Stanford University, the Camargo Foundation, the National Endowment for the Arts, and the Fine Arts Work Center in Provincetown. Originally from Lake Charles, Louisiana, Stephanie now lives in Chicago and teaches at the University of Chicago.

    * The situation—an old man whose quiet morning of crabbing is rudely interrupted by a young family searching for a cat—was a gift from my old Cajun grandfather, who suffered such a morning himself. The thematic concerns of the story—whose suffering we grace with our sympathy and whose we deny, how we sometimes turn our own suffering into cruelty—came out of what I heard and observed in the time following Hurricane Katrina's and Hurricane Rita's landfall in Louisiana in 2005. Hurricane

Rita's devastation just a few short weeks after Katrina's prompted, in someone like Haguillory (white, working class, and generally spiteful), not a
deeper empathy for the suffering in New Orleans but rather a sense of
grievance, a perception that he and others like him were being slighted
by the media in favor of "New Orleans" (i.e., urban Black people). This
attitude seems to be a pretty clear, if euphemistic, expression of endemic
racism, and demonstrates how deeply both private and institutional racism
divides people with common interests. Never mind that New Orleanians
drowned in their own homes, waited *days* on roofs for rescue. Haguillory
still feels aggrieved that his own (relatively minor) suffering—the loss of
his remote control and the vibrating pad for his back, the annoyance of
evacuating with his irksome family—has not been adequately represented
or alleviated.

MADHURI VIJAY is the author of the novel *The Far Field*, which, among
other honors, won India's JCB Prize for Literature and was a finalist for
the DSC Prize for South Asian Literature. She is the recipient of a Pushcart
Prize, and her fiction has appeared in *The New Yorker, The Best American
Nonrequired Reading,* and *Narrative Magazine.*
   · I'm fascinated by what I see as the fundamental alienness of children.
Even the most affable, well-adjusted child seems to me unknowable in a
way that many adults are not. But outside of fairy tales and folktales, which
allow children the degree of darkness and opacity they deserve, most fiction tends to treat them either as dim innocents to be protected or, if they
are the troublemaking type, wild creatures to be tamed and won over. I
wanted to write about a child who refuses to fall into these categories, who
is immune to protection or taming, who retains her privacy and her un-
knowability to the very end, even if it comes at a painful cost to all involved.

BRYAN WASHINGTON is the author of *Memorial* and *Lot.* He's a National
Book Foundation 5 Under 35 honoree, a recipient of the International
Dylan Thomas Prize, the New York Public Library's Young Lions Award,
the Lambda Literary Award, and an O. Henry Award. He was also a finalist
for the National Book Critics Circle Award for Fiction, the National Book
Critics Circle John Leonard Prize, the Aspen Literary Award, the Center
for Fiction's First Novel Prize, the Andrew Carnegie Medal of Excellence,
and the PEN/Robert Bingham Prize. He lives in Houston.
   · I'm always taken by stories within stories, and I'd wanted to write a
narrative between this mother and her son for years. I've thought about

these two characters for a while, along with the literal and imaginative distances between them. But I couldn't land the narrative's voice for anything. It always felt a little too distant. So it was only after I allowed the story's structure to relax, giving it breathing room and flexibility for both characters to reveal themselves, that the writing began to feel less like an impossible thing than something that I could maybe navigate.

From there, the goal became to write the sort of story that I wanted to read, and the sort of story that I myself *needed* to read—which is always the highest bar. I don't always get there, but I felt pretty close with this one.

KEVIN WILSON is the author of two story collections and three novels, most recently *Nothing to See Here*. His stories have appeared in *Ploughshares, A Public Space, The Southern Review, Subtropics,* and elsewhere. He lives in Sewanee, Tennessee, and teaches at the University of the South.

• A lot of my writing in the last few years features characters looking into the past, trying to come to terms with things that happened to them and figure out how to connect it back to who they are now. This is probably because, now that I'm in my forties, I'm doing this all the time. The thing about adolescence, for me at least, was that I wasn't necessarily capable of understanding what was going on around me. I just absorbed whatever strange thing and tried to keep moving forward. And now, with some context, I try to write my way back into those moments.

The story began with something from my past—a teacher I really cared for who was involved in an ill-advised sporting contest for money with bad-ass middle school girls—and I just started building the other elements around that. And I think what kind of amazes me about writing these stories is how, when I work my way through the confusion and the weirdness, at the heart of these stories is tenderness, of wanting to somehow tell the character, and maybe myself too, that they made it. That they're still in this world, still alive. Maybe that's all I've ever wanted from a story.

Born in Beijing, C PAM ZHANG is mostly an artifact of the United States. She is the author of *How Much of These Hills Is Gold,* winner of the Asian/ Pacific American Award for Literature and the Academy of Arts and Letters Rosenthal Foundation Prize and nominated for the Booker Prize, the PEN/Hemingway Award, and the National Book Critics Circle John Leonard Prize, among others. Zhang's writing appears in *The Cut, McSweeney's, The New Yorker,* the *New York Times,* and *The Pushcart Prize Anthology.* She is a National Book Foundation 5 Under 35 honoree.

• It was a spooky fall in a slightly shabby college town and the news was flooded with yet another grisly scandal involving young girls. I don't remember which. There are too many. What does it mean to grow up as a girl when the models for girlhood that you see in the media are dead, or maimed, or "ruined," or abused, or endangered—and when the public's rapt attention on these girls gives them an aura of desirability, even sexiness? I don't know any woman or girl, however strong and educated, who hasn't been subliminally warped by the constant narrative of girls as victims and sex objects both. For that matter, I don't know any living human who hasn't been warped by it. In "Little Beast" I amplify this creepiness with the creepiness inherent to any very insular society: here, an elite all-girls school.

Other Distinguished Stories of 2020

American and Canadian Magazines Publishing Short Stories

Across the Margin
The Adroit Journal
African American Review
After Dinner Conversation
Agni
Air/Light
Alaska Quarterly Review
Alta Journal
American Bystander
American Literary Review
American Short Fiction
Antioch Review
Apple Valley Review
Arch Street Press
Aster(ix) Journal
The Baffler
The Baltimore Review
Bayou Magazine
Bellevue Literary Review
Beloit Fiction Journal
Big Fiction Magazine
Big Muddy
Black Warrior Review
Blood Orange Review
Bluestem Magazine
BOMB
Boulevard
The Briar Cliff Review

Cagibi
Capsule Stories
The Carolina Quarterly
Catamaran
Catapult Magazine
Causeway Lit
The Chattahoochee Review
Chautaqua
Cherry Tree
Chicago Quarterly Review
Chicago Tribune
Cimarron Review
The Cincinnati Review
Coffin Bell
Colorado Review
The Columbia Journal
The Common
Conjunctions
Consequence
Coppernickel
Craft
Crazyhorse
Cream City Review
The Cut
Cutbank
The Dalhousie Review
Deep Wild: Writing from the
   Backcountry

Denver Quarterly
Dr. Cicero
Driftwood
805 Lit and Art
Electric Literature
Emry's Journal
Epiphany
Event
Fairy Tale Review
Fantasy and Science Fiction
The Fiddlehead
Fireside Magazine
Foglifter
The Forge
Freeman's
F(r)iction
The Georgia Review
The Gettysburg Review
Gold Man Review
Granta
The Gravity of the Thing
Greensboro Review
Guernica
Gulf Coast
Harper's Magazine
The Harvard Advocate
Harvard Review
Hayden's Ferry Review
Heavy Feather Review
High Desert Journal
Hip Mama Magazine
The Hopkins Review
The Hopper
The Hudson Review
Hypertext Revew
The Idaho Review
Image
Indiana Review
Intima: A Journal of Narrative Medicine
Into the Void
The Iowa Review
Iron Horse Review

Jabberwock Review
Jelly Bucket
Jellyfish Review
Joyland
Juked
Kenyon Review
Kestrel
Lady Churchill's Rosebud Wristlet
Lake Effect
Lightspeed Magazine
Lit Hub
LitMag
Litro Magazine
Longleaf Review
The Los Angeles Review
The Louisville Review
Massachusetts Review
The Masters Review
Maudlin House
McSweeney's (Timothy McSweeney's Quarterly Concern)
Meridian
Michigan Quarterly Review
Midnight Breakfast
Midwest Review
The Missouri Review
Monkeybicycle
Montana Quarterly
Mount Hope
n+1
Narrative
Nelle
New England Review
New Flash Fiction Review
The New Guard
New Letters
New Ohio Review
New Orleans Review
The New Yorker
New York Review of Books
Ninth Letter

Noon
The Normal School
North American Review
North Dakota Quarterly
O, the Oprah Magazine
The Offing
Okay Donkey
One Story
Orion
Oyez Review
Oyster River Pages
Pank
Paper Brigade
The Paris Review
Passages North
Pembroke Magazine
Pigeon Pages
Pinyon
Playgirl
Pleiades
Ploughshares
Post Road
Potomac Review
Prairie Schooner
Prime Number Magazine
Prism International
Prism Review
Puerto Del Sol
The Rappahannock Review
Raritan
Reed
Room
Ruminate
The Rumpus
San Francisco Chronicle
Sci-Fi Lampoon
Scoundrel Time
The Sewanee Review
Shenandoah

The Southampton Review
South Carolina Review
Southern Humanities Review
Southern Indiana Review
The Southern Review
Southwest Review
Spice Today
Split Lip Magazine
Stoneboat
Story
Strange Horizons
Stranger's Guide
Subtropics
The Sun
Sycamore Review
Tahoma Literary Review
Tampa Review
Territory
The Threepenny Review
Trajectory
Triquarterly
Upstreet
Valparaiso Fiction Review
Vida Review
Virginia Quarterly Review
Vol. 1 Brooklyn
Water-Stone Review
West Branch
Wigleaf
Wildness
Willow Springs
Witness
World Literature Today
X-R-A-Y
The Yale Review
Zoetrope: All-Story
Zone 3
ZYZZYVA

THE BEST AMERICAN SERIES®

FIRST, BEST, AND BEST-SELLING

The Best American Essays

The Best American Food Writing

The Best American Mystery and Suspense

The Best American Science and Nature Writing

The Best American Science Fiction and Fantasy

The Best American Short Stories

The Best American Travel Writing

Available in print and e-book wherever books are sold.

Visit our website: MarinerBooks.com/BestAmerican